"Compelling from start to finish, this fast-paced thriller combines engaging characters, sharp dialogue, and a plot so gripping that the pages seem to turn themselves. A handsome job." —Richard North Patterson

"Terrific legal suspense—a great debut." —Lee Child

"An impressive debut. Written with urgency . . . The climaxes and about turns and surprises just keep coming until the final showdown . . . Watch out Grisham."
—*The Sydney Morning Herald*

"*Undertow* is all handled with dexterity and no little style . . . her locations have the right sense of place, her plotting is economical and concise . . . Bauer is credibly packaged."
—*The Australian*

"Bauer has done a Grisham, producing a fast-paced and suspenseful legal thriller." —*The Melbourne Age*

"Sydney Bauer has hit the crime scene in fine style with a legal thriller that is confronting, touching on relevant and controversial issues with absolute confidence. This is the kind of story that legal-thriller fans everywhere would eat up with a spoon and then go looking for more."
—*Australian Crime Writers' Association*

"A creditable, enthralling, legal suspense drama following firmly in the footsteps of Grisham and Patterson."
—*Good Reading*

"One of the most accomplished Australian crime novels to date. Look out John Grisham." —*Sisters in Crime Australia*

"A deeply compelling political/legal thriller . . . with a series of ingenious twists." —*Crime Down Under*

UNDERTOW

SYDNEY BAUER

BERKLEY BOOKS, NEW YORK

THE BERKLEY PUBLISHING GROUP
Published by the Penguin Group
Penguin Group (USA) Inc.
375 Hudson Street, New York, New York 10014, USA
Penguin Group (Canada), 90 Eglinton Avenue East, Suite 700, Toronto, Ontario M4P 2Y3, Canada
(a division of Pearson Penguin Canada Inc.)
Penguin Books Ltd., 80 Strand, London WC2R 0RL, England
Penguin Group Ireland, 25 St. Stephen's Green, Dublin 2, Ireland (a division of Penguin Books Ltd.)
Penguin Group (Australia), 250 Camberwell Road, Camberwell, Victoria 3124, Australia
(a division of Pearson Australia Group Pty. Ltd.)
Penguin Books India Pvt. Ltd., 11 Community Centre, Panchsheel Park, New Delhi—110 017, India
Penguin Group (NZ), 67 Apollo Drive, Rosedale, North Shore 0632, New Zealand
(a division of Pearson New Zealand Ltd.)
Penguin Books (South Africa) (Pty.) Ltd., 24 Sturdee Avenue, Rosebank, Johannesburg 2196,
South Africa

Penguin Books Ltd., Registered Offices: 80 Strand, London WC2R 0RL, England

This is a work of fiction. Names, characters, places, and incidents either are the product of the author's imagination or are used fictitiously, and any resemblance to actual persons, living or dead, business establishments, events, or locales is entirely coincidental. The publisher does not have any control over and does not assume any responsibility for author or third-party websites or their content.

UNDERTOW

A Berkley Book / published by arrangement with the author

PRINTING HISTORY
Macmillan Australia Pty Limited trade edition / 2006
Madison Park Press hardcover edition / 2007
Berkley mass-market edition / July 2008

Copyright © 2008 by Sydney Bauer.
Interior text design by Tiffany Estreicher.

ISBN: 978-0-425-22290-4

BERKLEY®
Berkley Books are published by The Berkley Publishing Group,
a division of Penguin Group (USA) Inc.,
375 Hudson Street, New York, New York 10014.
BERKLEY® is a registered trademark of Penguin Group (USA) Inc.
The "B" design is a trademark belonging to Penguin Group (USA) Inc.

PRINTED IN THE UNITED STATES OF AMERICA

10 9 8 7 6 5 4 3 2 1

PROLOGUE

"If a tree falls in the forest and there is no one to hear it, will there be a sound?"

It was a rhetorical question, an age-old conundrum.

"Yes and no," Judge Isaac Stein answered it for himself. "For *sound,* like most other things, is a matter of conjecture."

Boston attorney-at-law David Cavanaugh knew when not to interrupt, and so he stood in the judge's chambers, still in shock at what had just happened and impatient for him to go on.

"For a start, the word *sound* has two different meanings: one is a description of a particular type of physical disturbance and the other an auditory sensation. In other words, one is the cause, the other the effect. Thus the answer to the original question is, in the first case, 'yes,' in the second, a deafening 'no.'"

"Judge, no offense but I don't really give a . . ." David took a deep breath. It took all of his strength to keep his anger in check. "I can't believe what just happened. You know this is wrong. No, more than wrong, it's outrageous, criminal."

"So here is another conundrum," the judge went on. "If two people are at sea and have a conversation heard by only those two, did the conversation actually take place? If the two confirm it, then the answer is most definitely yes. But if one of them should die, before the confirmation is made, it really comes down to conjecture once again and whether that one witness is to be believed."

"What are you saying, Judge? That the DA can pull this sickening stunt and get away with it? That they actually have a chance of—"

"Nothing is impossible."

"So this is what? A warning?"

"No," replied Stein with a shake of his head. "I am a judge of the Massachusetts Superior Court; it is not my job to hand out any form of advice to either side. It is merely an observation from an old man who has seen too much and still understands little."

"That's not good enough."

"A girl is dead, David, and not just any girl. Human nature is both a wonderful and terrible thing. Her father," the judge paused before going on, "he will want someone to—"

"And my client is the most obvious option," interrupted David, not believing what he was hearing.

Stein did not answer, merely walked toward his fifth-story window, the midday sun accentuating the crevices on his tired and world-weary face. "Sometimes, perhaps more often than not, life comes down to luck, or in your client's case, the lack thereof. It is not the troubles we anticipate in life that undo us, but the unexpected horrors that creep up on us like traitors in the night."

Judge Stein turned toward the young attorney with one last thing to say before sending him away. "Do not underestimate him, son; he is a powerful man. Just be careful."

1

Three Days Earlier

She was running.

Not because she was being chased, but because it was the only thing she could do at a time like this.

She had left the house quickly, the early morning sun forcing her to squint as she turned to look back, just once, before sprinting down the sandstone steps of her family's expansive 1912 colonial. The breeze from the back of the house had met with the air now flowing in from the front and compressed the door like an invisible hand squeezing their images from view.

She focused on the sound of her footfalls as they crunched down the red pebbled driveway. Counted them, and then took her first new breath as she heard the click of the well-oiled, six-foot wrought iron gates behind her.

She reached Chestnut Hill Avenue, leafy and quiet, the last tree-lined corridor leading out of her privileged world and down toward Highway 9, which ran all the way into Boston. She would try to catch a cab, and hopefully be at her best friend Teesha's house within the half hour.

She looked at her watch. It was later than she thought. She would have to be quick, or they would leave without her.

She did not know what hurt the most, the fact that her parents had forbidden her to go, or the fact that her father had finally admitted his reasons outright. She had never openly defied them. God, she doubted anyone had ever openly defied her father—ever. Until today.

She shifted her bag over her left shoulder, pulled her long blond hair over her right and raised her arm to hail a Checker cab. Once inside, she wiped her face and noticed the hair at her temples was damp. Her tears had trailed sideways. She had been running fast.

"Victoria Square, South End, please, and would you mind hurrying? I'm running a little late. Thank you so much."

Christina Haynes listened to herself and realized just how much she sounded like her mother. But that is where the comparisons would end. She was not like her parents and never would be.

She sat back in her seat, fastened her belt and decided at the very least to try to enjoy this day with her friends. And after that? She was not sure.

· · ·

How was it that teenagers could wake at six and still be running late for an outing at ten? Rayna Martin pondered this as she threw bottles of water, soda and juice into a wicker basket and placed an assortment of sandwiches on top.

"Teesha, come *on*," she yelled. "We have to go. I only have the boat from eleven till four."

It was a few weeks before Teesha's seventeenth birthday, but they were celebrating early as final exams were looming and Teesha wanted to have this day with her friends Francie Washington and Mariah Jordan before they hit the study trail and then went their separate ways for the summer.

Rayna had said no to the girls' chartering a boat on their own but yes to Rayna's hiring a cruiser from which they could launch their own outboard in the waters north of the historic fishing port of Gloucester, Cape Ann, about forty minutes northeast of Boston.

She would pick up the cruiser at Cape Ann Marina, sail up the picturesque Annisquam River toward Ipswich Bay and then drop anchor, allowing the girls to putter around the unspoiled white-sanded beaches for a while, like grown-ups, have their own minipicnic and pretend there were no such things as parents.

Then the doorbell.

"Mom, can you get that? We're just helping Francie pack her bag."

"Okay, okay, but get moving, you guys."

Rayna rushed down the stairs to the front of her renovated three-story South End terrace, wondering what this further delay would be, and was surprised to see the pretty, red-faced teen standing in her doorway. Christina Haynes—the fourth musketeer.

"Hi, Mrs. Martin."

"Christina, I thought you had to go out with your mom. We weren't expecting you."

"I know," said Christina, avoiding eye contact, her face flushed and wet. "Mom and Dad, well, you know the drill. I decided I wanted to come after all, if that's okay." She gave Rayna a small embarrassed smile before moving past her, down the hallway and up the stairs toward her friends, who had congregated on the landing above.

"Chrissie," said Teesha. "You made it."

"Yeah. Change of plans. Hey," she said, seemingly determined to change the subject, "you better take that swimsuit off because I brought the exact same one." She managed to smile.

"But I told you *I* was buying the blue one," laughed Teesha, her voice trailing off down the upstairs hallway.

Christina had been crying, thought Rayna. *Something to do with her parents no doubt.* But at this point she was more concerned about how four girls would fit into an outboard built for three. And she was somewhat annoyed at Christina's parents, who seemed reluctant to let the girl out but happy enough to have her decline a birthday invitation to go shopping, and hurt Teesha's feelings in the process. And now she turns up unannounced at the last minute. But this was Teesha's day and it was no big deal. *The more the merrier, right?*

"Come on, girls, we have to go—*now*."

• • •

Boston police officer Susan Leigh was pissed.

"I can't believe this," she said for the fifth time in the past half hour. "I mean seriously, what is the Coast Guard for?"

Leigh and her partner, Officer Tommy Wu, were on their way to Gloucester Harbor to undertake a mandatory water safety training course as part of an education program instituted by the current commissioner of police.

The commissioner's memo spoke of an "opportunity to multitask and partake in ongoing instruction for the greater good and safety of officers in the force and the community of the harbor city of Boston as a whole."

"Listen to this," said Leigh, quoting from the memo again. " 'The program will also foster interpolice community relations and provide an opportunity to share multibeneficial educational resources.' Educational resources? With that bunch of small-town deputies? Jesus Christ, what a load of crap."

Leigh smoothed the sides of her dark, shoulder-length hair back to where it was confined in a short, tight ponytail.

"At least we're on duty," offered Tommy Wu, who had the annoying habit of finding the bright side in even the dullest of circumstances. "I mean, we had to work a shift today in any case. You never know—it might be interesting."

"Sure, Pollyanna, while the rest of the precinct is out solving crimes."

Leigh was on the career fast track and determined not to miss a beat when it came to finding perps, making arrests and assisting the detectives in their investigations. At twenty-six she had her big brown eyes set on a gold shield by the end of the year, and giving a blow-up dummy mouth to mouth for six hours was not her idea of career advancement.

"Here we go," said Tommy, who didn't appear at all irritated that his buddies might be solving crimes in his absence. "Gloucester PD."

"Hicks by the sea," rhymed Leigh.

"Come on, Susan, it's a nice day; we'll be by the water. Let's make the most of it."

"Sure, Wu. Just don't expect me to blow into some god-damned mouthpiece after those two-bit fishermen dressed as cops. Everyone stinks of fish up here, and I hate fish at the best of times. They give me hives."

■ ■ ■

"So," said Francie Washington, unable to hold it in any longer. "I thought you weren't coming?"

The four girls were lazing in the overcrowded outboard, dangling their feet over the sides.

"Francie," said Teesha, knowing it was coming but trying to stop her before she upset Christina.

"What? I was just asking. She said she had to go shopping."

"My mom had a last-minute errand," Christina replied quickly.

"Oh, okay. I thought maybe you'd decided we meant more to you than some stupid dress, but I guess that's not—"

"Francie, give it a rest will you?" This came from Mariah Jordan, the voice of reason in their little group.

Teesha didn't think Francie set out to be malicious with her barbed comments. She suspected that it drove Francie crazy that Christina seemed to be everything she was not. Francie was short and round with dark bangs and braces on her teeth. Christina was tall and lean with long blond hair and huge blue eyes. Francie was a mediocre student with little or no athletic ability whose parents earned a reasonable living selling real estate. Christina was a straight-A student who excelled at every sport she tried and her parents were . . . well, everyone knew who they were, and on top of that, they were loaded.

"Chrissie," said Mariah. "You'd better put some more sunscreen on your legs. They're turning pink."

Mariah, the eldest of the four girls, was tall, poised and intelligent, with the innate ability to calm things down. She pressed her thumb against Christina's thigh and left a white impression.

"You're right, throw some over, Teesh."

Teesha did as asked, relieved by the change of subject.

"Who wants a drink?" said Francie.

"You didn't!" said Teesha, a smile on her face. She suspected Francie sensed she had gone too far and now was trying to slide back into favor.

"I did, and it's French. Moët." She pronounced it to rhyme with "boat," and Teesha gave Christina a quick half smile.

"Where did you get it?" asked Teesha.

"Some megarich client sent my dad a whole case. Dad sold him some huge mansion in Brookline for some unbelievable price and even though the guy was like totally loaded, he was also totally grateful. Dad saved him millions so I guess it was the least he could do. There were stacks of bottles so I figured, you know, Dad's not going to miss *one*."

Francie, always fond of superlatives, used the words *rich, loaded* and *millions* a lot. She liked the sound of them, and Teesha got the feeling her parents did too.

"I'm in. Thanks, Francie," said Christina, accepting the bottle from her friend and offering to pop the cork.

The noise made them jump, and Teesha instinctively looked around for the cruiser. They had drifted around Castle Neck Peninsula, the natural outcrop separating Ipswich Bay from Essex Bay, and toward Turtle Beach, a beautiful seven-mile expanse of white sand and spinifex. The cruiser, which was too heavy to enter the shallower shoals of Essex Bay, was anchored on the other side of the outcrop, now just beyond their sight. Her mom would be pissed.

"Quick, Mom will kill us if she sees this." The girls each took a long sip, enjoying the feeling of the bubbly, semichilled liquid sliding down their throats.

"I'm hot. Let's go for a swim, and then I'll tell you who called me last night."

Teesha undid her life jacket, pulled off her hat and shook her long brown hair out of its ponytail. She stood up, her light frame tilting the boat a little to the left, and dived into the water.

"Who? Who called you?" asked Christina, leaning over the edge of the boat. "Not Justin. Teesha, was it Justin?"

"Ah, it's beautiful," said Teesha, drawing out the suspense. "Come on in."

"Okay, okay," said Christina just as Mariah dived in.

"Wait for me," said Francie, tugging at the jacket around her waist.

"It's okay, Francie," said Christina with a smile. "I'll wait. Let's hold hands and we'll jump in together."

■ ■ ■

Rayna Martin sat in her blue-and-white-striped deck chair, looking out upon the mesmerizing expanse before her. The water was a mercurial shade of silver. It looked like a glassy canvas upon which someone had dropped tiny spots of color.

The rainbow reflections caught on the small wavelets in the salty inlet breeze.

Unlike the more picturesque ports of Cape Cod or Martha's Vineyard, Cape Ann, Massachusetts, had a character of its own, forgoing a clichéd "traditional resort beauty" for a more rustic aesthetic carved from its island topography and a historic respect for the sea. It was America's oldest seaport, home to generations of fishermen with big catches and even bigger nerve. It had survived the "perfect storm" of 1991, having built a reputation grounded in strength and toughness, and was home to a special breed of people who cherished their wood-shingle houses and ramshackle marinas with an unspoken pride and camaraderie.

But today, most important to Rayna, it smelled fresh and new and full of promise. It had the feeling of freedom and she wanted to absorb every minute of it. Perhaps it was the fact that her little girl was growing up, but something told her this was a time of change for her too—a new stage in her life, a new independence.

Rayna took a deep breath and closed her eyes to the blue skies and calm waters around her. It was more than a month until the official start of summer and weather like this in early May was nothing short of a blessing. She had picked up *The Cruisader* on schedule and was now anchored at the mouth of Essex Bay, just off the southernmost tip of Castle Neck Peninsula. The girls were about a quarter of a mile southwest, squashed in and sunning themselves with octopus legs dangling over the sides of the outboard. No doubt they were talking about their plans for summer and three months of freedom from Curtis Academy, one of Massachusetts' most respected and exclusive high schools and one of the most sought-after educational institutions in the country.

Rayna had made sacrifices to send her daughter to Curtis: long hours at work, weekends in the office, too much time away from her daughter. But this school was special. It had an admissions program based on excellence in both character and academia, striving for diversity in a city known for its—how would she put it?—unique racial structure. It was a school with ideals Rayna admired, especially a mission statement calling for the development of "inspired and resourceful thinkers dedicated to building a better universe for themselves and their fellow human beings," and a school motto, "Seek Justice with Compassion" that she lived by. Bottom line: it was one of the best and, as such, one of the most expensive options in a state renowned for its fine schools and universities.

Ten years ago, Teesha's father, a respected Boston attorney, had died suddenly from a brain tumor and Rayna had spent the past decade working around the clock to establish her own legal career. Determined to give Teesha the financial security she would have enjoyed if her father were still alive, Rayna had managed to build her own practice and divert into the niche area of African American legal support. She was now deputy director of AACSAM, the African American Community Service Agency of Massachusetts, and spent her days helping African Americans negotiate everything from legal aid and insurance payouts to health benefits and educational assistance.

While Boston was the birthplace of American independence, built on the principles of "Justice and Liberty for all," it was also a city of hyphenated Americans—Irish, Italian, Asian, African—each with their own cultural differences, often living in neighborhoods with people of similar backgrounds and needs.

It was Rayna's ambition to break down such barriers that had led to her rise through the ranks of AACSAM, where she gained the respect of all she came in contact with: white, black, Hispanic, Chinese. The agency even ran a sailing school, which is how Rayna and Teesha learned to sail. All this meant years of vocation dedication and the guilt that goes with it, and that's why this birthday outing was so special.

She took a sip of ice water to soothe her dry throat and leaned back in her chair, pondering the proud but heartbreaking thought that in a little over a year, her daughter and her friends would be off to college, living God knows where with Lord knows whom. She lifted her head to see that the outboard had drifted around the outcrop closer to the beach and sat up, squinting to distinguish the boat against the now golden ripples of water.

"Stay in sight, Teesha," she whispered to herself.

She contemplated pulling up anchor and following the little dinghy into Essex Bay—the tide was starting to come in and she was pretty sure the waters would be deep enough to chance a trip into the inlet—but she knew Teesha wouldn't stray too far, so she decided to wait a few more minutes in the hope they would motor back into view.

Ten minutes later, Rayna was on her feet and hauling anchor. *Kids,* she thought. *Why did they always have to stretch the boundaries?* It was then that she heard a voice off to her left, so she ran to the front of the cruiser. Christina Haynes was treading water about fifteen yards off to the port side.

"Mrs. Martin," she called, catching her breath.

"Christina, what are you doing? Where are the others?" yelled Rayna.

"They're, um . . . they need you, Mrs. Martin. Our boat capsized and Francie says she bumped her head when she fell out. Now she has a cramp and Mariah isn't strong enough to hold her up and Teesha is trying to do up her life jacket and we tried to pull the boat back over but Francie didn't want us to let her go and she was crying really loudly and . . ." Christina caught her breath again, her legs working hard beneath the crystal clear water. "I volunteered to swim out and get you to pick them up."

"Get in the boat now, Christina," said Rayna, before realizing the cruiser was pointed directly toward the beach, which meant the ladder was at the opposite end, a good thirty yards from the young teenager. "Swim that way," she called, pointing east. "And I'll turn the cruiser around so you can climb on board, quickly."

"*No,* Mrs. Martin. I mean, I don't think we should waste any time. I'm a really good swimmer. Best in my year."

Rayna was having trouble hearing Christina. There seemed to be a white noise, from above, but she ignored it, recognizing the trace of panic in Christina's voice and finding it contagious.

"I'm worried, Mrs. Martin," called Christina. "Francie was screaming. I don't know how long they . . . Please, it'll only take you a few minutes. I'll be fine. I just think you'd better go."

"Are you sure?" yelled Rayna.

"*Yes*. You're already pointed toward shore. Please."

"Okay, I'll be right back. Stay where you are."

Luckily, the anchor was up and the cruiser pointed directly toward the inlet. Rayna put the engine in full throttle, defying the shoals to threaten her lifted bow. As she headed west she craned her neck to see over the top of the sandy dune that ran down the middle of Castle Neck Peninsula, forming the two-sided strand that was Turtle Beach.

She pictured Francie gasping for breath, Teesha struggling to put on her life jacket, Mariah crying as she tried desperately to hold her head above water. She felt in that limbo between knowing and not knowing, between hope and fear, where dread is controlled by the practicality of getting from A to B in the shortest time possible.

After what seemed like an eternity she turned into the cove and saw them, all three of them, alive and well, their life jackets zipped up, holding on to the bottom of the capsized boat. Rayna finally let out a breath she had no idea she had been holding as she approached the three bobbing up and down in the water. They looked more than okay. In fact, Teesha and Mariah seemed to be enjoying some joke at Francie's expense. Rayna's relief became tinged with anger as she pulled up alongside and signaled for them to climb onto the cruiser.

"I can't believe you girls. Teesha, I told you not to lose sight of the cruiser. I was so worried. Francie, are you okay? What the hell were you thinking?"

"It's okay, Mom," said Teesha, trying to stop giggling and apologize to her mother. "We took our jackets off so we could jump in for a swim, and the boat turned over on us. Then Francie said she bumped her head, and got a cramp and . . . Where's Chrissie?"

"What am I supposed to think happened when Christina turns up floating alongside the cruiser?"

The veins in Rayna's temples and arms bulged as she turned the cruiser's steering wheel a full 180 degrees and shouted at the three girls.

"Come on, get in. When you act irresponsibly, you put

lives at risk, Teesha. Accidents happen all the time; you three were just lucky. Just get on board, quickly. We'll come back for the outboard in a few minutes. Christina is still in the water."

Teesha whispered a "Sorry, Mom," which was followed by apologies from the other two girls. Rayna turned her back on them and maneuvered the boat around to head northeast.

The girls moved to the edge of the cruiser in silence. The sun was reflecting brightly off the water's surface and they squinted downward, trying to spot Christina through the millions of fluid lights that flickered back up at them.

"Where is she, Mom?"

"Here somewhere. She has to be close by." Rayna turned off the engine so that they might hear Christina calling from somewhere nearby. All four called out for her—but there was no answer.

Francie started moaning about her leg, claiming the cramp was returning. Mariah fell silent, and Teesha's face started to wear the early signs of concern.

One minute went by, then two, three.

It was so quiet. The seagulls seemed to have disappeared, the engine was still and all they could hear was the peaceful sound of water lapping up against the edges of the boat. A cold chill started to grow in Rayna's stomach. It made its way up her spine and down her arms to her fingertips. Her brain teetered on the precipice between the logical need not to overreact in front of three scared teenagers and a more primitive desire to scream in the seconds that precede a catastrophe.

"Christina! Christina!"

"God, Mom, this is weird."

"She must have swum off a little farther." Mariah spoke at last. "She's a good swimmer. Maybe she wanted to stretch out a little, to keep warm."

"She has to be here," said Rayna. "She has to be."

It was then that Mariah pointed toward the starboard. "There she is. God, that was scary. She must be looking at some fish or something. Christina. Hey, over here," she called out to her friend.

A relieved Rayna headed to the front of the boat, but she sensed the stillness and silence, and the fresh flow of fear that came with it. The first thing she noticed was the long blond hair floating out around Christina's head, which was facing downward. She looked like an angel hovering in a sea of fairy lights. Her lower body hung loosely in the water like a night-shirt suspended on a clothesline. Her arms were stretched out as if ready to embrace. Her pink nail polish glistened at the end of her graceful fingertips.

Christina Haynes was not breathing.

Rayna Martin was sure of it.

■ ■ ■

Christina was heavy.

She wore a white Gap T-shirt over her blue hipster bi-kini (*the same as Teesha's!*) and it dragged in the water. Francie and Mariah helped Rayna pull her on board while Teesha repeated her Mayday call into the two-way. Her skin was clammy and hard, like the cool, glossy plastic feel of a Barbie doll. It was blotchy, as if her whole body were blush-ing, and her fingers were wrinkled from the water expo-sure.

They laid her faceup on the deck. Her body made a loud plopping sound as water ran from her clothing and onto the wooden boards. Teesha screamed into the radio, finally con-tacting the Coast Guard and giving their location and direc-tion back to the marina. That done, she took the wheel and sped east toward the northern mouth of the Annisquam, keep-ing an eye out for the rescue vessel that would be heading north from Gloucester Harbor in an effort to meet them half-way.

Meanwhile, Rayna and Mariah commenced CPR. Chris-tina seemed to be leaking seawater and other foamy fluids. Her tongue and lips appeared swollen and her eyes remained shut.

Every three breaths, Rayna tilted her head to the side, making sure that when . . . *if* . . . Christina revived, she did not choke on her own vomit. Mariah was calm and effective, pushing down rhythmically on her friend's chest, rocking back and forward in practiced determination. Francie stood off to the side, clutching her stomach.

"Oh my God. Oh my God. Oh my God," Francie repeated in what sounded like some hysterical gospel chant. "My parents are going to kill me."

"For God's sake, Francie," snapped Rayna in between breaths. "You're not the one with the problem here. You were never the one with the problem. Snap out of it."

Ten minutes later a small wave on the port side told Rayna the Coast Guard had pulled up next to the cruiser. Neither boat stopped as two paramedics leaped from one vessel to the next. Within seconds they had taken over the CPR and attached Christina to all sorts of monitors that seemed, for all their importance, unusually quiet.

The paramedics fired questions at Rayna and the girls.

"How long was she unconscious?" asked the female paramedic.

"I don't know. It can't have been long."

"Has she taken anything—drugs, alcohol?"

"No," said Rayna.

"Yes," came a voice from behind her.

"Shut up, Mariah," said Francie.

"We were drinking champagne."

Rayna closed her eyes.

"How much?" asked the male paramedic.

"Christina was drinking straight from the bottle," said Mariah. "I'm not sure. Maybe half a bottle."

"She drank from my cup," said Francie, and Rayna noticed how easy it was for this young girl to lay blame.

By this stage they were about half a mile from Gloucester Marina. Rayna looked up to see the flashing lights: a red one above an Addison Gilbert Hospital ambulance, a yellow one above a Gloucester PD van and a blue one above a BPD blue and white. *Boston Police . . . a long way from home.* The thought raced through her mind.

The next few minutes happened as if in fast forward as Christina was lifted off the cruiser, onto a gurney, into the ambulance and off to the local hospital. The siren faded in the distance and the silence seemed even worse than its deafening wail.

At that point time seemed to stand still. It was as if no one existed but these four females—the commotion around them detached by their closeness to the agony of the moment. And there they stood, wet and bedraggled and unable to speak on this picturesque jetty, under this glorious sunshine, on this beautiful day.

2

Boston district attorney Loretta Scaturro removed her wire-rimmed glasses and rubbed hard at her bloodshot brown eyes.

It was Saturday and she had been putting down a thick pile of case files and contemplating an evening walk down to the harbor and up to the North End for some Italian takeout when the phone had rung with the bad news.

Christina Haynes was dead. The official cause of death, according to Boston's head of Homicide, Lieutenant Joe Mannix, was drowning.

Lieutenant Mannix, who had two cops on the scene and two detectives already working the case, had just arrived at Christina's parents' home to inform them of the untimely death of their only daughter.

Lucky Joe. Better him than her. Loretta quietly scolded herself for callousness in the wake of such a tragedy but realized that the case was going to cause all kinds of trouble.

Christina's father, Senator Rudolph Haynes, was one of the most influential men in the state. Hell, he was one of the most powerful men in the country, and Loretta knew he would be all over this—and more specifically, all over her. This was an election year and the case was going to be tricky. After all, the death occurred way beyond her field of influence— Gloucester, Cape Ann—a long way from Suffolk County and the jurisdiction of the Boston Police Department. But she knew Haynes would have his say in that too, and Mannix was smart enough to keep a foothold on things until the dust had settled.

She moved to the kitchen, the thought of a walk long forgotten as she opened a bottle of her finest Merlot. And then, glass in hand, she moved back into the living room without turning on the lights and sat down in her chintz-covered chair, focusing on the telephone before her and counting down the seconds until it screeched with his call.

. . .

David Cavanaugh swung his feet up onto Arthur Wright's desk and lifted the icy cold beer to his mouth, the refreshing liquid stinging the fresh cut on his lower lip before making its way down his throat. Arthur was right; there is no better way to drink a beer than straight from the top of an almost frozen longneck bottle. David's boss claimed to have spent at least some part of his colorful past in Australia, where, he told David, they drink beer the only way it was meant to be drunk: coldly, quickly and in copious amounts.

"Now I know why they call it the game they play in heaven," said Arthur, referring to David's weekly fix of rugby with his old Boston College buddies.

"Why is that?"

"Because the entire brutish code is designed to send its players on a fast track to the pearly gates or, in your case, in the opposite direction."

David smiled. It was rare that he and his boss/mentor/ friend had time to hang out like this, but it was Saturday evening and they had just put in four long hours of criminal-precedent research.

"We'll both be in hell before these two parties reach some form of agreement," said David.

David had worked for Wright, Wallace and Gertz for twelve years. The firm, located in a low-rise heritage building on Boston's historic Congress Street, was an old one, with Arthur, at sixty-seven, being the youngest of the three partners. Howard Wallace was semiretired, Walter Gertz was more administrator than lawyer, and these days Arthur spent much of his time tag-teaming it with his young up-and-coming associate, David Cavanaugh.

Arthur was one of those rare creatures who had achieved great respect among his peers without ever having walked the conservative Boston legal fraternity line. He was one of the best criminal attorneys in the city, but he looked more like a weather-beaten sailor fresh from a solo trip around the globe. He preferred jeans over trousers, open-neck shirts over button-downs and beer over bourbon. He was bright and brusque, stubborn and opinionated, and was David's rough-around-the-edges hero.

Luckily for David, Arthur's sometimes limited patience had stretched far enough to foster the career of the overenthusiastic associate who had worked his way up through the ranks to become one of Arthur's most trusted employees. David was in the process of earning a good reputation of his own as both a solid legal negotiator and competent trial lawyer. As such, he was becoming a cash cow for the firm and a partnership was certainly not out of the question.

David took another long swallow and jumped a little when a knock at Arthur's door was followed by the swift, no-nonsense entrance of Arthur's assistant, Nora.

Nora Kelly was fiftyish. She was sharp as a tack and spoke with the thickest Irish accent David had ever heard, or misunderstood, as was more often the case. She was dedicated, hardworking and dripping with Irish wit that served to douse her prim and proper facade in just the right amount of humor.

Today she wore her customary tweed skirt and snow-white blouse, despite the fact that it was Saturday and David and Arthur were dressed down in jeans and collared T-shirts.

"Hey, Nora."

"Is what horses eat, lad, and would you please remove your shoes from Mr. Wright's nineteenth-century mahogany table. You need to get up anyway. You have a phone call."

"I do?" David smiled, immediately dropping his feet to the floor. "But no one knows I'm here, Nora. Sure you aren't bluffing to steal a minute alone with me?"

"Never in your reasonably short but unfortunate life," she returned. "C'mon then, lad, move it. The lady won't hold forever."

"Lady, hm?" Now Arthur was interested.

"No accounting for taste," said Nora.

Arthur and Nora had been trying for the past decade to set up David with every single, breathing female they came across. David had married his college sweetheart at nineteen, divorced at twenty-three and spent the past twelve years buried in his work and stumbling from one uncommitted relationship to the next.

"Are you both finished?" he said, signaling to Nora that he had no intention of moving to his office but would take the call on Arthur's direct line.

"You can live in hope, dear boy," said Nora, always needing to have the last word.

And then David smiled, looking past her to her screensaver, which she changed daily. Without fail, it consisted of an uncannily prophetic proverb. "There's always a calm before a storm," it read, and while half of him wondered why she had chosen this particular maxim today, the other had a strange feeling he was about to find out.

"This is David Cavanaugh."

"Mr. Cavanaugh, my name is Sara Davis and I am an attorney. I work for AACSAM." David knew of AACSAM. He had done some pro bono work for them a couple of years ago. "I'm at police headquarters. I am calling to ask your help."

"I'm listening, Ms. Davis."

"Rayna Martin is my boss."

"I remember her."

"And she you. That's why I called."

David had worked with Rayna on a health insurance case, something about a young kid who was being denied a payout for kidney surgery. He remembered liking her, thinking she was gracious, and smart.

"There has been an accident. And Mrs. Martin is currently being questioned by the Boston PD."

"Has she been charged with something?"

"No charge, at least not yet, but Rayna is anticipating a problem. You see, a teenager in her care drowned this afternoon."

"Where?" asked David.

"Essex Bay, just north of Gloucester, Cape Ann."

"But Boston has the case?"

"Yes," said Sara. "Apparently, there were two Boston cops on the scene."

"Okay. But she's a teenager, so she can swim, right? We're not talking a toddler here."

"There are circumstances. The girl drowned on a boating trip, a birthday party for Rayna's daughter."

"So we're talking—"

"We're not talking anything specific as yet. But the detectives are hovering."

"Are the police claiming Mrs. Martin was negligent in her care of the girl?"

"I'm not sure. It's possible, but the girl's father will certainly have a hand in all that."

This was getting more interesting by the minute.

"Who is the girl, Ms. Davis?" asked David, now looking up at Arthur who was leaning forward on his desk, curious as to what was going on.

"Christina Haynes. Her father is Senator Rudolph Haynes."

David said nothing, just took it all in.

"Mr. Cavanaugh, are you there?"

"Yes, I'm sorry, Ms. Davis. I was just thinking."

"I know. There is a lot to think about. In any case, as I said, Rayna is asking for you."

"Ms. Davis," said David.

"It's Sara."

"Okay, Sara, I'm gonna hang up now and walk out the door. I can be in Roxbury in about fifteen. Tell Rayna I'm on my way and not to say anything until I get there. Tell her not to worry and that we'll work this out."

• • •

David Cavanaugh pushed through the front glass doors of the Boston Police Department headquarters and looked around for anyone who might be Sara Davis. Within seconds he felt a firm tap on his shoulder and turned to see a woman standing behind him.

Sara Davis had a slim build and long brown hair framing her narrow, high-cheekboned face. David knew this was not the time to be distracted by her mocha skin and pale blue eyes and immediately collected himself to shake her outstretched hand.

"It's nice to meet you, Mr. Cavanaugh; I'm glad you're here."

"Call me David."

"Thanks." She steered him toward the check-in desk before they headed for the elevators at the end of the large, marble-floored lobby. "It's getting rather tense up there. Rayna gave an initial statement to a uniform but has since refused to talk to the detectives."

"Who are the detectives involved?" David knew most of the plainclothes team at headquarters.

"Detectives Petri and Rico, I think."

"I know Petri," said David, now getting a little concerned himself. "He's homicide. Go on."

"Well, there's a certain . . . vibe."

"What vibe?" he asked.

"The one where you feel a simple matter could be on the verge of becoming something a lot more complicated."

"Sara, forgive me for asking this up front, but Rayna must know scores of lawyers, so why me?"

"Rayna remembered you from the Jamal Digby case. She admired your work."

"But I'm a criminal attorney and she hasn't been charged with anything as yet, so—?"

"No. Not *yet,* but . . ." Sara stopped. "The police are interviewing the three girls who were also on the cruiser; they are still up at Addison Gilbert Hospital in Gloucester. Christina's body is on its way to the ME's office, and the autopsy is being scheduled for tomorrow."

"On a Sunday? Fast work. Have they put someone in charge of the case?" David knew some major clout was needed to organize an autopsy this early.

"Yes, Lieutenant Mannix."

Joe Mannix was the commander of the Homicide Unit. David knew him well and liked him. They'd been friends for years, but he was as high as you could go on the ladder of death at Boston PD. He was a good man, hardworking, loyal and more interested in solving crimes than pandering to the politics that went hand in hand with his position.

"What's wrong?" asked Sara, obviously noticing David's worried expression.

"Joe Mannix is head of Homicide," he said. "The DA probably asked for him personally."

"I have a bad feeling about this," she said.

"Okay, Sara, let's head upstairs. Mannix is a friend, and at the very least should be able to give us some indication of what the hell is going down."

■ ■ ■

"David." Lieutenant Joe Mannix looked up as the elevator doors opened.

"Hey, Joe. How's the family?"

"Good. They're good. I was just about to come find you. Got a minute?" asked Mannix, his head angling back toward his office as he stole a glance at Sara.

David asked Sara to excuse him while he got the background from the lieutenant. He was anxious to get the police take on all of this before he met with Rayna. Things were moving way too fast.

■ ■ ■

Joe Mannix's office in the new Roxbury Police Headquarters Building was arranged in what could only be described as an assembly of minimalist chaos. The pale gray carpet formed a base for four walls—three glass and one solid and painted off-white, the latter of which acted as a partition between the Homicide Unit and the main corridor behind it. The glass walls were backed by venetian blinds that ran to the floor and, judging by the dust on their slats, were set permanently open, just like the door pushed back against the wall, which had worn a groove in the office carpet.

The overcrowded desk was a birch laminate with metal legs that were already scuffed with shoe polish. On top was a phone, various pieces of stationery, three manila folders and a framed photograph of Joe's wife, Marie, and his four sons. At the back right-hand corner sat a metal basket marked In, which was overflowing with paperwork while the complementary Out tray was pretty much empty.

The chair behind the desk was one of those ergonomically

correct offerings, all gray and squat and uninviting. It looked newer than everything else in the room and David guessed it was because his detective friend spent more time perched on the edge of his desk than he did passing out orders from behind it. This afternoon was no exception.

"Okay," said David, leaning his back against the front glass wall. "Let's have it."

Mannix went through the basic story Rayna had given the police on the scene, starting with the cruiser hire and ending with their arrival back at port.

He told David about the two Boston cops, and their water safety course, and their establishment of jurisdiction over the scene. He said Rayna gave an initial statement to Officer Tommy Wu but then refused to speak further until she saw her lawyer—David Cavanaugh.

"Bet the local cops were impressed," said David, referring to Boston PD's commandeering the case.

"This is a sensitive situation. The media will be all over it. They were probably happy to pass."

"Sure, Joe. More like you guys saw the red flag on this one, and knew the girl's father would want it handled down here."

Joe hesitated.

"Okay," said Mannix. "If it was accidental death, why was Mrs. Martin so afraid to talk to us?"

"Come on, Joe. She gave Tommy the facts. After that, she was probably smart enough to realize there was no need for further explanation until she lawyered up. She's a respected counselor with solid legal training. The woman isn't stupid, and given the girl's parentage . . ."

Mannix looked at David and shrugged his shoulders. They both knew how these things worked.

"I suppose the DA will be involved," said David, fishing for more information.

"Does a bear shit in the woods? Scaturro asked me to look after this one personally."

"But you're chief of Homicide, Joe, and as you aptly pointed out, the media will be all over this one. Your involvement gives the immediate impression my client is—"

"Look, David, no one is gunning to take this woman down. If the death was accidental, then that's what we'll find."

"How can it be anything but? What is she supposed to have done, held the girl under water because they ran out of party food?"

"No, but she may have played favorites when it came to their rescue."

"That's crazy. You've heard her story; it makes perfect sense."

"To you and me, maybe, but we're not the DA and we're certainly not Senator Rudolph Haynes."

David realized that Mannix, in his own way, was giving him a subtle warning.

"What are you getting at, Joe? If something is up, I deserve to know. I *am* the woman's attorney, after all."

"It's the four girls," said Mannix, lowering his voice before going on, "or more specifically, the three who are alive and the one who is dead. Teesha Martin, Mariah Jordan and Francie Washington are all African American, and Christina Haynes is . . . well, Christina Haynes was white."

• • •

It was almost nine by the time David got to see Rayna Martin. She sat in the corner of interview room 1, the pale green cinder-block walls making it feel even colder. She looked even smaller than David remembered; her normally bright eyes now red with tiredness and her neat navy dress crumpled and damp from the long day's events. Sara was sitting by her side and a plainclothes cop stood sentry at the door.

David knew time was running out for the police. They had to charge her with something soon or let her go home.

"David, how nice of you to come." She managed a smile. "It's been a while."

"Too long, Rayna. Given your extensive connections in the industry, I have to admit I'm flattered you called, if that's an appropriate thing to say under the circumstances."

"It is and thank you, but you have to remember I've seen how you work, David, and to be honest, it was an easy decision to make. I'm just glad Sara found you, and that you're here."

She gave a quick sideways glance toward the cop at the door, and David took her cue, asking him to leave.

After the officer had gone, Rayna stood up from her chair to shake David's hand with both of her own. He noticed how cold and clammy they were.

"I want to see my daughter," she said, her grip on him tightening.

"Isn't she back from Gloucester?"

"The police keep saying the girls are resting, being treated for shock, but we get the feeling they're stalling us," said Sara.

David patted Rayna's hands as if saying it was okay to release him, before leaving the room momentarily and returning with the news that Francie's and Mariah's parents had already picked up their daughters and taken them home and that Teesha was on her way to headquarters in a Gloucester PD patrol car.

This seemed to calm Rayna a little, but she admitted she was still concerned at how long the girls had been held for treatment, wondering if it was a tactic for the police to tire them with endless questions.

"Not that that should be a problem, right?" said David.

"No, not at all," she said, her brow now fixed and tight. "But these are teenagers, David—scared, impressionable, emotional kids who have just witnessed the death of their good friend."

David suggested they get themselves a fresh cup of coffee and start from scratch. Sara offered to go down the block for the real thing, leaving David and Rayna to get to it.

* * *

Twenty minutes later, Sara returned with the coffee. Teesha was sitting next to her mom, their hands held tightly, Teesha's head resting on her mother's shoulder. Rayna was describing their arrival back at the marina, and Sara quietly took a seat by the door.

"The police officer . . . Officer Wu, he was very polite, gave me a blanket, some coffee. The other officer, the woman . . ."

"Officer Leigh," said Teesha.

"Yes, she was speaking to the girls. I told Officer Wu exactly what I told you, David, just as it happened. He was thorough. He took notes."

"Wu's been involved with some of my cases in the past. He's a good cop."

"I got that feeling too."

"He . . ." she went on, as if trying to remember something.

"He what?" said David.

"Well, he seemed to be annoyed by his radio. It kept interrupting our conversation and he was getting up every few minutes to talk into it."

"Who was he talking to?"

"Someone back at Boston HQ, a detective, Petri, I think." Rayna rubbed her temples as if trying to massage away the fatigue and clear her head.

"I remember hearing bits and pieces, but to be honest, I'm having a little trouble recalling all the details."

"Understandable. Go on, just take your time."

"The next thing I know he asked me to come down to the station, back to Boston. I told him I wanted to see my daughter, but he promised he would have someone drive her back down. By the time I got here, two detectives were waiting for me at the front door. It all happened so quickly. They were treating me like a perp. I have seen the routine too many times, but I'm usually the one who comes to the rescue. That's when I got wise."

Rayna explained how she told the big detective—Petri—that she had given Officer Wu her statement and would not be answering any further questions until she made a phone call to her lawyer.

Petri sang the usual "why do you need a lawyer when you haven't done anything wrong" song, but that made Rayna all the more determined to find David and secure legal representation as soon as she could.

"I called Sara and asked her to track you down."

Sara explained how directory assistance gave out his home number, but when there was no answer, she guessed that he might be at his office—and luckily he was.

"And that is basically it," said Rayna, looking at David apologetically, as if knowing it wasn't enough. "It was an accident, a horrible, tragic accident, but I can't help but think they . . ."

Rayna's eyes started to pool with tears as she swallowed a silent sob lodged deep in her throat. David took her hand and they sat for a moment before Rayna spoke again.

"You know, it's true what they say."

"What's that?" asked David.

"That the events of one day can change your life forever."

David saw the fear in his client's eyes and wanted desperately to reassure her. "It's okay, Rayna. You will get your life back."

"Do you think so? Somehow, I'm not so sure."

• • •

By the time Rayna had finished her story, their coffee cups were empty and Teesha had fallen asleep against her mother's shoulder. David looked at his watch. It was almost eleven. This was crazy. His client had given a full statement and as far as he was concerned, there would be no more questions tonight. If there was no charge, Rayna should be allowed to go home with her daughter.

David rose from his chair to go tell Mannix just that, and found Tommy Wu standing immediately outside the door.

"Hey, Tommy."

"Hi, Mr. Cavanaugh."

"What is it?" This came from Detective Paul Petri, sitting at his desk just three feet away and smirking behind mounds of untidy paperwork and countless dirty cups of coffee dregs.

"Where's Mannix?"

"He's busy."

David glanced at Mannix's office and immediately noticed the change. The venetians were drawn. Joe had visitors and David's guess was his client was the subject of their discussions.

"You got something to say?" Always the charmer was Petri.

"My client has given her statement. No charge has been laid

and we certainly won't be answering any further questions tonight. So unless you guys have something else, I'm taking Rayna Martin and her daughter home."

Petri told David to wait with his client while he checked things out, and within minutes Tommy Wu was knocking on the interview-room door.

"Mrs. Martin, I'm sorry about the delay. You and your daughter can go home now."

Tommy glanced at David. "I'm sorry about all this; everything seems to take longer on the weekends," he attempted.

David noticed that Tommy looked straight at the floor and decided to do a little more fishing.

"Long day, Tommy?"

"Yeah, my shift finished hours ago. But you know what it's like; when the DA's around, we all jump."

Tommy's eyes hit the floor again and his brow furrowed slightly, as if he realized that maybe he had given too much away. But then his eyes lifted briefly to meet David's straight on. The comment about Scaturro was not a slip. It was a tip-off.

"Scaturro's here?"

"Ah . . . yeah, she popped in for a bit. Anyways, we'll drive you home if you like, Mrs. Martin."

"It's okay, Tommy. I got it," said David.

"You sure then? Okay. Mrs. Martin, I'm sorry for . . . you know."

"I do, and so am I, and thank you, Officer, you've been very kind."

"No problem."

And with that, Tommy Wu slinked backward out the door as if embarrassed that he had ever been involved with the whole unruly mess.

. . .

David dropped Rayna and Teesha at their home in the South End before heading uptown toward Sara's brownstone in the historic North End. It was a neat-looking building with window boxes and a painted mailbox, located between a small Italian restaurant and another family brownstone so common in this culturally rich harborside cranny. It looked warm and inviting.

He turned off the engine and they sat there in silence for a moment before she spoke.

"Thank you," she said, looking straight ahead.

"There's no need."

"This isn't the end of it, is it?"

David paused before answering. "No."

"Should we be preparing for the worst?"

By "worst" David knew Sara was referring to a criminal charge—most likely involuntary manslaughter. In order for this charge to stick, the DA had to believe they had a chance of proving Rayna was grossly negligent when she left Christina alone in the water, and that this one decision ultimately led to her death. Involuntary manslaughter could carry a jail term of up to twenty years, but first-time offenders usually expected a three-to-five-year sentence.

David hated to admit it, but while the charge seemed horribly unjust, it was not totally unreasonable in the eyes of the law. He had seen similar cases where ordinary people had been placed in extraordinary circumstances over which they had no control and had ended up facing a jury.

"Yes," he finally answered. "We should prepare just in case." He turned to look at her. "What are you doing tomorrow?"

"You mean today, don't you?" It was past midnight.

"Today then," he said.

"You tell me."

"Why don't we meet at my office late morning, say about ten-thirty. I'll try to get my boss, Arthur Wright, to be there too. He has a knack for heading off trouble. Can I pick you up?" he asked, not sure if the offer was inappropriate.

"No, thanks, I know where you work; I'll meet you there. But thanks again, you know, for everything."

Her smile almost made him forget the horrible circumstances that had resulted in their sitting here, alone, in the early hours of a spring Sunday morning.

"Tomorrow then," she said before turning to get out of the car.

Tomorrow, he said to himself, watching her go and sitting there a moment longer, as if unwilling to disturb the quiet that had settled over the old, narrow streets. He waited as her automatic entrance light went on, and then off, the last of the neighborhood lights extinguished, before turning on the engine and heading for home.

3

Rudolph Haynes closed his eyes and allowed the memory to consume him. For some reason his father's words had been looming in the back of his brain all day—today of all days, the worst day of his life, the day of his daughter's death. Haynes was not one to reminisce, but over the years he had come to acknowledge that memories such as these resurfaced for a reason and, considering that his father had been the man he was, he realized he would be foolish to ignore what could be a valuable insight.

"You know what the most ridiculous Americanism is, son?" Alistair Haynes had asked his five-year-old son over sixty years ago. "You can count on it. You can count on it!" He had said it twice, the second time with gusto. "That, young Rudi, is rubbish, claptrap, tripe, utter nonsense! If you want to get ahead in this world, son, you count on nothing," Alistair Haynes had continued. "For there is no such thing as fate, and any man who tells you otherwise is a liar and a fool."

Haynes remembered the smell of malt and sweat and perhaps a trace of regret that had accompanied his father's late-night visits.

"Life isn't going to cut you any breaks, Rudi. You make your own way like your father and his father before him. Of course you must play the game," the older Haynes had gone on. "As doing the dance is just as important as getting the applause. But know inside, son, in here . . ." he had pressed his hand against his son's chest, hard enough for Rudi to swallow a cough, ". . . that you are a Haynes, better than the rest of them, with a clear mind and determination to succeed."

Young Rudi had looked at his father then, his brain absorbing the advice like a hungry sponge, his back straight, his expression intense and his respect beyond question.

"Finally," the older Haynes had said in conclusion. "You must set goals. Know your plan from beginning to end and don't ever let some weak-kneed son of a bitch think they can get away with cheating you. Mercy is a weakness and pity even worse. You're a good boy, Rudi," he had said as he took his only child in his arms, in a rare show of affection. "Just don't take any crap."

Haynes ached—physically, mentally. For his entire career, his entire *life,* he had prided himself on remaining focused at times of extreme pressure, and yet now, at the very time when he needed it most, his ability to concentrate seemed to have abandoned him.

He forced his thoughts back to his father, to what he would do at a time like this, to his belief in the power of strategy and his mantra: "A man with a plan is a man in command."

And he was right. In fact, it was upon this philosophy that Rudolph Haynes had based his long and successful political career. A loyal Republican, he had been elected a U.S. senator almost thirty years ago—an amazing feat considering Massachusetts had been a Democratic powerhouse since JFK won his congressional seat back in 1946. He, a blue-blooded conservative in a city of Irish liberals, had conquered Boston and still, after all these years, held his seat with an unbeatable majority.

Like his father before him, Haynes had learned the art of "tap dancing." He had mastered the skill of demanding perfection without alienating the public and could lead a campaign that no political opponent could rival. He had a reputation for strength, consistency and getting things done—and he still didn't take any crap.

Even so, he knew the timing of this tragedy could not be worse. U.S. senators were elected or reelected on a cyclic basis once every six years, and his seat was up for reelection next year. His campaign strategy was about to begin, and this violation, this "attack" on his family, was completely unforgivable.

So now, as he sat at his hand-carved, cherrywood desk in his painstakingly arranged library, in his beautifully appointed home, he knew he must call upon every iota of his organizational genius to set things right—for his own sake; for his wife, Elizabeth; and most of all for Christina.

He could hear the faint moans of Elizabeth's sobbing in the living room and immediately swallowed the wave of emotion that had stolen into his thoughts and attempted to cloud his focus. He must stay calm. There was no time for grief. First things first. One step at a time. His daughter was dead, and the explanation was unacceptable. So he knew it would be left to him to carve out the road to justice and ensure that those running this show were driving in the appropriate direction.

He had great respect for the legal process and its many ambiguities—for Harvard had taught him the rules, and politics had shown him the possibilities. Katz had called twice and he had spoken to Verne, and so he took some relief in the comfort of action.

Justice, he said to himself. "Justice." He said it aloud and then followed it with another word: "Control."

• • •

They called him the Kat because he was slick and quick and always landed on his feet. Not to his face, of course, but behind the secretarial partitions and closed office doors of the DA's office. And now, sitting across from him in her Martha Stewartesque sunroom, in her tastefully decorated harborside condominium, on this sunny Sunday morning, Loretta Scaturro had a silent laugh to herself as she had to agree the name fit.

ADA Roger Katz was her second in command, a meticulously groomed man with expensive tastes, a George Hamilton tan and Armani sunglasses that rarely left his dark, almond-shaped eyes. He was confident to the point of arrogance, smooth with the ladies and one of the boys. He drove a red Corvette, shopped on Newbury Street and lived in a condo in Back Bay's fashionable Copley Place. He was also one of the smartest attorneys she had ever worked with and if there was one thing she needed right now, it was a sharp mind to help her sort through this mess.

DA Scaturro had spent most of last night at headquarters trying to get her head around every piece of information relating to the Haynes case. Senator Haynes had called her within minutes of receiving news of his daughter's death and, cool and calm as usual, had asked her to personally investigate the circumstances surrounding Christina's drowning. His voice was cordial but strong, and she knew that when Rudolph Haynes asked for something, he expected results quickly and efficiently.

So she had called the coroner and organized a weekend autopsy, the results of which she should have within twenty-four hours. She met Mannix at headquarters and questioned Officers Wu and Leigh. She called Katz and briefed him on the situation. She wanted him to focus on Rayna—her job, her home life, her personality. She knew Katz would jump at this one—it was high profile and gave him the chance to impress Senator Haynes. Right up the Kat's alley, so to speak.

She brought her attention back to Katz, fully decked out in his Sunday Ralph Lauren. He was telling her what he had discovered so far.

"Everyone at work loves her," he said. "But this is a niche group, racially and socially. In other words, they don't get out much." Katz flashed one of his perfect-teeth smiles. "She has a reputation for being smart, savvy. She's gracious without being sycophantic. She is happy to burn an insurance company CEO one minute and console a crackhead the next."

God, thought Scaturro, this woman was beginning to sound like the Second Coming, which, from their point of view, would make things difficult.

"She is forty-two, widowed, one daughter. She has a wealthy older sister who lives in Brookline, a divorcée named Delia Banks, who often keeps an eye on the kid when she's busy at work, which is often.

"Martin is independently quite well off herself. She sends the kid to Curtis Academy, owns a million-plus property in the South End and drives a Lexus 4WD." Katz went on to explain that Rayna had at least three years' sailing experience and was well trained in all areas of nautical safety. "Which sounds pretty rosy, but it is only Sunday morning and there is plenty of digging to come." Katz smiled some more.

"Look, Roger," said Loretta, getting to the crux of the matter. "Senator Haynes is breathing down my neck—make that *our* necks—on this one." There was nothing like a threat from lofty heights to get Roger fired up. "We don't have much time—it's already making the front page. If there is a case for involuntary manslaughter, we have to find it fast. We're already behind the eight ball for not booking her last night. But Mannix claims there are no solid grounds for the charge. He also warned that if we harass this woman, we're in for some serious flack from her colleagues, who, you may have noticed, hold some serious clout in this community."

"With all due respect, Loretta, Mannix is full of crap and it doesn't help that he's good friends with her attorney. We don't need an ironclad case to book her. All we need are the grounds for a potential case."

He was right, but this was a tricky one and Loretta still had her doubts.

"Look." The Kat took the floor, smoothing down his pants in the process. "First of all, she leaves a teenager—no, a *drunken* teenager—floating over five hundred yards out to sea."

"She didn't know about the alcohol," countered Scaturro. "And I don't think the girl was drunk, a little light-headed maybe."

"Come on, one glass at sixteen and you're on your way, right? And this is not about what she says but what we might be able to prove. Let's not forget these kids were underage, in her care and drinking booze on a small boat in the middle of historically treacherous waters. Secondly, she has that whole mother/daughter protection thing going on, so she decides to dump the friend to go and save her own kid. Understandable maybe, but still irresponsible, or some might say grossly negligent."

Loretta was now on the edge of her chair, listening to the arguments that had been going through her own head all night. Hearing Roger play them out started to give them validity.

"Okay, let's think of all the things she *didn't* do that she should have. She let four kids on an outboard built for three, and these are adult-sized kids, Loretta, not babies. She failed to check their bags for alcohol. She let them out of her sight, which meant the capsize occurred beyond her field of vision. She believed a drunken teenager when she said she was (a) a good swimmer and (b) sober enough to play Flipper way offshore for at least five minutes. We have more than probable cause—we have the foundations for a very strong prosecution, and we've only just scratched the surface."

Loretta sat back in her pink and white floral chair and considered her colleague's reasoning. Add this to the senator's determination and it certainly sounded more than plausible to at least charge the woman and proceed with formal investigations.

"Then there's the other matter," said Katz quietly, his eyes avoiding contact.

"No, Roger, we are not going down that road," she snapped. "It could be a disaster for all concerned. It could be fatal for us."

"So it's involuntary manslaughter then?"

Loretta could see the excitement in his eyes. He was willing to take what he could get, at least for now. "Call the District Court and talk warrant. Then call Mannix. Better still, hand me the phone and I'll make the calls myself. Let's do this now, before I have a chance to change my mind."

• • •

Vincent Verne had a love-hate relationship with computers. On one hand, they allowed incredible access to information—and not just the free-for-all kind but the confidential stuff, which was exactly the sort Vince was interested in. On the other, they left a trail. They had powerful hard drives with infinite memories that seemed all too permanent for a man who enjoyed the reassurance of anonymity.

Vince felt the same way about telephones, great for accumulating knowledge but landlines were too easy to trace. So he always used a cell that was registered to a fake name and, at times like this, he would change the number every twenty-four hours.

He found it easy to be anonymous. He had learned the art of being nobody from a very early age. His mother was only sixteen when he was born and thirty when she died. She took more notice of the liquor cabinet than she did of him. Looking back, he knew it had been good training for his career in obscurity. She had actually done him a favor.

And so this morning as he sat at his hotel room desk, having cleared it of brochures and note pads and other useless paraphernalia, he drew on such experiences and considered the significance of what was to come: his most important assignment yet. He had based his career, his entire adult life on protecting those more important than him. From the moment he left his poor excuse for a home, he'd set out to create a new life for himself by joining the Secret Service, and eventually he'd met the man who would take the place of the father he never had.

Now he had the ultimate opportunity to assist the man he respected more than any other. True, it was an opportunity doused in tragedy, but an opportunity nonetheless. And so he set out on his task. It had been only eighteen hours and he had already obtained extensive information on Rayna Martin—everything from her social security number to her health records, from her family background to her entire career history, her Boston University law school graduation marks, her car registration number, her home and cell phone details and a wealth of other intimate information extracted from her e-mail in-box. He even discovered that her favorite food was sushi, which he had never taken a liking to himself.

He had not slept but he wasn't tired; in fact, he felt invigorated. He took great pride in knowing the neatly compiled file before him was accurate, detailed and more than enough to get things started. Soon he would start on the other witnesses: the Martin girl, Mariah Jordan and Francine Washington. As the senator always said, information was your friend, and he was more than happy to provide such friendship to the man who had once saved his life.

. . .

David arrived at his office to find Sara waiting out front. She was wearing a pale blue dress the same color as her eyes. Her hair was pushed back from her face by her sunglasses, and she smiled as she rushed forward to help him carry the food and coffee trays.

It was just before ten-thirty and David used his security key to let them into the old federal-style building. He loved this part of town, so much so that his own high-rise apartment was only a block away. There was something inspirational about working on the street where the Declaration of Independence had first been read aloud, a stone's throw from where Samuel Adams had called upon the revolutionaries to throw Britain's highly taxed tea into the harbor and a short stroll from where Benjamin Franklin had gone to school.

They entered the office to find Arthur looking his usual scruffy self, already at work with various law books strewn across his beloved old desk. David had called him early in the morning knowing his boss would be anxious for an update, after which Arthur must have come straight to work, no doubt eager to get a head start on what they needed to cover.

Introductions were made and brunch unpacked as Arthur dived into his initial summation. "Okay, so we're supposing that the DA and her merry men may succumb to what we believe may be significant pressure from Senator Haynes to find someone to blame for his daughter's death."

"In a nutshell," said Sara.

"All right then, let's start with what we know. The DA was personally involved with the holding of Mrs. Martin at headquarters yesterday. She must have already spoken with Haynes and spent the best half of last night stalling so that the police could help her find probable cause and arrest Rayna while she was still at HQ. That failed, but David's subtle tip from Tommy Wu would suggest the DA is most likely still dedicated to finding such probable cause and issuing a warrant for arrest on the charge of involuntary manslaughter asap. By this stage she would have involved her ADA Roger Katz, who will be salivating at the political and publicity potential for such a case. Add this to Haynes's tenacity and, in all honesty, I would expect our client to be arrested before the day is out."

Sara shifted uncomfortably in her seat.

"Okay, so let's talk about their probable cause," said David.

"We must remember that Christina's last words were to Rayna," said Arthur. "So everything Rayna describes regarding that last conversation is hearsay."

"In other words," interrupted David, "the prosecution could claim Rayna blatantly abandoned Christina to seek out her daughter and the other two girls. In fact, that is their most likely scenario, a straight case of negligent abandonment—or in this case favoritism—which resulted in a helpless teenager being left alone in historically dangerous waters at a significant distance from shore."

"Creating the likelihood that her life would be put in imminent jeopardy," finished Arthur.

"This is crazy," said Sara. "You are making this sound like an open-and-shut case. When you put it that way, it sounds . . . I don't know, hopeless."

"No, my dear," said Arthur. "Just more interesting. In any case, Rayna must be prepared for scrutiny at all levels. If my guess is correct, Scaturro and Katz will be after a grand jury indictment within the week. The commonwealth will depend on finding character flaws or incidences that show a pattern of irresponsibility."

"Well, they won't. I know Rayna; she's a good woman," said Sara.

"I'm sure she is," said Arthur, lifting his gray eyes above the half spectacles that settled on the end of his nose, "but so was Joan of Arc, and look what happened to her."

• • •

They worked on possible prosecution scenarios until three in the afternoon, when David got the tip-off. Petri and Rico were on their way to Rayna's house with a warrant for her arrest.

Strictly speaking, Mannix was walking a fine line by calling with this information, but David knew his friend would have weighed the pros and cons of making such a call and would not have done so unless he believed Rayna Martin had the right to some form of legal backup upon her arrival at headquarters.

Mannix had told him he predicted an all-out frenzy, considering that the press had been calling all morning looking for the next installment for tomorrow's newspapers. And now, one look at the gathering crowd outside the new glass and granite police headquarters facility told David and Sara that he had been right.

The game was on. The circus had come to town. Television vans blocked traffic on the busy intersection of Ruggles and Tremont, while reporters and photographers grappled for position on the large, open-plan entryway leading up to the glass front doors. Cameramen divided themselves between the main and side entrances, unsure which way the unmarked detective's car would approach, while a third group hedged their bets by covering an alternative access at the building's rear.

David and Sara moved inside the building, just beyond the garaged back entrance where high profile prisoners were admitted. They knew the detectives always avoided the front doors, or "red carpet drive" as it was sometimes called, in cases of high media interest. Occasionally they would use the main doors, usually when a cop killer or pedophile saw them abandon any regard for the alleged criminal, but a case such as this would definitely be an undercover delivery.

But for some unknown reason, the detectives took Rayna through the front. Petri approached headquarters with lights flashing and siren blazing, and parked the car near the TV vans on Ruggles Street, more than four hundred feet from the crowded main entrance. A seemingly frustrated Rico pulled a handcuffed Rayna from the backseat and led her through the minefield of media who pushed and shoved, cameras held high.

It took over five minutes for them to negotiate the distance, giving the press their pound of flesh and then some, before

ADA Roger Katz, all seriousness and importance, opened the front doors and shepherded them into the building.

David and Sara rushed through the building trying to catch up with the action out front and saw Katz doing his best performance for the hungry audience milling around him. That explained the grand entrance. The Kat was making a curtain call and David headed straight for him.

"You bastard. How dare you parade my client through that mob." David grabbed Katz by the arm and spun him around hard.

"What's the matter, Counselor, your detective buddy give you a bum steer on the back door?" Katz said low enough and with a thoughtful look on his face so that any reporters looking through the front doors would assume Mr. Cool was as collected as ever. He told David he would be able to see his client once she had been processed, but until then he would have to sit tight.

"You know the drill, Counselor, but forgive me in advance if the processing takes a little longer than usual. This is a rather high profile matter and we want to make sure everything is done by the book. Don't you agree? So if you'll excuse me, Mr. Cavanaugh, Ms. . . . ?"

"Davis. Sara Davis," said Sara through gritted teeth.

"A pleasure," said the Kat before turning to follow Petri and Rayna down the marbled passageway.

Sara looked up at David. "That man is the lowest."

David didn't need anyone to tell him how low Katz could go. They had worked on opposite sides of the fence for a long time, and every case seemed to see the Kat find a new meaning to the word *shallow*.

"Don't let him get to you," said David. "Consider him an asset to the defense."

"An asset? How so?"

"He gives us another reason to fight. A few minutes ago I just wanted to win this thing. Now I'm going to enjoy doing it."

• • •

Luckily, Rayna's sister Delia had been at Rayna's home when the detectives arrived. She and Teesha had followed the unmarked car in her BMW. David and Sara met up with them in the front lobby and did their best to reassure Teesha, who was shaking in Delia's arms.

Delia was a larger-than-life version of her sister—in fact, thought David, everything about Delia was big. She was at least a foot taller than Rayna, with big hair, colorful clothes and a large diamond ring on her large left hand.

Sara introduced them and Delia immediately grabbed David by the shoulders, pulled him toward her and engulfed him in a hug. It seemed Delia Banks had a big heart too and was not afraid to show it.

"Your mother is in processing," said Sara, taking Teesha's hand. "You will be able to see her as soon as the paperwork is completed."

"Will she have to stay in jail tonight?"

"Probably," said David. There was no point in lying. "Your mom will most likely be arraigned tomorrow. This means she will stand before a judge who'll read the charge to her. That's when she gets to tell everyone she is not guilty. Then we get your mom out on bail," he said, looking toward Delia, sensing that she might have a hand in organizing the bond money, "and back home to you."

Delia gave him a nod.

"I want to tell them it wasn't her fault," said Teesha, breaking from Delia's embrace to look David directly in the eye. "It was my fault; it was my party. It was my idea to take the boat into the cove. We should never have drunk Francie's champagne."

"Stop that, girl," said Delia, hitching up her skirt so that she might bend down to Teesha's level.

"We've been over this all night. Your momma knows how much you love her, and this is nobody's fault. It was an accident—a tragic one, indeed, but all part of God's plan. Sara and Mr. Cavanaugh are good lawyers, Teesha, and more important, good people. They're gonna make sure your mom is free of all of this nonsense real soon."

With that Delia gave David a look of pure admiration and squeezed Sara's hand, the bracelets on her right arm jingling with approval, before taking Teesha to buy something to eat.

"Talk about pressure," said Sara, and he caught the small shudder at the intake of her breath.

"Come on," he said. "Let's go wait up in Homicide."

• • •

"Enjoying your weekend, Joe?" David and Sara tapped on Mannix's office door and walked in.

David was tempted to have a go at his friend over the afternoon's front door fiasco but decided against it. He knew Katz was behind the pathetic parade, and Petri was most likely acting under the ADA's orders. Joe was Petri's boss, but the lines of authority were becoming increasingly blurred in this case—and Joe had tipped them off, after all.

"Yeah, sure. My eldest kid was in his baseball prelims today. Don't even know the score."

Joe and his wife, Marie, had four sons, all of whom looked exactly like their mother. Mannix claimed it was his greatest gift to them, a mother with looks.

"Look, David, I'm sorry about the—"

"It's okay, Joe."

"I'm gonna have a word with Petri. I had no idea what he was going to do."

"It's okay. Thanks for the tip-off," David interrupted him.

Joe managed a smile. "What tip-off?"

David smiled back. "This is Sara Davis, by the way; she's working on the case with me."

"Hi." They shook hands and Mannix looked out through the glass of his office partitions before shutting the door. "You see the Kat out front?" he asked.

"Yeah. We had a few words."

"Watch him, David." Mannix paused, looking at Sara.

"It's all right, Joe. She's okay."

"All I'm saying is, Scaturro is one thing—she plays the political game, but she's pretty straight up. Katz, on the other hand . . . Haynes will want to pull the strings on this one and Katz will let him."

"But Scaturro's in charge, right? You told me that yourself."

"All I know is the Kat is looking very happy with himself.

I wouldn't be surprised if he and the senator were having some private dialogue of their own."

"You know this for a fact?" asked Sara.

Mannix looked at David again for reassurance of Sara's loyalties.

"All I know is, a cop can't help it if he walks into the coffee room to pour some more black mud and overhears part of a conversation."

"What? Katz and Haynes? Do you think they—" David was cut short by the sight of Katz and Detective Petri rounding the corridor.

"You better get going."

"Okay. Thanks, Joe."

"For what?"

· · ·

When Elizabeth Haynes was a child, she thought that all black people had the same first name: The. There was The Chauffeur, The Gardener, The Butler, The Maid.

As she sat in her living room, cold and alone, she watched the television images of Rayna Martin walking toward the front doors of police headquarters and decided she was The Murderer.

Elizabeth's upbringing had protected her from life's darker side. Her childhood was one of sailing boats and white ponies, tennis courts and pool parties. Then she'd been lucky enough to find Rudi, even if he wasn't, at first glance, the obvious choice for the fifth and final daughter of Preston "Percy" Whitman and his beautiful wife, Christine. But Rudolph had risen to the occasion and proven himself more than worthy, despite his Yankee heritage and political affiliations.

Elizabeth realized at that moment how much she needed Rudi right now and rose from her chair, turning off the television before heading downstairs to look for her husband in his study. He was busy. There would be so much to do. But surely he could stop for dinner, spend some time with her. After all, this was the worst time of their lives and without him she did not think she could go on.

"They've arrested her," she said, standing at the door.

"I know," he said flatly, pointing at the TV he had muted on the other side of the room.

She looked a little bewildered, as if she were wrong to feel some form of relief at the arrest.

"It's good, and it's just the beginning, Elizabeth."

She smiled at this, but it was a poor effort riddled with pain and exhaustion. "Are you coming down for dinner? It's after eight."

"I'll be there in ten."

"Good." She managed a half smile before turning to walk slowly down the hall. "Good."

■ ■ ■

Rudolph Haynes watched his wife leave and noted that, even in grief, she was the picture of elegance. But that was to be expected, considering her upbringing, her lineage, and perhaps more important, the position in life she had long ago accepted as her "duty."

Elizabeth Whitman Haynes was the youngest of five girls in a family loaded with money and flush with connections. She grew up in Greens Farms, Westport, the exclusive Connecticut town originally called Machamux, or "beautiful land," by the local Indians. The Whitman estate was a centerpiece of the local community, a large, traditional white colonial overlooking the glistening waters of the Long Island Sound. Her father played golf with the Kennedys, her mother was chief fund-raiser for the Connecticut Women's Auxiliary and her sisters—Eleanor, Edith, Eunice and Evelyn—all married appropriately.

So it was a miracle that she should find love not among the country club set she frequented but with Rudi, a brash young Bostonian with big ambitions and the brains to back them up. Not that Haynes was from the wrong side of the tracks, he was indeed very wealthy. His ancestors traced back to the first families of Boston, the Brahmins, as they came to be known.

Young Rudolph, his mother having died in childbirth, grew up the only child of an affluent, emotionally detached single parent and was sent to the best boarding schools money could buy. He studied law at Harvard and entered politics at the tender age of eighteen, running errands for the then Republican governor of Massachusetts. In fact, he recalled, reclining in his seat and closing his eyes, it was his work as a young campaign strategist that led to his first setting eyes on Elizabeth.

It was 1960 and Elizabeth's father, a die-hard Democrat, was a major contributor to the Kennedy campaign, while an ambitious young Haynes was similarly devoted to securing the presidency for his opponent, one Richard Milhous Nixon.

Haynes found himself unable to suppress a smile as he allowed the memory to rush over him. He recalled jumping on a plane to LA and scamming his way into the site for Kennedy's Democratic nomination acceptance address, decking himself out in JFK paraphernalia and forcing his way to the front of the Memorial Coliseum, determined to get a bird's-eye view of the "enemy" and in the process, ideally, come up with counterstrategies to impress Nixon and the influential Republicans around him.

True, it was hard to listen to the sandy-haired Catholic denigrate his man, but halfway through the speech his mission was all but forgotten, for he found himself face-to-face with the most lovely thing he had ever seen: the fifth E, Elizabeth Christine Whitman.

Rudolph could remember maneuvering his way back to row 5, behind the Whitman clan of endless blond heads and their complementary husbands and children. He could not, however, remember hesitating—probably because he did not—before leaning forward to whisper in the youngest girl's ear: "He'll never win. The man's an impostor; he doesn't stand a chance."

"I beg your pardon," she had replied as she turned to lock her wide blue eyes on the brazen young man behind her.

"My name is Rudolph Haynes. I am a Republican, and you are the girl I am going to marry."

That was forty-six years ago and the rest, as they say, is history.

They were husband and wife by the end of the following year, married on Elizabeth's twenty-first birthday. Percy Whitman, while initially pained at his new son-in-law's political persuasions, soon had his anxieties eased by Haynes's fine manner and even finer bank account. In short, Rudolph slipped as smoothly into the Whitman fold as butter onto bread.

That, he knew, was when it had started—when his wife had seen the importance of fulfilling her destiny, moving to Boston with her dear housemaid Agnes, becoming active in the appropriate social circles, and immediately assuming the role of the perfect politician's wife.

He spent the next decade negotiating his way up the local party ladder, biding his time, expanding his realm of influence, until the right opportunity came along. And it did. In 1978, the soon-to-retire U.S. senator Rufus Fonte went looking for a successor young enough to energize the Grand Old Party with vigor and old enough to comfort them with experience. The choice was obvious.

Rudolph was elected at the age of thirty-nine and had held his seat ever since, a remarkable achievement in a state dominated by the powerful post-Kennedy Irish American contingent, a state where, despite its conservative roots, Democrats drove local politics and working-class rhetoric ruled.

Now he realized how important his wife had been. All those years working at his side, hosting dinner parties, attending rallies, chairing charity committees and following his stride on the grueling campaign trail without a word of complaint. She had been—she *was still*—the perfect political companion, and he knew he owed a good proportion of his success to her.

And so as he sat in his darkened personal sanctuary, late for dinner and frustrated at the thought, he realized this latest turn of events had the potential to "unsettle" her. Christina may have been his prized prodigy, but she was also her mother's miracle. They had all but given up hope of having a child when Elizabeth fell pregnant at forty-eight. Losing her daughter would leave a massive hole in his wife's life—no more trips to ballet class, no more tennis club fund-raisers, no more school committees or summer fetes.

And as much as he understood her pain, he also knew that her falling into a pit of uselessness fed by the bitterness of grief was not an option. The next few months would require the utmost of his concentration and he could not afford to be distracted by his wife's lack of purpose—no matter how genuine her anguish might be. He had to protect everything they had accomplished; he had to make sure she was kept busy with various tasks and commitments so that she did not compromise his strategy and, along with it, the future they had worked so hard to secure.

His eyes drifted upward, toward the evening news, his thoughts now consolidated by a series of archive images showing the three of them—he, Elizabeth and a waist-high Christina—standing on the steps of the golden-domed State House. He saw the vision of Rayna being herded into headquarters, with Roger Katz lording over the proceedings just as he'd known he would.

Perhaps more interesting was the breakout story that saw a female reporter interviewing Francie Washington and her parents. Mr. and Mrs. Washington took the righteous role as they held tight to their daughter, who seemed more interested in fixing her hair and smiling at the camera. Haynes pressed the mute button once again so that he might hear the Washingtons express their deepest sympathies, speak of their admiration for the senator and stress that this tragedy would affect them for the rest of their lives. Haynes could sense that the girl and her parents liked a little attention and this could definitely work in his favor.

It was quarter past eight and Elizabeth was expecting him in the dining room. Just one more call, he thought as he closed Rayna's file and tapped in Verne's latest cell phone number.

Funny, he thought as the line connected. Two days ago he was furious at Christina for associating with the likes of Miss Francine Washington. Now she could be just what he was looking for.

• • •

Rayna Martin had made a discovery. If you sat completely still, reduced your breathing to a slow, steady rhythm, shut your eyes and tried to relax your body as much as possible, there was only one sound you could hear. It was the beating of your heart.

Then, if you allowed the panic to creep slowly into your

brain so that it spread like poison through every vessel in
your body, the sound of your heart would grow louder until
you could feel it pounding furiously in your chest like a wild
animal trying to escape. It was an illusion, of course, but a
terrifyingly realistic one at that.

Rayna desperately wanted to remain calm, but the past
thirty-six hours had been so frightening that she was not sure
she could maintain any semblance of composure. She knew
why David had given her this list of questions to consider
overnight. It was to keep her mind active, to prevent her from
dwelling on the horror of her circumstance. But the questions
were actually making things worse.

*Did you call each of the girls' parents to invite their
daughter to Teesha's birthday?* She had spoken to Mariah's
mom, Elise Jordan—they were friends—but Teesha had invited Francie and Christina herself.

*Did you inform the girls' parents where you would be tak-
ing the girls, that is, the exact location of your sailing destination?* She had told Elise of her plans, but once again Teesha
had spoken directly to the other two girls.

*Did you ring the Meteorological Society to check weather
conditions the morning of your departure?* That was a yes.
This had been part of her coastal safety routine.

*And did you speak with the harbormaster regarding tides,
rips and any other coastal conditions that may have had some
or any effect on your journey that day?* Well, no. She had called
the Coast Guard's recorded message line but had not spoken to
anyone directly.

She could see what was happening—and it only got worse.

*Did at least three other people know of your destination
that day?* Well, Delia had known—she was planning to come
until her plumber accidentally burst a pipe in her bathroom.
She had told George Livingston, the owner of Livingston
Charters, when she had picked up the cruiser, and Elise Jordan would have had a vague idea where they were headed
but . . .

Did you check the girls' bags for drugs or alcohol? No.

Did you lecture them on the importance of life jackets?
No, but she had assumed they . . .

Did you ask either their parents or the girls themselves about their swimming ability? No, but they had all done swimming at school so . . .

Did you tell the girls not to leave your field of vision? Yes, I mean, no. Not all of them. She had told Teesha.

When they left your field of vision, did you pull anchor immediately? Well, no, not immediately, but . . .

And so on it went, question after question—no, no, not really, not exactly, no, no, no.

Rayna was a good attorney. She didn't specialize in criminal law, but she knew the signs of a potentially strong case for the prosecution when she saw one. These questions were tough, and they came from *her* lawyers, so she could just imagine what the commonwealth would be dealing up.

"What have I done?" she said aloud. "Teesha, I am so sorry."

Her mind raced ahead to the arraignment, the indictment, the trial, the guilty verdict, the sentencing, the *years in prison*. She had to concentrate on holding the meager contents of her stomach. She had to steady herself for fear she would pass out.

And then she did the only thing she could do. She got down and knelt by her small, hard bunk and prayed like she had never prayed before as the tears flowed steadily down her cheeks and her angry heart banged like a deadly drum inside her.

■ ■ ■

He had chosen Ristorante Fiore, a small but popular Italian restaurant not far from Sara's house in the North End. It was noisy in a comforting way, allowing them either to sit in silence without feeling awkward or to talk without being overheard.

David and Sara had left Rayna after a long evening of reasoning, planning, consoling. There was little they could do for her tonight and they promised she would be out on bail within twenty-four hours. They decided to have dinner and talk about tomorrow's arraignment. But neither had the energy to do much strategizing, and they both seemed to need an excuse to relax.

"My brain is fried," Sara said just as the waiter came to take their order.

"Mine too. Some wine?" David asked, taking the wine list.

"To be honest, what I really need is a cold beer," she said.

"Make that two," he said to the waiter before turning back to Sara. "And if Arthur were here, he'd be congratulating you on your fine taste in refreshments."

The waiter left them to consider their menus and they both sat back, breathing in the comforting aromas coming from the restaurant kitchen. After a few minutes' silence, David looked up at Sara and smiled.

"So," she said. "Tell me the David Cavanaugh story."

"Is it a cliché to say not much to tell?"

"Yes, and I know that's not true. You have a good reputation in this city, Mr. Cavanaugh, and I would imagine there's an interesting story behind it somewhere?"

"Okay. Well, for starters, I'm from Jersey—Newark to be exact. Everyone at home calls me DC, and by everyone I mean my mom, my brother and his family, my sister, my old school friends."

David explained how he had been brought up in an Irish Catholic household, the second of three kids. His father, Sean senior, was a hard worker who had spent his life on the docks of Newark, bringing home with him the smell of salt and the trace of an after-work pint.

His father's complement was Patty Cavanaugh, née O'Reilly, a green-eyed, strawberry blonde who seemed born to her chosen profession of teaching. Together they were like two pieces of jigsaw, nothing alike when they stood alone but making a perfect whole when placed together.

"When I look back now, I realize how hard it was for my dad. All those long hours, the physical work, the financial strain. Every night at around seven, we'd listen for his heavy boots in the hall and race downstairs to hear Mom ask him about his day. He'd always say the same thing, which was something like 'Better than most and not as good as others.' And then Mom would smile and kick our butts for climbing all over our dad." David stopped, the memories rushing back.

"Sounds like you got lucky."

"Yeah," he said, now refocusing on Sara. "I guess I did.

"Ah, what else . . ." he said, taking a breath before moving on. He usually felt awkward sharing so much about himself. He may have had his mother's fair hair and pale green eyes, along with her unshakable idealism, but he also had his father's edge, a toughness reinforced by a protective need to hold what was dear to him close to his chest.

"I'm thirty-five, a lawyer, eater, sleeper, watcher of ESPN, sometime runner, rugby player, Celtics fan—"

"Rugby? You mean that insane game where everyone seems set on stomping each other to death?"

"The same," he said.

"And the Celtics?"

"An Irish team in the Scottish Premier League."

"And you play?"

"Nothing like the Celtics." He smiled. "I played a fair bit in college and a bunch of us still get together for a semiregular Saturday morning game."

"Thus the lip."

"Thus the lip." He smiled again.

"Okay, so what else?" Sara went on, her blue eyes reflecting the muted glow of the candlelight. "Tell me more about your brother and sister."

"Well, I have an older brother, Sean junior, who took over my dad's shipping business when he passed away five years ago, and a younger sister, Lisa, who is a nurse at Mass. General."

"Did she follow you to Boston?"

"I guess in a way. We're pretty close. Sean and his wife have three kids of their own, but Lisa and I are sort of like a pair of strays. We hang out together in between long days in court and odd shifts at the hospital."

"So why Boston?" she asked, the expression on her face one of genuine interest. "Why not New York?"

"That's easy. Boston has always been like a second home to us."

"How so?"

"My mom grew up here, in South Boston. Her father, my

grandfather, lived in the same two-story garrison his entire life. Mom kept the house after Pop passed away and now Lisa lives there."

"But not you."

"No, I have an apartment downtown, close to the office. Hell, sometimes I feel as if I might as well move into the office. Like I said, it's a pretty boring story."

"So no wife, no kids, no pets even?"

Their conversation had been flowing at such an easy pace that the question did not come as much of a surprise—more as a natural progression. But David had not been asked such a question in a long time and Sara must have read the expression of hesitancy on his face. He looked at her then, sensing her concern that she had gone too far. And in that moment he felt a strange need to put her at ease. To let her know that despite the tug of discomfort he still wanted to answer her question.

"Actually, I'm divorced," he said.

"Oh." She looked down, as if wondering if she had touched a nerve.

"It's old news," he said. "I married my college sweetheart. We were nineteen. I was divorced by the time I was twenty-three."

"Does she live . . . ?" Sara began.

"Here in Boston?" finished David. "No, Washington." He stopped wondering how much he should say, realizing these were just details about his past and had nothing to do with who he was now.

"Have you ever heard of Dr. Karin Vasquez Montgomery?" he asked.

"The cardiac surgeon? I've seen her on TV talking about transplants. She's amazing."

"I thought so too, but that was before she added the first and the last bits to that name."

"Didn't she marry that professor who operates on presidents?" she asked.

"That would be the one," answered David, looking up at her and stopping short. Sara smiled, as if letting him know it was okay to change the subject.

"Anyway, I studied law at Boston College," he said. "Passed

the bar and spent the past twelve years being bossed around by Arthur."

"Impressive."

"Actually, it's pretty pathetic. I have no life. I spend more time with my boss than I do with any other human being. But don't you dare tell him I admitted to that. It makes me sound desperate.

"As for the pet thing," he said in an attempt to lighten the mood, "I did own a guppy a year or so ago, but let's just say I wasn't the greatest of dads to old J Lo."

"You called your fish J Lo?" She smiled. "Somehow I wouldn't have picked you for a Jennifer Lopez fan."

"No." David laughed. "The fish was downright ugly. Oversized, misshapen. I would have been doing Ms. Lopez a serious injustice. J Lo was black and white; I named him after Jonah Lomu, you know, the New Zealand Rugby player. The All Blacks . . . black and white . . . team colors, get it?"

"I didn't, but I do now, and it makes perfect sense."

Within minutes their beers arrived and David turned the conversation to Sara. "Okay," he said as he put down his drink, "your turn."

"Right, well," Sara smiled, leaning slightly into the table. "I was born in Atlanta."

"Nice city."

"To be honest, I wouldn't know. To me it's just the POB listed on my birth certificate. I was adopted at two months by a couple, Alec and Dorothy Davis. Grew up in Cambridge. My dad's a dentist and Mom was his technician."

"That explains the straight teeth," said David.

"Thank you, sir." She smiled. "Anyway, they didn't think they could have kids but six years later gave me a baby brother the natural way. His name is Jake and he's an economics major at MIT."

"Good for him."

"He's twenty-three, full of optimism, hasn't been spoiled by life if you know what I mean."

"And you have?"

"I didn't mean that; it's just that I had my fair share of challenges as a kid." She paused before continuing, and he waited patiently for her to decide how much of herself she wanted to reveal.

"My parents are white and I'm . . . well, somewhere in between. Mom and Dad never made it an issue. Jake used to say he envied me every summer vacation when he would fry like a lobster. But others growing up . . . kids can be cruel."

"Did you ever want to look for your birth mother?" David asked.

"Yes and no. One day, maybe. My parents have always been very open about it. They told me she was African American, seventeen and single."

"And your father?"

"I have no idea. He was white, obviously, but that's all I know. Let's just say I have the feeling I was not created out of love."

She picked up her drink then and David sensed that perhaps Sara had built up her own defenses over the years. Once again he felt a need to relieve her discomfort. And so he smiled before asking: "So what does Sara Davis do when she's not working?"

She seemed grateful for the change of subject. "Well, besides all the usual stuff like hanging out with my friends and family, I can often be found at the shoe department at Neiman Marcus. My shoe cupboard puts Imelda Marcos's to shame."

"And mine is not something we should discuss over dinner."

She laughed. "And I rent a great little brownstone not far from here, which you already know. I share it with one of my best friends, Cindy Alverez, and the man in both our lives, her dalmatian, Sylvester."

"And you thought J Lo was a ridiculous name for a fish."

By the time they'd finished their meal, they seemed to get a second wind and were back on the case. David expected the arraignment to be the next afternoon. He knew the court docket was loaded, but he was sure a case with this much public interest would be bumped up the running order.

"And you're sure we'll secure bail?" Sara questioned.

"As sure as I can be. First of all, I'll be pushing for the charge to be dismissed. This was accidental death and Rayna shouldn't even be in some courtroom but at home consoling Teesha. Secondly, Rayna is a woman of high standing in her community—a hard worker, a single mom. Her flight risk is zero; she has a clean record and a close family with the means to supply the bond money."

"You have me convinced, but we both know the bail is just the beginning of what could turn out to be a hell of a fight."

They both agreed that while Scaturro would take the reins up front, Roger Katz would play a major role in any preliminary hearing and even the trial, if it came to that. David also put his money on Roger keeping his alleged chats to Haynes a secret from his boss.

"I gather you and Katz have a history? What happened?"

David frowned and paused before answering. "Let's just say every decent lawyer in Boston has a history with the Kat."

"He's good isn't he?"

"Very. But we all live in hope that one day he will trip over that huge ego of his and fall flat on his face."

Sara smiled. "Maybe we can give him a hand, or should I say a push in the right direction."

"Counselor," David said as he lifted his glass to hers, "I think you just said the magic words to launch an extremely successful partnership."

"To Rayna," she said.

"To Rayna," he replied.

4

Her name was Stacey Pepper.

After David had walked Sara to her car, he headed back for his Land Cruiser and started thinking about Roger Katz. Sara had asked about their history, but he just couldn't bring himself to tell her about Stacey Pepper. It was still too close. She had only been dead three years.

Stacey Pepper had been a large girl with unruly black hair and a drooping stature. She had deep, dark eyes that hid beneath heavy lids, and she wore oversize clothes that hung off her frame like a shroud of defeat.

Stacey had been eighteen when David met her and nineteen when she died. She had been charged with murdering her eight-year-old stepsister, Lara, a wide-eyed, blond-haired child with an angelic face and the gentle disposition to match. There was no disputing the charge, for the evidence was plain and clear: in the middle of the night Stacey had shot her sister through the heart with a shotgun.

Five years earlier Roger Katz had been touted as the perfect running mate for hotshot prospective DA Loretta Scaturro. They made an impressive team, Scaturro promising strength and stability and Katz adding the sparkle. Loretta stood for justice with compassion while Roger vowed to keep the conviction rate up and the critics, all too ready to label her soft, at bay.

That was mid-2001 and all was sailing smoothly until that catastrophic day on September 11 when the whole world was turned upside down. Suddenly the national psyche changed from one of clemency to one of fear. Scaturro's reformist attitudes became seriously out of sync while Katz's stance on tough justice became even more important to her campaign.

A new hard-line strategy saw them win the election, but talk meant nothing if they could not back it up, and they knew they needed a case to prove their administration meant business. The Pepper case was perfect. Big, ugly stepsister murders sweet and defenseless child. It was a PR dream, a no-brainer, a political gift. Until David Cavanaugh agreed to represent the defendant.

It was Mannix who had persuaded him. He'd said he had a feeling about this one, and Joe's feelings, combined with his incessant nagging and talk of an "attorney's duty to represent those less fortunate" had made it impossible for David to refuse.

He took the case pro bono and spent two months trying

to gain Stacey's confidence. Then he asked for help from an independent psychiatrist who examined Stacey and diagnosed her as a classic abuse victim. The doctor suspected that Stacey had been abused sexually, physically and emotionally from a very early age. He also concluded that the girl was incapable of cold-blooded murder, particularly of her sister Lara, toward whom she exhibited extreme protective tendencies. So David asked Mannix to do some digging, certain his client was hiding something important.

The case started and the press lapped it up. Pictures of the two girls ran on the front page. Dolores Pepper, the mother of the two girls, played the loving parent whose family had been torn apart by her uncontrollable daughter, and her husband, the Reverend Pepper, took his righteous role as the forgiving stepfather, devastated by Stacey's actions but buoyed by his faith in an "all-loving and all-forgiving God."

Katz claimed Stacey was the ultimate bully. He called in his own psychologist, who testified she was a crazed, unstable, green-eyed monster who could just as easily have emptied her bullets into a school playground or a McDonald's restaurant. He claimed the commonwealth had a responsibility to "set a precedent" and seek "conviction without reservation." And, unfortunately, many agreed.

While David had finally won Stacey's trust, she still hadn't told him the truth. She was so horrified with what she had done, and so emotionally incapable of seeing past her guilt and desperation and loneliness, that she almost welcomed the inevitable: a guilty verdict and the subsequent punishment.

And so, without any help from his seriously depressed client, David lost at trial, the greatest loss of his career and a personal defeat from which he had never fully recovered. Two days later Stacey was sentenced to life without parole, and one day after that Mannix cracked the case.

Stacey had been born in Pensacola, Florida. Her biological father, one Leroy Levane, was a drunk. Her mother claimed to have left him ten years before after realizing he was a no-good bum.

Dolores had taken up with the Reverend Thaddeus Pepper

when Stacey was eight. She married him a year later after becoming pregnant with Lara.

They moved five times in the next seven years from Florida, across the Midwest, over to California and then back across the country to Boston. Reverend Pepper claimed he was "spreading the word," but David later found out otherwise.

Thad Pepper, alias Nigel Hooper, alias Philip Cripps, born Ernest Schiff, was a pedophile who abused his way across the United States, using his front as a reverend for the fictional Church of Little Flowers as a means of gaining access to unsuspecting children. He was the lowest of scum, who now rotted in a Massachusetts maximum security correctional institution.

The psychiatrist surmised that Stacey Pepper had most likely been abused by both Leroy Levane and Thaddeus Pepper, only finding the courage to fight back when she discovered her stepfather had started on her younger sister.

According to teachers and friends, Lara Pepper had been a happy child, considering her circumstances. But her demeanor had changed in the months leading up to her death. Her grades had slipped and her smile had faded. Stacey guessed what was happening and decided to take matters into her own hands.

That dreadful night, Lara was sleeping over at her best friend Polly's house, the stay having been orchestrated by Stacey without her parents' knowledge. Stacey's plan had been to lie in Lara's bed and wait for the Reverend Pepper to come, as he had started to do after midnight. She was ready, hiding under the thin blankets with his huge, rusty rifle firmly in her grip.

What went through the young girl's head as she heard the door handle, listened to his footfalls, and finally sat up and fired was anyone's guess. For within hours she had lost the will to speak, having been charged with the murder of her little sister, who had run home seeking comfort from her older sibling after a silly midnight fight with Polly.

For months Mannix had been trying to get a lead on the Reverend Thaddeus Pepper, suspecting there was more to the man's facade than met the eye. Finally he got a positive photo ID from a seven-year-old in San Diego who named Pepper as the man who had abused her after a prayer meeting. After that, it was just a matter of retracing his evil criminal exploits across the country.

That Stacey had intended to kill her stepfather in order to protect her sister was clear. This was still murder one, but a jury would have had a hard time convicting her under the circumstances. David had planned to petition for acquittal. He never got the chance.

Stacey committed suicide in custody the night before Mannix broke the case. She had made a primitive knife out of a discarded soda can and cut away at her wrists until she lost consciousness and bled to death under the concealment of a dark gray prison blanket.

Katz was all shock and horror, devastated by the death, horrified by the new evidence, stricken with grief for the girls' mother and ready and willing to prosecute Thaddeus Pepper to the full force of the law. If only poor Stacey had spoken up.

A month later, Mannix told David he had information that Roger Katz knew of Pepper's perverted past at least two weeks prior to Stacey's conviction and Mannix's exposé.

He knew. He *knew.*

Right at the end, when David knew the case was unwinnable, he had tried to plead it out. But even then Katz wanted to take it to trial. He wanted to bury this girl and the evidence concerning her stepfather just so he could stand in the spotlight and continue to score those beloved political points.

And all the time he knew.

David asked Mannix to beg his source to come forward and expose Katz, but the informant, who worked in the DA's office, wanted to remain anonymous. To this day David did not know who had ratted out Katz. Worse still, he had no proof that Roger had foreknowledge of the Reverend Pepper's perverted activities. Even Katz was unaware that David knew the truth. It had taken all his restraint not to head over to Katz's office and beat the crap out of him, but on Arthur's advice he decided to hold on to the information in case he needed it in the future.

Maybe that time had come.

. . .

"Mr. Washington."

"Yes."

"This is Senator Rudolph Haynes."

It was ten on Sunday night and Haynes had decided to take a calculated risk.

"Senator Haynes," said Washington, and Haynes visualized the man juggling his handset as he gathered himself for this all-important, unexpected telephone call.

"This is such an honor," Washington went on. "I am *so* sorry for your loss, Senator. My wife and I are two of your biggest supporters."

The level of risk was reducing with every word.

"Thank you, Mr. Washington. My daughter certainly thought the world of young Francine." This was a lie. While Christina would fight to see Teesha Martin and the other girl, his feeling was that Francine Washington had been more an accessory to this distasteful group of inappropriate friends.

"Likewise, Senator, likewise. Oh, Senator, I can only begin to imagine your . . ."

"Yes, Mr. Washington, I was actually calling to ask a favor."

"Anything, sir."

"Would you meet me for breakfast tomorrow? Say the Regency Plaza at eight? Don't give your name; just ask for Charles, the maître d', and he'll direct you to a private table."

"Why I'd be delighted, Senator. Delighted. Anything I can do to help."

"Thank you, Mr. Washington. Tomorrow then."

And Haynes promptly hung up, knowing Washington was running to tell his wife and already deciding what suit to wear for tomorrow's much anticipated engagement.

There was now no doubt in Haynes's mind that Washington would bite at his offer, subtle as it was. The senator always marveled at how men like trustworthy Ed could bend their ideals for personal gain and then convince themselves it was all in the best interest of others. Haynes would not be asking much. He would start by flattering the man with false reports of his stellar real estate reputation. He would suggest that he had many friends who could not seem to find an honest realtor and were in desperate need of assistance in selling their properties. And then he would move on to the subject of Teesha's party and how while Christina was the victim on that day, it could well have been one of the other girls—Mariah or, God forbid, his own dear Francine.

He would say how grateful he was that the Washingtons had put aside their distress to speak honestly to the media, and he would hope they would continue to do so, as a favor to the senator; his wife, Elizabeth; and his dear departed daughter. In fact, the senator had a friend who worked at the *Boston Tribune*. Perhaps he could call on Francie and get her side of the story, say tomorrow morning, as a sort of tribute to Christina.

After all, it was really a matter of duty. There were millions of good American fathers who wanted to make sure that all teenagers in this fine country were protected from irresponsible people who failed to watch over their children. Yes, indeed. God Bless America.

5

Loretta Scaturro was in a very awkward position. It was early Monday morning and she had just hung up a call from Senator Haynes. Rayna Martin's arraignment was scheduled for four that afternoon. She had spoken with Judge Stein himself. He had done as she requested and cleared his busy docket in recognition of the public interest in the case and as a personal favor to her.

Now she was in the embarrassing situation of having to call Stein back and ask for a delay. Worse still, she would have to tell Cavanaugh his client would be spending another night in jail. All potential defendants charged with a crime were entitled to a speedy arraignment, within forty-eight hours of their arrest. While Tuesday morning was still within this window, it seemed ridiculous to knock back an opening for this afternoon and she had no idea how she was going to explain it.

Damn Haynes. He knew he had her in the palm of his hand. Two years ago Loretta had fallen to one small indiscretion in the form of a romantic liaison with a reasonably well-known Boston attorney. Professionally, this should not have been a problem, but the fact that the attorney was defense counsel in a major case she was prosecuting was. Not to mention the fact that he had been, and still was, married with two children.

Eventually her Catholic conscience (and his roving eye) won out and they went their separate ways. The liaison was brief and she had been fool enough to believe it would never get out, but Haynes had a way of discovering skeletons in closets—and was even better at producing them at appropriate moments.

The conversation had been short and simple. He requested that the DA take another twenty-four hours before formally laying the charge of involuntary manslaughter.

"Senator, there is no need to delay," she had said. "ADA Katz and I are ready, and as you know, this is just a formal reading of the charge. We'll do our best to block bail, but Cavanaugh has a good case. Mrs. Martin has no priors."

"Ms. Scaturro, I appreciate your efforts to secure a speedy arraignment, but another twenty-four hours will not harm the prosecution in any way. On the contrary, it might rattle Mr. Cavanaugh and his client and act to your benefit."

"How is that, Senator?" She had tried to keep the frustration out of her voice.

"I believe I will have more information by this afternoon. You and I both know that there are instances where the police miss a detail or two and, on occasion, it can be difficult for the people of your busy office to step back and see the big picture."

That had been it. Senator Haynes may lunch with presidents, but she was the DA in this city and he had no right telling her how to run her office, dead daughter or not.

"Look, Senator, I'm afraid a delay is both unnecessary and impossible. With all due respect, sir, you have a strong emotional attachment to this case and I have every confidence in my people."

"How is Jim Elliot?" he interrupted suddenly, and paused before continuing. "Do you see him much these days? Good man, Jim. Solid Republican. Saw him and his lovely wife, Cecilia, at a charity dinner last weekend. They have a son the same age as Christina. Oliver, I think his name is. Yes, that's it, Oliver."

She could not find the words to answer.

"Tomorrow morning it is then. Let's make arrangements to touch base later today so we can go over a few details regarding the direction of the case. I truly appreciate your keeping me informed about all of this, Loretta. I'll have my assistant call you before midday."

And with that he was gone.

• • •

David was listening to Katz on the other end of the line, but he could not believe what he was hearing. He was telling him the arraignment had been delayed. He was saying his client would be spending another night in jail.

"You have *got* to be kidding."

"Now, Counselor, you know that kidding is a euphemism for lying and I take offense at the suggestion. Unfortunately, there was no opening in the court docket today."

"That's bullshit, Katz. Don't treat me like an idiot. I know the judge would have cleared time for this case."

David knew Judge Stein to be rigid but fair; he also knew he hated interference from the press and would go all out to move things along if it meant denying them an extra day's speculation.

"I'm sorry, Cavanaugh, the DA's office can do a lot of things, but I am afraid we are yet to conquer creating extra time in the day."

"You insolent bastard." David had had enough. "I know this stalling tactic is some macabre notion on your part to further torture my client, who shouldn't even be in jail right now. No doubt it also has something to do with your little conversations with Haynes."

He could almost see Katz freeze at the other end of the phone.

"That's right, you heard me. I wonder if your boss knows about that, Roger. If I get one ounce of evidence that you are collaborating with the girl's father to secure a conviction on this one, you'll be thrown in jail faster than I can say the word *conspiracy*."

David looked up to see Arthur staring at him, the corners of his lips forming a slight smile. He glanced through his office doorway to Nora, who sat straight up at her desk looking like a proud mother, today's proverb revealing itself as "If you can't take the heat, get out of the kitchen."

"If you have finally finished your childish tirade, Mr. Cavanaugh," said Katz, a sharp surge of anger fostering his recovery, "I would suggest you consider that this delay may work in your favor. I think you may need all the time you can get. After tomorrow's arraignment we'll be going straight to the grand jury for an indictment."

David was not surprised. In the Commonwealth of Massachusetts there were two ways by which a case got scheduled for trial: through a probable cause hearing, after which a judge decided whether the evidence was strong enough to go to trial, or by the grand jury, which could come to the same conclusion in minutes by issuing an indictment.

It made sense that the ADA would push for an early indictment; probable cause hearings were by nature less sensational than jury trials, and the Kat never missed a chance to strut his stuff on the grander stage, especially if he thought he had a strong possibility of winning.

"This is not going to go away, Cavanaugh. You may want to tell your client that sometimes things catch up with people. You can't live in your own little world, deciding who should stay and who should go based on your own skewed idea of utopia. Sooner or later it catches up with you. I'll see you in the morning, Counselor. Good day."

David hung up the phone, his mind racing as he deciphered Katz's last comments. He recapped the conversation for Arthur and they both sat silently, knowing where this was leading and terrified at the implications.

Everyone had been tiptoeing around the race issue. Mannix had mentioned it briefly, but from David's point of view it should be irrelevant. The charge was *involuntary* manslaughter and the fact that the girl who drowned was white should have no bearing on the case whatsoever.

From the DA's perspective, even mentioning the word race could be disastrous. Scaturro was seen as pro minority and any suggestion that they were crucifying Rayna because she was black could mean political suicide.

Then there was Haynes. David and Arthur had heard rumors of Haynes's racial preferences. He certainly moved in white circles, the land of country club parties and unspoken bigotries. But there was no solid evidence of prejudice. He had African Americans on his staff. Maybe not in his closest clique of associates, but they were there.

No, David actually felt any play of the race card would only benefit the defense. The minute the words *black* or *white* were mentioned, he could argue Rayna was being persecuted because of her color. So why would Katz even allude to the issue? It didn't make sense. Maybe he was just trying to push David's buttons.

At least Sara had not heard these remarks; somehow he figured she would have been even less impressed than he was. He had said this last thought aloud and heard her voice in the doorway.

"What didn't I hear?" she said, looking stunning in a navy-blue suit and white shirt, her hair pulled back in a bun at the base of her neck, her face filled with let's-go-get-'em enthusiasm.

David filled her in on Katz's call and, as predicted, she was furious.

"I don't believe this. What are we going to tell Rayna and Teesha? We promised them she would be out on bail by tonight. This is insane. What the hell are they playing at?"

David told her of Katz's last comments and he saw her brow stiffen as if a random thought had just entered her head.

"I know Haynes must be burning to bury the black woman," she said. "But I thought Scaturro would be just as determined to underplay the race thing."

"Our thoughts exactly," said David.

Sara paused for a moment before continuing. "Have you guys ever heard of the one-in-six rule?"

Neither of them had.

"It's a term we use at AACSAM. It basically refers to companies or persons we know who have a problem with hiring minorities, usually African Americans or Latinos, but still have to play the PC game and thus try to hire at least one in six."

"And Haynes?" said David.

"Oh, come on, the guy is a classic one-in-sixer. I swear if you went through his staff list, it would be almost to the number."

"How do you know this?"

Sara hesitated as if she were unsure where she should start.

"Look around you," she said, gesturing toward Arthur's old federal-style windows. "This is Boston, the city of neighborhoods, of unspoken racial segregation. The Italians are in the North End, the Irish in the South, the blacks in Roxbury, the Asians in Brighton. Okay, so I am generalizing a little, but you know what I am saying is true."

"Some would say that adds to the city's charm," said David. "It's cultural diversity, a mini United Nations, people of different backgrounds living side by side."

"True, but that's just it, isn't it? They live side by side but not together." She took a breath and went on, trying to explain. "The sad thing is, the system works. Crime is low, prosperity high. People don't like being forced into one another's backyards. They stick to their own little patch and all is fine with the world. The debacle of compulsory school desegregation back in the seventies certainly taught us that."

David remembered reading about the utter chaos that followed when black children were bussed to white schools and white to black, the result being rioting, violence and bloodshed.

"This city was built by people like Haynes: the white, Protestant elite whose tolerance level is less than zero. He may appear to be walking the walk, but he is what he is, and that isn't about to change."

The room fell silent, leaving her harsh assessments to hang in the air like unwelcome visitors.

"Don't take this the wrong way, David," she said quietly, moving toward him. "But sometimes people like you don't live in the real world. You've been brought up to believe that people are basically born good and ninety-nine percent of them stay that way."

"And that's a bad thing?"

"No, it's great, but it's just not true, even the good guys have their hidden prejudices. They bubble inside them for years and when something like this happens, it's like pulling the pin out of the grenade."

David looked at Arthur, afraid of where this was taking them.

"She's right," said Arthur, removing his glasses to massage his eyes. "We have to understand Haynes before we move on. Even if Katz is just being precocious, we must remember he's being steered by Haynes."

"So what the hell are they up to?" asked David, bringing the conversation back into the now.

All three looked at one another before Arthur spoke. "I have no idea, and we only have twenty-four hours to work it out."

■ ■ ■

Vince Verne still had the golf ball that had started their friendship. Ridiculous as it was, this little white sphere covered in tiny smooth craters and signed by one of the world's greats was responsible for a relationship that had given him a reason to go on living.

The gods must have been smiling on him that day nine years, six months, two weeks and three days ago, for it was on that day he had met Senator Rudolph Haynes. For years the senator had played golf at the exclusive Westport Country Club in Connecticut, and on this particular Sunday, Haynes was playing with the vice president of the United States, a one-on-one that had been going on for some months. So far, the vice president was one game ahead and on this day, one stroke under and four strokes ahead of Haynes on the sixteenth hole.

"I hate to say it, Rudi," Verne had heard the vice president say, "but it looks as if you'll be buying the drinks this evening." This was followed by a guttural laugh that scared some nearby sparrows out of their tree.

The senator managed a smile for the vice president, who took obvious delight in one-upping the blue-blooded senator on his hallowed home ground. "I think you're right, Larry; I can feel your handicap burning a hole in my pocket. In fact, I think it's time I pulled out my lucky ball."

Verne knew this was no light decision for the senator. That morning he had overheard Haynes tell Vice President Howell that the ball had been a gift from Jack Nicklaus, who had used that very orb to win a Masters Tournament. It was personally autographed "To the S from the B"—"To the Senator from the Bear."

"Whatever you feel you need to do, Rudi," Howell had replied.

Haynes lined up the shot on the seventeenth tee. It was a par 4 with a long curving fairway. The green was invisible slightly off to his left, surrounded by a bunker on its front side and backed by a swamp.

He decided on the driver. His intention was to draw the ball left and, with the help of the healthy northwesterly breeze, curve it up and onto the green. He certainly had the drive; he hit the ball with full force, so hard, in fact, that he overshot the green, his ball barely touching the ground before it landed with a plop in the thick, muddy swamp behind.

"Looks like the Golden Bear let you down there, buddy. Never mind, plenty more balls where that came from, right?"

• • •

Secret Service agent Vincent Bartholomew Verne had watched the entire scene from the sidelines. He was on the vice president's detail, one of the youngest on the team. At twenty-five his ambition was to make it to the A-team, to guard the president, and the general feeling was that it would not take him long to get there.

Truth be told, he thought the vice president was an ass and most of his team agreed. He had overheard some of the players' conversation and wondered how the hell Senator Haynes kept his cool. He felt an immediate admiration for the man who obviously had twice the decorum and three times the brains of his egotistical competitor. *That is a man who deserves respect,* he thought as he stood back and watched the senator's lucky ball fall gracefully to its murky grave.

The following night the senator had been back home and sitting down to dinner with Elizabeth and a seven-year-old Christina.

"Do sit still, Christina," said Elizabeth. "Agnes has made some wonderful berry pudding for dessert, but there won't be any for young ladies who decide to impersonate monkeys at the dinner table." Christina found this hysterically funny and laughed aloud until her father called for silence.

Their housekeeper, Agnes Gilroy, entered from the hall-way. "There's a young man at the door for you, Senator . . . a Mr. Verne. He says he has something for you."

"I don't know anyone named Verne, Agnes. Tell him to leave it with you and take his number."

"I did that, sir, but he says he wants to deliver this package personally."

For God's sake, thought Haynes, *they do climb out of the woodwork.* Since becoming a man of the people, he'd been convinced that half the population of Massachusetts took this literally.

"All right, Agnes, I'll see him for a minute. Show him to the library would you?"

The senator was not lax with security, but in his many years in politics he had never been threatened and was sure this man simply wanted some sort of favor, or maybe he was just an admirer wanting to give him a gift. There were quite a few of those about and, as sweet as the sentiment may seem, he found them a constant annoyance.

"I'm Senator Haynes," he said, striding into his library. "How can I help you?"

The young man turned and Haynes was struck by his strong presence—tailored suit, crisp shirt, polished shoes, perfect hair.

"Senator, my name is Vincent Verne. I am a Secret Service agent on Vice President Howell's detail. I was working yesterday when you played golf with the vice president."

Where the hell was this going? Did Howell send the boy to rub salt into his wounds? He wouldn't put it past him.

Verne took the pause as a signal to continue. He moved forward swiftly as if sliding across the parqueted floor, so fast, in fact, that Haynes took a small step backward.

"I believe this belongs to you, sir."

He pulled it from his right inside jacket pocket. Haynes's lucky golf ball . . . all clean and shiny with the black ink note from Nicklaus as clear as day across the bumps of its recently polished surface.

"Where did you . . . ?"

"I saw where it landed, sir."

It was rare that the senator found himself lost for words. He realized Verne must have been wading around in a muddy swamp just to find his treasured golf ball. He was unable to move for a second or two as he stared at the sphere held out in Verne's long arm.

"Why?" was all he could think to say.

"Because I believe this item means a lot to you, sir, and life is all too devoid of such possessions, is it not?"

Haynes took the ball and looked at the man again. "Would you like a drink, son?"

Verne looked at his watch. "Well, my next shift doesn't start for seven hours, so yes, sir, that is most kind of you."

"Not at all. Scotch okay? Straight up?"

"Yes, sir."

And so it began. Over the next twelve months Haynes kept an eye on Verne's career, and while Verne may not have been seen at any of Haynes's dinner parties, he was invited to the house at quiet times. Verne, who had been raised by an emotionally unstable single mother, discovered he had found a father figure in Haynes. He enjoyed his conversations with Elizabeth, who mothered him when he visited, and would spoil the young Christina with little gifts and birthday trinkets from his travels around the world.

Five years passed, and in that time Verne rose through the ranks of the Secret Service, eventually being assigned to the president of the United States. Verne kept Haynes abreast of political goings-on. He fell into the habit of doing small favors for the senator. It was amazing how much you could learn in the White House just by watching, listening and knowing whom to ask the odd discreet question. He didn't exactly break any rules, just gathered information, deciphered it and passed on what might be beneficial to the senator, who was, after all, a respected politician and patriotic American.

Then, two years ago, his whole life went to hell.

Verne, who lived alone in a small but neat rented Georgetown apartment, was accustomed to late-night strolls down to his local convenience store to buy the essentials and pick up the earliest edition of the next morning's paper. On this particular night he was taking a Diet Coke from the freezer when two men entered the store. The first man jumped over the front counter and climbed its left corner, ripping out the surveillance camera and demanding that the proprietor open his cash register.

In the confusion and gunfire that followed, Verne remembered feeling pain as he tackled the second thief in a crash to the ground, causing the criminal to accidentally shoot himself in the right thigh. One of the bandits panicked as the second man bled onto the linoleum floor and fled the store penniless.

For Verne it all went black. He spent the next week in and out of surgery. The bullets had torn both his kidneys, spleen and upper liver. They had severed his femoral artery and lacerated his abdominal wall. He earned the title of local hero until another brave, more pressworthy individual came along, and he spent all of this time in and out of consciousness, completely unaware of what was going on.

He received a new kidney, just hours after the shooting, a transplant procedure that normally took months to organize with waiting lists long and donors all too rare. The senator had organized it privately. He had used discreet means to pay for the specialists and then funded the entire extensive rehabilitation program, never asking a cent in return. He did not visit the hospitals or clinics and never even had a conversation with Verne regarding the situation.

There was no need. Verne knew of his generosity and respected the senator's distaste for open gratitude. So rather than shower him with thank-yous, he decided to dedicate the rest of his life to repaying his debt to the man he admired more than any other. His career with the Secret Service might be over, but his dedication to duty grew tenfold.

Now, as Verne, alias *Boston Tribune* reporter Max Truman, turned onto Queensbury Street and pulled up outside the Washingtons' neat, pale blue, wood-shingled home with white gloss trim and late-blooming daisies in the window boxes, he vowed to do whatever he could to destroy Rayna Martin and those willing to help her. Not just for the senator, or for his wife, but also for the little girl who used to look up at him and smile when the rest of the world had a tendency to look straight through him.

■ ■ ■

Over the past two days, David's respect for Rayna Martin had grown a hundredfold. Her ability to stay calm and focused, to think solely of her daughter's welfare and maintain a sense of grace was nothing short of amazing. This morning his admiration for her grew again as she showed she was human. When given the news of the delayed arraignment, she turned in her chair, fell into the arms of her visiting older sister, Delia, and broke down and cried.

There was no point to empty promises. Rayna was an attorney and way too smart for the usual placations David would give to a client unused to the complications of the law. David recounted Katz's conversation, knowing Rayna was entitled to the full story and hoping she may be able to shed some light on his allusions to the race issue.

"Tell me what you know about Haynes," said David.

"She knows he's a goddamned liar," interrupted Delia, who, David had discovered, was prone to such emotional outbursts. "He has my sister locked up in here while she should be home with her baby, who needs her. It just isn't right."

"It's okay, Delia," said Rayna, patting her sister's hand before taking a deep breath, wiping her tears and turning back to David to say, "I know the campaign spiel, that he is a man of the people, strong, direct, determined, conservative. I know he's been around for a long time. I know the people that work for him are polarized, meaning they either love him or hate him, and I know he's a bigot."

"I told David he's a one-in-sixer," said Sara, who had removed her jacket, undone her top button and was leaning forward on the vinyl interview room chair.

"Right," said Rayna. "There is no concrete evidence, of course, but AACSAM is a pretty good place to hear the unspoken."

"Would anyone at AACSAM have evidence of such prejudices?" said David.

"Probably not. The man is very careful. I do believe, however, that if you polled his staff, those at the negative end of the polarization would be largely African Americans, Latin Americans, Asian Americans."

Rayna paused to think of how best to describe a man like Haynes. "You have to understand that Haynes has been a politician for decades. He is a master of illusion. If he is a bigot, then he would never have admitted it directly. People like Haynes exude their racial preferences subliminally. They give more opportunities to white employees while still patting the black ones on their backs. They have a circle of close friends, all white, but make sure they have the odd public dinner or game of tennis with a respected Latin American. Their wives mix in white, socially acceptable, upper-class circles while waving the flag of tolerance at their expensive charity dinners. They give to minority causes and claim the contributions on their tax returns, but then encourage their children to form friendships with those whose skin is the same color as their own."

This last remark hit a chord as David realized Rayna was making an accusation of a more personal nature.

"Was Christina under pressure to stay away from Teesha?"

"Of course she was," interrupted Delia again. "That poor child was a victim of the worst kind of prejudice. She was stuck in the middle with no place to go."

"I think Delia's right," said Rayna. "She never spoke ill of her parents and I respected her for that. But there were times when we sensed she was under pressure to forgo her African American friends. The party was a perfect example." Rayna explained how Christina initially had declined Teesha's invitation and then turned up at the last minute.

"So you think her coming to the party was an act of rebellion?"

"Probably. At first she said she couldn't come because her mother wanted to take her shopping for a dress to wear to a dinner in honor of her father—a Fifty Years in Politics banquet—you probably read about it in the paper."

David had. It was scheduled for some time later in the week. In fact, Arthur was invited, not because he knew Haynes personally but because of his legal standing in the community. He also assumed that given Christina's funeral was scheduled for Wednesday, it would be canceled until further notice.

"Anyway, when she turned up, she mentioned her mom and dad hassling her and I figured she had come not just to have fun with her friends, but also as a stand against her parents. God, the irony of it all now."

"Did Christina ever say anything more specific about her father's racial preferences?" said Sara.

"You'd have to ask Teesha, or maybe Mariah. I'd say those two were her closest friends."

"The senator would have loved that," said Sara.

"Exactly."

David wanted to take advantage of Rayna's experience and so had no qualms about asking her opinion straight out.

"Given your experience with race-motivated crimes, where do you think the DA is going with this?"

"Well, most of my dealings in crime are more to do with discrimination in insurance matters, employment, stuff like that, but I could make an educated guess." Rayna's brow furrowed in concentration as if she were trying to think of a way to voice concerns steeped in the ugly and often unspoken realities of racism. "I agree with you that the race card appears to be a dangerous one for the prosecution, but from Haynes's point of view, it is the only card to play. Don't forget that Haynes is up for reelection next year. He can't afford a setback. Winning is everything to him and his drive to succeed is vehement.

"I believe that at this point, Senator Haynes and his wife hate me more than any living being on the planet. The fact that I am black makes it that much easier. He wants to hang me out to dry, David, and he will not rest until it is done. This may be tough, given the nature of the charge, but that makes it all the worse."

"Why is that?" asked Sara.

"Because Haynes loves a challenge and he never, ever loses." Rayna looked at them both. "I don't want to appear melodramatic. I have been trying to keep a clear head through all of this mess, but I truly believe they will go for broke."

Delia reached across to her sister to cover her hands in her own. "So you good people have a job to do," she said. "My sister's life is in your hands. She never hurt a single person in her whole entire life. So you go work your miracles . . . and set things right."

• • •

The autopsy report came in at midday. David and Sara had both skipped breakfast so they decided to take the file and head to Myrtle McGee's for a quick lunch. Myrtle's was a popular harborside café run by their good friend Mick—a six foot four carrot topped Irishman with a wide girth, ruddy complexion and colorful disposition to match. David and Sara sat next to each other hunched over the document while Mick, knowing better than to interrupt, brought them some sandwiches and mineral water with two mugs of strong, hot coffee on the side.

Christina Haynes had died of suffocation due to submersion. There was salt water in her lungs, and since this liquid was saltier than her body fluids, water had left her blood and entered her lungs to help dilute the salt. The air in the lungs then mixed with the fluids and formed a frothy foam, which acted as a barrier to oxygen exchange. The coroner had concluded that she probably struggled to inhale as much air as possible, eventually inhaling the water. This resulted in a lack of oxygen to the brain, loss of consciousness, and most likely convulsions and cardiac arrest followed by death. In other words, she had drowned.

The coroner also reported that these events usually took a maximum of five minutes. Meaning Rayna must have been away from Christina for at least this amount of time. If she had reached Christina within the first five minutes, her chances of resuscitation would have increased considerably.

Her blood alcohol level was .051, which, considering Christina weighed roughly 115 pounds, meant that she had consumed approximately two drinks. This may not seem like a lot, but it would have been enough for Christina to be feeling the calming effect of body warmth and perhaps the beginning of some reduced small muscle control. At a distance, she could well have seemed sober, but she was definitely high enough to be experiencing at least some loss in judgment, especially at the age of sixteen. This reduction in reasoning ability could have led to panic or, on the opposite end of the scale, complacency, either of which would have decreased her chances of survival.

"Five minutes," said Sara, taking the first bite of her egg salad roll. "The timing will kill us. This report gives the state their case. They'll just say Rayna shouldn't have left her, that she was away for too long. And from what you tell me about Katz, he'll milk the emotion so that all the parents on the jury visualize *their* son or daughter alone in the water, abandoned and gasping for breath."

"So we have to try to keep the case on a platform of logic," said David. "Rayna had to make a split decision regarding all four girls' welfare and we have to prove, given the information available to her, that she made the most reasonable choice," said David.

"And that means convincing a jury they would have done the same thing," she said.

"Exactly," said David, going straight for the coffee.

"You know," said Sara, "that all sounds fine except for one major problem. *Christina* is the one who told Rayna to go af-

ter the others. She is the one who said Francie was in trouble.
She is the one who also said she'd be okay treading water.

"Our whole case is based on Christina's last conversation
with our client, and our number-one witness is dead."

∎ ∎ ∎

He had called her. "Just wanted to see how you were doin' ,"
he had said. "And find out what happened. You were there,
right? Everyone is dying to know."

Francie could not believe it. Mitchell Dresco. *The* Mitchell
Dresco. Curtis Academy's star quarterback—tall, dark and
seriously hot, who drove a fancy red sports car called a Wasp
or a Spider or something like that. He had called her and it felt
good.

In fact (dare she admit it?), everything felt pretty
good right now: all the attention, the lights, the cameras,
the reporters and Mitchell Dresco! Truth be told, the last
twenty-four hours had been the most exciting in her entire
life. Her dad was proud, her mom had something else to yap
on about besides the usual crap, and the cameras were focused on *her,* not on Chrissie or Teesha or any of the white,
super skinny, big-breasted bitches in the "popular" crowd at
school.

She could hear her dad now. He was down the hall telling
her mom about the new clientele and once-in-a-lifetime opportunities, and all because of her, the receiver of calls from
Mitchell Dresco, the center of attention, the brave survivor of
tragedy. Of course, it came at a price. Chrissie was gone. But
she was the one who wanted to swim to the boat, wanted to
show off yet again. And that was Chrissie all over, wasn't it?
So typical. Mrs. Martin would have come for them at any
minute; it was just another case of Chrissie trying to prove
she was . . .

Francie took a deep breath and avoided her reflection in
her bedroom mirror as she went to her window to look out on
the shadows falling on her mother's hydrangeas. She swallowed hard, needing to rid her throat of something bitter that
lingered behind. Maybe what that reporter said was true.
Maybe her dad was right. Maybe Teesha's mom was a bigot.
Yes, yes, she must be. Why else would she leave her like that?
Seriously, what a stupid thing to do.

Now all Francie had to do was—how did her dad put it?—help Chrissie's mom and dad find peace, justice. She could do that. She could even help things on a little, at least that's what her dad had said. It was only fair after all.

Francie closed her eyes and tried to conjure up the image of Mitchell Dresco on the back of her eyelids. But the lump in her throat had returned and with it, a burning sensation that clutched at her chest and restricted her lungs. She took a deep breath and swallowed again, praying it would disappear and the sickness in her stomach would go with it.

■ ■ ■

Sometimes, fate was on your side and you came up lucky, and as much as he hated to admit luck actually played a part in life's twists and turns, there was no other way to explain the good news the senator had just received. Francine Washington was not just a potential ally, she was a verifiable gold mine.

Haynes had set on this route with reasonable expectations but had no idea he would pull out an ace so early. The breakfast with Washington had gone as expected, with trustworthy Ed playing right into his hands. Haynes would probably have to call in a few favors to get the man some extra real estate business, but that was a small price to pay for his daughter's surprise contribution.

He had to see Scaturro. Timing would be important. He wanted to leave Cavanaugh as little reaction time as possible. He would see the DA and Katz this evening and try to delay informing the defense until tomorrow morning. Hell, he'd love to drop the bomb at the actual arraignment, but he wasn't too sure how far he could push the duty of disclosure.

He would have his secretary, Louise, call Scaturro's office and set up a meeting for six. Louise could tell Scaturro he would be unavailable until that time, as he was busy organizing his daughter's funeral.

He surprised himself when he realized that he'd been smiling through this thought. But then, he knew, revenge was the sweetest way to dull the pain of grief.

6

The courtroom was packed. The early morning sun poured softly through the east-facing windows, throwing alternate stripes of light and shadow across the worn hardwood floors. On its way it captured millions of floating dust particles as they entered and left the pale yellow beams.

David and Sara squinted as they came through the back doors just as a court clerk moved to lower the blinds. Arthur was already at the defense desk on the left-hand side of the room. He sat across from Loretta Scaturro, all businesslike in a navy suit, pale blue blouse and sensible matching shoes.

The Kat was dressed to the nines. The suit was charcoal Armani, his crisp white shirt playing backdrop to a subtle designer tie of blue and gray, and his Italian leather shoes screamed straight out of the box. David knew his gold cuff links read RTK. His hair was combed flat and shone in smooth black strips under pendulum lights that hung from the high courtroom ceiling. His face was clean shaven, his nails neatly manicured.

"Good morning, Counselor. Ms. Davis." Katz nodded.

"Roger," said David, noticing the Kat eyeing Sara up and down.

Sara mirrored Scaturro's professional attire in a pale gray suit.

"Big morning." Katz smiled, no doubt realizing the gallery was packed and feeling the need to put on a show of confidence for his public.

"Surprised you hadn't rolled out the red carpet to make your entrance," said David.

"Very funny, Counselor. Make the most of your wit while you can because I get the feeling it is about to dry up."

With that, Katz turned to Scaturro and shuffled the papers in front of him. David turned to acknowledge the DA, but she immediately looked away. Was it his imagination or was Scaturro looking particularly nervous this morning? Actually, he decided, she looked more guilty than nervous and David had a feeling this did not bode well for events that were to come.

The gallery comprised a mixture of familiar faces and unrecognizable members of the public. Teesha, Delia and another man, whom Sara introduced as Delia's ex-husband, Tyrone Banks, were sitting directly behind the defense table. Next to them sat two of Arthur's younger associates, Samantha Bale and Con Stipoulos.

Sitting behind them and to the right were a large group of African Americans who, Sara explained, were AACSAM colleagues, including the AACSAM director, an elderly gentleman named Macarthur Dodds. Behind them sat the Jordans: Mariah and her parents, Elise and Ewan. The Washingtons, David noticed, were sitting in the far right-hand corner of the room, behind the prosecution, and beyond them at the back entrance stood Joe Mannix, who caught David's eye and gave him a nod.

Rudolph and Elizabeth Haynes had just entered and sat immediately behind the prosecution's table, he in a conservative dark navy suit and she in a stylish ensemble of mourning black; her soft azure blouse, the only hint of color, captured the sorrow in her blue eyes.

The rest of the crowd were reporters or interested citizens curious about the case that had dominated the news during the past three days. David had the horrible feeling that if he rose above this room and looked down, there would be a noticeable color-block effect embracing the room: mostly white on one side, mostly black on the other.

The side door to the holding cell that led into the courtroom opened, and Rayna was led in to join the defense table. She wore a conservative cream suit with a pale pink blouse; her hair was neatly groomed and her face lightly made up. The room went quiet as everyone waited in anticipation.

"How are you doing?" whispered David to his client.

"I'm not sure," she said with the slightest of shudders. "Okay, I guess."

"All rise," said the bailiff.

Judge Isaac Stein entered from his chambers at the front left-hand side of courtroom 17. He was a tall, thin man with tamed graying hair and bushy eyebrows that acted as a canopy over his pale gray eyes. He was lithe and agile for his roughly sixty years.

David had been before Stein before and knew that the best way to proceed in his courtroom was to act with respect and efficiency. If there was one thing the judge hated, it was someone wasting his time. Well, maybe two things: he hated the press and anyone who pandered to them, which put Katz right up there on his list of most despised.

"All right then," he said, flipping his robe over his chair and taking a seat behind the bench. His large leather chair was framed by the American flag to his right and the Commonwealth of Massachusetts flag to his left.

"Ah, Ms. Scaturro, glad to see this time suits you."

"Of course, Your Honor."

So David was right: the prosecution had delayed this arraignment to their advantage. But why? At least the judge had tipped him off.

"Mr. Cavanaugh."

"Good morning, Your Honor."

"You represent the defendant?"

"Yes, sir, along with Ms. Sara Davis, and you know Mr. Wright."

"I do, indeed. Hello, Mr. Wright."

"Your Honor," said Arthur in a half stand.

Arthur and Judge Stein went way back, but David knew their long-term friendship would not sway Stein's view on the case.

"All right then. Mrs. Martin, as I am sure you are aware, today is simply a formal charging procedure whereby we—"

"Your Honor." It was Scaturro.

"Interrupting already, Ms. Scaturro?"

"I'm sorry, Your Honor, but before you continue, the prosecution has some new information that may alter the course of these proceedings."

"Ms. Scaturro, as DA you are aware, I am sure, that this is an arraignment, not a hearing or a trial and not the place for case argument or raising of evidence."

"Yes, Your Honor, but this new information relates to the nature of the charge."

"Your Honor." David was on his feet. One minute into proceedings and they were already trying to call the shots. "What is this all about? The prosecution has already put an innocent woman through two nights in jail and now I'm hearing they have sat on some so-called new information affecting a charge that was ridiculous in the first place."

"I am as curious as you are, Mr. Cavanaugh," said Stein. "This better be good, Ms. Scaturro."

"Yes, Your Honor." Scaturro stood up and started to walk in the direction of the bench. "During the past twenty-four hours the DA's office has become aware of new evidence that suggests the original laying of the charge of involuntary manslaughter may have been a little, shall we say, off base."

"So are you saying you agree with Mr. Cavanaugh? Do you want me to dismiss the charge before it's even been read, Ms. Scaturro?"

"No, Your Honor, we are saying that this new evidence changes the nature of the charge."

"Please spell it out, Ms. Scaturro. If you were after a buildup for your audience, you've got it."

"We are changing the charge, Your Honor, from involuntary manslaughter to second degree murder."

"*What?*" David was up, out of his chair and bounding toward the judge's bench.

The gallery went wild. Rayna grasped the edge of the defense table as if trying to steady herself. "What are they saying?" she said, turning to Sara. "I don't understand."

"Your Honor, this is unbelievable," said David, raising his voice over the din. "The unfortunate death of Christina Haynes was an accident. My client has been wrongly charged with involuntary manslaughter, a charge that we can prove is completely unfounded. Now they pull this sickening scam, just so they can do their dance in front of the media and crucify an innocent woman."

"Counselor." Judge Stein was trying to regain control of his room. He banged his gavel several times until the gallery quieted and David had stopped his advance on the bench. He turned to glare at Scaturro.

"You had better explain yourself, Ms. Scaturro, and fast, because right now I tend to agree with Mr. Cavanaugh."

"Your Honor, we realize it would have been preferable to have had this information earlier, but it came as the result of an interview conducted late yesterday. As I could not reach Your Honor when I rang last night, and considering this arraignment was scheduled for first thing this morning, I spoke to Judge Fitzgerald, who agreed the information warranted the further charge of murder two."

"Did you leave me a message, Ms. Scaturro? At home, at work? I was in a private conference until eight, but I certainly would have returned your obviously urgent call if—"

"A message," interrupted Scaturro. "Well, I may not have."

"There *was* no message, Your Honor," said David, getting more frustrated by the minute. "Just as there was no message left for me—no call even. Why wasn't I contacted regarding this insane development? Mrs. Martin is my client and this is an unfair surprise."

"We apologize to the defense, Your Honor." This came from Katz, who had been quiet up until now. Obviously, he felt it was time to stand and take a bow. "But the new information came from a source close to Mrs. Martin's family and we felt it best to protect this witness from any undue pressure until the charge was formally laid."

"So now you're accusing my client and her family of potential witness tampering. Who is this mystery witness anyway?" said David.

"Your Honor, the witness is a minor and the parents of this witness have requested as much discretion as possible. We would prefer that any further information be divulged in closed quarters," said Katz.

David immediately looked to Stein to see his normally cool complexion tinged with red.

"My chambers—*now*," said the judge.

David moved quickly back to the defense table, leaning

over it toward Rayna and making sure they could not be heard. "Don't panic," he said quietly. "They can't make this stick."

"But . . ." Rayna grabbed David's wrist and he could see that her hands were shaking. "They have a witness? Who? How? David, I'm—"

"It's all right, Rayna. Sara and I will go back to Stein's chambers and sort this out. Arthur will stay right here with you. Okay?"

David turned to leave the courtroom and as he did he cast a quick glance toward the prosecution's table to see Scaturro already scurrying behind Stein, with Katz slinking like his namesake after her.

It was Haynes who caught his eye. The senator was staring directly at him, not just in his vicinity, but eye to eye. There was no emotion there, just the straight face of purpose, daring him to a challenge. David stared straight back as if in acceptance and then followed Sara into the room beyond.

■ ■ ■

"No one speak," said Stein before anyone could open their mouth. "I am the judge and I get to go first." He flipped his robe up at the back, obviously a habit, and sat down. "Let me get this straight, Ms. Scaturro. Yesterday you interviewed a witness who I am assuming to be one of the other three girls on the boat that day?"

"Yes, Your Honor. Francine Washington."

"And she gave you information to suggest that Ms. Martin's role in the death of Christina Haynes was such that it warranted the more serious charge of murder two."

"Yes, Your Honor. I—"

"I haven't finished, Ms. Scaturro."

"Yes, sir."

"Did Miss Washington give you sufficient reason to believe Mrs. Martin acted with premeditation? Because I find this extremely hard to believe and think a jury will too."

"Your Honor," Katz couldn't help himself. "In the Commonwealth of Massachusetts, a person can be found guilty of second degree murder even when there is no obvious intent to kill or even intent to harm, so long as we can prove the accused placed the victim in a situation where there was a plain and strong likelihood that death would occur."

Katz was right, in fact he was quoting Massachusetts law almost word for word. But this was impossible. "Your Honor, I have to protest."

"Shut up, Mr. Cavanaugh," snapped Stein. "You'll get your turn. Thank you for the legal lesson, Mr. Katz." Judge Stein turned away from Katz to address Scaturro. "So Francine Washington is saying she knows for a fact that Mrs. Martin left Christina Haynes with the full knowledge that she would most likely drown? I am as confused as the defense, Ms. Scaturro."

"I understand the confusion, Your Honor, but Miss Washington has revealed a discrepancy in the defendant's testimony that can most likely be confirmed by the other two girls, who, we suspect, are withholding information or lying to protect Mrs. Martin."

"Don't keep us waiting, Ms. Scaturro. What discrepancy are you talking about?"

"Mrs. Martin's entire defense is based on her alleged final conversation with Christina Haynes. Mrs. Martin claims it was the fruits of this said conversation that led her to leave Christina and pick up the other three girls before returning to pull the Haynes girl on board."

David almost spoke up in protest at Scaturro's assuming to know how the defense would play its case but decided he would wait for her punch line.

"But we believe Christina Haynes never had a final conversation with the defendant."

"What?" said Sara.

"We believe that when Mrs. Martin saw Christina, she was already unconscious in the water. And rather than try to rescue and revive her, she turned her boat around and sped off to get the other three. Further, in all likelihood, Miss Haynes, while unconscious, was still very much alive when Mrs. Martin first saw her, but her failure to stop and attempt resuscitation effectively assured her demise. In other words, Your Honor, she left the girl for dead."

David's head was spinning. Why would Francine Washington concoct such a story? What would she have to gain?

Teesha and Mariah would certainly pull her up on it. It just didn't make sense.

"All right, Mr. Cavanaugh. Your turn," said Stein, obviously realizing David was about to burst.

"Your Honor, for starters, there is no way the other two girls will not deny these allegations. You have one girl's word against the testimony of three others."

"Really, Mr. Cavanaugh, I would not call the testimony of Rayna and Teesha Martin reliable on this issue. No jury—"

"Shut up, Mr. Katz."

David went on: "*No* jury will believe a good mother and solid citizen like Rayna Martin would leave an unconscious teenager floating in the water. It just didn't happen that way. You have one unreliable witness, no motive."

"No, Mr. Cavanaugh, in fact, we have two motives," said Katz, smiling like a hyena at feeding time. "The first motive relates to her desire as a mother to go to her daughter—a natural instinct, maybe, but still criminally negligent given that Christina Haynes was in obvious danger and on the precipice of death."

Here it comes, thought David. Haynes had found a way to play the race card.

"The second involves prejudice, Your Honor. We believe Mrs. Martin's decision to rescue her daughter, Miss Washington and Miss Jordan was based on racial preference. She chose to go after the three African American teenagers, totally disregarding the welfare of Christina Haynes."

Stein removed his glasses, rubbed his forehead and looked the ADA directly in the eye. "Are you calling this a hate crime, Mr. Katz?"

"We certainly are, Your Honor, for that is exactly what it is."

David looked at Stein and could see by his expression that he knew he was between a rock and a hard place. He could almost read the dilemma playing across the old man's mind. On one hand, the new charge was extreme—so far there was no real proof any crime had been committed at all. On the other hand, a girl was dead and her family deserved full investigation into the events surrounding her death. There was also the matter of Judge Walter Fitzgerald, who had read the

Washington girl's statement and given the DA the nod on murder two.

David knew Fitzgerald, as did most of the city's lawyers and politicians, because the man was a player who, rumor had it, considered his position on the state bench as a stepping-stone to the federal court. He carried a lot of clout in Boston legal circles, largely because he nurtured friendships in high places. Perhaps that was why he—

"All right," Stein said at last, "I will allow the arraignment to continue with the charge now standing at second degree murder. But I want to remind you, Ms. Scaturro, that the prosecution holds the burden of proof, and I fear you are setting yourselves a mighty task."

"Please, Your Honor," interrupted David in desperation. "I cannot go out there and tell my client the legal system she has spent over half her life honoring has turned to stab her in the back. She is a single mom, a decent human being who helps others for a living. This hate crime stunt is a load of crap and you know it."

He took a deep breath. There was no other way to play this but straight down the line. "I believe the prosecution may be experiencing undue pressure from the girl's father to push this thing way beyond the point of reasonable," he said. "I also believe they enjoy the celebrity that comes with such a sensational misuse of justice. I would suggest they have no idea of the extent of damage this racial argument will cause: for Rayna, for themselves and for the greater community as a whole. And further, I warn them that when we throw this case out of court, and we will, I will be encouraging Mrs. Martin to sue the commonwealth for damages."

The judge leaned back in his chair. "I understand your plight, Mr. Cavanaugh, but I must stress again that this is just an arraignment. All we are doing here is reading a charge."

"And denying bail," said Sara.

"True, Ms. Davis. Unfortunately, until this mess is sorted, Mrs. Martin will remain in custody. You will have to have faith in this system and your own abilities as attorneys to see that justice is done. I would suggest for all concerned that this matter be moved swiftly through the system so that the fanatics do not use it to cause further racial unrest in our community. I would also suggest that the prosecution be extremely sure of their ability to win this case before dragging us all through that nasty minefield known as bigotry."

Judge Stein turned to David and Sara.

"We have a courtroom of vultures out there waiting for us to return and throw them a few more bloody crumbs for lunch. If we are quick and efficient, we can keep theatrics to a minimum."

"Try telling that to a sixteen-year-old girl who has to sit there and watch her mother being charged with murdering one of her best friends," said David. He was sweating now, his throat dry, his hands clenched, his chest tight. "There's your crime right there, Judge. One girl is dead and now we are going to witness another have her soul ripped out and her innocence destroyed forever. I hope you can live with that, Roger," he said, turning to the ADA. "Because I sure as hell couldn't."

7

There was one "The" who was white. His name was Spencer Bloom and he was The Mechanic.

He was different from the other The's. Not just because of his skin (which was white, but tanned almost as dark as the others) but because he was funny and sweet, and treated her more like a friend than a Whitman. And so she called him Spence.

"Spence," she said in her sleep. And she could see him now, standing on the bottom veranda step of their large white Greens Farms estate, his hands glistening with grease, his brow shiny with perspiration and a look of embarrassment on his face as her father retold the story of how Spence had saved his life.

"We were stationed in the East Solomons, on the USS *Enterprise*," she could hear her father say. "I was captain of the artillery unit and Spence was the best damned lieutenant on the carrier. He treated those turrets like his very own children: respectful of their power and mindful of their quirks."

"Tell us about the battle, Daddy," she heard herself say, now not sure if she was actually asleep or not. And her daddy would smile and Spence would take his cap from his sunburned head and screw it up in his hands, embarrassed by the attention.

"There were over a hundred fighter pilots," he would begin, looking up as if the action were playing out above him, "launched from our ship and the USS *Saratoga,* and they were soon joined by hundreds more from the *Shokaku* and the *Zuikaku,* the Japanese airmen weaving and dive-bombing in a sky filled with fire and smoke.

"Spence was moving as fast as he could on his way to give me an update in the chief petty officer's quarters. And that was when the first bomb hit."

Elizabeth shifted in her bed, a faint sense of anticipation in her expression as her dream played out like a movie, the characters familiar, the colors bright and the warmth of her memories all encompassing.

She could hear her father recall the explosion that "ripped six-foot holes in the hull" and how Spence "broke his right arm and three ribs" and still managed to rescue his captain, who lay "unconscious under a collapsed steel strut."

A noise in the hallway broke her focus and opened the door to reality, which reared its ugly head and invaded her temporary respite. She forced it away, determined to stay in this safe, familiar place as long as possible.

Spence, the man who saved her father's life and was repaid with a job for life . . . Spence, the man who never spoke of his past or the places and people in it . . . It seemed to Elizabeth, who was surrounded by possessions, that Spence was grateful for what little he had, and most important, cherished the one person who gave his life meaning: his ten-year-old son, Topher, with the long dark hair and the deep brown eyes. He was . . . he was . . .

"Elizabeth," he said, standing at her door, newspaper in one hand, glasses in the other.

"Rudolph," she said, jolted from her dream, the guilt of her memories sending a hot flush throughout her entire body.

"It's after nine. You'd better get up. Agnes has laid out your clothes."

"The Chanel?" she asked, not knowing what else to say.

"I have no idea." He stood there, looking at her.

"It's all right, Rudolph. I'm getting up."

"Right." And then he paused a few seconds longer before turning to walk down the corridor.

She sat up in bed, searching the corners of her brain for something to send him away.

The bag should be Prada, she pondered: *simple, small, black. And the shoes . . . Gucci: modest heel, understated. Yes, yes, that was it. The perfect attire for a society funeral. They would do just fine.*

■ ■ ■

When, she wondered, did it happen? When did a child become an adult, a little girl become a woman?

She was seventeen. Well, almost, close enough, and maybe this was it? Maybe that was why this morning she looked at her reflection and knew the little girl inside her was dead.

Teesha Martin used her hand to wipe away the steam that sat like a thin veil on the surface of her aunt's bathroom mirror. Her long hair was piled on top of her head and as she released it, she realized that the change was internal. She didn't look any different. She used her index finger to push a strand away from her left eye. She looked the same but different, unchanged but affected.

They had allowed her to make the decision herself, and she had decided to go. Her mother had advised against it, worried what some might say or do. Her aunt had agreed it was dangerous and that it might be best if they offered their prayers for Christina in private. But this was her best friend's funeral and this decision, they agreed, had to be hers.

She had led a charmed life. Sure, her dad had died when she was little, but to be honest, there was little pain there. Her memories were few but sweet and she had been too young to suffer the grief that comes with years of closeness and familiarity. Her mom was the best, her aunt Delia like a second mom and her uncle Tyrone was always there for her, even though he lived a few hundred miles away.

She was smart, getting straight A's in school. She was on the debate team, the track team and, thanks to her mom's job, didn't want for anything. She didn't have a boyfriend, but last Friday night Justin Winter had called and she was going to find the right time to ask her mom if she could go out with him. But first she would tell her best friends. They would be happy for her, they would laugh and give her advice and tell her what she should wear and hang out for all the details of the date the next day.

She hadn't even had the chance to tell Christina that it was Justin who had called, and that he'd asked her to a movie the following weekend, which would have been this coming Saturday. But that was in her other life, when Chrissie was still alive, before Francie had betrayed her and when the little girl inside her still smiled.

And so she had decided to go, for that is what an adult would do, and today she was older and wiser than she had ever been before.

• • •

"It's a bad idea, David. No, it's not just bad, it's insane."

It was early Wednesday morning and Lieutenant Joe Mannix had spent the past half hour trying to talk David out of going to Christina Haynes's funeral.

"It will look like harassment. You're a good lawyer, David, one of the best, but you have a problem when it comes to knowing when to pull back—and this, my friend, is one of those times."

David sat in Mannix's office, drinking a disgusting potion disguised as black coffee in an effort to stay awake and fuel himself for the day ahead. He had not slept. He and Sara had spent the rest of Tuesday between the Suffolk County Jail, with Rayna, and David's offices, trying to make some sense of Francine Washington's claims and what they meant to their case, or rather, how they'd destroyed it.

"Look, Joe, I'm not going to harass the Hayneses. I just want to observe. I need to see who is there and who isn't. Who is sitting where, what is the ratio of black to white, is Francine Washington in Rudolph Haynes's pocket?"

It had not taken long for David, Sara and Arthur to work out that the Washingtons had been "reached" by Haynes. David was pretty sure the senator was pulling the strings and feeding Katz the ammunition. They would have to talk to Francie, of course (if her father would allow it), and to Teesha and Mariah, but today was going to be hard for all three of them, so the plan was to lie low and watch from the sidelines.

David knew Mannix would be there in his role as commander of the Homicide Unit. This was customary, considering the charge was now murder two.

"Okay," said Mannix with a sigh. "If I can't talk you out of it, just make sure you stay out of sight. I'll be hanging around the back of the church with Petri."

"Lucky you."

"Paul's not so bad, David," said Mannix, and David could see he was a little miffed at David's attempt at sarcasm. "His wife is sick. The guy's just going through a rough time."

"Whatever you say."

"Just stay close to your car. Anyone else from your legal team going?"

"Sara will be inside with Teesha."

Mannix shook his head.

"She's like a big sister to Teesha."

"And you need a set of eyes inside the church," finished Mannix. "Jesus, you guys are gluttons for punishment. I really don't think it's smart, the kid turning up and all, for her own sake."

"She'll be with Sara and Rayna's sister, Delia."

Mannix got up from his desk and took David's stained coffee mug before starting for his office door.

"All right, but one word of warning: if I see your sorry ass anywhere near that church, I'll kick it from here to hell and back."

"That your way of saying you want to protect me, Joe?" David couldn't resist a smile.

"Sure, because you sure as hell can't look after yourself."

* * *

She should have worn the Saint Laurent.

Elizabeth Haynes sat in the back of the black town car next to her husband. The Chanel was too big; she must have dropped five pounds in the last five days, because the skirt was swiveling around her waist.

"You're pleased with yesterday then," she said softly, as much to make conversation as anything else.

"Yes, of course. It's a good first step, Elizabeth. Fitzgerald is a good man; I knew he would get the ball rolling for us."

They sat in silence as the car crawled out of the long, red gravel circular drive and headed toward the city and Trinity Church. She felt him looking at her.

"Are you all right?" he asked.

"Yes," she said, both of them knowing it was not true.

"All the formalities will be over soon; then we can get back to it," he said.

She knew "it" was her husband's obsession with going after Rayna Martin, and while she was glad it was giving him some form of comfort, she could not understand how he could think it would make things better.

She would like the Martin woman to feel the full fury of the law but knew that even life imprisonment was a walk in the park compared to her own new lot in life. Five days after the fact, somewhere in this gray sea of confusion, she had come to one simple, obvious conclusion. *Losing a child was the ultimate hell.*

It was worse than a million life sentences. It was condemnation to endless years of nothingness, an existence filled with agonizing memories and dreams of what might have been. And for it to end as it did . . . How could he not see this?

She took a deep breath and fixed the small black hat on her

groomed golden hair, checked her makeup in her compact mirror and straightened her skirt yet again.

She should have worn the Saint Laurent.

■ ■ ■

It truly is impressive, thought Sara as she stopped in the middle of Copley Square to look up at the breathtaking structure before her. She could remember reading somewhere that Trinity Church, with its rough-faced stone walls and clay-tiled roof, had been an innovation for its time. Designed in the early 1870s by the young architect H. H. Richardson, who shunned the traditional Gothic style, it was a masterpiece of what became known as Richardsonian Romanesque.

Delia and Teesha had gone ahead, allowing Sara the opportunity to take in the activity surrounding the church. Copley Square, an oasis normally filled with mothers and their children, professionals eating lunch and tourists admiring the church's historic grandeur, was today packed with different sorts of observers: those with zoom lenses and live-to-air TV cameras, conservative suits and microphones, and a mishmash crowd of curious passersby being urged by uniformed police to steer clear of the entrance and move along.

Once inside, Sara could see why the stained glass windows had earned their reputation as some of the most beautiful in the world. This morning the sunlight filtered through the northeast windows, throwing splashes of muted color across the crowded pews, with hundreds of dark suits and dresses providing a dark canvas for the splotches of reds, blues, greens and golds.

Sara joined Delia and Teesha in a pew toward the middle of the church. Next to them sat the Jordans: Mariah, her parents and her little brother, William. They would normally be joined by Francie, but today, if the Washingtons were here, they had decided to sit elsewhere, which, under the circumstances, was no surprise.

Sara knew that as mercenary as it might seem, she was here not only for Teesha but to do a job, and she set about taking in as much detail as possible. She noted that despite its expansive interior, the church still could not accommodate all the mourners. The overflow spilled out onto the street.

Many in the crowd were middle-aged or older, obviously friends and associates of the senator and his wife. Many had famous faces, including White House chief of staff Maxine Bryant; Boston mayor Moses Novelli, who, Sara knew, was one of the senator's oldest friends; and former vice president Larry Howell.

Scaturro and Katz sat about six rows from the front, across from her on the left-hand side of the church. The former kept her head down while the latter managed to look up every now and again to give an appropriate nod to the more important of the VIPs.

Behind her fell row upon row of students from Curtis Academy wearing the school's colors of blue and gold. Impressive as a whole, some held leatherbound prayer books, others sought solace in each other's embrace, many whispered quietly as they waited for the service to begin. There were other young people scattered throughout who must have known Christina in one way or another: a young man in a tennis camp blazer, a poised young woman in a dancer's crossover wrap who might have been her ballet teacher. Sara estimated that, disregarding the mixed nature of the Curtis Academy students' origins, still disproportionately white, the congregation in general was approximately 90 percent Anglo.

Haynes and his wife entered last. Both wore black.

They walked down the aisle toward the casket and sat in the front row to Sara's left. The senator walked with head high, holding on tightly to his wife's elbow. Sara's heart went out to the woman who was trying desperately not to look at her daughter's coffin.

Sara had met Christina a number of times and now saw where the girl had gotten her prettiness. Elizabeth Haynes was the picture of elegance. The horror of the past week was etched on her face, but she still looked incredibly beautiful.

The casket was white and covered with pale pink roses that seemed to pour down its sides like strawberry milk. It was simple, without the usual carvings and embellishments, as if paying homage to the angelic being inside who needed no adornment.

The service itself was moving but conservative, with readings offered by everyone from Mayor Novelli to a white student named Cassandra Cummings, who was introduced as Christina's closest friend. Sara wondered how that reference would be received by Teesha and Mariah.

In his homily, the bishop urged all present to thank God for what little time they had had with Christina and trust that, although impossible for us to conceive, the brief nature of her life was all part of the Almighty's greater plan. He preached about God's teachings of forgiveness and mercy, of compassion and understanding—a subtle reference to Rayna (and one which insinuated guilt), which, Sara knew, was falling on deaf ears.

As well as monitoring the details, David had told Sara to soak in the atmosphere, to get a feeling for the level of emotion surrounding the case, so she tried to define the sentiment around her. She could feel something beyond the throb of grief, something more powerful. It was something dressed up as sympathy and disguised as sorrow. It lacked compassion and cried out for revenge. There was no other word for it . . . she could feel hate. This was a hatred any normal person *would* feel for someone they thought, or were told, was responsible for such a travesty. Their anger at Rayna, their condemnation of her actions, was unspoken but screamed like a siren through the silence of the ceremony.

At the end of the hour, six young white pallbearers from Curtis Academy carried the casket to the back of the church, where it was placed in the rear of a Rolls-Royce hearse. The crowd started to fold out into the street.

David and Arthur had parked a block north on Berkeley Street. Arthur had agreed with Mannix that it was a mistake for David to be here. Sara had a legitimate reason for attending, and Arthur had the ability to blend in with the crowd. But whether he liked it or not, as Arthur had lectured, David was the public face of the defense—the enemy—and he was too damned tall and good looking to play the curious bystander.

So David had promised to stay on the other side of Boylston Street, to listen to the people milling around the square and get a feeling for their take on this whole crazy mess. Arthur had stressed the importance of public opinion. The case was already being tried in the media, and he knew this would intensify. The photos of Christina showed a golden-haired angel, the photos of Rayna a dark-skinned, tired-looking woman holding a number. There was no contest when it came to the aesthetics.

David knew the African American community would rally behind his client, but even this could play against them. If the case became a forum for racial debate, the public, and more important, the jury, could lose track of the core truth, the fact that Rayna made the right decision in dire circumstances.

David would do everything to make sure this case did not turn into an us-against-them. He had seen hate crimes turn a mild-natured community into a bunch of savages, and this one had the potential to do that and more. Overall, David and Arthur both noted the obvious: a general rift in opinion based on color. This was no surprise; it just confirmed their fears of the growing emotional debate.

The crowd started dribbling through the back doors of the church, a flow that soon became a throng of mourners adjusting to the sunlight and the world of the living outside the huge hand-carved doors. The students from Curtis had formed a guard of honor, and the congregation moved in an orderly fashion down the stairs and onto the front grass, where they milled around, looking up every now and again to see if the Hayneses, who had chosen to leave last, were at the back doors.

The press, who had been asked to remain behind temporary barricades positioned around the periphery of the square, began clicking and filming from the footpaths. This was a society funeral after all.

David looked up to see the senator and his wife emerge, and it became a case of who could get to them first. Elizabeth was soon surrounded by a large group of well-dressed women, social clones of herself who held her hands and fussed quietly about her like a group of well-mannered worker bees. The senator received a procession of mourners, mostly fellow politicians and businessmen, giving quiet nods and strong handshakes.

David noticed a young girl in a school uniform handing Elizabeth a small bunch of white tiger lilies while her mother almost curtsied in the background.

And then David saw him.

Edward Washington was moving fast through the crowd toward the senator. He walked with his back straight, as if he belonged in this herd of white men, his wife taking quick, excited steps behind him and Francine, unsure of herself, bringing up the rear.

Arthur moved alongside David.

"You see them?" asked David.

"Sure do," replied his boss. "I think he's moving in."

"Just as we suspected."

"Now the only question is, how friendly he thinks he can get."

David found Sara in the crowd and was pleased to see her eyes were also following the Washingtons. Now all three could see Edward Washington and his family elbow governors and senators and corporate chiefs out of their way so that they could get to their best friend, Rudi.

Haynes saw them too and the look on his face was pure horror. At first he turned his back, hoping they would move on, but when the annoying Edward Washington poked him on the shoulder, he had no choice but to turn and give his best impression of an appreciative smile. Luckily, Sara had moved close enough to hear the conversation.

"Senator," began Washington in a rather loud, deep voice. "As I have said before, we are so sorry for your loss. Please do not hesitate to ask if there is anything else we can do."

So there it was . . . "as he had said before" . . . "anything else" they could do.

"Ah, thank you, Mr. . . ."

"Washington, from the other morning. Surely you . . ."

"Yes, thank you, Mr. Washington."

Sara processed the enormity of the words just spoken while noticing Haynes desperately trying to cut the handshake short. She was not surprised when he started to look around as if trying to determine who might have been close

enough to overhear their conversation, and took grim satisfaction at the look of shock on his face when he turned in her
direction and they locked eyes.

Teesha was watching Cassandra Cummings and getting
angrier by the minute. No way was Cassie Cummings Christina's best friend. In fact, one of the last things Chrissie had
said to her was that Cassie was a stuck-up bitch who only
sucked up to her because her dad was famous. Christina had
told the girls how Cassie's mom would call her mom and invite Christina over. Christina's mom thought it was a great
idea and Chrissie thought it sucked.

Teesha suspected that Chrissie had fought with her
parents about her choice of friends the very morning she
died—turning up at the party unannounced, the distinct
tinge of red in her moist blue eyes. She had no doubt this
argument would have been about Teesha, Mariah and Francie. Chrissie may not have said this outright—she wouldn't
have wanted to hurt their feelings—but the girls knew where
they stood.

Teesha's mind was made up. If Cassie could stand there
holding Chrissie's mom's hand, then Teesha had every right
to tell Mrs. Haynes how much she was missing Christina too.
Surely she would understand. They could break down the
silly black and white thing to share in their grief, a sort of
solidarity in pain that would hopefully bring some comfort to
both.

Teesha looked around for Sara. She knew she would stop
her. But she was over near Chrissie's dad. Delia was at least
four bodies behind her, and Mariah and her family had left
straight after the service.

That's when Cassie stepped back and Teesha met Elizabeth Haynes face-to-face.

"Mrs. Haynes, my name is . . ."

"I know who you are," said Elizabeth, her soft features
turning to stone.

"I just wanted you to know . . ."

Elizabeth lowered her voice. "How dare you show your
face here."

Teesha took a small step backward, unsure of what to
say, and then she thought of Chrissie and took a deep

breath before stepping forward again and extending her hand in an attempt at conciliation. But Elizabeth reacted quickly, slapping Teesha's wrist and forcing her arm downward.

Teesha instinctively pulled back, but her hand was stuck, caught on something. Her silver charm bracelet was entwined in threads on Elizabeth's black skirt and an embarrassed Teesha yanked hard to release it, wanting to get out of there as quickly as possible.

Teesha soon realized Elizabeth had no room to move, and covered her face as her best friend's mother twisted around making rapid shooing gestures. Elizabeth's skirt swung about her waist, the twisting doing nothing to loosen Teesha's bracelet.

"Please, Mrs. Haynes. I only wanted to . . ." said Teesha, now starting to panic. There seemed to be no escape. Elizabeth's flailing arms had triggered a chain reaction as half the women around her, unsure of what was going on, started to flee, while the others, thinking Teesha was trying to attack their friend, joined the fray and tried to pull the two apart.

The press on the pavement had picked up on the fracas and clicked away with enthusiasm. They were not completely sure what had caused the commotion but knew that whatever it was, it was front-page fodder.

David saw Haynes look directly at Sara and instinctively moved in. In that split second he noticed Haynes's head turn from Sara toward the road. David followed his line of vision and saw a dark-haired man dressed in a suit springing out of a parked car directly across the street from the main gate. David took note of the fact that Haynes shook his head quickly as if telling him to stay where he was before turning back to Sara. He mouthed something to her, which David could see made Sara freeze. But by the time he got to her, Katz had entered the picture, his arm moving around her waist pulling her backward.

David reached for Katz, grabbing him by the right shoulder, pivoting him around. "Get away from her, Roger."

"My God, you're all here," said Katz. "I don't believe it. This is the girl's funeral, for God's sake. Leave these people alone, Mr. Cavanaugh, or I'll have you arrested for harassment."

David could tell that Katz realized the surrounding press would hear every word and was playing this one for effect.

It was about now that Elizabeth's arms took full flight and her friends started a tug-of-war with Teesha. A new commotion behind David caused him to turn around. It was the Secret Service—and they were moving in.

There was a fresh circle of chaos in the middle of the crowd where the Hayneses and, coincidentally, the White House chief of staff were standing. David knew the Secret Service were trained to act immediately with any indication that their charge was in danger, and they certainly wasted no time. Four men in black suits with dark glasses, buzz cuts and earpieces burrowed through the crowd at record speed with complete disregard for everyone except the woman they were here to protect.

David saw them grab Maxine Bryant under each arm and run her to a nearby government limo, all the time yelling at police to clear the access to the road so they could get out of there . . . *now*!

The police, not to be outdone, followed their lead. David was pushed aside by four zealous uniforms as Haynes and his wife, who was now free from Teesha and holding her skirt tightly at her waist, were shuffled quickly into their town car. They stumbled as the officers forced the congregation farther back into the park and the government car carrying the chief of staff screeched down the pavement, onto Saint James Avenue and out of sight.

Next came the screech of a new set of tires as the driver of the hearse, obviously deciding to follow the government car's lead, swerved in an attempt to make as hasty an exit as possible. David saw Elizabeth Haynes grasp her husband's arm as their driver started their car and immediately accelerated after the hearse, across the square and down the sidewalk with no regard for the customary decorum.

The two funeral cars, now desperate to avoid one slow, elderly parishioner standing stock-still in the middle of the roadway, veered up onto the grass, their wheels plowing deep burrows into the perfectly manicured lawn and crushing a sea of wreaths that had been laid row upon row at the top of the square in front of the church's main entrance.

The next thing David registered was the sound of falling barricades as the press joined in the general disregard for order and attempted to follow the frenzy. Flashes went off everywhere, reporters stood yelling frantically into live cameras while police tried desperately to push them aside so that the funeral cars could enter the street.

"Look what you've done," a voice said from behind and David turned to see Katz with a smirk on his face.

David did not hesitate, just pulled back his right arm aiming directly at the ADA's perfectly proportioned nose. But just as he was about to connect, Mannix grabbed his shoulder and yanked his arm back in a classic police hold. Before he knew it, he was being dragged to the pavement and forced into an unmarked police car.

"Get him out of here," he heard Mannix say to the young officer. "Drop him at his car and escort him back to his office."

Then Mannix slammed the door and banged on the roof twice with his right hand leaving David, still fuming, to turn back in his seat and see what looked like the process of a war zone evacuation.

It was one almighty mess and, worse still, he knew it had handed Roger Katz his motive of "hate" on a platter. He also knew it was an incident that would have serious repercussions, fired as it was by Haynes's rage, which was aimed unequivocally at destroying their case and putting their client away, for good.

8

"I swear, Tyrone," said Delia Banks down the line to her ex-husband in Washington. "It was pure bedlam. I've never seen such chaos—a whole lotta so-called civilized white people fussing about like loons in a lockup. They all blame Rayna, Tyrone," she said, and he knew she was starting to cry. "They think my baby sister is a goddamned murderer and if she would've been there, I swear, they would have held a good old-fashioned lynching."

Tyrone felt the familiar sensation of guilt wash over him. He should have stayed in Boston for the funeral, but his job as a senior research analyst for the Democratic Party was a demanding one, and he was already feeling the pressure of a backlog after taking two days' personal leave to be by his ex-wife's side.

"I'm so sorry, Delia," he said, the apology so habitual that its genuineness was lost in its familiarity. "I should have taken the extra day."

"*Of course* you should have, Tyrone. But a leopard never changes his spots and we all know those precious politicians in D.C. cannot cope a minute without you."

And so it began, the sarcasm, the hurt, the familiar routine of one-upmanship that had ended their marriage. In all fairness to Delia, she had made it clear from the outset that she would never move to Washington, and in the early days Tyrone coped with the regular commutes. But the promotions got bigger, the trips got longer and before long Delia was giving him the ultimatum—Boston or Washington—*me or them.*

In the end, Tyrone took the easy way out, burying himself in polls and statistics and the loneliness that was Capitol

Hill. Professionally it was the best decision he ever made, as he worked his way up within the party, earning some serious clout and the dollars to go with it. Personally it was a disaster, for he had lost the only woman he could ever love and rarely saw the niece whom he thought of as a daughter.

"I'm owed plenty of vacation time," he said now, hoping to make amends. "I'll finish up on my current projects, and then I'll come home for a while." *Home,* he noticed he'd said—after all these years he still thought of Delia's home as his own.

"Since when have you been thinking about anyone but yourself, Mr. Banks?" his ex-wife asked, but he could hear the relief in her voice and took comfort in the knowledge that despite the proud facade, she still needed him—at least just a little bit.

"I guess Teesha could use the support," she said, determined not to show any sign of frailty. "So, if you want to come, I suppose I could do up the spare room."

"I do. And thanks, Delia."

He hung up the phone, turned on the TV and sat back in his lonely apartment to watch the chaos of the funeral on the evening news. He felt completely helpless. There must be something he could do.

Being there for Delia, Teesha and Rayna was one thing, but he had to be able to contribute something more. He may not have been a hotshot lawyer, but he was good at research, meticulous in fact. Trials required plenty of research, didn't they? Perhaps he could use his skills and contacts somehow?

His mind was made up. Tomorrow he would call David Cavanaugh and offer his services. Anything was better than sitting back and watching this terrible thing happening to the people he loved the most.

. . .

Vincent Verne had always believed that a true leader was one who knew how to delegate. He also believed that a leader's strength lay in his ability to allow his people to execute their expertise unhindered. That is probably why he respected the senator so much—because he would assign an instruction without interference or, more specifically in this case, give Vince a broad directive and leave the details of implementation to him.

Haynes had taught Vince that the reason most people failed to advance in life was because they were too easily distracted. "Distraction," he would say, "is your enemy's greatest weapon."

He believed the majority only had the ability to concentrate on one thing at one time with 100 percent efficiency. Throw in a little disturbance here, an interruption there and their 100 percent focus would drop to 85. Hit them with an emotional obstacle, one that would screw with their head and their heart simultaneously, and the concentration level was down around 65 percent. Distractions were the negatives to the positives of commitment. It was a basic mathematical formula where you simply continued to subtract from the total.

Vince was not one to argue. Experience had shown him that the senator was right. So if the senator wanted distractions, he would have them—delicately placed, growing in intensity and untraceable.

He dialed the number committed to memory and gave a few specific instructions into the cell phone. The whole conversation, one way that it was, took all of thirty seconds. He put down his cell phone and allowed himself a smile. He would start with Sara Davis and go from there.

• • •

"You know you are breaking the law," said David.

"Hm," said Mick McGee, scratching his head in mock confusion. "I don't see how that's possible, Davy, my boy, given my good friend here"—Mick gestured at Joe—"obviously has no problem consuming alcoholic beverages on my hospitable premises."

Myrtle's was a breakfast and lunchtime café that closed at 5:00 PM. It had no liquor license and a little late-night gathering like this might have made the proprietor nervous if the clientele had not included the commander of Boston PD's Homicide Unit.

"I thought this was ginger beer," said Joe, putting the Bud to his lips.

"Aye, that it is," said Mick, downing his own icy cold brew. "This fella is just out for a tussle today," he said, pointing at David. "I saw him on the news. Throws a good right hook by the look of things. It's the Irish in him, Joseph. We all have hot tempers, so try not to be too hard on him."

"Yeah, well," Joe began, "I hate to say I told you so."

"Then don't," said David, who opted for a Coke and passed another to Sara before throwing a glance at Arthur, daring him to agree with his detective friend.

"This is no joke," said Arthur. "We may know the Hayneses showed their true colors today, but all the public saw was Rayna's daughter and the defense team harassing the dead girl's parents, at her funeral no less. It was inappropriate. It was a serious setback, and we will pay for it."

They sat in silence knowing Arthur was right.

"All right, we messed up. Now we have to start thinking about how to gain from what we learned today."

"If you guys are gonna talk strategy, I better take off," said Joe, draining his beer and grabbing his jacket.

"Me too," said Mick. "Otherwise I'll sell my story to the papers and head for Vegas."

"I can lock up," David told Mick, standing to walk Joe to the door.

"That you will, lad, and you'll also promise not to start any fistfights in future without including me." Mick went to turn off the kitchen lights while David walked outside with Mannix.

"Thanks for the emergency rescue today, Joe."

"Don't mention it. But David . . ." Mannix slowed, turning to look at his friend.

"Yeah." David expected Joe to have another go at him for attending the funeral in the first place.

"What I am going to say to you now stays between us, and only us," Joe said.

"Okay."

"I mean *just* us, not Arthur or Sara, and if you ever repeat this, I'll deny I ever said it."

"Okay, Joe, what is it?"

Joe looked around the quiet street and took a deep breath. "Haynes knows people."

"He knows people . . ." repeated David, scratching his head, not too sure where this was going.

"What I am saying is, you can't be a cop in this city for as long as I have and not notice things, see a pattern."

"Go on."

"When Haynes wants something, he gets it," said Mannix. "He makes things happen. The guy is a zealot when it comes to fulfilling election promises, growing his financial interests, protecting his inner circle, punishing those who let him down. He walks all over people, David, and he does it with a smile on his face."

"Can you give me an example?"

"Okay, take this guy, an accountant at Locke and Baum, midthirties, wife, two kids, rosy future, right? One day he gets himself in a car accident, breaks his arm, his pelvis. Leaves him in traction for six weeks."

"So?"

"So the accident happens in his own driveway. He claims some crazy drunk sped up there by mistake and then took off. Didn't get the plates or the make of the car, couldn't even say what color. But the neighbors see it different. They see a black Mercedes swerve into his house and nudge him up his own drive while he's fixing his kid's bicycle. The driver winds down the window, says something to the accountant and takes off."

"Who was the accountant, Joe?"

"He was handling Haynes's finances at the time and there was some suggestion of embezzlement. The fraud squad was investigating him, but after the accident, they were called off.

"And don't forget, next year Haynes is up for reelection," Joe went on. "And believe you me, *no one* is gonna get in the way of him winning another term. Whether you like it or not, this case is a forerunner to his campaign. You defeat the prosecution and you defeat Haynes by default—he'll either come off as a loser or a man to be pitied—and both perspectives, I can promise you, have no place in the great Rudolph Haynes's predetermined road to victory."

"I hear what you're saying," said David, his head down as he scuffed his shoes on the pavement.

"Do you?" asked Mannix, placing his hand on his friend's shoulder and forcing him to look up. "Well, just to make sure, let me put it another way. If I found myself on Haynes's hit list, I would take Marie and the boys and change cities. Hell, I'd migrate to Fiji. Don't underestimate him, David, because he'll stop at nothing, and no one will ever be the wiser."

"Except you."

"Except me," said Joe, perhaps realizing he had scared his friend enough to at least keep him on the alert. "And by then I'll be sailing a yacht off some idyllic, tropical island paradise without a care in the world."

• • •

It was late. Arthur told David and Sara to go home. They should get some sleep and start again early tomorrow.

Sara had driven to the church with Delia, so her car was still at home. David liked it that Sara didn't wait for the offer for a lift home; she just climbed into his Toyota Land Cruiser as if knowing he was going to insist anyway.

"We made a mess of things today," she said.

"Yeah," he replied.

They sat in silence as he pulled out and headed north toward Sara's brownstone.

"David?"

"Yep."

"I didn't tell you what he said to me."

David had forgotten seeing Haynes mouth something to Sara. So much had happened so quickly. He now remembered the horrified look on her face just before he'd reached her.

"What was it?" he said, turning to look at her.

"He said, 'Forget or regret.' "

David knew what Haynes had meant, forget Washington's conversation or suffer the consequences.

"Look, Sara, the guy is all bluff. He was emotionally distressed, he was just trying to rattle you."

But David knew better. These three words scared the hell out of him, especially after his conversation with Mannix.

But there was no point in alarming Sara unnecessarily, and he wanted so desperately to alleviate her fears. "I wouldn't let it worry you."

"I'm sure you're right," she said. "Silly isn't it? I mean what can the guy do?"

"Exactly."

They sat quietly as David approached her terrace, the front light left on by her friend Cindy.

"The guy just wants to unnerve us, keep our minds on everything else but defending Rayna."

"I know. I just . . . I really want to win this, David. For Rayna, of course, but also because we have to fight for what's right. This case has nothing to do with race. Rayna is one of the most tolerant people I know; she doesn't even notice the color of people's skin, just who they are, what they do, how she can help them.

"I have seen bigotry at work; that's one of the things that drew me to Rayna in the first place. She is so incredibly free of any form of bias. And I worry what this is doing to Teesha. I just hope I'm a good enough lawyer to help you pull this off."

He took her hand, and without thinking brought it up to his lips and kissed it. "You're more than good enough," he said. "Everything you just said proves that."

She brought up her other hand and touched his cheek.

"Thanks," she said, leaning in toward him ever so slightly.

They looked at each other then, inches apart, and David felt an all-consuming need to kiss her. He sensed that she felt the same way, her eyes locked on his, her breaths long and slow and warm against his face.

"Sara, I . . ."

"I know," she said, cutting him short. "It's just that there is so much happening right now."

"I didn't mean to . . ."

"It's okay," she said, and then paused before going on. "I have to go. But David, I need you to know that . . . I guess there is a time for everything and this is, well . . ." She paused again. "As I said, thanks for everything."

And then she turned and climbed out of the car, closing the door behind her, moving quickly up her front walk, without looking back.

He had no idea how long he sat there. Seconds, minutes, longer. He was so tired, so terrified, so overwhelmed, so confused.

This is what it is like, he thought to himself, realizing that he had forgotten. And then he turned the ignition key and pulled out toward home, feeling more alive than he had in years.

9

Arthur leaned forward and put the paper down.

"Not good," he said.

"Could have been worse," offered David, who then turned to page three to see a photo of himself rearing back to punch Roger Katz in the face, "or maybe not."

"No, maybe not," said Sara, looking over his shoulder, the scent of perfume on her neck.

They had started early, and neither had mentioned last night's "moment." It was as if they both realized that work was the priority; but there was no awkwardness, and this in itself was reassuring.

"Anyway, what's done is done," said Arthur. "We should get back to work."

The strategy they had devised for Rayna's defense had originally been based on the charge of involuntary manslaughter, but the new charge of murder two required a different tack. Initially, they were to focus on Rayna's reputation as a responsible person, and while this was still the case, they now also had to prove that Rayna was not a racist and this is where the lines became foggy.

For starters, Rayna worked for a minority support organization. Despite the fact that AACSAM was a respected community establishment, it was still associated with racial division. Secondly, she had managed to build a good reputation as a talented civil rights lawyer. But this meant that 90 percent of the time she represented the little guy—meaning minority—against the bigger guy—usually meaning a corporation run or owned by powerful, wealthy, white people. The commonwealth could claim her actions "against" Christina were representative of her feelings toward the affluent white establishment as a whole.

Finally, while Rayna had white friends, her larger social group was African American. The only time she had to socialize was on the odd occasion after work, with her workmates, or on the weekends, which she usually spent with Teesha, Delia and people associated with Teesha's friends, like Elise and Ewan Jordan.

"All black," said Sara as Arthur outlined his reasoning.

"All black."

"So where does that leave us?" asked Sara.

"With two options," said David. "First up, we paint a picture of our client that proves she is incapable of murder. Remember, all we need is reasonable doubt. Secondly, we establish that the laying of the charge itself was racially motivated, and that the girl's father is a bigot seeking retribution for his daughter's death."

"You want us to expose Haynes as a racist?" asked Sara, her expression indicating how difficult she knew this would be.

"Yes. Nothing's impossible, Sara."

"I see where you are going with this, David," offered Arthur. "But above all else, we have to remember that Haynes is not the one on trial here."

"True, but if we can prove to a jury that the initial laying of the charge was driven by Haynes's influence over the DA . . . If we can show how his bigotry is the driving force behind his determination for revenge . . ."

And Arthur nodded.

"Exposing a powerful, popular politician as a white supremacist is not going to be easy," said Sara.

"*Nothing* about this is going to be easy," said Arthur.

"Okay," said Sara. "So where do we start?"

"By talking to the three girls," said David.

"I can talk to Teesha if you like. You can take Mariah," said Sara.

Arthur interrupted. "I don't think that's a very good idea. No offense intended, Sara, but you are too close to Teesha."

Sara looked at David.

"Witnesses answer with a greater degree of detail when questioned by people with whom they have no emotional attachment," said David. "When they know you too well, they leave out the finer points because they assume you can fill in the gaps. I think I should speak to Teesha alone."

"I understand," she said with just the tiniest hint of disappointment.

"As for Mariah and Francine," said Arthur, "I think the two of you should be present at both interviews. I am sure their parents will want to be in the room and I think one of you should ask the questions while the other observes the parents. If Ed Washington is in Haynes's pocket, you'll see it in his eyes and hear it in Francine's answers."

"That's if he lets us near his daughter in the first place. We have to assume Haynes has advised him against it," said David.

"True, but we have to try."

"Okay, so what about Rayna?" asked Sara. "One of us should check in with her daily, get her take on things, make sure she's okay."

"You're right," said David. "But Rayna will have to understand that her immediate emotional well-being can't be our priority. The prosecution wants a speedy trial and Judge Stein agrees. We can drag this thing out if we want, but I can't help but think that the less time we give the press to turn this into a racial war, the better."

"You don't think a groundswell of African American support can help us?" asked Sara, and David wondered if this whole issue was becoming a personal one for her. "It might remind the DA who put her in office."

"No," said David a little too quickly. "You have to step back from it, Sara. Minority groundswell can just as easily be interpreted as prejudice. We don't want a situation where the Hayneses become the underdogs. You more than anyone should know this." He regretted it the minute it came out of his mouth.

"Can you excuse me for a minute?" said Sara, and David could see that her pale blue eyes were starting to pool with tears.

"Sure," they both said.

The office door was open and Sara walked out toward the ladies' restroom. Nora smiled at her as she passed and then turned to give Arthur and David the look from hell.

"What?" said David, playing innocent but feeling terrible.

Nora walked around her desk and into the office.

"Honestly, you two. The girl *is* attached to this case no matter what. She cares for the defendant and her daughter. She even knew the victim, for goodness sake. That might make her a little emotional, and she is young to be sure, but I've seen you both win cases *because* you cared. She gives your defense some heart. Since when did you two he-men become so callous?"

Nora was right.

"I understand what you're saying, Nora, but that doesn't mean we won't have to keep an eye on her," said Arthur. "For her own sake as much as anyone else's. You know her better than we do, David. Is she up to this?"

David thought about it for a second or two. "Sara may not be the world's most experienced attorney, but she is certainly a lot better than I was at twenty-nine. She might care too much, but that just means she'll work her butt off to get the verdict we need. Yeah, she's up to it," he said. "She might even surprise us."

"I'm sure of it," said Nora. "You mark my words."

■ ■ ■

Boston mayor Moses Novelli stared at the blue message paper one more time. He even picked it up, passed it back and forth between his thick olive-skinned hands, and then stared at it again.

It was identical to two others on his desk, all three with the name Senator Rudolph Haynes at the top, all three with Haynes's home, cell and work numbers below and all

three with a tick in the box next to the words "Please
call." Although this third one also had a tick in the box
marked "Urgent."

It was late Thursday and he knew he would have to call
before the day was out. He just couldn't bring himself to pick
up the phone. The whole thing was just too awkward. The
funeral had been a disaster, an almighty embarrassment for
Haynes, and God knows how that was playing out in that ob-
sessive mind of his. Truth be told, Moses had not wanted to
read at the service. He loved Christina, and her father was one
of his oldest friends, but that was the problem, wasn't it? He
knew Rudi too well.

His deputy mayor had hinted at the problems any association with Haynes might cause. Normally, Haynes was a man
to be seen *with;* but the past few days—the arraignment, the
funeral—had seen a shift in Boston's conservative social
clique. Word had it Haynes was coming off as a little extreme.
And the talk (gossip) among the wives was that Elizabeth had
become quite "vague." And Boston being Boston, unfair or
not, those who "counted" were sitting back and waiting until
the dust settled before they started wearing any badges of
support.

A slight smile crossed his face as he realized how
fickle a community they had become or, perhaps, had always been. Boston, the city of paradoxes—on one hand, the
land of liberals, the birthplace of revolutionaries, the capital
of education, the Athens of America, and on the other, the
custodian of conservatism, the citadel of self-importance,
the Hub of the universe. Moses knew Bostonians liked to
think of themselves as progressive, but this was a city with a
history of banning books. Hell, tattoos had been illegal here
until 2001.

He knew reading at the service would send out the message that he stood by Haynes and therefore was against the
Martin woman and her growing minority support group. Imagine, the blue-collar Italian American Moses Novelli siding
with the rich Brahmin! Worse still, he knew where he stood
in his heart. If he had to choose sides, he would go with the
defense. He had done a fair bit of investigating of his own

since the weekend and thought that Rayna Martin should not have been arrested in the first place. But that was not his call, nor should it be.

He leaned back in his ridiculously large leather chair and closed his deep-set brown eyes so that he could remember the sweet little girl who had grown into an idealistic teenager with no regard for the small-mindedness of bigotry. Then he thought back to two other teenagers many years ago, a pair of very unlikely friends who spent a good deal of the greatest years of their lives together. That was almost half a century ago, but right now it felt like yesterday.

They called Rudi Haynes Clark, as in Clark Kent, as in Superman. "Clark" was tall and handsome, with the physique of an athlete, the brain of a professor and the confidence of a politician. He was born and bred on Beacon Hill, his heritage pure Brahmin with an accent to match. He was at the top of his class at Harvard Law, and at Harvard College he had been on the swim team, the rowing team, and the debate team. He was a favorite of the faculty, a hit with the women, a hero of the men and a sure thing for a big future.

As for Moses, he was dark and swarthy, short and stocky, shy and self-conscious, and totally inept at anything that required physical exertion. He was at Harvard on a scholarship, his father a leatherworker, his mother a homemaker and his address working class. Bottom line, he was Rudolph's unlikely shadow, his awkward alter ego, his odd choice of friend. Clark oozed confidence while Moses oozed sweat. Clark was Superman and Moses his Jimmy Olsen.

True, Moses was bright—he could match Rudi grade for grade, but he had to study night and day to do it. In lots of ways he had his popular friend to thank for his success in life, for it was his dire need to keep up with him that saw him graduate with honors. His high distinctions got him a job at Foley, Simmons and Grasso, a small but respected Boston law firm, and he grew his career from there.

But now, as he looked around his expansive but conservatively decorated office, realizing how far he had come, he understood that the seeds of the future were firmly planted long ago. It had taken decades for Moses to finally hang up those all-too-comfortable rose-tinted glasses and see Rudi for what he really was. And he hated himself for not acknowledging it sooner.

Clark always avoided the black kids in the locker rooms, or he would accidentally kick their sweats into the shower or absentmindedly knock their gym bags onto the floor. Clark never sat next to the Latinos in tutorials, avoided the study groups with the Asian kids and transferred from classes given by colored professors. Clark slept with every girl on the debate team except one, a pretty dark girl named Molly Pope, who like the rest of them, would probably have said yes if she had been asked.

Then there were the racially based throwaway comments, the meaningless banter that meant nothing and everything all at the same time. It seemed harmless enough back in the days when PC meant Pepsi Cola, but it wasn't then and it wasn't now.

Not long after graduation, Moses experienced Rudi's shallowness firsthand. It wasn't long after Rudi had met Elizabeth and slid smoothly into the Connecticut country club set. The phone calls stopped, the correspondence waned and the visits were canceled and never rebooked. He wasn't even invited to the highly publicized, much anticipated, Westport society wedding. It was as if he had vanished from Rudi's life altogether and could only be seen through windows provided by the society papers and upmarket magazines.

Over time, Moses wondered if their friendship was a friendship at all, or if it was just a case of Rudi's needing a lap dog in college. Back in college he thought the relationship made him look cool; now he realized it made him look like a chump. In fact, it wasn't until years later that Rudi resurfaced, as a U.S. senator—rich, famous and powerful to boot, his friends all in similar categories.

In 1992, attorney-at-law Moses Novelli left Foley, Simmons and Grasso to set up his own practice downtown. He became involved with local politics, attending public meetings at City Hall, befriending city councilmen and -women with similar sensibilities and eventually acting as a legal counsel to the then mayor of Boston.

By the late 1990s he had become one of the more popular

and influential fringe figures in local government. He was seen as a man with vision and energy, his strength in conviction enhanced by his personable manner and obvious love for the city. And so when the opportunity arose, it seemed only natural that he run for mayor. His victory, driven by his working-class supporters, was overwhelming. Little Jimmy was now a force to be reckoned with—and that's when Clark reappeared.

The Hayneses had moved, meanwhile, from Beacon Hill to Chestnut Hill, keeping the old family residence as their home in town while enjoying the newfound luxury of a mansion expanse New England style.

"You must come to Highgrove for dinner," Rudi had said, in his best rendition of the "we should have done this sooner" song, to a tune as unoriginal as it was contrived.

Moses guessed that asking him to be his daughter's godfather was linked to his strong Catholic background. The Hayneses were Episcopalians and Moses was a conduit to the powerful working-class Catholic element, which, in a post-JFK era, held its own political sway in Massachusetts. Not that Moses didn't take his responsibilities seriously. Christina grew up calling him Uncle Mo, and he made sure he was very much part of the little girl's life.

But he was not stupid. He knew the request to read at the service was Rudi's way of telling the people of Boston that their mayor was behind him. He wouldn't be surprised if Rudi had a little something on White House chief of staff Maxine Bryant too; otherwise, he doubted she would have attended the funeral. But then Rudi made everybody else's business his own. It was how he got things done.

One thing was for sure: he would hate to be in David Cavanaugh's shoes right now.

Novelli looked at the message again, knowing he should call, and took a deep breath before reaching for the receiver and poising his finger to punch the number. *It will all be over in a few minutes,* he told himself, *just dial the number.* He watched his hand retreat as he put the receiver back on the hook. Then he told his secretary he would not be taking any more calls for the day. He felt the irony of guilt seep into his veins and did his best to chase it away before Jimmy Olsen returned. "I'm not his little man anymore," he said out loud before tidying his desk, gathering his coat and his brief-case and walking toward his office door. "So long, Jimmy," he whispered to himself. "The superhero ain't so super after all."

10

"It could just as easily have been us." Mariah's mother, Elise Jordan, was an attractive woman in her forties who could have passed for thirty-five. She smiled graciously at David and Sara as she led them through her sprawling two-story Providence home and onto the sun-drenched back patio.

The past week had been hectic as the defense team had started to put its case plan together. The success of any de-fense often came back to administration: keeping up-to-date files and well-labeled folders, accounting for every piece of discovery and evidence. These clerical duties sounded mun-dane, but they more often than not became the savior of an attorney at trial who had to access small details at a minute's notice. Further, every file and folder would all be used again if there was need for an appeal, which they were hoping would not be the case.

Sara and David had thrown themselves into their work this past week, falling into a rhythm that well-oiled teams often do. Neither of them had mentioned that night in his car, and there were moments when David wondered if he had imag-ined what seemed at the time to be a mutual attraction. And then there were those insensitive comments he had made in Arthur's office. Comments he wished he could take back. Whatever the case, he knew this was no time for distractions, and if Sara did not feel the same way he did, then he would have to settle for the solidarity that came with the determination to set this thing right.

Today's "chat" with Mariah was their first major interview and as such would be recorded and noted, scrutinized and tabled.

"Honestly," Elise Jordan continued. "It could have been Mariah's birthday. Ewan sails quite a bit. He could have taken the kids to the Cape and he could be sitting in prison right now."

"We know what you mean, Mrs. Jordan," said David.

"Call me Elise, please."

"Elise, that's the frustrating thing about this case, it could have happened to anyone, but Rayna is being placed as the scapegoat."

"Rayna Martin is one of the best people I know. Her daughter is a delight. Do you have children, Mr. Cavanaugh?"

"It's David, and no, ma'am."

"Well, when you do, you'll know how wonderful it is to see your child befriend other good people. Mariah boards at Curtis; the commute from Providence is just that much too far. But just knowing Rayna is a short drive away from the school gives me comfort. I know my daughter is safe at the Martin home and I hope Rayna feels the same way about us."

"I'm sure she does," said Sara.

"Well, that's nice to know."

Elise Jordan passed a tray of cookies and went on. "All right then, I understand you two are very busy and as much as I am enjoying your company, I know you want to speak with Mariah. If it's all right with you, I'll play silent witness, just for moral support. She's had a tough week and I think it might relax her a little if I sit quietly in the background."

"That's fine," said Sara.

"Thank you. I'll just go call her. Help yourself to some more iced tea."

A moment later Elise returned with her daughter: a tall, poised, younger version of her mother. Her arms were long and graceful, and she walked with a calm assurance that most young girls did not acquire until they were older and more comfortable in their own skin. She had shoulder-length brown hair and large brown eyes.

"Hi, Ms. Davis," said Mariah, recognizing Sara from her visits to Teesha's house.

"Hi, Mariah, and you know you can call me Sara. How are you doing?"

"Okay, I guess."

"This is my friend David Cavanaugh; he's the guy trying to get Mrs. Martin home to Teesha," said Sara, obviously trying to put the girl at ease.

"I know. How do you do, Mr. Cavanaugh?"

A teenager with manners—now there's a treat, David thought.

"I'm fine, Mariah. Has your mom explained that we want to ask you a few questions about what happened at Teesha's party?"

"Yes, I'll do anything I can to help."

David immediately realized that this girl, at sixteen, should not be treated like a child. She stood tall, sat with a straight back, held her arms neatly on her lap and relaxed her shoulders. She was slightly nervous but determined to help and, according to Teesha, one of the smartest girls in her class.

"I know what Francie has been saying. I have read all the papers and watched the news."

"Okay," said David. "Then if it's all right with you, let's start with one of the most important issues we have to cover and backtrack from there."

Mariah nodded.

"Mrs. Martin was the last person to talk with Christina. Christina urged Mrs. Martin to leave her in the water so that she might go to you three immediately. Christina said she was worried about Francie and the fact that you girls had taken off your life jackets."

"That's right. Chrissie would say that. She was very considerate. She was also a great swimmer. Me, I'm pretty hopeless, but she was on the A squad at school and could swim a fifty freestyle faster than most of the seniors."

"Right. Now you are probably aware that the prosecution

is claiming that this conversation never happened. They say Mrs. Martin saw Christina from *The Cruisader* but that she was already unconscious. And that she chose to leave her there so she could rescue you three. Because you are black . . ."

"And Christina was white."

"That's right." David nodded. "So you can understand how important it is that we establish the true content of that final conversation to confirm that Mrs. Martin is not a racist."

"Yes."

"Right, well, that's a good start. Now let's go back to the beginning, from the time you arrived at Teesha's house."

"I'm happy to do that, Mr. Cavanaugh, but before we go on, I think I should tell you something."

"Sure," said David.

Mariah took a deep breath and sat up even straighter. "I cannot confirm that Mrs. Martin had a final conversation with Christina."

They all paused a moment, waiting for her to go on.

"I have wracked my brain trying to remember something, anything that gave me that impression. But she didn't mention the conversation." Mariah obviously noted the horrified looks on their faces. "I never assumed it *didn't* take place, but it's just that she never really told us about it."

David and Sara were speechless.

"Believe me, Mr. Cavanaugh, I want to remember it. I am sure that it happened, but all I remember is Mrs. Martin saying that Chrissie was floating next to the cruiser . . . floating," she said the word again. "I am so sorry, but my mom and dad told me to tell the truth. They said, 'Tell the truth and everything will be okay.' But it won't will it? I am just as bad as Francie." A single tear started its way down her left cheek, gliding smoothly over her young, unblemished skin.

"It's okay, baby," said Elise, wrapping her arm around her daughter.

"I am so sorry, please forgive me," she said again. "I'm so sorry."

The silence was broken by the simultaneous shriek of two

cell phones chiming in uninvited clashing tones. Everyone flinched as the jarring sounds sliced into the quiet.

"That's me," said Sara, who had jumped an inch out of her white patio chair.

"Me too," said David. "Would you excuse us for a minute, Mariah, Elise?"

"Sure," said Mariah, glad for the break and wiping her eyes with a small white handkerchief her mother had pulled from her pocket.

David pressed Receive. "Cavanaugh."

"David, it's Arthur. Katz has his indictment."

So Katz had waltzed Francie Washington straight from the arraignment to an audience with the grand jury, and her statement had been convincing enough to give the DA the go-ahead. It was official. They were headed for trial.

"How much time do we have?"

"I would expect Katz or Scaturro to contact us on Monday. They'll want a trial before the year is out, and Judge Stein will probably clear his docket to accommodate them. I tend to agree with you, David, a speedy proceeding might work to our benefit as well."

There was a pause. "David, are you there?"

"Yeah, sorry, Arthur. I was just thinking. We have a problem with Mariah Jordan."

"What is it?"

"I'll explain later. You around this evening?"

"What else would I be doing on a Friday night, dancing the tango with Ginger Rogers?"

"I think poor old Ginger is dead, Arthur."

"Then I am definitely free. See you then."

Sara had come up behind him. He turned to tell her about the indictment but stopped short when he saw the look of shock and confusion on her face.

"What is it?" he said, instinctively putting his hand on her shoulder.

"That was my dad on the phone."

"Is he all right?"

"Yes, I mean no . . . it's my brother Jake. He's been arrested."

"What?"

"For possession—cocaine. I know him inside out, David; my brother doesn't do drugs. There must be an explanation."

"Where did they find the cocaine?"

"Dad wasn't making much sense—something about Jake being pulled over and the drugs being in the glove compartment of his car."

"Why was he pulled over?" David was already thinking like a lawyer. Could they prove the search was unlawful?

"I asked Dad the same thing. He's at police headquarters. He's confused, so I got him to get the charge sheet and read it to me."

"And . . ."

"That's what's weird. He wasn't pulled over by uniformed cops but by an unmarked car—detectives."

"What? Why would they pull him over?"

"That's not all. The detective who pulled him over and found the drugs . . . it was Detective Petri."

"A homicide detective playing traffic cop?"

"Apparently he said he thought Jake's right-rear brake light was out. But he's the same guy that arrested Rayna. It's not right. Tell me I'm being paranoid, but . . ."

"We'll soon find out. Let's apologize to the Jordans and—"

"No, David, you stay. I'll be stuck in processing all afternoon. God, he'll probably be held overnight. There is nothing you can do right now. Finish the interview. You know it's the most sensible thing to do. I'll call you later."

David knew she was right. There was probably nothing either of them could do until tomorrow and he didn't want to break Mariah's momentum.

"Well, you take my car. It's over an hour's drive," he said.

"How will you get back?"

"I'll work something out. Just go."

She moved forward and wrapped her arms around him in an embrace so natural it caught him by surprise.

"Give my apologies, will you? And David, thanks."

"It'll be okay. Just promise you'll call."

* * *

"Now . . . the napkins," said Deloris Du Bois. "We could go with either red, white or blue. My personal preference is a combination of all three so the overall appearance gives a scattered effect of our national colors."

The senator could not believe he was sitting here listening to this.

"Of course the flowers will be white. No question. But I think the . . ."

"Ms. De Bra," he said calmly.

"It's Du Bois, Senator."

"With all due respect, Ms. De Bra, I don't give a crap about the color of some goddamned napkins. Red, white, blue, pink . . . hundreds of little American flags, I couldn't care less."

"Well, sir, we couldn't go with the flags because people would be wiping their mouths on them and it might be a little inappro—"

"Don't you get it? I'm busy. I have staff for these matters. Go see my wife; see my secretary, Louise; see any of my endless number of employees who probably know a hell of a lot more about organizing a banquet than I do." She sat a few seconds longer as if stuck to the chair before jolting up and out of his office. *My God,* he thought, he would kill Louise for this.

The long-awaited banquet to celebrate his fifty years in politics originally had been scheduled for tonight but had been postponed to June 28 for obvious reasons. Some bright spark had sacked the original function organizers and hired a whole new group—Ms. Du Bois included—so the preparations were starting from scratch. A few days ago he was going to cancel it altogether, but the funeral had changed all that. God, the funeral. What a nightmare.

The senator was not blind to public opinion or, more important, the exclusive inner-circle gossip that permeated the political scene in this city. He knew that while the press had largely gone his way, painting the defense as a bunch of unscrupulous savages, the rebound effect had people talking about his possible bias and that of his wife's.

He intended to use the banquet as a PR exercise; the guest list would be racially balanced, even loaded their way if necessary. He had already told Louise to include two more senators from California—one black, the other Hispanic—and the seating would be carefully arranged to give, in Ms. De Bra's words, "a scattered effect."

A smile crossed his face as he realized that this *was* a lot like choosing napkins, except of much greater importance. The funeral chaos was a setback, but many great strategies had setbacks and they could, in fact, be used to keep one focused. The sad truth was, these days all this bullshit about the rights of the defendant had turned this country into a pathetic playground for criminals who roamed the streets because of technicalities, suppressed evidence, plea bargains and other feeble legal tripe that had no regard for the damage done to victims and their loved ones. He would not allow this to happen in this instance. And so it was left to him.

Verne had begun his new phase of the operation and the prosecution was still in his pocket. Scaturro had not returned a call today, which concerned him, but he knew he had the goods to keep her in line, especially considering that she was up for reelection in a matter of months. He would get Verne to send her a little reminder.

As for Katz, he was fairly confident the ADA, so blinded by ambition, would follow his instructions to the letter. He had put all of his staff on the case, so the senator knew there were plenty of overzealous young clerks digging like rats into Rayna's background. They would find witnesses willing to give evidence of her bigotry and he would reward them for their time.

Novelli had called at last, although the conversation was rushed and distant. But then he had always controlled little Moses and always would. The mayor would support him if for no other reason than that he wanted a second term. Moses understood that his old buddy Rudi still knew how to get him on the A list and keep him there.

Logically, he saw only three potential problems: Ed Washington; Cavanaugh; and, he hated to admit it, his wife.

Washington would be spoken to and watched closely. The senator suspected this would be enough, but being the cautious man that he was, he allowed for the possibility that some secondary action might be necessary. He would wait and see.

Cavanaugh was good, very good in fact. Verne's research

had confirmed this. But he also had a history of allowing his emotions to cloud his judgment. He hated Katz, which could fuel his will to win, but it would also inevitably interfere with his clarity. The girl Davis was not a threat. She was young and inexperienced. If Cavanaugh was as smart as he suspected, he would not use her a great deal in trial. She was, after all, one of them, so everything she said would be tainted.

As for Elizabeth, he would have to keep an eye on her. Her behavior at the funeral was unacceptable and extremely high risk. There was that look in her eye, the vague behavior, the memory lapses, the idle chatter. Elizabeth had always been prone to daydreams, and such behavior often came hand in hand with grief, but she seemed a little . . . unstable. And this made him nervous.

He would have a word with Agnes and find ways to keep Elizabeth close to home, occupied with the banquet and other menial tasks. He needed her shipshape for the upcoming electoral campaign and as such would make sure she was rested and protected. After all, it would not be for long. This trial would be fast-tracked so that he could concentrate on his reelection. By the end of the year, Rayna Martin would be well settled in her new home, serving the first months of what would be a lifetime in prison. Just where she belonged.

• • •

David did not get back to Boston until late Friday night. After spending another two hours talking with Mariah, he had accepted an offer to stay for dinner and was even more grateful when Ewan Jordan offered him a lift back to the city. The successful veterinarian who, according to Sara, had made a good deal of money from inventing a nationwide vets' online consulting service said he hadn't driven the Porsche all week and wanted to take it for a decent spin.

Not one to turn down an hour-long drive in a 911—or even better, the chance to get behind the wheel, which Ewan offered halfway through their journey—David called Arthur and postponed their meeting. He was also relieved to get a call from Sara on his cell. They both agreed something was definitely not right about Petri's involvement in her brother's arrest and arranged to meet at the district court the next morning to try to get Jake arraigned and released in the Saturday morning rush.

After he hung up from Sara's call he turned his attention to Ewan Jordan, the two of them talking about everything: the news, the Red Sox and eventually sailing. Ewan Jordan didn't just dabble in the sport, he was actually a very accomplished yachtsman. He was part owner of a thirty-two-footer moored at Rockport, Cape Ann, and he knew the waters of the area very well.

"So I guess you're familiar with Ipswich and Essex Bay, where Rayna took the girls?" said David.

"Sure am. Calm waters, mild winds—the perfect place for a safe weekend sail."

"And you would doubt climatic or tidal forces had anything to do with Christina's death?"

"Highly unlikely, in my opinion. As you know, Gloucester and some of the areas around it are still working fishing villages. Even the immediate harbor used to be a fisherman's haven with schools of bluefish, cod and haddock swimming into the more protected inlets where waters were warm and currents less threatening. Fishermen used to set their nets overnight and pull in loads of the stuff every morning. It was a trawler's gold mine.

"Of course these days they have to travel a little farther out for any decent sort of catch. The closer inlets have been pretty much fished out. Some of the old nets are still there but do little more than act as a hindrance to charter boats that get tangled anchors at low tide. Nowadays places like Gloucester, Rockport and Essex rely more on the tourist dollar: boat charters, helicopter rides, craft shops, art galleries—that sort of thing. It's a nice spot. Well worth a visit."

David made a mental note of Ewan's comments so he could pass them on to Arthur's associates Samantha Bale and Con Stipoulos, who were currently investigating the physical forces in play on the day of Christina's death. They were researching the tidal and weather conditions, canvassing the locals, interviewing the Coast Guard and so on.

"It's a popular destination then?"

"Yes and no. It's no Cape Cod, but it has its own sort of

earthy charm. Summers are busy, but May is a sweet time—
warm enough for a great day's sailing, but a whole lot quieter
than June or July."

"Hm," said David.

"Yes, sir, I see your problem," said Ewan, reading between
the lines. "No witnesses. And no explanation as to why a
teenage girl drowns in the middle of a relatively quiet and
peaceful waterway."

"Exactly."

11

Friday night brought the best sleep David had had in a week,
due more to exhaustion than anything else. He woke early on
Saturday feeling refreshed enough to tackle a long run before
grabbing a juice at Myrtle's, jogging home to shower and
change, and heading out to meet Sara.

Luckily, Sara had worked her magic with the court clerk and
managed to get Jake's arraignment squeezed into the heavy
weekend docket. Sara's father paid the five-thousand-dollar
bond and Jake was free to go home, pending a hearing to be
scheduled in the next few months.

By two, David and Sara were starving, so David suggested some takeout and a late picnic lunch on Boston Common. Sara was anxious to hear about Mariah's interview, but
David thought they should allow themselves a quiet lunch
before they rang Arthur to set up a time to go through it as a
group. For the moment they were enjoying the sun on their
faces and the comforting sound of children playing around
them.

"Do you think we should talk to Joe about Petri?" Sara
broke the silence.

"That's what I was planning. We have to be careful,

though; Petri is one of his men and Joe is pretty protective. He seems to think the guy is straight up, just a little jaded after years on the job."

"I don't like accusing an experienced cop, David, but there just doesn't seem to be any other explanation, and the link with Rayna . . . it just seems a little too—"

"I know. We'll get to the bottom of it, don't worry."

David immediately thought of Joe's warning about Haynes and his ability to reach into people's lives. *Perhaps I should tell her,* he thought, but then he looked at her profile as she gazed out across the park, her eyes squinting in the afternoon light, her hair back in a ponytail blowing in the breeze, and he felt an all-consuming need to protect her.

She turned to see him looking at her. "David, I think we need to . . . um . . ."

"Look, if it's about the other day in Arthur's office, I'm sorry. I didn't mean to—"

"No, no. It's not that."

She turned toward him and took his hand. He looked at her, not knowing what to say.

"The other night in the car . . . I didn't want you to think that I—"

"I know," he interrupted, somehow preferring to say it himself than hear any form of rejection coming from her.

"It's not that I didn't want to."

"It's not?" he interrupted, feeling surprised, pleased.

"No. I mean, I *did,* but I just think that right now we have to focus one hundred percent on the trial."

"It's okay, Sara," he said, relieved she had felt something. "I understand and you're right. First things first." He squeezed her hand. "But I am sorry," he went on, "about what I said about your needing to take a step back."

"Don't be. I know I am too close to this thing and I've been trying to toughen up and disassociate myself, but I can't seem to stop this feeling of anger. The mess with Jake just made it worse."

"You don't have to stop being angry. You might find this hard to believe, but I've been known to let my temper get the better of me."

"Oh, really?" she said, and he could hear the playful

sarcasm in her voice. "If your performance at the funeral is anything to go by, my guess is that temper of yours has had more than its fair share of run-ins. To be honest, I was pretty annoyed at Joe when he pulled you off the ADA."

"Me too," he laughed.

They sat in silence a minute longer, David not feeling the need to fill the pauses.

"You hate him, don't you?" she asked at last.

"Katz? Well, yeah, I suppose I do. Not very grown-up of me, is it?"

"Will you tell me one day what he did to you?"

"It wasn't really to me; it was to someone a lot more vulnerable. And yeah, I will tell you one day." He squeezed her hand again. "I promise."

• • •

"You were right," David heard Arthur say as he leaned back in his old, scratched-leather chair. "Mariah is a problem."

He was almost hoping the older, wiser member of their team might find some redeeming feature in Mariah's interview, but in the end they all agreed the girl they were hoping would be their star witness had turned out to be a major disappointment. Mariah's heart was certainly in the right place, but putting her on the stand would be a huge risk. The commonwealth could tear her apart, and their client's case along with her.

"Maybe it's not as bad as it first seems," said David. "She's not saying the conversation didn't take place, just that Rayna made no direct reference to it. It all happened so quickly. She was maneuvering the cruiser, relieved to find out they were okay and desperate to get back to Christina. There was no time for chitchat."

"David's right," said Sara.

"Maybe," said Arthur. "But it still would have been a hell of a lot easier if she'd made some allusion to it."

They sat in silence for a moment trying to re-collect their thoughts.

"Okay," said Sara, standing to walk toward the windows, obviously determined that this latest setback would not affect their enthusiasm. "Maybe we're looking at this the wrong way. We're so busy trying to paint a picture of what *did* happen, maybe we should be focusing on what *didn't*."

They looked at her, confused.

"Think about it. What if Rayna hadn't rushed to the other three?" she asked.

"Be careful, Sara," said Arthur. "Katz will just say Christina would be alive and the girls would have been waiting for the cruiser with their life jackets on."

"No, that's not what I mean." She was on a roll now, pacing around the office. "The jury has to see this from Rayna's perspective. All Rayna had to go on was Christina's urgent warning that they were in danger—immediate danger. What if Christina was right? For all Rayna knew, she was. In this scenario Christina would be safe, but three other teenagers could be in serious trouble."

The two of them looked at her without interrupting.

"Francie said she hit her head, right? And she had a cramp. She couldn't move and she was panicking big time. Mariah isn't a great swimmer; she was trying to hold her up but getting weaker by the minute. Teesha would probably have been okay, but who knows what lengths she would have gone to in order to support the other two. Christina told Rayna she was one of the best swimmers at school so . . . *This* is the scenario Rayna was seeing and we have to make the jury see it this way too."

"And as for Haynes—" began Arthur, now sitting forward in his chair.

"He must be carrying a hell of a lot of guilt for allowing Christina to go to the party in the first place," said David.

"Or rather," said Arthur, "not trying hard enough to stop her."

"Exactly," said Sara, moving across the room again before stopping short in front of Arthur's desk. "To Haynes there can be no other suspect. Rayna is black. In his mind that alone is predisposition of guilt. He isn't even considering an alternative. He doesn't know how."

"And so he is manipulating the legal system to make sure she goes away," said Arthur. "The question is, can Mariah help us establish Haynes's bias?"

"Well," said Sara, "Mariah had no doubt Christina was under pressure to drop her African American friends. She even suspected that Christina originally befriended the three girls as an act of rebellion. The fact that they all became fast friends made her parents even more furious."

"None of these girls have ever been to Christina's house?" asked Arthur.

"Mariah went there once," said David, now rising from his chair across the room to join the other two at Arthur's desk, completing the huddle of three. "But only when Christina's parents were out and only for a few minutes. She described a family room with one wall acting as a gallery for photographs—you know, politicians, movie stars, relatives, friends, that sort of thing. Of the eighty or so pictures on the wall, there was not one black face in the mix."

"That isn't normal," said Sara.

"It is also useless," said Arthur, bringing his fist down on his desk and simultaneously dropping a bomb on their enthusiasm. "This is not concrete evidence. Christina Haynes was a minor. Her parents had every right to stop her from going to a party. They also have the right to choose what photos they put on their goddamned family room wall."

"But their decisions were based on skin color," said Sara.

"So what?" countered Arthur, playing devil's advocate. "Even if they were, there is no real evidence of it. We are clutching at straws. We bring up stuff like this in court and we look petty, or worse, desperate. Go over to Rayna's house and find a white face on her mantel."

Arthur was right. They needed something more tangible.

"Arthur," said Sara, her arms up in a gesture of futility. "What you are asking is impossible. We are not going to find someone who'll stand up in court and call Haynes a racist."

David could tell she was getting worked up.

"Let's face it, our key witness is the victim, our main accuser is a wealthy and popular politician and our client is black. We are behind the eight ball here, big time. My bet is Katz and Scaturro are halfway to locking up Rayna for life, and we're . . . well . . . we're sitting here talking about birthday parties and picture walls."

Sara took a deep breath, looked to Arthur and then to David before shaking her head in defeat.

"It just feels so pointless. There's an invisible undertow of deceit here that is pulling us under. It's as if we're drowning, or already dead in the water."

They realized the significance of her analogy the moment it left her lips, and David saw Sara look across at Arthur once more, no doubt hoping this smart, experienced, opinionated man might have some sound bite of wisdom that would save them all or, at the very least, give them some small piece of hope.

Arthur looked at them both and opened his mouth in reply, but for once he couldn't think of anything else to say.

■ ■ ■

"Just finishing?"

Officer Susan Leigh had just changed into her casuals and was heading for the front door of headquarters when Lieutenant Mannix came up behind her.

"Ah . . . hello, Lieutenant. Spent the day with the ADA, so I picked up an extra shift tonight. We're short staffed."

"What else is new?"

Lieutenant Mannix was a respected figure in the department, known for his ability to get things done minus the fuss and bravado exercised by many other senior detectives. The guy carried a lot of clout in the building and, from what she heard, down at the DA's office as well. Even more important, he was also commander of the Homicide Unit—*Homicide*! Exactly where she wanted to be when she got her gold shield. And so Susan Leigh, quick on her feet and never one to miss an opportunity, decided she should make the most of this timely encounter.

"Busy coupla weeks," she said.

"You can say that again. Is the ADA cutting into your work time?"

"Not really. But Mr. Katz is thorough and I am happy to work doubles if it means assisting them in their pursuit of justice."

Jeez, she thought, *pursuit of justice*—it sounded like a bad line from one of those overrated TV dramas. *Tone it down, Susan.*

"I mean to say . . ."

"I know what you meant, Officer. The ADA can be . . . ah, shall we say, zealous in his pursuit of all sorts of things."

"Just trying to help, Lieutenant."

"I am sure you are."

They reached the front doors and Susan, now cursing herself for saying the wrong thing, turned to try to make amends. "I believe our role as police officers is to try to assist both the detectives and the district attorney's office as much as possible. The case doesn't stop after the arrest, Lieutenant. I don't believe in the theory that we should wash our hands of a perp as soon as our report is typed and filed. That attitude is both lazy and negligent. I certainly do not want to shirk the responsibility of seeing a case through. And if that means putting in the extra hours, then so be it."

Mannix smiled.

"May I offer a little advice, Officer?"

"Yes, sir. Please, sir."

"Well, not everyone's motives are as noble as yours," he said. "And sometimes certain people can be so determined to nail a perp that they forget everyone is innocent until proven guilty. And you're right, your job is to help. But you have to be careful not to be played as the pawn in the process."

"Yes, sir," she said, delighted to be getting a one-on-one with the head of Homicide. Taking mental notes. A look of complete concentration on her face. "Anything else, sir?"

"Yeah, Susan. Lighten up."

"Lighten up?"

"Yeah."

"Yes, sir," she said as Joe turned to walk toward his car. "Goodnight, Lieutenant, and thank you." Her voice trailed off in the distance. "Thank you very much."

● ● ●

She was on *The Cruisader*. The day was still bright and sunny and the yellow light danced like little fairies over the rippled surface of the water. On closer inspection, she saw they were fairies, millions of them so happy and free, diving, leaping, turning, skipping on their glasslike playground.

She was alone. Where were the girls?

That's right, she remembered, the fairies had taken them by the hand and shown them how to do their pretty dance. She could see them now. Francie and Mariah were smiling, tiptoeing across the water's surface, waving to her as they ap-

proached the cruiser to hop back on board. She heard Teesha
laughing and turned to see she was already safe on the cruiser
behind her. Her long brown hair decorated with seaweed,
which sparkled like Christmas tinsel dripping with beads of
silver stars.

Christina was still dancing. The fairies had her by both
hands, spinning and spinning in circles of such pure delight
that Rayna almost felt cruel calling her back in.

"It's time," she heard herself say.

But Christina did not hear her; she just smiled and waved
as she spun farther and farther away into the distance. Then
Teesha spoke behind her and she turned to face her daughter.
Only it wasn't Teesha anymore but Christina. Her skin was
like porcelain, the long dark hair now closer to white than
blond.

"Where's Teesha?" she said.

"Out there." Christina smiled. "See."

Rayna strained to see her; she caught flashes of her wet
hair whipping up in the wind as she spun in a dance of joy.

"Come back," she called. "Teesha, come back."

She felt the tears stinging her eyes as she forced them to
make out her daughter, now a single spark among millions.

"Don't leave me," she yelled through her sobs, knowing
she was lost forever. "Teesha, I'm so sorry. Come back."

She realized that she had spoken those final words aloud
as dream merged with reality in one elongated extension of
horror. She was awake now and the feeling of loss was all too
real, and then for some reason it came to her. Something
about Christmas, the tinsel—Christmas was about snow and
good cheer and Santa Claus and sleigh bells.

Officer Wu was talking to Detective Petri. He repeated
something about Rudolph . . . Rudolph the Red-Nosed Reindeer. Then there was a second reference. When was it? The
day she was arrested?

This is what she had been hoping for—finally, a question
she could answer that did not cast her actions in guilt but shed
new light on the activities of the real criminals. Finally, a
fresh insight that might give them an edge. For the first time
in weeks, she felt a welcome wave of hope. Well, maybe not a
wave, but certainly a ripple.

This has to mean something, she whispered to herself as she lifted her feet onto the too-small prison bunk and lay her head on the flat, narrow, prison-issue pillow.

Rudolph Haynes. Petri had been talking about *him*. Haynes had people everywhere. He had been calling the shots from the very beginning.

12

She was in love with him.

"Ma'am . . . ma'am, are you all right?"

It was Agnes. She was behind her.

How long had she been standing there holding this white magnolia? She had been examining its perfect petals and pondering the fine balls of moisture that sat like mercury on the pale cream crests and falls when *he* entered her thoughts again. He hadn't for years, but so often of late. Perhaps it had been the magnolias—Louisiana's flower and all that.

"Yes . . . yes of course, Agnes."

Elizabeth Haynes got the feeling that Agnes had been watching her over the past few days, and it was really starting to anger her. Anger! The emotion came as quite a surprise. She had never felt anger toward Agnes before. The mild-mannered housekeeper had been with them for years and Elizabeth knew that she, too, would be experiencing grief.

"I was just arranging the flowers." She managed a smile. "Would you mind asking Nelson to prune the side hedge this morning? It is looking a little untidy."

"Yes, ma'am. Can I get you anything?"

"No. No, thank you, Agnes. I'm fine."

Agnes nodded her perfunctory gesture of goodwill before moving along the corridor to tackle the vacuuming in the master bedroom. Elizabeth heard her open the bedroom door and plug in the vacuum cleaner. She took solace in the cover of its drone.

Topher Bloom, so tall and dark and handsome. Just like a movie star. Not the macho variety, more the brooding sensitive type like . . . like Montgomery Clift. *Yes, that was it! Montgomery Clift.*

He was Spence's son, the boy with no mother who attended the local public school and helped his pa work on their cars on weekends. Elizabeth had known him for as long as she could remember. He had been her friend, her confidant, her first true love.

Unlike his father, Christopher Bloom was not born to overhaul engines or recharge batteries. He was destined for greater things: as an actor, an artist and, perhaps one day, a director. She could remember the Saturdays they would sneak away to O'Connor's Movie House. How old would they have been? Thirteen, maybe fourteen? Topher had found a broken air vent that led down behind the stalls, and there they would sit, at the back, on the floor, watching the newsreels and cartoons and holding hands as they anticipated the start of the main feature.

She shut her eyes and saw them: Rita Hayworth, Clark Gable and so many more. For those few hours they would feel like Hollywood royalty, taking part in their dreamlike adventures with Topher feeling like Errol Flynn by sweeping his girl in the back way and gallantly avoiding the one-dollar ticket fee every single time.

Such daring, such romance.

Of course, old man O'Connor knew what they were up to and, luckily for them, found their spirit more amusing than aggravating. It was, in fact, O'Connor who had given Topher his first real job, as a theater usher, Friday nights and weekends, which meant he got to see the movies for free, and even better, he got paid to watch them. She knew his name would be magnified on that screen one day, she was sure of it.

The vacuum cleaner stopped and took Topher with it. She looked down and realized she had pulled three flowers from the vase, allowing water to drip on the carpet and petals to fall near her feet. She felt a mild panic flood through her veins. If Agnes noticed, she would tell her husband, and that was the last thing she needed.

Topher, she said, as if needing to validate her thoughts and remind herself that he actually did exist. She picked up the petals, wiped the side table with her handkerchief and replaced the magnolias before turning to move quickly along the hallway to the washroom. He could have lived his dream. Could have, would have, should have. If only she had not stolen it from him.

■ ■ ■

"Something isn't right about her," said DA Loretta Scaturro, taking another sip of her lukewarm chamomile tea. "She's just too rehearsed."

Scaturro was having Sunday brunch with Roger Katz out on her large, harborside, sun-drenched balcony. She found it hard to believe it was only a week since they were last here together. They said the wheels of justice moved at a snail's pace, but whoever "they" were, they obviously had never done business with Rudolph Haynes.

"Teenagers, Loretta, they're all like that these days: sassy, overconfident."

Katz and Scaturro had spent Saturday afternoon with Francine Washington and her parents. Loretta was concerned about her robotic performance in front of the grand jury and wanted to sit down with the girl face-to-face.

"It's more than that, Roger," she said, returning her china teacup to its matching saucer. "Her testimony has changed a little from the initial statement."

"Only to our benefit."

"That's just it. It feels as if she were trying too hard to help us. Why would she do that?" She said this suspecting she knew the answer, but wanting to see how Katz would respond. All she got was a shrug.

"First of all," Scaturro went on, "Francine said Martin used the word *floating;* now she says it was 'floating facedown.'"

In her statement she said Martin told her, 'You three were just lucky.' Now she's saying it was 'Look at yourselves; you three are lucky,' which she says she took to mean they were saved because they were African American. For God's sake, it's all becoming a little too melodramatic, don't you think?"

"Most murders are, Loretta," said Katz, his hands up in a gesture which indicated she should know this better than anyone. "Don't look a gift horse in the mouth."

"Speaking of mouth, her father is a huge liability," she went on. "He keeps interrupting her as if he's prompting from a script."

"Look, she ain't the sharpest tool in the shed; she needs a little reminding, that's all. I'll have her prepped for trial. I don't see what you're complaining about. Our case is getting stronger by the minute."

"All I'm saying is, we need more than Francine Washington. Girls like that cannot be trusted. Any jury, particularly one with a reasonable percentage of African Americans, will find it hard to believe this woman is capable of murder. And if Francine Washington is our main witness, well . . ."

"Look," said Roger again, topping up her tea and serving her some more strawberries with her Danish, "we cannot forget the core issue here. A teenage girl is dead because this woman decided to bypass one girl's welfare to save three others who didn't need saving in the first place. Think of Christina. She didn't even get the option of resuscitation, just because she was white. No one has the right to play God, least of all a bigot like Rayna Martin, good track record or not."

Loretta wiped the corners of her mouth, contemplating her deputy's reasoning. She had to give it to him, he was good. He played the heartstrings like a virtuoso. The jury would lap it up. But Cavanaugh was good too, very good in fact, and they would be extremely naive to think he—

Her thoughts were interrupted by the ring of her telephone. She excused herself from the balcony and went inside.

"Scaturro," she said, a greeting normally reserved for the

office, but these days she found it hard to distinguish between work and home.

"It's Jim Elliot."

Her first response was to walk farther away from the balcony—in fact, all the way into the kitchen.

"Jim, I . . . How are you?"

"What the hell are you playing at?"

She didn't know what to say. The last time she had spoken to Jim Elliot was their last night of lovemaking, the night they both agreed the affair had to stop. It pained her to realize her heart was racing—she still had feelings for this man.

"I don't understand," she said.

"Look, I have no idea what the hell you were thinking, but the tie was a mistake—a *big* mistake. My wife opened the box. She wants to know why a 'Loretta' is sending me a tie for my birthday with some ridiculous personal note attached."

"What did it say?"

"*What?* You wrote the damned thing. Listen, I don't have time for this; my family is waiting for me in the car. It's over, has been for a long time. It was just sex, Loretta, so get over it and leave me and my family alone."

She clung to the receiver, listening to the beep, beep of the disconnected call. Then, still in a daze of confusion, she turned to see Katz standing in her kitchen doorway and the receiver leaped from her grip in a moment of pure horror.

"Loretta, are you all right? Who was it? Was it a crank call? Should I call the police? We can trace—"

"*No!*" she shouted, and it was Katz's turn to jump.

"I'm sorry, Roger, it was just a family matter. Nothing serious, but if you wouldn't mind I—"

"Sure, sure, let's pick this up tomorrow morning. You sit down, take a load off. Families can be a bitch, right? I'll let myself out."

She heard the door click behind him and then walked slowly to her room. She picked up a tissue to blot her lipstick, tidied the perfume bottles on her bureau and then made eye contact with herself in her dresser mirror. Not knowing what else to do, she moved over to her bed and fell on it facedown, burying her head in her pillow. And then she cried, from deep inside, sobbing like a teenager in the throes of the depths of rejection.

• • •

You have to hand it to him, thought Katz as he skipped down Loretta's front steps and clicked on his car key to unlock the doors of his red Corvette convertible. He was smooth. An evil son of a bitch but very, very smooth.

Katz knew that whatever had just happened upstairs was orchestrated by Haynes and would no doubt have his boss back in line by the morning. He patted himself on the back for being smart enough to side with the winning team on this one. If Loretta continued to rock the boat, although he suspected she would be back on board after this morning's little surprise, she'd just fall out, leaving more room for him.

Women, he thought. *Why the hell did they have to go and complicate things by getting all moralistic?* He bet that Davis girl was like that—scruples up to her eyeballs, and what pretty eyes they were too. When this was all over he might give her a call. Not now of course, God no, imagine the trouble that would cause. But maybe after all this settled down? Something sweet and discreet.

He smiled to himself and swung into the driver's seat, settling on the cool, soft leather; he turned on the ignition, reveling in the soft but powerful purr, and turned his face upward, feeling the sun on his cheeks and the sea breeze on his hair. Then he put on his sunglasses and slid his foot over toward the accelerator before pressing down, smiling, and burning some serious rubber all the way home.

• • •

Rayna was so excited to see David and Sara enter the Suffolk County Jail interview room. She could tell by their expressions that her newfound enthusiasm was written all over her face as she hugged Sara and shook David's hand with both of her own. She had had a rough night but could not help but think the dream had been some kind of gift. It may not be much, but it could set them on a road to proving some form of conspiracy.

"I'm so glad you're here." She smiled. "I thought of something last night. On one hand it scares the hell out of me, but on the other, it could help us prove Haynes is interfering with this investigation."

"What do you mean?" said David, now visibly excited and signaling for them all to sit down.

"Well, last night I had a dream—it was horrible, but that's not the point. It helped me remember something. It took me back to the day of the accident and something Officer Wu said. Not to me but to the detective."

She wanted to be articulate, so she took a sip of the latte David had brought for her and slowed down.

Rayna had been talking to Tommy Wu.

"I remember his radio kept buzzing. He started to walk away from me to take the calls, so I couldn't hear them too well. But those radios are loud and even though I probably wasn't listening on a conscious level, I could tell that the officer was frustrated, upset even. It seemed he was being hassled by a detective. I am pretty sure it was Detective Petri."

Rayna told them she heard an exchange that went along the lines of:

> *Officer Wu: Look, Detective, I'm busy. I am trying to get a statement. For all we know she could be going into shock, so just let me do my job.*
> *Detective Petri: Just do as I say. Get a cell phone and ring me on a secure line on this number: 555-3705. Did you get that? Do it now.*
> *Officer Wu: Petri, I don't have the . . .*

"So Officer Wu comes over to me and apologizes for the interruption and goes to borrow a cell from one of the paramedics. He calls the number and it picks up right away. But now I can only hear one half of the conversation.

> *What is it, Detective?*
>
> *No, I am standing here on my own.*
>
> *I'm sure. What is this all about?*

No, Leigh and I have it. But this is Gloucester's jurisdiction and . . .

Okay, okay. I heard you, it's our case. But unless you plan on coming up here to question her yourself, you had better let me get on with my job.

What? I can't do that, she hasn't been charged with anything.

Susan is busy with the girls.

Look, the woman is an attorney. I can't ask her that. It will sound ridiculous, especially coming from an Asian American.

Are you saying what I think you're saying, Detective, because in case you hadn't noticed, Petrovski, your ancestors didn't exactly arrive on the Mayflower either. What the hell is this all about? Who wants to know this stuff?

Is that meant to be funny? Rudolph the Fucking Reindeer? Look, Detective, a girl is dead and I'm trying to speak to the woman who just spent half an hour trying to bring her back to life. I'll have her at the station within the hour and you can talk to her then.

Officer Wu had hung up the cell, returned it to the paramedic and walked back to Rayna.

"That was the first reference. Then there was the day I was arrested, a week ago today."

Rayna explained how Petri and his partner, a young detective named Victor Rico, had come to her home, read her her rights, and bundled her into the car.

On the way into the station Petri had told Rico to pull over so he could use a pay phone. Rico seemed annoyed, but he was obviously the subordinate of the two so he pulled over. Petri got out for maybe three minutes, then he came back in and told Rico to deliver the prisoner up front. Rico complained, but Petri said there was some kind of obstruction to the back entrance and it was the only way in.

"Who told you that? It was fine this morning," Rico had said.

"Rudolph the Red-Nosed Reindeer, that's who. Now shut the fuck up so we can get the lady into the system."

"He must have thought he was being funny; maybe he is just stupid, but it had to mean something," said Rayna.

David agreed. "So if Petri was referring to Haynes in both instances, the senator was told about his daughter's death as soon as the accident was called in. Petri probably told him before Joe even got to the house."

"They must have a prior relationship," said Sara.

"Probably." David turned to Rayna. "He must have wanted Tommy to force you into saying something incriminating regarding Christina's color, give away your racial preferences."

"Not that I have any," said Rayna. "But even if I did, why would I be stupid enough to say something of that nature after what had just occurred?"

"That's just it," said Sara. "That may have been the perfect time for you to say something incriminating. Thousands of perps lose their case and their freedom by saying too much immediately after the crime. Think about it—you're in shock, cold, frightened, you haven't lawyered up. You might have been panicking, trying to relay blame, like putting it onto the stupidity or disobedience of the white girl. If you were going to say something that gave away your prejudices, it would have been then."

"Haynes wanted this to be a hate crime from the start," said David. "He was looking at murder two before Rayna had even been charged with involuntary manslaughter, which also means he spent the next two days orchestrating a charge of murder."

"Does this mean we can also assume Haynes told Petri to take me through the front of headquarters after my arrest?" asked Rayna.

"Looks like it. And he arranged for Katz to be there to meet you. That's probably what Mannix overheard in the coffee room."

"First Jake and now this," said Sara.

Rayna looked confused, so Sara filled her in.

"Do we go to Joe?" Sara asked David.

"No," he said. "At first I thought that was the right thing to do but now . . . If we go to Joe, we place him in a very awkward position. We can be pretty sure Petri is dirty, but we don't have any real proof. Joe is protective of his men, and rightly so; they're a good bunch as a whole. Also, Joe has already stuck his neck out for us on this one and every time we run to him, the DA thinks he's batting for the opposition. No, I don't want to go bothering him until we have something more substantial."

"So what do we do?" asked Sara.

"We go to Tommy Wu," finished David.

"Doesn't that put Tommy in an even more sensitive situation?"

"Yes, but we need him to substantiate what you heard and fill in the blanks."

"Officer Wu may be a good man, but he won't talk. Why should he?" said Rayna.

"Because he is just that—a good man."

Rayna saw Sara exchange glances with her cocounsel and sensed something between them. A past disagreement? A clash of ideals? A difference in perspective on human beings, positive and negative, black and white? Rayna knew Sara tried hard to see the good in people and sometimes fell short, erring on the side of caution. But then Sara smiled and Rayna saw something else, an understanding between them—perhaps more. David seemed to have the ability to get Sara to question her somewhat skeptical view of the world, and Rayna knew it was good for her.

"But first," said David, turning to Rayna, interrupting her thoughts, "we have some work to do. Let's start by bringing you up to speed on Mariah, and then you have to go back to last Saturday and start remembering everything—detail for detail, word for word, second for second. It will be the details that save us and we can't afford to miss a thing."

. . .

There were twelve messages on his home machine. David threw his backpack on the sofa and contemplated the mess before him. This really was the stereotypical bachelor apartment—big but largely unfurnished, clean but messy, lived-in but not homey.

At least the twenty-third-story view down to Back Bay and across the Charles River gave his rather bland apartment some character. Otherwise, it seemed pretty soulless. But he guessed that's what happened when you used your place of residence as a dormitory between days at work.

There were times when he missed Jersey, his old friends, his mom's cooking. He could have stayed and gone into the family business with his brother. But while Sean loved the shipping industry, David was more interested in other things, like people and why they did the things they did.

Most nights he would come home to one or two messages, usually one from his sister, Lisa, about work or some new guy or some complaint about his lack of calls; maybe one from a friend wanting to go for a run or a beer; or Arthur calling with one last anecdote for the day.

The truth was, David didn't have much time for anything besides work and his lack of messages usually reflected this. *No dates, no mates,* he thought to himself. But not tonight. Tonight his machine told him he was very popular.

He got a pad (kitchen drawer) and pen (living room floor) and took notes as he deleted the messages one by one. The first was from Lisa, wanting to catch up this weekend—too late for that. One from Sara, trying his home before she tried his cell on Friday night—Delete. The beeps of a hang up, someone changing his or her mind about leaving a message— Delete. One from his niece Katie with the news that she had gotten the lead in her school play—good for her. "Ring Katie—congrats," he wrote on the small pad in a lawyer's scrawl. One from his rugby buddy Tony Bishop asking why he missed Saturday morning's game. *Shit,* he thought and wrote down, "Call Tony."

The sixth message was interesting. It was from Tyrone Banks, Delia's ex-husband, apologizing for bothering him at home on the weekend, but he'd gotten his number from Delia and wanted to know if he could help. He left a D.C. number. David wrote it down.

Another call from Lisa. Another hang up. A third hang up. David got the feeling someone wanted to say something but kept changing his or her mind at the last minute.

He moved about the living room, picking up stray items of clothing he really should either fold or wash or . . . that's when the tenth caller stopped him in his tracks.

"Mr. Cavanaugh . . . David . . . it's Tommy Wu. I need to speak to you. I, um, think it could be important, but I don't know what to . . . Look, if you get this, just give me a call, okay? I'm off all weekend, back on duty Monday, but don't call me at work. My home number is 555-2206. Um, well . . . talk soon."

David wrote down the number and looked at his watch. It was after ten-thirty—too late to call? Probably. Damn it. Someone had once told him Tommy shared a place with his sister and her little boy. No, he'd better wait until tomorrow afternoon.

The eleventh message was from his mom. She rang to tell him she was doing some substitute work at Saint Francis Elementary, his old school. She was teaching first grade while the teacher was on maternity leave. She sounded excited, which was great.

The all too familiar feeling of guilt settled on him again as he tried to remember the last time he had called his mother—a week ago? Two weeks maybe? Or was it closer to a month? He had a habit of forgetting to return her calls and taking her patience for granted. He kicked himself for not being more attentive and made a mental note to call her first thing tomorrow.

The last caller must have rung just before he walked in the door. It was Sara telling him she had decided to go straight to her office at AACSAM in the morning. The guys at AACSAM had given her all the time she wanted to work on Rayna's case, but there were always some details to clear up. She signed off by thanking him for, well, she wasn't quite sure—for just being him. This made him smile and feel something he had not felt since . . . since . . . Karin.

He shook this thought from his brain, knowing he was too tired to go anywhere near that pathetic emotional minefield again, looked around at his singular existence and instinctively started shoving clothes into a laundry bag, promising himself he would get to a Laundromat at some stage in the next twenty-four hours. Then he showered, ate some scraps from his close-to-empty refrigerator and went to bed. He was asleep exactly two minutes after his head hit the pillow.

· · ·

All the calls were interesting, thought Verne as he put down his own pad and pen, the details listed neatly in numerical order down the right-hand side of the page. Especially Banks and Wu. He would make some inquiries about Banks, and Wu, well, he could be a problem. He put a small, neat red asterisk next to caller number ten, realizing that this would have to be dealt with immediately.

Cavanaugh was obviously close to his sister and his mother—good; the closer the better. And the last call—well, that was precious. Cavanaugh and his cocounsel were obviously getting cozy, and Verne knew this could play to the senator's advantage.

Yes, it was a good list. Thank God he'd gotten the bug in before Cavanaugh played them all back and erased them. Some days, you just got lucky.

· · ·

It was late on Sunday night and Ed Washington could not get the name out of his mind.

Ivan Lipshultz. Ivan Lipshultz. He had not thought of him for over a decade. But one call from Haynes had brought it all back.

Lipshultz was a grumpy old miser. All that money stashed in the bank, and under the mattress and God knows where else, and living like he didn't have a penny. *I didn't do anything wrong,* Ed told himself. *It's not like he didn't have enough to live on—if you call that living.*

Ten years ago he had felt mighty proud of himself for buying Lipshultz's advantageously positioned, four-bedroom Fenway home at a steal (a good one hundred thousand under the market price!). But now the thought—and the potential repercussions—of any investigation by the Massachusetts Board of Registration of Real Estate Brokers made him nauseated. Haynes knew all about it and now Ed was swallowing gas.

While the senator had begun his late night call by thanking Ed and his family for attending the funeral, the subject of the discussion soon moved to real estate and, more specifically, to Ed's white-washed, picket-fenced, flower-box-festooned Fenway home.

"Yes, sir," Ed had begun, delighted the senator had shifted the conversation to his area of expertise. "We love it here, Senator. We're on Queensbury Street, just north of the Back Bay Fens. It's a big property, huge potential. Fenway may not be Chestnut Hill, but it certainly—"

"You bought it from a man named Lipshultz, didn't you," said Haynes, interrupting Ed midsentence. The senator even pronounced the name correctly: "Lip-shits," as opposed to the more obvious "Lip-shooltz."

"Or more specifically, I believe you bought two properties from Mr. Lipshultz—adjoining homes, if I am correct, the smaller of which you sold to your brother at a tidy profit."

Haynes was right. Lipshultz was a client and Ed had convinced the old Russian that an exhaustive (nonexistent) marketing campaign had turned up zero interest in his property. But being the "dedicated" agent that he was, and hating to see an elderly gentleman "lumbered" with the "burden" of two large homes before moving to a retirement complex in Jamaica Plain, Ed was willing to take the properties off his hands for a more than generous price. Which of course he did.

Within weeks Ed had moved his family into the larger of the two homes and after a little sprucing, had sold the house next door to his older brother George. He made fifty grand plus on the later transaction, but he hadn't charged George any commission so . . .

"Did I mention to you that I have a friend at the Board of Registration of Real Estate Brokers?" asked Haynes.

Ah, the world of coincidences!

"His name is Grainger, Bob Grainger. In fact, I think he was recently appointed chairman. Perhaps I should get you two together. You could discuss Bob's concern about the current deterioration of some agents' standards of practice and

ethics. Big problem according to Bob—especially the rising
incidence of underselling and misrepresentation of the market to the vendor."

So there it was, plain and simple—and so came the
bottom line. Ed would pull his head in, keep Francine in
line, make sure their confidential discussion remained exactly that, and not talk to any press except for the *Tribune*'s Max Truman (whose story had never even run). In
return, Haynes would unfortunately be way too busy to
organize a meeting between Ed and his good friend Bob
Grainger.

No need to think about it. Ed knew a good deal when he
saw one. And this was a damned fine deal.

13

Monday was a blur. While Sara was tidying up some loose
ends at AACSAM, David and Arthur began compiling a potential witness list and working on an estimated time line for
the trial. Arthur surmised that the DA would be asking for
some time in early November, before the cold and the Christmas season set in.

They both acknowledged the importance of Tommy Wu's
testimony, especially given the rumor that his partner, Susan
Leigh, was being courted as a witness for the prosecution.
While they doubted Leigh was in Haynes's pocket—her reputation was one of aspiration rather than suspicion—they had
no doubt Katz would be sweetening her contribution with the
promise of "career advancement." Arthur made a note to get
Con and Sam to make some further inquiries about the ambitious young police officer as soon as they had finished their
physical report.

It was after three when they finally took a break, so

Arthur set about returning his messages and David decided to do the same. He figured he would give Tommy another half hour to make sure he was home from work before making the call. He dialed Tyrone Banks and got his voice mail, so he left a message suggesting they catch up as soon as he returned to Boston. He had forgotten to call Lisa and his mom, but he could do that from home tonight. He was tempted to ring Sara to check on how her day had been but decided she probably needed a break from the case, at least for today.

He leaned back in his chair, balancing on its back legs, his feet on his desk, his pen in his mouth.

"I've got half an hour up my sleeve," he called out to Nora, knowing the whole feet on the desk thing would annoy her. "How's about you and I go out for a quick afternoon cocktail?"

"How very nice of you," she replied, her strongly accented words dripping with sarcasm. "But I don't date out of pity."

And with that she turned her computer screen around to reveal her proverb of the day: "Forbidden fruit is the sweetest."

Twenty-five minutes, then he'd call Wu.

Ten minutes later Arthur poked his head around David's door.

"Judge Stein wants us in chambers at ten tomorrow morning."

"To set a trial date," said David. "You're still thinking . . . ?"

"Scaturro will ask for six months give or take. We could ask for more time."

"I know," said David, tapping his chewed pen on his desk. "You still think we're better off going for sooner rather than later?"

"Well . . ." Arthur took a seat in front of his friend. "I know that in most cases it is in the defense's best interest to delay, particularly when their client is guilty. Cops lose their notes, witnesses forget details, the prosecution is so busy that any delay just shifts that one case farther down in the pile of priorities. But this one is different."

"Go on," said David.

"For starters, there's the public interest. The press is all over this and it will only get worse as the black versus white thing gathers momentum. Rayna is innocent, so we have to trust the fresh memories of the police involved and those of our witnesses to act in our favor."

David agreed and pointed out one other advantage to agreeing to an early date.

"It wins us the first points with Stein. Katz will assume we want to delay, so he'll have his 'speedy trial' speech ready. He also knows he'll have Stein on his side. So we play the good guys, concede to the DA's wishes, give Stein his fast track to justice. The judge thanks us for our cooperation, we start in the box seat, and at the very least, that will piss off the Kat."

"Can't think of a better reason to do anything really," said Arthur with a smile.

"Me neither."

. . .

Ten minutes later David picked up the phone and called Wu's number.

"Tommy?" a woman answered.

"Ah, no . . . Is this Ms. Wu?"

"This is Vanessa Wu."

"Hi, my name is David Cavanaugh; I'm a friend of your brother's. He left a message for me to call him and I was wondering if he's in."

Vanessa explained that Tommy had been due about an hour earlier, so she expected him any minute.

"Running late is he?" David went fishing.

"Yeah, not like him either—probably having a beer with the guys."

"Probably. Vanessa, have you spoken to him today?"

"Well, not since he left for work early this morning. Is there something wrong, Mr. Cavanaugh? Tommy always calls if he is going to be held up."

A horrible feeling started to rise from the pit of David's stomach. He swallowed in an effort to force it back down.

"No, no, I'm sure he's okay—probably having a drink, as you said. Will you tell him I called then? He has my numbers."

"No problem."

"Thanks," and he hung up.

* * *

Tommy Wu looked at the note again and closed his eyes. The quiet was disheartening. Bunker Hill was normally much busier than this; Monument Square was usually abuzz with camera-carrying tourists, picnickers routinely taking advantage of one of the best views in the city.

He had been sitting here, in the driver's seat of his car, for almost an hour, oblivious to the view or the sweet summer weather or anything else besides the piece of paper in his left hand. He had found the envelope in his locker at the end of his shift. He had walked calmly to his car, driven across the river, making sure he wasn't being followed, and pulled the letter from his shirt pocket before opening it to read in private.

> Officer Wu:
> I have no time for pleasantries; I only deal in facts, so here are some for you.
> You know nothing.
> Even if you think you know something, you don't, for it is none of your business.
> A sense of duty should not transpire to stupidity. Successful police officers, future detectives and lieutenants protect their own. Just as fathers protect their sons, brothers protect their sisters and uncles their nephews.
> Did you learn something, Officer Wu?
> I hope so.

The note had been typed on an old-style typewriter. He had no doubt it was free of prints. It was typed on the back of a black-and-white photograph; its computerized date showed it had been taken that morning. The photo itself was covered in little bumps, like braille, formed by the whack of the typewriter's letters from behind. They somewhat distorted the picture, which was of a mother kissing her son good-bye before he walked into Alexander Hamilton Elementary. Her face was obscured by the boy's, and his was turned to the side so you could only see his beautiful profile. Vanessa and his nephew, Mikey.

They were his family. His sister had given up a scholarship to study medicine at Tufts to bring up the child she had not expected. Now she had been granted admission on a mature-aged student program at Boston University, and Tommy was determined that she get a chance to see her dream to its completion. Six-year-old Mikey was like his very own, and he was smart, funny and full of life. He would do anything to protect them. Even turn a blind eye to the corruption of a system of justice he once swore to defend.

He folded the note and put it back in his breast pocket; then he started the engine and headed for home. Vanessa would be worried. He was late, and he hadn't called. He practiced his calmest smile in the rearview mirror and listed a few facts of his own.

He knew nothing.

Even if he did, it was none of his business.

He needed this job—for his sister and her son.

And Rudolph the Red-nosed Reindeer was a myth, just like Santa Claus.

14

David glanced at Sara when he knew no one else was looking and rolled his eyes. Katz really was something. The suit was another Italian: a light wool in deep brown with matching leather shoes, a crisp white shirt and discreetly patterned beige tie. The hair was slick, the face shaven, the fingernails manicured.

"Good to see you again, Your Honor. How's that golf game going—still working on your handicap?"

"My day is filled with handicaps, Mr. Katz; unfortunately, none of them have to do with golf."

That put a lid on Roger's enthusiasm, at least for a few seconds.

Normally the two parties would meet in open court to set a trial date, but the judge wanted to avoid the media circus and thus recommended a short, closed proceeding in his chambers. They all agreed—even Katz, who must have been disappointed that he and his beautifully cut summer-weight ensemble would not get a bigger audience.

There were nine of them squeezed into the small office: David, Sara and Arthur, who sat at the back of the room with Rayna and the obligatory security guard; and Katz, Scaturro, a court reporter to record all of the proceedings and, of course, Judge Stein.

"All right then, let's get down to it," said Stein.

"Your Honor," Scaturro was standing right in front of the judge's desk, taking the floor as if in the courtroom, "the commonwealth believes this case should be heard as a matter of priority for a number of reasons. First, there is the growing concern about escalating media coverage and the subsequent potential for jury tainting. Even at this early stage it would be difficult to find a group of twelve people who have not already formed some sort of opinion about the events surrounding this case."

Scaturro paused for an objection from the defense. The fact that she heard none seemed to rattle her a little, but she cleared her throat and moved on.

"Second, there is the very nature of the crime."

"Your Honor," this was Arthur, "surely Ms. Scaturro means 'charge.' Ms. Martin is not guilty of any crime until proved so. Perhaps her trial is moving so quickly she has jumped to the verdict and left us all behind?"

"Very funny, Mr. Wright," said the judge. "He's right, Ms. Scaturro, please rephrase."

"I apologize, Your Honor. My point is, there is no question about how Ms. Haynes died, there is no question about a murder weapon, and witnesses are limited to the defendant and three girls who saw the body after the fact. Many of the usual time-consuming aspects of the average murder investigation are not applicable here. This should reduce the need for discovery. The DA's office is happy to reduce such time due to the controlled circumstances in which this crime . . . I mean to say, alleged crime . . . took place."

Scaturro was right. Most murders were committed under much more confusing circumstances. Often it would take weeks or months for crime scene investigators—better known as CSIs, thanks to the popular TV show—to go over every inch of a crime scene for blood, fibers, body fluids, prints and a million other pieces of the puzzle that the prosecution would normally use to secure a conviction. This case was more cut and dried because the defense and the prosecution agreed on most aspects of it. No one was arguing over the cause of death, just over the few minutes prior to Christina's drowning.

Scaturro paused again. Still no objection.

David glanced at Katz. The ADA obviously hadn't known whether to be pleased or suspicious. By the look on his face, he'd chosen the latter. David guessed he would have to say something soon and he was right.

"Your Honor, I—"

"Mr. Katz, I would say Ms. Scaturro is doing a fine job here, wouldn't you agree?"

"Of course, Your Honor."

"Right, well let's allow her to finish then, shall we?"

"Yes, Your Honor. Certainly."

"Your Honor," Scaturro continued, "there is also the issue of compassion. This trial will involve testimony from a number of young people. Indeed it centers around the death of a sixteen-year-old. The parents of the girl need some closure on the matter. We believe a speedy trial will at least reduce the period of uncertainty and distress that looms between every arraignment and verdict. We realize the courts cannot always accommodate trials on compassionate grounds, but in this case it might be possible."

David knew this final point would hit a chord with Rayna, and this was probably why Scaturro had used it in her argument. Scaturro would know Rayna would be wanting to make this period as easy as possible for her own daughter and would be guessing Rayna might push her counsel for an early trial in an effort to do so.

"All right, Ms. Scaturro, what are you suggesting?"

"Six weeks from next Monday, Your Honor, July twenty-ninth."

The defense were speechless. This was a whole three months earlier than they had expected. It was unheard of. July!

July is a vacation month, kicked off with the Fourth of July long weekend. It is midsummer, in the month where the atmosphere breathes good karma—friends; family; plain, old-fashioned fun. Everyone joins in with the reminder of how lucky they are to live in this country, in this city, the birthplace of independence.

And then David got an idea.

It was insane.

One part of him said, *Shut up, don't even think it,* but another part of him, his gut instinct, told him it might work to their advantage. It was a huge risk, but, hell, at the very least it could catch them off guard. Before he knew it, the words were out of his mouth.

"We recommend Monday, July first, Your Honor."

Everyone was silent. Including Arthur and Sara, who looked at him in shock. Katz's mouth had dropped to the floor, and for once it appeared that the normally eloquent ADA was completely lost for words.

"You are aware, Counselor, that today is May twenty-first. That leaves you a little under six weeks."

"I realize that, Your Honor, but we agree with everything the commonwealth has put forward. Further, we know that no crime has been committed here."

David stood up and moved to the center of the room. "The prosecution has called this a hate crime, a murder based on a decision made by a woman they claim is so predisposed to an abhorrence of Caucasians that she chose to leave a sixteen-year-old girl alone to die. Not only is this preposterous, it is unprovable; and since the prosecution bears the burden of proof . . ." He let this thought hang for a few seconds before pushing on.

"We know our client, we know the way she lives, how she

is bringing up her daughter, how she treats her colleagues and friends. The extra time may seem necessary to the commonwealth because creating fiction is more laborious than stating facts. They say they want a speedy trial; they point out the potential for jury tainting, the straightforward nature of the events surrounding the case and the argument for compassion. We agree on all three points—especially the last.

"Rayna Martin deserves to be home with her daughter. The longer this drags on, the longer a good woman's reputation is under unfair scrutiny. We would be happy to begin jury selection during the last week of June and start the trial on the first of the month. We can work through the long weekend and complete this matter before it drags the city any further into the ugly pit of prejudice."

The room was silent. David could see a small line of saliva starting to appear at the corner of Katz's gaping mouth, which was still in fly-catching mode. He saw Sara and Arthur both turn to Rayna, who was looking at David with such respect and admiration that he knew their client had decided the matter for them.

"All right then, Mr. Cavanaugh, do you agree with this, Mrs. Martin?"

"Yes, Your Honor."

"Ms. Scaturro?"

"Your Honor, I, um . . . we didn't expect such a short . . ."

"You were after haste, were you not?"

"Yes, sir, but our suggested date already cut the usual trial preparation period by some months. This new proposal is a fair bit faster than . . ."

"Your Honor." Katz had finally shut his mouth and mopped up the damage with a monogrammed handkerchief. "With all due respect to Mr. Cavanaugh's noble motives, conducting a murder trial a mere two months after the crime—excuse me, sir, alleged crime—is unheard of. The DA's office is swamped during an average week, but vacation periods are particularly awkward with court staff and other officials taking leave. Surely it would make more sense to—"

"Are you free from July first, Mr. Katz?"

"Of course, Your Honor."

"Ms. Scaturro?"

"Yes, Your Honor."

"Well, the defense suggests they are also available and I am free as a bird so I don't see the problem. The DA's office cannot have their cake and eat it too, Mr. Katz. You came in here demanding speedy justice and you have it with a bonus."

The judge turned to David. "By the same token, Mr. Cavanaugh, I admire your confidence in your client and in your case, or rather in the inability of the prosecution to prove theirs. But you are placing yourself in a very, very tight squeeze here. Your client is an attorney, a good one I'm told, so I trust she understands the implications of your recommendations."

"Yes, Your Honor."

"All right, the first of July it is. Now move along all of you; it's getting more than a little claustrophobic in here."

"Thank you, Your Honor," said Scaturro.

The defense filed out behind the prosecution with David at the rear.

"Mr. Cavanaugh," said Stein, "a quick word before you go."

David stayed behind and the judge asked him to shut the door.

"Mr. Cavanaugh, are you sure about this?"

"No, sir."

"I didn't think so. Did your client know about your recommendation before you entered this room?"

"No, sir."

The judge took off his glasses and rubbed his eyes. "One word of warning, David. A girl is dead. People are going to want someone to pay for this. It's part of human nature, an eye for an eye—but we have had this discussion before."

"Yes, sir."

"I am worried about you and your client. The DA is not stupid and neither is her cohort, despite his unwitting efforts to appear otherwise. I see what you are trying to do—the Fourth of July and all that. But remember, patriotism takes many forms, even that of bigotry. In fact, the very idea of nationalism could be construed as a form of prejudice.

"I admire your chutzpah, but do not expect any leniency from me in court. In there, my personal opinion counts for nothing. From here on in, you are on your own. Do you understand, son?"

"Yes, Your Honor."

"All right then."

* * *

The trip back to their offices was a three-way shouting match with each of them jockeying to get a word in. Sara was panicking about the terrifying lack of time. Arthur was outwardly furious but seemed unable to wipe the half smile off his face. He declared David to be one of those rare individuals who hovered dangerously between genius and insanity.

David concurred with them both and admitted his on-the-spot strategy scared the hell out of him too. They all agreed they had to believe in their client, who supported David's decision, and take heart in the fact that the prosecution only had six weeks as well.

Rayna wanted this thing over, largely for Teesha's sake. Before returning to her cell, she had reinforced her support of his Fourth of July strategy, arguing that the longer the trial preparation period, the longer Haynes would have to condition his "soldiers" and recruit new ones in his quest for revenge.

She, too, was concerned how the case was affecting the community and agreed with David that each day saw an escalation of public debate, and a distortion of the basic fact that this was accidental death. She told her team that she had used time—or lack thereof—to her defense strategy advantage in the past and found that generally it was the prosecution who came unprepared. The DA's office was an arm of the public service, just like any other government body, and by nature tended to get bogged in bureaucracy, making it more difficult to work on a fast track.

Most of all, she had faith in her attorneys' ability to win this thing. More faith perhaps than David had in himself.

Arthur warned it meant late nights, weekends, work,

work, work every living, breathing minute for the next six weeks and what could turn into months beyond. This was agreed to without a hint of hesitation, and they hit the ground running.

15

The theory was not a new one. Hannibal, Khan, Caesar, William the Conqueror, Napoleon—all the great warriors had used it at one time or another: attack the heart.

Senator Haynes looked up from his newspaper, which was proclaiming the date of the trial, and leaned back in his gray leather office chair. This really was a beautiful city, and on days such as these, when he surveyed its grandeur from the fifty-eighth floor of the John Hancock Tower in Boston's affluent Back Bay, he felt as if it were his own. A king in his glass castle, a sovereign on his throne, a ruler of the people.

He liked this time of day, early, before his staff arrived, the sun rising over the harbor and with it the challenge of new battles to win. It gave him time to think, to breathe, and lately, a small respite from his mourning wife and the shroud that covered his home and cast his life into shadow.

The distractions had begun and were now entering their second phase. Verne had discovered Cavanaugh's weakness: a sentimental attachment to his family, which was, at this very moment, being manipulated to their advantage. Haynes's father had taught him well.

"Love," he would say, "is a man's greatest weakness, and that weakness, a soldier's greatest weapon. It is no coincidence that love is associated with the heart, the biological key to our survival. That is why a clever enemy targets the heart—it is where he plants his flag and damns his foe to hell."

"All you have to do, my son," the memory came flooding back, "is find out what matters to people—what, or who, drives them. And there, my dear Rudolph, is your mark. Remember this and you will never know defeat."

Haynes wished his father were here now. He could use such a man on his team. Still, in the end, kings breed kings, and he had been trained by the best. In truth, it had been a long time since he had needed anyone. Some would say this had made him lonely or emotionally restricted, which was rubbish. On the contrary, he knew it had made him invincible.

. . .

"I don't understand, Lillian," said Patty Cavanaugh, now sitting across the desk from Mrs. Lillian O'Shae, longstanding principal of Newark's Saint Francis Elementary.

"Please, explain it to me again. What is it she said I have done?"

This was very hard for Mrs. O'Shae. Patty Cavanaugh was one of her oldest friends. Lillian had taught all three of her children, and she knew Patty was one of the best teachers, one of the best people, she had ever met. She also knew her friend might be a little lonely with her husband gone, two of her children in Boston and the other very busy with his own family. So she had thought the job might help fill in the odd empty hour.

"Maybe it is because I am new? You know, I made the decision not to teach at Saint Francis while my kids were students here. I thought it would be unfair to them. But that was a long time ago. Maybe this woman has me confused with someone else. Is there another substitute teacher on staff right now? Not that I would think for one minute that any teacher would . . ."

"Patty," interrupted Lillian, "I am so sorry. It isn't me, really. I know you would never strike a child. But the complaint wasn't made to me. It was made directly to the Division of Youth and Families and they have a legal obligation to investigate."

"My Lord, how could this have happened. You know I would never lay a finger . . ."

"Of course not, and I have told them as much, but there really isn't much I can do. I have the name of the DYFS representative who will be looking into the matter, and I have already placed a call to her. Believe me, I will not rest until this is resolved. But in the meantime, I am afraid you cannot teach here."

Lillian O'Shae had received the call from DYFS about two hours earlier. They told her Mrs. Nell Putty had complained that the new first-grade substitute teacher had struck her son Louis during a painting session a week ago. According to Mrs. Putty, Mrs. Cavanaugh had grabbed her son and struck the back of both his legs with a paint stirrer before sending him to sit in the corner. Mrs. Putty said Louis sported two red welts, which had turned into nasty black bruises, across the back of his thighs and knees. Mrs. O'Shae suspected that such bruises, which were not uncommon on poor little Louis Putty's blotchy skin, were the result of a beating from another source closer to home. She had told the woman from DYFS as much and planned to do a bit of reporting of her own.

"I understand, Lillian, I know it isn't your fault."

"Patty, I am not asking this because I suspect anything but because I want to know how Mrs. Putty came up with such a story. What happened?"

"He is such a nice little boy but quiet, timid. I gave him the job of putting the paints away because I felt he needed a little confidence boost, a little bit of importance. He only dropped a couple of jars. I cleaned it up quickly so none of the other children could make too much of a fuss.

"I didn't hit him. In fact, I bent down and gave him a kiss on his forehead and thanked him for being my number-one helper. Even put a gold star on his day sheet. Poor Louis."

"Yes. Poor Louis indeed."

The two women sat there silently for a moment, both of their backs straight, too distraught to look each other in the eye.

"There'll be a report then. My name is now in a DYFS investigation report."

"Yes. And . . ."

"And what, Lillian?"

"And I believe Mrs. Putty also made a report to the police."

Lillian O'Shae watched as a small but deep-seated shiver vibrated through her friend's entire body.

"Well, I never," said Patty Cavanaugh as the lump in her throat rose and fell in an effort to swallow back the tears that threatened to escape her. "Well, I never," she said again.

• • •

That was four out of six. How could you hold an afternoon tea when over half of your guests had canceled at the last minute. It was so embarrassing; it was unheard of. My God, what was happening to her life?

"I don't know what to do, dear." Elizabeth tried to hold back the tears as she spoke to her husband on the telephone. She had called Louise, saying it was an emergency, and the senator had run from a budget meeting to take her call.

"Agnes just hung up a call from Lucinda McGrath. She claims to have the flu. Amelia Bilby-Smith says she accidentally double booked herself and has to attend a charity lunch for the Boston Leukemia Foundation, which is preposterous because I am on the board of the foundation and I *know* there is no lunch. At the very least she could have been more considerate in her choice of lie."

The day had gone from bad to worse, first Agnes tiptoeing around and spying on her, and now this.

"Elizabeth, calm down. You must . . ."

"I can't calm down, Rudolph, I don't understand what is going on. They were the ones who asked to see me, to offer their condolences. I simply suggested we get together here so that I could thank them for their good wishes, their flowers . . ."

"Look, my dear . . ." her husband hesitated, "there are some people who feel it is best to steer clear of controversy and I fear some of your so-called friends fall into that—"

"What do you mean 'so-called'? They *are* my friends; that

is why I don't understand it. My daughter has not been gone for two weeks and they appear to be avoiding me?"

"Well, Sophia is still coming, isn't she?"

Sophia Novelli was Mayor Novelli's wife, and despite Elizabeth's view that she lacked a certain level of decorum, she had been more supportive than most, calling Elizabeth every second day since the drowning.

"Yes . . . and Caroline."

Her husband immediately cut in. "Darling, you must listen to me. You must pick up the phone, call Sophia and Caroline and cancel tomorrow's gathering."

"What? How can I . . ."

"Don't argue, my dear. It will be less embarrassing for all concerned if you delay the little get-together for a month or two, until things settle down. That way you won't have to explain why the other four are absent."

"Rudolph, you simply cannot uninvite people at twenty-four hours' notice, no matter what the circumstances." Elizabeth was at a loss to explain her husband's attitude.

"Of course you can. You said it yourself—you have been through too much. Besides, I really think you should get some rest. You should be looking after yourself rather than waiting on that group of social scavengers."

And there it was. This was the first time in all their years together that Rudolph had suggested their friends were anything less than genuine. Elizabeth was lost for words. On one level she was horrified that he could propose such a thing, and on the other, she was terrified that he was right—a fact she probably had known for most of her socially acceptable life. But admitting this was admitting that they, too, were part of that shallow roundabout called society, and agreeing with him would mean she would have to deal with the very foundations of her entire existence. No, she was not ready for such concepts, true or false. It was much safer to stay in her privileged little world with her designer-suited, face-lifted, air-kissing "friends."

"I have to go," she said quickly.

"Elizabeth."

"I have to go, darling, Agnes is calling me."

"Just call off the tea."

"All right, my dear, now I really must go. I shall see you after work."

* * *

Haynes held the receiver away from his ear and listened to the beeps of the disconnected call. This was a problem. He knew she would obey him and cancel the soiree. She had never disobeyed a request from him in all their years of marriage. But Caroline Croft? If that woman was after a story, it would take more than a canceled tea party to put her off.

Caroline Croft was a big name on American television, a respected journalist who was one of the high profile presenters on the acclaimed news magazine program *Newsline*. She was married to Bernard Jefferson, *Newsline*'s executive producer. Caroline was white and her husband was African American.

God, he thought, imagining his wife left alone with the sugar-coated dominatrix of mass consumer journalism. He had no doubt Caroline would pass on any conversation with Elizabeth to her equally zealous husband, and the next thing they knew, they would be the lead on CBC's prime-time news program for weeks. But he had diverted that disaster, at least for the time being. Now he must press the point with his wife, forbidding her to speak with her "friend" until all of this was over.

All the talk of the tea party and Sophia Novelli had reminded him of his friend Moses and the next step in his strategy. Moses—dear Moses. It is time to use your influence for the greater good. He sighed before buzzing Louise and asking her to set up lunch with the mayor—tomorrow if possible, if not, Friday. Hell, as soon as she could nail him down. Time was short, after all, and there was still so much to do.

* * *

Tommy Wu's freshly painted, white-shingled house was a compact testament to the man's approach to life—simple, neat, clean. The garden was small but tidy, the grass trimmed and watered, the windows shiny and clear. In other words, a lot of care went into this house. No, not house, this Brighton three-bedder was definitely more like a home, even if this morning it looked decidedly empty.

David knocked again. There was no answer. It had been two days since he had spoken to Vanessa, and Tommy had not returned his calls. He decided the only way was to confront Tommy in person.

In the driveway there was a car, a Toyota with a freshly dry-cleaned police shirt draped over the back of the front passenger seat—Tommy's shirt, Tommy's car. He pushed the buzzer, this time leaving his finger on it for a good five seconds. Still nothing. He could have sworn he saw some movement behind the front curtain. Maybe it was his imagination. He was tired. Then he heard Tommy's voice.

"Mr. Cavanaugh, you have to leave."

Tommy was on the other side of his front door whispering through the crack, talking low with a quiver in his voice.

"Tommy, I don't understand; you were the one who called me. I am just trying to . . ."

"I know. I'm sorry, but you really have to go."

They had gotten to him. The man was terrified.

"Tommy."

David knew he probably had one shot at getting Tommy to talk. His experience as a trial lawyer had taught him that the longer people had time to think about offering information, the less likely they were to do so.

"Tommy," he said again, "listen very carefully. I know about Petri and I know about Haynes. I know you are scared and I understand you are only trying to protect your family."

This was a punt. David was guessing Haynes's people had threatened the one thing that would prevent a good cop like Tommy Wu from coming forward.

"But you must know what is at stake here—a woman's life. Rayna Martin is innocent, she is being railroaded by a pack of bullies who stoop to threats and blackmail to get their way. I know you love your sister and your nephew, but you also know they love you *because* you refuse to pander to such low-life bastards. You're a good cop, Tommy. Don't let them change that."

There was silence. At the very least he had Tommy's attention. He decided to play one more card.

"We can protect you." Even as the words left his mouth, he did not know what they meant. Who were "*we*"? Mannix? Himself?

"I'll talk to Joe; we'll make sure you are . . ."

"Bullshit," said Tommy. "You and I both know you can't hide from these people. No, I'm sorry, David; I have Vanessa and Mikey to think about. I may be a good cop, but I am also responsible for their future. And when it comes down to it, that's all that matters."

"Tommy, please. I don't want to have to subpoena . . ."

"Go ahead. I'll just lie. I'm sorry, Mr. Cavanaugh, I truly am, but you really have to go."

David heard Tommy's footsteps back away from his front door and realized he was losing his one true link to the real Rudolph Haynes. *It's over before we even begin,* he said to himself. *Shit.*

• • •

That afternoon David did something he had never done before. He played hooky.

He left Tommy Wu's at midday and drove directly home, where he changed into his running gear and hit the streets. He started north toward the Charles River and then turned left down the embankment and along Storrow Memorial Drive. From there he turned south on Massachusetts Avenue, then all the way up Commonwealth and through the Public Gardens and Boston Common.

He felt the perspiration drip from his face as his legs, now red from exertion, pumped through the picturesque running paths. The smell of the harbor spurred him on as he ran faster, harder, listening to his feet hit the pavement in successive strides so swift it felt as if he were flying. He felt his heart driving blood into his lungs, feeding them with oxygen, daring him to push on.

By the time he hit Atlantic Avenue, his legs were starting to cramp, forcing him to slow to a jog, a fast walk, until finally he bent double, leaning against one of the weathered awnings that circled the waterfront like a squadron of soldiers holding rusty hands. He stood up and took a deep breath, sucking in the salt air, hoping for some form of inspiration, some clue as to how he could solve this mess.

He did not know why his feet had carried him this far south. He had done a full circle of the city and he should have continued north from the Common, headed home, showered, gone to the office. But for some reason this afternoon he needed to smell the salt.

Then it hit him; this was where it had all happened—here on the corner of Atlantic and Congress. This was once a wharf, before Boston started its relentless expansion into the Charles River Basin. This was where those first brave revolutionaries had thrown the tea into the harbor as a symbol of independence. They had risked their lives for the freedom of others, and though it might be a cliché, that was what independence, the Fourth of July, was all about.

It was history. It set the record. *The evidence was in the past. That was it.* He was making a mistake by looking at the present. He had to go back. He had to find out exactly what Rudolph Haynes was made of. The senator might be careful now, but there must have been a time when his bigotries were more obvious, when they were worn as a symbol of his superiority. What did Sara say? Once a bigot, always a bigot.

If they could show a precedent for Haynes's current manipulative behavior, if they could prove Haynes had a history of using his ingrained racial intolerance to influence people and situations to his benefit, then perhaps they could also prove that he was driving the prosecution with an eye toward securing his revenge.

He looked at his watch; it was after four. He had been running for hours. He turned north along the waterfront with a new vigor. He did not know what this meant, only that it was something to hold on to. There was no point going back to the office today; he needed some quiet time to think this through.

He ran home and showered and changed before heading out again to the Boston Public Library in Copley Square. It was a beautiful building, with an Italian Renaissance facade that gave testament to its dedication to the pursuit of wisdom. It was in itself another source of inspiration, home to more than six million books and hundreds of thousands of historical manuscripts, the first public library in the United States.

The hours went by as he plowed through reams of newspaper articles and scoured shelves for old magazines, social columns, political reports, election notices. Then, hungry and thirsty, he borrowed such titles as *Who's Who of Boston* and *Massachusetts: A Recent Political History* as well as some Harvard yearbooks and community periodicals before heading out for something to eat.

He chose Grill 23 and Bar, a popular nearby steakhouse with a great menu and an even better selection of beers. It was a little more upmarket than he was used to; in fact, he felt downright scruffy among the set of cigar-smoking, pin-striped suits. But he was tired, and it was close, and the food was delicious. He requested a corner table, ordered his first icy cold Heineken and selected the rack of lamb with potato, Parma ham and goat cheese gratin before opening his first journal and starting to take notes.

He pored through it all, writing down details of Haynes's youth, his education, his time at Harvard, his marriage to Elizabeth Whitman, his political career. He scribbled random thoughts: places, dates, names of friends, alleged adversaries, political opponents.

It was almost midnight and a good six beers later when he finally looked up to find the restaurant close to empty. Realizing his eyes could no longer focus on the pages in front of him, he put away his scratchy ballpoint, gathered together the piles of paperwork and signaled for the check. He was exhausted, he had drunk way too much and all he could think of was sleep.

He left his car and hailed a cab for home, where he headed straight for his bedroom. He didn't even change, just took off his shirt and fell onto his unmade bed, unable to contemplate moving again until morning. He knew he should check his messages—he had turned off his cell phone sometime that morning before he'd gone to see Tommy, before the day had taken him on a roller-coaster ride from disaster to revelation. But it was late, and all that could wait until morning. He just needed a few hours' sleep, just a little shut-eye to recharge the batteries. Then, at sunup, he would go at it again.

16

David woke to a loud banging on the front door.

"Okay, okay. I'm coming." *God, what time is it?* The sun was up. He was squinting at the bright stripes that shot through the cracks in his vertical blinds and cut across his face like blinding daggers forcing him up, out of bed and toward his living room at the front of the apartment.

The banging started again.

"All right, all right," he said in a hoarse whisper, which was all he could manage at this point. He looked through the peephole to see an anxious Sara fidgeting on the other side of the door. For a split second he contemplated at least trying to make himself look a little more respectable, but he could tell she was not in the mood for waiting.

"Hey," he said as he unlatched the door. "What are you—"

"What am *I*?" her voice escaped her in one almighty shriek. She pushed the door open and bounded into the apartment, turning to face him, her right index finger now pounding against his chest.

"Where the hell have you *been*? My God, David, no one has heard from you for twenty-four hours. Arthur is fuming; Nora is sick with worry. Lisa called and I pretended you were in a meeting. Your brother has called three times."

Sean? Now *that* was unusual. Sean was a man of few words, and although he called every now and again, it was unlike him to call three times in a day. The truth was, he and his brother tended to rub each other the wrong way and . . . His brow furrowed, bringing a fresh surge of pain and the thought left him as Sara plowed on.

"Arthur is on the verge of calling Joe. I was . . . I *am* . . . furious. How could you just disappear like that? You know we are treading on dangerous ground right now. You are so inconsiderate. What the hell did you do? Decide to go out and get drunk, ignore everyone who cares about you? Look at you, you obviously slept in your clothes. I mean . . . is there someone in your bedroom right now? Should I leave and give you your privacy? I just don't—"

He grabbed her right wrist and held it firmly, wanting to do something to calm her down. "Sara, I'm okay. I'm okay. It's all right."

"No, it's not," she said, trying to pull away from him. "It's not all right, it's unforgivable."

"Sara, Sara, look at me. *Please.*"

She took a deep breath and turned to face him. Slowly her hand stopped trembling as she relaxed in his grip. Her shoulders slumped as she exhaled from deep inside her lungs. He reached out and pulled her close, his arms enveloping her, holding her tight. He felt her whole body shake with silent sobs. Her quick short breaths were warm against his skin, her hair smooth around her face.

"I'm sorry," she said. "I have no right to yell at you like this. It's just that I knew you went to see Tommy, but Tommy has not been answering his phone. Your cell was off and I kept thinking about Petri."

"No, I'm the one who should be sorry," he said, stroking the back of her head. "I should have called. I got home late, I had too much to drink, I fell asleep. But that's no excuse."

Slowly she lifted her head to look up at him, her breathing now slow, her tears settled in small pools in the corners of her pale blue eyes. He reached up to hold her face, drawing her closer, pulling her up toward him, and then he bent to kiss her, slowly at first, and then deeper until all that mattered was her smell, her touch. It felt so natural, so right, and in that moment they allowed themselves to forget—about

Rayna and Teesha, about Tommy and Petri, about Katz and Haynes.

His hands moved down and around her waist, lifting her up. She tugged at her jacket, pulling it off her shoulders and letting it fall to the floor. He felt the beat of her heart against his chest, and the softness of her hair trailing across his shoulders and then they were on his couch, pulling at each other's clothes, breathing hard, not wanting to think, not wanting to consider whether this was—

And then she stopped, looking directly into his eyes, and he felt the slightest movement of uncertainty. He knew then what she was about to say and hated himself for knowing she was right.

"I'm sorry," she said. "I don't think we should. I want to. I *need* to. But—"

"It's okay," he said.

"It's just that I feel as if my head is about to explode, and we have so much to do, to focus on and I don't want to jeopardize—"

"The case."

"Yes. No, not just the case. I don't want to jeopardize *us.*"

He stood up, taking her hand and wiping one final tear from her cheek. "It's all right," he said, smiling, filled with disappointment but buoyed by her words of promise. "I'm sorry."

"Don't be. You didn't. It felt . . . it feels . . ."

"I'm glad," he said, kissing her gently on the forehead, now feeling the full force of the dull pain in his own. "Can I at least ask one favor? Well, two actually."

"Sure."

"I want you to promise me that when this is over, we will try to give this—give us—a chance."

"I promise."

"I know how important this case is. But it has been so long since I—"

"I promise," she said again, placing her finger on his lips, putting an end to his doubts. "Now what was the second thing?"

"Oh." He smiled at her. "My head is killing me. I was wondering if you could brew up some seriously strong coffee."

"Coffee I can do. But then you have to fill me in on everything that has happened in the past twenty-four hours. Deal?"

"Deal."

. . .

Showered and changed, David walked back into his living room, the strong smell of coffee soothing the dull ache in the back of his head.

"Thanks," he said as he turned toward the big bay window, the daylight hot on his face, the sun high in the sky. And then it hit him.

"What time is it?" he said.

"After midday."

"Shit," he said, struggling to remember exactly where he was meant to be right now. He knew he had an appointment. Thursday, lunch. That's right. Tyrone Banks, Delia's ex. He had made a booking at Radius.

"Shit, I'm going to be late," he said, absentmindedly clutching at his collar, looking around for a tie to put on. Trying to remember where he put his keys.

"David, where are you going? I want to know what happened with Tommy. You have to call Arthur."

"Okay, but first I have to meet Delia's ex for lunch. I think he might be able to help us—with research."

"Slow down. What research?"

"Sara, I have an idea, but the thing is, I'm not even sure what it means. I just have this feeling that I'm on the right track, that we have to start way back at the beginning."

"You're not making any sense," she said, finding a tie on his living room sofa and tossing it to him across the room.

"Thanks. I'm sorry," he said, his head mentally ticking off his long to-do list. Something Sara had said before leaped to the front of his brain: Sean, his brother, calling three times. He made a mental note to ring him back this afternoon.

"Listen, if you don't mind dropping me down to High Street, we can talk on the way."

"Okay," she said as he tossed her his keys.

"My briefcase?" he said, looking around him.

"By the coffee table," she said, scooping it up before heading for the door.

"Thanks. You know what? We make a good team," he said.

"You got that right." She smiled. "In fact, I am beginning to wonder how you ever managed without me."

"No idea," he said as they moved out the door. "Seriously, I have no idea."

• • •

"I want you at the head table, Moses. I want you and Sophia there, with Elizabeth and me."

Novelli could not help noticing that the senator's eyes were planted firmly on the 1996 Grange Chardonnay that sat in the elegantly understated crystal glasses placed on a perfectly set table at the ultraexclusive Somerset Club on Beacon Hill as he uttered these words of comradeship. Haynes picked up the glass and swirled the pale fluid around precariously close to its smooth rim before taking another sip.

"You are my oldest and dearest friend, Moses. And Elizabeth feels the same way about Sophia."

Now that was definitely a lie. Sophia always felt uncomfortable around Elizabeth, who she said had a tendency to treat her as a fortunate inferior—lucky to be included in Elizabeth Whitman Haynes's circle of friends, if only on the periphery.

"Of course," Haynes went on, "this banquet is all a lot of detestable ballyhoo and, normally, I'd avoid it at all costs. But it is a positive event for the party and I cannot rob them of a reason to celebrate in these uncertain times."

"Everyone would understand if you decided to cancel," said Novelli, the first words he had spoken in minutes. "You and Elizabeth have been through so much. I almost wonder if it would not be better to at least postpone . . ."

"Nonsense," said the senator, now looking his old friend squarely in the eye. "Why would you suggest such a thing, Moses? You know we are a stoic pair and it is important to show my coworkers, my fellow party members, my voters that I am as strong as ever."

And next year is an election year, thought Moses, before

responding. "You don't need my approval to have the banquet, Clark."

"No, no, of course not, old friend. I just want you to know how important you are to me—to us. We value your friendship just as Boston values your guidance."

So here it comes.

"Moses." The glass was on the table now, the senator's hands firmly in his lap, his back straight, his pale eyes meeting the dark counterparts of his companion. "You are no doubt aware of how this Martin case is playing out in the press. People are being forced to take sides. It is not just those involved with the case, but also the general public, the good people of our fine city. They are being asked to *choose*."

Novelli said nothing so Haynes went on.

"And it's not just a black and white thing. Forgive me, an African American/white American issue. It has crossed the lines of race and become a moral argument. Some publications are painting that woman as the victim—a poor single mother being bullied by the almighty politician. But it simply isn't true. The woman is a murderer, Moses. She killed your goddaughter, your beautiful, innocent, sweet goddaughter, and she must pay."

Haynes lifted his glass to his lips, and this time, Moses noted, his movements were not as smooth.

"Look," he said, placing the glass on the table a little harder than was necessary, "let's stop playing games shall we?"

"I didn't know we were."

"Bullshit. You know the press is waiting for your views on this case. The public lives by your goddamned opinion. You . . . *little Jimmy Olsen,* imagine that." He sighed.

"Rudolph, what can I do? It is not my place to influence a judicial proceeding, *especially* one that involves the death of my goddaughter. Yes, I loved Christina, she was like a fourth child to us."

"I am not asking you to bribe the jury, for God's sake, just offer your opinion."

"But it is precisely because you ask me to offer such opinions that I cannot. I do hold clout. I do sway the public. It would, therefore, be extremely irresponsible, even criminal, for me to step into this already overcrowded debate."

The senator sat back and observed his old university buddy

with a look that wavered between contempt and disgust. "Are you forgetting, my friend, that you are who you are because of me? Jimmy would be no one without Clark. Oh, you might think you rolled up your sleeves and got down with the lesser members of our community to garner their support and with it their valuable votes, but it was I who taught you what was possible. If you had not had me as a benchmark, you would still be some pissant misfit in some pissant misfit law firm with pissant misfit clients.

"There would be no thousand-dollar suits, no dinner parties with the president, no limousines, no houses in the South End or pictures in the social pages. No high profile job to compensate for your short stature, no powerful friends to boost your flailing little ego, no perfect white goddaughters to compensate for your dark Italian brood."

"That's enough," said Moses, his eyes watering with a combination of sadness and anger, his head willing his fists not to burst across the table and cover this all-too-white tablecloth with spatters of red.

"But I haven't finished," said Haynes. "You do not understand. This is not a request. It is an order. I have friends in high places, Moses, and perhaps more important, associates in not-so-lofty quarters who are always looking for an opportunity to assist. A rumor here, a suggestion there. Lord knows in our capricious society it only takes one scurrilous anecdote—true or otherwise—to bring a man down.

"So let's be plain, shall we? Speak out in favor of our case and your career will continue to flourish. Say nothing—or worse, support the Martin woman—and your future, your reputation . . ." The senator paused here to let his threat sink in. "Let's just say your professional life will be over."

Moses Novelli rose from the table. He pulled out his wallet and placed two crisp one-hundred-dollar bills on a stark white napkin. He removed his dark blue, off-the-rack suit jacket from the back of his chair and put it on before opening his mouth to say one last thing and turning to leave.

"There is one mercy in all of this: that Christina is not here to see what her father has become—or what he already was." Moses took another deep breath and looked directly at the man he once called his closest friend. "I pray to God each day that he blesses her soul—her wonderfully pure, idealistic, untainted and innocent soul. And I also pray for one other thing: that the Lord have pity on you, Clark. For your soul was discarded a long time ago, an unnecessary hindrance in your callous pursuit of power. Friend? How can I be your friend? I don't even know you and, to be honest, I am not sure I ever really did."

• • •

Lunch went well. Tyrone Banks was an interesting man. He was hospitable but straightforward, gracious but direct and, David suspected, used to having things done his way.

David was impressed with Banks's career record. He was one of the most powerful administrators in the Democratic Party. He headed a staff of over five hundred research analysts around the country and made it very clear to David that he was willing to do anything he could to help Delia's sister and his niece Teesha.

They spoke of politics and the law, Boston and Washington, baseball and football and finally of Delia, and Banks's high regard for his ex-wife and her family.

"Forgive me if this is too forward," said David, "but if you are so close to Delia and her family, shouldn't you two still be together?"

"Short answer is yes. Longer answer is . . . well, not so short." Banks hesitated before going on. "You ever hear the saying 'Be careful what you wish for,' Mr. Cavanaugh?"

"Sure."

"Well, I'm one of those lucky people who love what they do. I found a career that fits me like a glove. You see I love everything about research—the initiation, the process, the correlation and, most important, the results. I aim high, Mr. Cavanaugh, and work hard to reach my goals. In the end I got what I wished for: one of the top research jobs this country has to offer and, I might add, I am very good at it."

"Nothing wrong with that," said David.

"Oh yes, there is. A lot wrong when your wife is one stubborn woman who refuses to follow you on your selfish quest for advancement."

"I gather Delia's not a big fan of our nation's capital?"

"No, sir. She's a Boston girl born and bred and I know I

have no right to tell her where to live." Tyrone had a sip of his sauvignon blanc before going on. "Delia's a good woman, Mr. Cavanaugh, maybe too good for me. Don't get me wrong, we've had our moments, but when it comes down to it, I've never met anyone who has so much to give. And I was stupid enough to let that go."

David wasn't sure what to say. "Well, from what I can tell, you're still a very important part of her life—and Teesha's, and Rayna's too."

"That I am, and I'm grateful for it. Could be there's hope for me yet."

Radius was renowned for its mouthwatering modern French cuisine, and the menu gave credence to its stellar reputation. Tyrone had the seared marine scallops while David ordered the slow-cooked prime *côte de bœuf*.

Soon they were ordering coffee and speaking openly about the case, and about David's suspicions that Haynes's determination to crucify Rayna was not solely motivated by the death of his daughter.

"Would it surprise you if I said we were considering a counterdefense aimed at proving the prosecution is being driven by the senator's need for revenge?" asked David. "And by his views on African Americans as a whole?"

It was a broad statement and a risky one, considering he had only met this man two hours ago, but something told David that Banks could be trusted.

Tyrone raised his eyebrows, and David sensed that it was not as much in surprise at being asked the question as it was an indication that he thought David and his team were extremely courageous to take this on. Courageous or crazy, David wasn't sure.

"Considering that this is a hate trial," Tyrone went on, "and knowing the parties involved, it doesn't surprise me at all. In fact, I think it makes perfect sense. I am an analyst, and one who concerns himself not as much with statistics as with human behavior. Our country is not run by machines but by men and women, each with his or her own opinions on this or on that." Banks spoke slowly and deliberately.

"Sadly, there are a million Hayneses out there. A million little boiling pots all determined to keep their lids on a bellyful of hatred for fear of being labeled politically incorrect. I have made a few initial inquiries for my own information, so to speak, and from what I can see, the senator is very skilled at keeping his lid on tight. But that just means the steam inside is ready to explode."

David sat forward, his elbows on the table.

"So you think that maybe we could find some evidence of the senator's past prejudicial behavior that could show a pattern of intolerance?"

"Perhaps," answered Tyrone. "But that won't be enough."

Banks was right. Any evidence of past discrimination would not only have to reveal the senator as a bigot, it would also have to prove he was willing to break the law or at the very least, do some serious damage to the lives of others in order to support his own skewed beliefs.

They sat quietly for a moment as Banks sipped his cappuccino and David downed his second black coffee.

"Tyrone, I know you have some amazing research facilities at your disposal, and I would never think of asking you to compromise your position to help us, but . . ."

"I'm the one who asked you to lunch, Mr. Cavanaugh. In fact, I was hoping you would—"

"Ask for your help? It's David, remember? And yes, that's exactly what I'm doing."

"Well, it's about time." He smiled. "You may not be Tom Cruise, but you still had me at hello."

17

When she had first received it, Elizabeth Haynes had thrown down the book in disgust. It had landed faceup on the chintz-covered sofa beside her and she had glared at the title—*On Death and Dying* by Elisabeth Kübler-Ross—with a combination of anger and embarrassment.

The book—which outlined Kübler-Ross's "five stages of grief"—had been sent to her by the supposedly well-meaning wife of an opportunistic political climber as a "gift," hoping it would "help you understand the process you must go through in order to go on with your life," and while she knew her anger stemmed from the fact that this presumptuous woman would deign to tell her how to deal with her intensely personal heartache, she also realized that her embarrassment came from the knowledge that all and sundry now considered her a complete and utter mess.

It was true. She was a wreck. And in a spirit of open-mindedness—or perhaps a desperation to try anything, *everything* she could to lift herself from this quagmire of relentless misery—she had picked up the plain covered book again and begun to peruse it, one page at a time.

And as much as she hated to admit it, it was actually starting to help, perhaps not in the way the audacious sender thought it would, but in a more constructive sense—it helped her realize that she had gone about everything the wrong way. The only reason her husband was avoiding her, Agnes spying on her and her friends shunning her company was because she was coming across as weak, unstable and, as such, socially undesirable.

She was stuck in stage one—denial—and needed to move to stage two.

Stage two—anger—was so much more tangible, stronger, more productive. Her husband was in stage two—no doubt about it—and he, unlike her, was working constructively to make sure their daughter's murder was avenged.

More to the point, the book made her realize that she had been neglecting him. She had always been there for Rudolph and had taken pride in her ability to carry out her role as his loyal and loving companion with energy and effectiveness. She had seen so many political careers fail, so many men fall by the wayside because of the inappropriateness of their partners, and she knew she was considered one of the best political wives in the state, perhaps even the country.

But not of late. No, not of late.

And so she made the decision then and there that her erratic behavior would stop. Truth be told she *was* angry and now sensed that she could use this somewhat foreign sensation to support the man she loved. In doing that, she reasoned as she looked at the book again, she might be able to negotiate stage three—bargaining—avoid stage four—depression—altogether and skip all the way to stage five.

But then she read the word next to the number five and realized just how ludicrous such a proposition actually was. For stage five—acceptance—was an impossibility. How could she, why should she, *ever* accept the fact that her daughter had been stolen from her by a heartless bigot like Rayna Martin.

No. Rudi was right. They should never accept what had happened. She would support her husband in his quest for justice and show everyone that she was the woman they all knew her to be: a bastion of devotion, constancy and poise.

* * *

Sara was sitting by Arthur's office window, the sun now high enough to sneak its way through, the early morning light flickering across her face, bouncing off her blue eyes and making them appear almost translucent. She was in work attire again: a tailored navy skirt with a fitted striped shirt, the jacket flung over the back of Arthur's worn leather couch.

"I understand what you are saying, David," she began. "But part of me is also worried we may spend a great deal of our limited time chasing ghosts."

"I agree," said Arthur. "We have to be sure we are going to find something worthwhile before we go looking for skeletons."

David knew these were all reasonable responses to his "history" theory. But he had this feeling, right in the pit of his stomach, that looking to the past was the only way of nailing Haynes.

"So where to from here?" asked Arthur, breaking the silence.

"Research," said David. "That means pure, old-fashioned cramming—interviews, contacts."

"But we know it will be hard if not impossible to get someone to go on the record," said Sara.

"Even so, that someone might point us in the direction of somebody else who will. And talking to people who knew Haynes back then might be a lot easier than confronting his current circle. He wasn't always as powerful as he is now."

Sara and Arthur both stared at David, unsure.

"Look," he said, approaching Arthur's massive wall of books on the far side of the room. "What is the law if not history? This nation's entire legal system is based on precedent. If we can prove that Haynes *was* a racist, chances are we can convince the jury he still is. Even better, if we can prove he has acted on such views in the past, it will seem all the more plausible that the man is capable of influencing the political process and perverting the course of justice."

"And then," said Sara, "the jump to threats, bribery and blackmail is not such a stretch."

"Exactly," said David.

David paused then, Joe's warnings about Haynes coming back to haunt him. He did not want to alarm his colleagues, or more to the point Sara, but he was the one taking them down this road and he knew he had an obligation to at least float the idea of possible repercussions.

"One more thing before we go on," he said. "We know Haynes is a man not to be trifled with. He's powerful, determined and used to getting what he wants. So if we decide to take him on, we have to be prepared for . . ."

"I'm not scared of him, David," said Sara, cutting him off.

"I know, but I don't think you realize how—"

"Rayna Martin is our client," interrupted Arthur. "And we owe it to her to do everything in our power to secure a 'not guilty' verdict. If that means taking on a man like Haynes, then so be it."

"As Arthur says," said Sara, a look of energetic determination on her face, "bring it on."

David nodded, half of him terrified of what "it" might be and the other feeling a swell of admiration for Sara's dogged commitment to save their client.

"This isn't going to be easy," said Arthur, breaking the moment. "Haynes is not the one on trial here. We run the risk of losing control of our defense by going on the attack. If we screw up, Scaturro and Katz will say we are chasing the victims because we have no case."

"He's right, David," said Sara. "It could backfire. I'm worried we'll spend all our time chasing Haynes and forget we are supposed to be defending Rayna."

"All right. I see your point," said David. "So let's break the plan in two. First, we make sure Rayna's case is as strong as it can be—and then we go after Haynes."

• • •

By seven they were exhausted. With Ed Washington still refusing to take their calls, they had spent the best part of the day planning for next Monday's interview with Teesha, and were just deciding to back off Tommy Wu until next week when Nora tapped at Arthur's office door.

"You are forgetting one other all-important issue," she said.

"Which is?" asked Sara.

"You all need to get some rest. There is still a month to trial and you do not want to embarrass the firm by toppling over like bowling pins the minute the bailiff says 'All rise.'"

"Well said, Nora," agreed Arthur, who was rubbing the bridge of his nose where his glasses had worn deep, red depressions. "And on that note, I'd say it's time for some Friday night refreshments." Arthur headed for the bar fridge in the corner before being interrupted by a voice at the office door.

"Ah, excuse me."

Sara looked up to see a good-looking man in workman's clothes standing behind Nora. He was about forty, tall, strong, with sandy brown hair and green eyes. In fact he looked a little like . . .

"Sean," said David, rising quickly as Nora moved aside, allowing his older brother into the office. "I've been trying to call you."

"Excuse me," said Sean to Nora, who nodded, replying, "No, please come in, Mr. . . ."

"Cavanaugh," said Sean.

"So you're the older brother," said Arthur, moving away from the fridge to shake his hand.

"Yes, sir."

"Arthur. Call me Arthur."

"And this is Sara," said David. "Sara, this is my brother Sean."

"It's so nice to meet you." Sara smiled, taking his large calloused hand in hers. "I can see the family resemblance."

"This is a real surprise," said David, who was now starting to worry. "Is everything okay? How are Teresa and the kids?"

"They're fine. Just fine."

But David could see the growing agitation on his brother's face. David knew Sean was not comfortable in places like this one. His brother used to feel uncomfortable in his school uniform, never mind in an office block full of lawyers and accountants. Something was up, and it was serious.

"Can we talk?" said Sean, turning to David.

"Sure, in my office. Excuse us for a second."

David led Sean outside, leaving a concerned Sara, Arthur and Nora behind. The three sat patiently saying nothing as they heard the growing volume of what was obviously a one-way conversation going on next door.

The brothers were in there for no more than a few minutes before returning to Arthur's larger room where the three stood quietly, concerned but not wanting to pry.

"I have to go home to Jersey," said David, his cheeks flushed with a mixture of anger, guilt and worry. "Mom's in trouble and I'm afraid we're the cause."

"*Jesus*, DC," said Sean, obviously not done with berating his younger brother. "I came here to kick your ass for ignoring my calls and not calling Mom in weeks. Now I find out Mom is in trouble *because* of your precious job."

"Is she all right?" asked Sara, obviously trying to defuse the conflict and find out what the hell was going on.

"She will be," said David. "It's a legal matter. Sean came down to get me when I couldn't be reached on the phone."

"Couldn't be reached?" said Sean, his suntanned brow

now shiny with perspiration. "Too busy to bother is more like it, DC. When was the last time you had more than a rushed conversation with Mom? You know how much she misses Dad. You would think at the very least you could have—"

"I said I was sorry, Sean." David took a deep breath, realizing that flying off the handle would not help them now. "These are my friends and I think they can help."

Sean looked at them then, still standing in the doorway, and David could see he was not too sure whether to walk on in and join their world of legal mumbo jumbo or grab David by the arm and drag him all the way to his car.

"Let's hear it then," said Arthur, walking over to Sean and directing him toward a comfy chair in front of his desk. David knew Arthur had picked up on his brother's discomfort and was grateful for the intervention. "But before we do, I'd say we all need that cold beer."

"Sean?"

"Ah," said Sean, standing next to the suede-covered chair, looking over at David one more time before making the decision to stay. "All right."

"That's beers all around then, and a sherry for Nora. No excuses, Mrs. Kelly."

"Wasn't going to offer any, Mr. Wright," said Nora, smiling at Sean and taking a seat by the window.

Arthur opened the bar fridge that was set on a temperature closer to a freezer's, allowing billows of cold air to escape in an inviting cloud of frost. He reached in, his arm now lost in the cool fog, and felt around for a couple of longneck bottles of imported Australian beer.

Nora moved to Arthur's desk to gather the mountain of open files strewn across the worn mahogany surface, stacking them neatly into the far corner in-box. She then proceeded to the glass-doored cabinet on the far wall to retrieve four beer tumblers and one crystal sherry glass for herself.

"Just what we need," said Arthur, collecting a bottle opener from his drawer before attacking the first longneck with gusto. But in his enthusiasm to unleash the cold amber liquid, he released the pressure from inside the freezing bottle a little too quickly, causing a flood of frothy beer to gush from its narrow mouth and cascade quickly across his recently cleared work space.

"Oh dear," said Nora, now rushing forward with the bar towel she had grabbed from the top of the refrigerator, her outreached hand clashing with Arthur's elbow as he tried to stem the flow. The result was one almighty mess, including an overturned desk lamp and a broken nineteenth-century vase that fell to its side and rolled slowly across the tacky, still-bubbling surface.

And in that moment Arthur flashed a look at David, who followed his boss's eyes to the upturned vase. And there it was, sitting snug and tight on the base of the cracked antique urn.

Arthur said nothing, just looked at the others in the room around him with a new expression of apprehension. "Shh," he said, effectively harnessing their full attention before opening his mouth to whisper, "No one say another word."

18

He was tired and frustrated and angry. It was late afternoon and David had just arrived back in Boston. He'd spent a few days in Newark, easing his mother's fears about the investigation and having Sunday brunch with Lillian O'Shae, whom he remembered from Saint Francis's and who appeared not to have aged a day. Lillian had recounted the entire story and David sat back to ask one final question.

"Mrs. O'Shae, what is your personal take on all this?"

"That's just it. I really don't have one. I have no idea why

Mrs. Putty would target your mother with such ludicrous accusations. If anything, Patty has been bending over backward to reach Louis. There is no answer to that question, David. None at all."

But there was, and David knew it. His mother was particularly distressed by a call from an attorney with the unfortunate name of Richard Butt, who said he would be "representing Nell Putty, who, on top of any criminal charges that might be laid, intended filing a civil suit against her son's teacher for emotional distress caused over the paint jar incident and subsequent inappropriate abusive punishment."

So David and his mother spent Monday at the Division of Youth and Families, speaking with a woman named Rosemary Farello, who was investigating the case. Mrs. Farello was a large, hearty, garrulous woman who, by the end of the day, seemed at least to some extent convinced that the accusations against Patty Cavanaugh were difficult to justify.

She had also discovered that the Puttys were once the subject of some suspicion themselves. About six months earlier a neighbor had called DYFS, concerned when he saw one of the children playing naked in the backyard in the dead of winter. This report had unfortunately fallen through the cracks in the ever-burdened system of case overload, and was yet to be investigated.

Of course Mrs. Farello, true to the "suspect until proved otherwise" mantra of a department riddled with the ever-present threat of litigation from both the accuser and accused, could not rule on any specific findings until investigating further. She would speak with Mrs. O'Shae and the parents of other children in Mrs. Cavanaugh's class, but "felt quite certain there would be no further action against Mrs. Cavanaugh." Further, she insinuated she might make an unscheduled visit to the Putty home sometime during the week. At least that was a start.

On Tuesday morning David went to see Sergeant Harold McNally at Newark PD, who assured him no charges had been laid and no charges would be laid unless DYFS found a case for abuse, which at this stage was unlikely.

That afternoon David made an appointment to see attorney-at-law Richard Butt and told him that under no circumstances was he to call his mother direct—that he must deal personally with David, who, after speaking with DYFS and the police, was ready and willing to represent Patricia Cavanaugh in the filing of countercharges against Mrs. Putty for false accusations and emotional distress.

He could have left on Tuesday evening but chose to spend the night with his family, largely to make sure his mom was okay but also to avoid Sean's constant snipes that he was too busy and too selfish to take time out with his family. His older brother was a hardworking man with strong views and set opinions, and while David was grateful for his watching after their mother while he and Lisa were in Boston, he was also a little tired of Sean's repeated jibes about David's career and "priorities."

"I suppose you're off first thing then?" he asked David at dinner.

David, seeing Lisa immediately looking up from her lamb casserole with a glare that said, "Don't turn this rare family dinner into a shit fight," tried to stay calm.

"The trial is less than a month away," answered David. "Rayna Martin is a good woman, a dedicated single mom who—"

"Glad to see there are some mothers who get your attention."

"Boys!" their mother said at last, tired of the undercurrent of animosity. It had been like this as long as David could remember—Sean and he having a go at each other, their mother letting it get to a point before finally stepping in. "Enough! We all have our responsibilities, Sean, and right now David's are in Boston."

"Yeah, well, sometimes I don't think my little brother knows what a responsibility is."

"Jesus, Sean," said David, slamming his knife and fork on the table. "Give it a rest, will you?"

"Shut up, both of you," interjected Lisa. "Can't we have *one* pleasant family dinner without the two of you going at it? Sean, get off David's case. He just managed to get Mom out of some serious trouble."

"Trouble he got her into in the first place."

"It wasn't his fault and you know it." Lisa turned to David. "DC, I know your job is important, but you gotta make the time to call Mom—and *me*, for that matter, a little more often. And every now and again, when I come home to Newark for a weekend, you can come with me. Okay?"

David said nothing, just nodded. And that was that.

The rest of dinner went on without any outward signs of aggression, with talk of Sean's kids, his mother's friends and Lisa's rundown on the latest from her work and social life, and David found himself happy enough just to sit back and listen. Although, he would have admitted, his mind was split between the dinner table and a grim cell in Boston where his client sat facing the possibility of never returning to the real world again.

Maybe Sean is right, he thought. Maybe I *am* obsessed with my work. Or maybe I just can't handle seeing assholes like Haynes using their power to trash the lives of innocent people. Either way, rightly or wrongly, he was looking forward to getting back "home."

The next morning he kissed his mom and shook hands with his brother before climbing into Lisa's Geo and heading north again—back to the Martin case and the all-important interview with Teesha. The entire office had been swept for bugs, but there was only the one found in the base of the vase. That made two altogether, including the one found in David's home telephone. Sara's house was clean, as was Arthur's big bachelor condo in Cambridge. They had decided against informing the police, knowing that it would only have bogged down investigations with more accusations and counterallegations, and besides, there would be plenty of time for payback.

While David told himself that he was still on top of things, he knew his focus had been compromised. His demeanor swayed between a controlled determination not to let them get the better of him, and a burning desire to head straight to Highgrove and smash Haynes in his arrogant, self-important, pompous-assed face—not just for delaying his trial preparations but for making this personal by involving his family. He now knew how Sara had felt after Jake's arrest, a frustrating combination of rage and guilt as you watched the people you loved being dragged into a mess they had nothing to do with, all because of you.

19

"Are you under the influence, Detective Petri?"

"What? No way. No, sir. Just tired. I pulled a double shift yesterday."

"Because given the situation and your part in it, that would be completely inappropriate."

"Yeah, sure. I know that."

Petri was on a pay phone at the corner of Dorchester and Geneva. Early this morning when he had climbed into his beaten-up Buick outside his tired-looking Dorchester house, he had found a note on the driver's seat asking him to call a certain cell number from this specific pay phone as soon as possible.

Petri was not a nervous person by nature. He had seen so much in his long and disturbing career that these days he sailed through even the most macabre of scenarios without batting an eyelid. But he had to admit that this dude had always made him a little chilly. His voice was a hollow monotone, robotic even. He got the feeling this guy would have no problem following through on any of his threats, without even breaking a sweat. Petri covered the mouthpiece with his right hand before letting out a raucous cough, the result of too many whiskeys and not enough sleep.

"Detective Petri?"

"Yeah, yeah. I'm here."

"This is simply a gentle reminder. Stay calm, watch your back, keep your ears open and your mouth shut."

"Right. No sweat, loose lips and all that."

Another cough. This one louder, deeper and straight into the receiver.

"Sounds like you need a checkup, Detective. But then again, you already have one Petri draining the medical resources and those private clinics can be frightfully expensive."

Pig, he had to mention his wife.

"Detective?"

"Yeah, I'm here."

"Good, we're all on the same page then."

Petri held the phone to his ear, listening to the beeps of the disconnected call before slamming the filthy receiver back on its greasy rest.

"Prick," he said, before getting back in his car and heading uptown to work. "Fucking prick."

• • •

Samantha Bale blew a small, fuzzy auburn curl out of her left eye before opening the manila folder in front of her.

Sam was twenty-seven, about five foot three and loaded with enthusiasm. She wore a deep green suit with well-worn, high-heeled shoes, which she never seemed to master. Her fiery mane was controlled in a tight bun that still managed to sprout wires of unruly auburn hair like little electrical threads alive with complementary vigor. Her counterpart, Con Stipoulos, sat next to her, ready to contribute when needed, his relaxed manner soothing her jack-in-the-box dynamism.

"Okay," she began. "Let's start with the weather conditions. On Saturday, May fourth, the sun rose at six-fifteen AM and set at six-thirty-five PM. There was little if any cloud cover except for a small band of wispy cirrus that strung out across the sky from the southeast in the morning only to be burned off by midday."

Arthur gave David a sideways glance. This was so Sam, so determined not to miss a beat. Samantha Bale had not been the obvious choice for associate; in fact, there had been at least twenty other applicants for her job who had better bar exam results and references. But Arthur had been impressed by her no-holds-barred spunk and enthusiasm, and no one was more shocked than Sam when six months earlier he had called to tell her she had gotten the job. She had been out to prove her worth ever since and more than made up for her slipups with an insatiable passion to learn and an unwavering determination never to make the same mistake twice.

"The temperature range was a cool fifty to an above average seventy-eight—a maximum reached at two o'clock that afternoon. Wind was mild, blowing from the southwest in the morning at six knots and lessening to a mild breeze by eleven o'clock. In other words, if they had been in a sailboat rather than a cruiser, the lack of wind would have prevented them from going very far."

Sam looked up and smiled before burying her head back in the report and moving on.

"High tide was at five-fifty-two AM and low at eleven-forty-four AM, so the accident occurred when the waters were close to their lowest of the day. The current was weak—a mere 0.75 knots to the northeast—basically still. The water temperature was about sixty-eight, cool but more than bearable, and a lot warmer than it usually is at that time of year. In other words, the weather was beautiful. Exceptional for early May, in fact. More like conditions seen in July or August. A perfect day . . . well," she paused, "not in this instance, of course."

Sam released a breath and sat back in her seat, prompting her partner, Con, all calm professionalism and brooding confidence, to lean forward toward the table and take a sip of chilled water before moving on.

"There are approximately one hundred ten licensed tour operators in the greater Cape Ann area, most of whom operate out of Gloucester—population twenty-eight thousand seven hundred sixteen. Some of them only operate from late May to early September, while others hold winter tours with a slight increase in activity at Christmas.

"The greater majority organize boat charters and harbor cruises, with fishing and whale watching being two of the major drawing cards. There are also a few who offer helicopter tours, flying over the greater cape area of Manchester, Gloucester, Rockport, Essex and Ipswich and giving the tourists a bird's-eye view of the many coves and beaches. These operate out of Beverly Municipal Airport just south of Gloucester.

"Others sell walking, hiking and biking expeditions, and there is the added attraction of the local art galleries and antique shops. But as a whole, about seventy-five percent of the cape's tourist income is made on or near the water and most of that during the months of June, July and August."

"Given all this activity, why is it that no one witnessed the accident?" said Sara.

"Well, early May is still fairly quiet," said Con. "And the waters are expansive. The cape doesn't feel busy at that time of year. Also, the accident occurred north of the main marinas in the more tranquil waters of Essex and Ipswich bays. Turtle Beach is private and protected. People go there to *avoid* the crowds."

They all agreed that if anyone had witnessed any part of the day's events, they would have come forward by now.

"We interviewed an endless number of tour operators and other locals," said Sam. "They all knew about the accident and the pending trial, but no one seems to have seen anything. We spoke to George Livingston, who leased *The Cruisader* to Rayna. He put them on board and saw them set off, but he didn't see anything else until they returned to port."

"Someone must have seen something," said David. "Let's check with Teesha tomorrow—see if she remembers anything."

"I'm afraid there is not much else to tell," said Sam, disappointed they could not contribute any more. "The good news is that Mrs. Martin's story checks out. The conditions are just as she told us. But it still doesn't shed any light on cause of death, or provide us with any witness to the conversation."

"You've been very thorough," said Arthur.

"So what now?" asked Con.

Arthur sat back in his chair and looked at his two associates.

"I need you to do a little background work on a couple of police officers," said Arthur. "Let's see what we can turn up on Detective Paul Petri and Officer Susan Leigh."

20

What the hell was wrong with that girl? This was the fourth time this month that his secretary had called in sick. Her name was Bessie Billings and she was nineteen. She had one of those horrendous navel rings that popped out between her blouse and her skirt whenever she reached up to access the A–E filing cabinet drawer. How anyone found those things attractive he would never know.

The phone rang again as Ed Washington cursed young Bessie and his wife, who had promised to come down straight after breakfast but had so far failed to show. His junior Realtor, a keen car-salesman type named Zachary Duck, was at an early showing and the phone just rang and rang, interrupting his efforts to concentrate on his end of financial year book-work.

"Hello!" he screamed at the phone, unable to stand the noise any longer.

"Hello, Mr. Washington?"

"Yes." Ed took a breath and lowered his voice, realizing this could be a potential client. "This is Ed Washington; how can I help you?"

Marc Rigotti sat up in his seat. This was the umpteenth time he had placed a call to Ed Washington and the first time Ed had answered the phone himself. Normally it was the monotoned secretary who kept saying he wasn't in, or Ed's wife, who had hung up as soon as he offered his name and place of employment.

"Mr. Washington, my name is Marc Rigotti. I am a reporter for the *Boston Tribune*. I have been following the Martin case and I was wondering if you would be free to meet with me."

"My wife has told me you have been harassing her, Mr. Rigotti," said Ed, and there was no mistaking the animosity in his voice. "We do not wish to—"

"Sir, I know you are determined to protect your daughter, and rightly so, but I also hear you are a man dedicated to helping others, to making sure accidents such as these will never happen again."

The first rule of getting a potential source to talk is to move quickly but smoothly. Present the facts, just enough to eliminate any confusion, play the concerned advocate of free speech, compliment your potential source for his or her public interest and act neutral with a slight lean toward your source's slant on the situation.

But Rigotti realized he may have just blown it. He had said "accidents," which immediately gave away his personal take on the case. A mistake. He held his breath, hoping Ed was as dim as he had been told.

"Mr. Rigotti, I do not speak to the press."

"But you did, sir, from the onset. I am just wondering why you decided not to continue your crusade for responsible teenage supervision. From what I am told, you hold the view that Mrs. Martin was negligent in the care of the teenage girls she took out on the cruiser that fateful day. I have also heard you are a supporter of Senator Haynes's."

"Look, Mr. Rigotti, the senator is a good man and I am extremely sorry for his loss. My daughter and his daughter were fast friends and it will take some time for Francine to get over this."

"Naturally. It must be very hard for your daughter, and for you, as her father, trying to console and protect her all at the same time."

"Yes," said Ed, obviously feeling that he was at last speaking to someone who acknowledged his position in this whole mess. "It could have been my daughter, you know, that's what the senator said, and he was right."

Now *this* was interesting. First, it showed that Ed Washington had spoken to Haynes, and second, it proved something far more powerful. That the senator's original take on the case was not as a hate crime.

If Haynes had seen this as a racially motivated crime all along, he would never have suggested that "it could have been" Francine Washington who was left for dead. Francie was black. Unless, of course, this was all part of Haynes's plan to win at least one of the three remaining teenagers into his camp.

Rigotti smiled. Sometimes you just got lucky. He had to get this guy in a room with a tape recorder.

"Exactly, sir," he agreed. "It could easily have been Francine. Mr. Washington, do you think we could get together, talk a little, clear the picture on this fog, and in the process help the Hayneses find some form of justice?"

Haynes—the very name brought Ed back into focus. Lord, what was he thinking?

"No, no, I don't think so, Mr. Rigotti. I really shouldn't be—"

"Shouldn't be what, sir? You are only doing what is right for your family, for the Hayneses."

"No, no, I am sorry. I have already spoken to the *Tribune* and the story was never published. Check with your editor. You have the interview. I mean, Max Truman has it; speak to him."

"Truman? Who is Max Truman?"

"He's a reporter from your paper. Don't you know what goes on in your own office, Mr. Rigotti?"

"Mr. Washington, there is no Max Truman here. I know every journalist in the building. I was assigned to this story from day one and have been following it ever since. Who did you speak to, Mr. Washington?"

Ed Washington was no Einstein, but he was no amoeba either. *Oh my Lord,* he thought to himself. *Max Truman wasn't a reporter; Haynes had arranged for him to . . . He was a friend of Haynes's.*

He had been set up. The breakfast, the talk of new clients, the cold shoulder at the funeral, Ivan Lipshultz!

"I don't know. I have to go."

"Mr. Washington, how well do you know the senator?"

"Don't call me again, Mr. Rigotti. Please, please do not call again. Just leave well enough alone."

• • •

Teesha was lying. And David knew it. Tyrone had cooked them a great dinner of honey-roasted spare ribs and baked vegetables, which was followed by Delia's mouthwatering homemade rhubarb pie, before David and Teesha moved into the living room for a more private chat. David started by asking her about school finals and telling her how he had once taken home economics as a dare.

"To my horror," he smiled, "I won the class prize for best quiche. You can just imagine how well that went down at football practice."

Teesha laughed and he saw her relax.

"I think it's cool when guys can cook." She smiled.

"Me too, only I'm afraid I never progressed past the quiche."

She laughed again and he took the opportunity to slowly introduce the subject of her birthday party and what she remembered of the day. Teesha jumped right in.

"It is very clear in my mind, Mr. Cavanaugh."

"It's David, remember?"

"David." She smiled. "Mom was very specific. She said, *'Christina told me to come and get you.'* I remember it word for word. She said, *'I spoke to Chrissie. She is fine, but the water is a little cold so I need you three to hurry.'* She was angry at us, but she was very clear. Mariah and Francie didn't hear her because they were already swimming to the back of the cruiser. But I was right in front of her.

"She told us about that conversation," she went on. "I may have been the only one who heard her, but she told us. There is no doubt about it, David. That is what happened. That is the truth." Teesha's eyes were downcast. She looked everywhere around her aunt's large, comfortable living room, everywhere except at David.

And in that moment David felt a new respect for this terrified young girl who was willing to do anything to save her mother.

"Teesha, let me explain something. Your mom is a good person, right? She has brought you up to be a good person too. You know the difference between right and wrong, the truth and a lie. The only way you can get your mom into trouble is by lying. You utter one untruth and the prosecution will know it, the jury will know it, and they will assume your mom has told you to lie for her. You think you are helping and I know that. But lying won't help your mom. In fact, it will do the exact opposite."

Teesha looked up at David. She was not stupid. She knew he was right. If the jury thought her mom coached her in a lie, it would only make her look worse. She could not protect her.

"David," she said, now looking him straight in the eye, her face a mixture of realization, hopelessness and despair. "You tell me not to lie, but what choice do I have? I know she spoke to Chrissie, but she just didn't spell it out to us." She took a breath. "We were behaving like a pack of idiots—sixteen-year-olds acting like a bunch of kids. It is our fault—no, *my* fault. I knew we shouldn't have sailed into the bay, or taken off our life jackets. I drank Francie's champagne, I agreed with Chrissie when she suggested she should swim out to the cruiser. Don't you see?"

David sat silently. Teesha wiped the tears with the back of her hand, pushed her long black braid behind her shoulder and went on.

"Have you ever watched those courtroom shows on TV?" she asked.

David nodded.

"Well, I watched one a few months ago where a daughter covered up for her dad, who killed her mom. She lied, saying she accidentally fired her father's gun. The dad got off and the daughter got off too, because she said it was an accident. Then they find out the dad really was guilty, but they couldn't try him again because of, um . . ."

"Double jeopardy."

"That's right."

Not so much Law 101, more like Law & Order *101,* thought David.

"Well," she went on. "I've been thinking maybe there is a way for me to take the blame. Maybe there is a story we can tell that can save us all. I have been trying to work out a scenario in which this could work. How we could use the whole double jeopardy thing, or some other law that would protect my mom and bring her home to me. But I keep coming up with the same problem. There is no crime to cover up. This really was an accident."

David looked at Teesha, seventeen going on forty-five, and felt the worst he had felt in weeks. For there was nothing he could say to make this better, no great legal solution, no rabbit out of a hat. So he said all he could say, knowing that false comfort would be unfair and she was too smart for it anyway.

"You're right, Teesha, there was no crime and that is our problem. We are starting with nothing and praying the truth will be enough."

David asked Delia for another cup of coffee, thinking it best they take a break before pushing on. Teesha was happy for the chance to catch her breath, and after a few minutes in the bathroom and a hot cup of cocoa with Sara, she returned to her seat by the living room window.

After another hour of questions it was soon clear that Teesha's recollection of events mirrored Mariah's, which was devastating for the defense. David had suspected this would be the case but was hoping against hell that Teesha could provide something more concrete. It was getting late and he was almost done when he thought of one more issue that had to be explored again. It was a long shot, but at this stage anything was worth a try.

"Teesha, can you remember seeing anyone else during the course of the day? Anyone who may have seen you on the outboard or seen Christina swim to the cruiser?"

"I remember it was pretty quiet. I remember thinking we could be as noisy as we wanted without annoying anyone. When Francie popped the champagne, we yelled at her to keep it down but there was no one there to . . ."

She paused.

"What? What is it, Teesha?"

"I think . . ."

"You think . . . ?"

"I think maybe there was someone. No, two people, a couple."

"Where? Where were they?"

"On the beach, Turtle Beach, up the other end. I remember thinking Mom might hear the pop, but she was too far away. So my head turned full circle, toward land. There was a couple. Asian, I think. Having a picnic on the beach. They looked like tourists. They were a way off, but I'm pretty sure . . ."

Her eyes came alive.

"David, maybe they saw Chrissie swim out, maybe they had a better view around the outcrop, out to the cruiser. Why didn't I think of this before?"

"Because you've had so much to cope with . . . *too* much. But that doesn't matter, you're remembering now. Try to think harder, close your eyes, picture them. Were they old, young, large, thin, short, tall . . ."

"They were young, a young couple. Both of them were slim, the man was pretty tall, I think, or the girl was short. She had long hair, tied back, and she was . . ."

"She was what, Teesha? Think."

"She was slim, but when she turned side on . . . David, I think she might have been pregnant."

21

"You're going to have to talk fast because my shift starts in an hour," said Lisa Cavanaugh over the clatter typical of a Monday morning at Myrtle's.

"No . . . wait, let me start. You are an awful, horrible,

neglectful brother and I hate you. There! It had to be said. You promised you'd call me over the weekend."

"I did call," said David.

"Sure, at eleven o'clock last night to invite me to a quick breakfast at Myrtle's."

"Eleven o'clock Sunday night is still technically the weekend."

"Can it, DC. This is me you're talking to." She gave him one of her feigned dark stares before grabbing her juice and swallowing half the glass in three seconds flat.

"Well, come on then," she went on. "Let's hear it; what's going on with you? What's happening with your case? All I know is what I read in the newspapers. This is big stuff, David. Seriously, I mean how are you, really?"

A wide-eyed Lisa said all of this while shoveling forkfuls of egg, tomato and sausage into her mouth. She was petite—five foot four—and David never knew where she put it.

"Everything all right over here?" said Mick, pouring David more coffee and smiling at Lisa.

"Great, Mick. Super as usual." Lisa grinned.

"He been neglecting you?" Mick asked in jest, cocking his head at David.

"See." Lisa smiled at her brother, blowing a strand of long, dark hair away from her green eyes. "Mick understands."

"All right already," said David, glad of the relief after a weekend of hard work.

"Just keeping you on your toes," grinned his sister.

"And fair enough too," said Mick, winking at Lisa before moving on to the next table.

"So . . . ?"

"So you're right. It's pretty big."

David went on to explain the basics of their case, all the while trying not to worry his sister in the process. Lisa liked to play it for laughs, but David knew her lighthearted banter was often a cover-up for concern.

He talked on for fifteen minutes, telling her of his anger at the charge in the first place and his crazy, self-imposed time limit.

"So are you going to win?"

That was Lisa, straight to the point.

"I . . . ah . . ."

Then it hit him. Usually he had a fair idea of his chances in court and, luckily, most of the time he could answer yes to such a question without too much hesitation. But no one had asked him this question with regard to the Martin case, and it scared the hell out of him that he did not know what to say.

Lisa saw the fear in his eyes and reached across the table to hold her brother's hand.

"DC, if it makes any difference. I think you will—no, I *know* you are going to win."

"Either that," he said, grateful for the encouragement, "or die trying."

. . .

It was early.

Senator Haynes was almost out the door when he heard her footsteps behind him. But it wasn't his wife, it was Agnes and, strangely, he felt a small wave of relief.

He had spent most of the weekend at the office, calling friends, lunching with media owners, touching base with associates—basically campaigning for his own cause, making sure the right people with the right amount of power were saying the right things to those who mattered. And by doing so, he knew, he had been neglecting Elizabeth.

"Senator."

"Yes, Agnes? What is it?"

"Sir, I just wanted you to know that Mrs. Haynes, well, I know you have been concerned, and rightly so under the circumstances."

"Agnes, I am running late."

"Yes, sir. Well, I just wanted to say that she has been so much better. I truly think she has found a way to deal with it all. She has thrown herself into the banquet arrangements and seems to be more . . . ah, focused. Yesterday she found the strength to go through Christina's things, start to pack them in boxes. I just thought this might make you feel a little more at ease, sir—knowing she was better."

Agnes had been with them for as long as Haynes could remember; she had worked for the Whitmans when she was a teenager, and then had come with Elizabeth when she moved to her new home in Boston. She was helpful, hardworking and, most important, loyal. She had been a good influence on his daughter—all in all, a team player. He made a mental note to give her a bonus in her next pay.

"Thank you, Agnes. I'm glad. Thank you for telling me."

"Anything I can do, Senator. I know it will take time, but I honestly feel she is on the right track. She will be all right, sir. I just know it."

. . .

In the Commonwealth of Massachusetts, and throughout the country, the preparation for any trial involved the filing of numerous motions. Many of these submissions were part of the pretrial routine, and most were filed as insurance against a negative result for the defense and the need to call upon them later when appearing before the appellate court.

The possibilities were endless—there were motions for discovery, production and inspection of evidence; motions to disclose evidence favorable to the accused; motions to suppress evidence; motions for a list of all the state's witnesses; and motions for the state to produce all criminal records of witnesses.

On the other hand, the state could also file any number of motions. These might include the motion for a speedy trial, or to dismiss information or compel discovery. It was all about insurance, hedging your bets, dotting the i's and crossing the t's.

While motions were generally brief and to the point, the process still took time and much of David's and his team's week would be spent making sure their "insurance" was paid up in full. David knew such paperwork could be done by associates, but Arthur agreed that in this case they should prepare the briefs themselves and make sure their chances, in the event of an appeal, were as strong as possible. Of course, this was depressing work, for it meant admitting there was a possibility of defeat, but it was also reality and therefore they approached it with the necessary stoicism.

Despite all this, Teesha's revelations regarding the Asian couple were definitely at the forefront of their minds and had, in effect, turned their course of discovery upside down. Con and Sam hit the phones first thing Monday calling and recalling every hotel and tour operator in the Cape Ann area. Sam in particular felt individually responsible for not discovering evidence of any witnesses earlier, and took on finding the Asian couple as a personal quest.

Three days of endless telephone calls turned up nothing and David realized that if they had any chance of finding the couple, they would need to go to Gloucester and talk to the locals firsthand. They all realized that if the young couple were tourists, chances were they were home by now, and home could be anywhere—here or abroad. The search seemed impossible, but given that it was the one piece of evidence that could prove Rayna's version of events, they clung to it and swore not to give up until the mysterious Asian vacationers were tracked down.

David couldn't help but feel that there must be another way; he needed an ally with contacts—ways and means of finding the impossible. And then the following morning the tide finally started to turn their way.

22

NO MOTIVE . . . TRY GOOD OLD-FASHIONED HATE
Legal Comment and Guest Editorial by Marc Rigotti

Hate is an unnecessary word.

I say this not because I do not think human beings are capable of strong negative feelings toward one another, but because there are so many more accurate words that offer greater clarity in definition.

In other words, it is not so much unnecessary as un-specific.

Think about it.

Abhorrence, revulsion, disgust, loathing, detestation, repugnance—these and many more refer to hate, but somehow hit the nail on each specific head with greater precision.

Hate is too general—it is like saying the sea is only one shade of blue.

Why then is it possible for our intelligent, superior system of justice to use this word—this erroneous oversimplification—as a motive for a crime as serious as murder.

The Martin case is evidence of this major anomaly in our legal process.

Rayna Martin is accused of leaving an unconscious white teenager in the water, leaving her to drown so that she might save three African American girls in her stead.

According to the state, her motive was hate.

Even if Mrs. Martin were guilty of the alleged crime, and many believe she is not, why is the motive hate? Why not desperation to save her own daughter? Why not pure mathematics: that it is better to save three than one? Probably because these motives require a charge of manslaughter rather than the sexier one of murder two.

One might be led to believe that a motive such as hate is used when no other seems to fit. It is the motive you apply when all others seem ridiculous, making it all the more ridiculous itself.

That, of course, begs the question why a respected citizen, who spends her life helping people of all races, should fall prey to the law's most absurd definition of *motive*.

Perhaps it is not the accused but the accusers who suffer from an overzealous case of abhorrence, revulsion, disgust, loathing, detestation, repugnance.

Then again, perhaps in this case none of the above words are hitting that proverbial nail on that proverbial head.

Perhaps the more appropriate word in this instance is *revenge*.

There, he had done it.

It had taken him almost a week to get the piece approved. It had been read and reread by at least twenty lawyers, and in the end, only half of them had given their legal nod of approval.

"The key," Rigotti's editor, Bud Wiseman, had argued, "is to run it as editorial. That way we are not printing it as fact but as a thought piece." Bud had looked at the room full of suits hoping to see a vote of unanimous agreement. What he got was dissent, warnings and another hour of legal mumbo jumbo.

In the end, it was Bud's call and Rigotti almost burst with admiration for his boss, who had looked at the room of discerning faces, turned to his editorial manager and simply said, "Run it—page six," before replacing the soggy cigar in his mouth and stomping off to his office.

Bud Wiseman—scruffy, overworked, short-tempered, opinionated hero! Marc knew the piece would, to put it mildly, "ruffle a few feathers," enough to trigger a reaction from one or both sides of the legal fence, and he and Bud hoped he was right.

Now it was a matter of time. He would wait a little, start making the right calls and pray the defense would finally agree to speak with him. He had probably scared the hell out of Ed Washington—nothing personal, but the guy had made his own bed, so to speak. What he really wanted was a reaction from Haynes or the DA.

There was merit in the theory that the media was the fourth arm of government. It wasn't particularly accurate, of course; it was more likely an understatement. The media was actually first in rank when it came to public influence.

Let's see where we go from here, he thought. Good or bad news, depending on where you stood, travels fast. He sipped his coffee and looked at his watch—a little after seven. He knew someone would knee jerk off his editorial. It would just be a matter of who.

. . .

Rayna Martin put down the newspaper and looked at David across the chipped, laminated interview room table. "This is good," she said. "This is—"

"Just what we needed," he finished.

"Rigotti is an ally," she said, her voice echoing around the small cinderblock room.

"Rigotti knows something. This is his way of getting his point across without landing his paper in court for influencing a matter sub judice. It's fact disguised as opinion, and if I know Marc, aimed decidedly at getting a rise out of the prosecution."

"I'm sure he won't be disappointed."

"I'm sure you're right."

They sat quietly for a minute enjoying their small victory.

"Is there any way we can find out why Mr. Rigotti ran this piece now?" asked Rayna. "Something must have prompted him to climb so far out on a limb."

"Something or someone," said David.

"Whatever the case, he certainly seems to be on our side."

"That's what I'm counting on—because I'm about to ask him a favor."

"What's that?" asked Rayna.

"I'll get to that later," he said, reaching into his briefcase to retrieve a miniature tape recorder. "First, I have some more good news for you, Mrs. Martin."

"You do?" she said with a half smile. "How so?"

"Let's listen to Teesha's interview tape. I want you to hear this for yourself."

• • •

Riddle me this, Batman: When is the Boy Wonder no longer the Boy Wonder?

Answer: When the Bat decides he wants to eat his Robin for breakfast.

It had been a long day, his mind was playing tricks on him and he had no idea why this ridiculous riddle had entered his head. He didn't even like Batman. Never went through the superhero phase as a kid. Thought it was stupid make-believe rubbish. A waste of time.

So why now was he, Roger Katz, the second most powerful prosecutor in the city (well, probably *the* most powerful considering his boss's lack of cojones), thinking about some stupid also-ran who never had a chance in hell of graduating to the top job. Probably because, as of early this morning when Haynes had treated him like a dim-witted lackey, his career prospects were looking frighteningly similar.

The *Tribune* editorial had hit him like a truck. Haynes had been on the phone at 6:30 AM, interrupting his morning calisthenics, scaring the hell out of him, dropping the subtlety and going straight for the jugular.

Unlike Scaturro, Katz didn't have any skeletons. He had no family . . . well, none of any consequence, and thus thought he was safe from the senator's usual hit-'em-where-it-hurts-most threats.

But then he did it anyway, hit 'em where it hurt most, that is. One word: *career.* Which, of course, led to other associated terms like money, status, reputation, power. The message was clear. Control the press, make sure the *Tribune*—Marc Rigotti and his goddamned editor—never ran a piece like it again.

Wiseman finally came out of the morning conference to take his call at about 7:30 AM and as usual with these journalist bastards, went on about that freedom-of-the-press bullshit served up in that superior, working-class tone newspaper dinosaurs seemed to think was macho. Katz had threatened legal action, and promised that if such an editorial ran again, he would go straight to Judge Stein for a gag order. The only consolation was that his boss had obviously been hit even harder than him. She looked like a total wreck when he got in at eight-thirty and seemed to get progressively worse as the day wore on. Her door was shut for most of the morning, and he could have sworn he saw her enter the ladies' room with tears in her eyes. Women . . . no control!

Come to think of it, it was no wonder Haynes had asked (told) him to deal with the press. Scaturro just couldn't hack it. Her days were numbered no matter which way you looked at it. He would get the job done and everything would be sweet.

Ironically, Rigotti's slanderous piece had actually given

him an idea—a proposal that had the potential not only to put
him back in the good books but also to shoot him all the way
to the top. It was risky, and he might have to bide his time
until things turned a little more in their favor. But the senator
was a man who demanded all or nothing. No compromises,
no second bests.

"Well, okay then," he said aloud. "Let's give the man what
he wants. No compromise. No halfway. Let's put this woman
away for good."

. . .

David turned off the tape, sat forward on the well-worn vinyl
chair, placed his hands on his knees and looked across at
Rayna. She was smiling.

"I am so proud of her."

"You should be," he said. "But I'm afraid her version
doesn't give us confirmation of the conversation."

"I know," she said. "I just thought she might have . . ."

"Lied?"

"Yes."

"She did."

"Oh."

She smiled again. "Well, I suppose that just means she'll
go to any lengths to protect me, so I am just as proud."

"As I said."

They had been at it all day, going over every single detail.
Cross-referencing Rayna's account with Mariah's and finally
with the additional information most recently supplied by
Teesha. They talked about the Asian couple—Rayna had not
seen them—and what they may or may not have witnessed.
David told her how he and Sara planned to drive up to
Gloucester and stay for the weekend to see if they could
track down any contact information on the mysterious vacationing pair.

Next they talked about Teesha's account of what occurred
at the funeral—her altercation with Elizabeth Haynes and the
subsequent frenzy.

"I feel so responsible for all of this. Teesha is a strong,
bright girl, but what happened at that funeral was nothing
short of humiliating."

They sat in silence for a moment before Rayna looked up, a puzzled look on her face.

"What is it?" David asked.

"Something Teesha said about Mrs. Haynes—her skirt. She said her charm bracelet—it was too big for her and it caught on a thread. Teesha loves that bracelet, never takes it off. There are four bracelets in all. Teesha has one, Francie, Mariah and Christina have the other three. They are quite chunky, with thick links and lots of dangling charms.

"Anyway, Christina is smaller than the other three, she wears—I mean *wore*—hers on her ankle, as an anklet. It would jingle when she walked. Teesha told me her parents hated it, thought it was crass. She had it on that day. On her ankle, I'm sure of it. But I don't remember seeing it later, after she—"

"It must have come off in the water," said David, not sure where this was going, but sensing it might be something significant.

"Yes," said Rayna, now sitting up straight, her eyes wide, her face animated. "The bracelet was gone, but her ankle was all red where it should have been. I remember because when we lifted her onto the cruiser, the girls took her upper body and I grabbed her feet—her ankles. She might even have been bleeding a little. But I'm not sure."

"Wait a minute," said David, getting to his feet. "That day I was with the Jordans, Ewan mentioned something about the fishing nets right near where you were anchored. He said it used to be a major fishing haven but the area around Essex Bay had been largely fished out. He also said there were still some old nets in place, and that sometimes boats would get caught in them."

"What are you saying? Do you think that—"

"The tide was low, right? In fact, according to Sam and Con's report, it was at its lowest at late morning—not long before Christina swam out to the cruiser. Maybe her foot caught and maybe she tried to pull loose, and if she couldn't, then maybe that's how she drowned."

Rayna looked up at David, who was already out of his

chair and packing his bag. "Where are you going?" she asked.

"Back to the office to check the autopsy report."

"Of course, they would have noted the ankle injury."

"Yes, and if they did, we missed it."

23

"You have made the right decision, Elizabeth," said Caroline Croft, coiffed and coutured from head to toe. Watermelon pink Anne Klein suit, white blouse, stockinged legs and conservative shoes. "You have been silent for long enough. You are Christina's mother, and if anyone deserves to have a say, it is you."

With this last comment she reached over and covered Elizabeth's hand with her own, giving it a little pat. Elizabeth noticed that her nail polish was red, far too red for the pastel in her suit, but this was an unimportant matter and she had more pressing things to focus on today.

Caroline had been phoning Elizabeth daily since their afternoon tea two weeks ago. She had planted the idea during that Thursday gathering. Not that you could call it a "gathering" she thought, considering there were only three of them in attendance, the rest of the fickle mob having canceled at the last minute.

As soon as Sophia had gone to the powder room (to correct the bleeding dark terra-cotta liner on her upper lip), Caroline had suggested that Elizabeth could use her television program, the Friday night ratings winner *Newsline,* as a means of expressing her point of view. She could talk of her grief, her rights as a mother to speak freely and her determination to see that justice was done.

At first Elizabeth had completely disregarded the idea. For starters, Rudolph would be furious that she had not canceled the afternoon tea, and God only knows what he would do if she went public with her feelings. It simply wasn't done, not now, not ever.

Two weeks ago she had ached for her husband's attention—watching him work in his study hour after hour and feeling so horribly useless, so stupid, a complete and utter nuisance. Two weeks ago this particular discovery—one of two she had hidden (the second of which she had not yet been able to bring herself to open), after finally finding the courage to sort through Christina's room—would have sent her over the edge. But that was then, before her welcome burst of strength, and her redefined purpose.

Now she felt empowered, and in the past twenty-four hours, fueled by a new dose of determination in the form of that horrible Mr. Rigotti's piece in the *Tribune*. So she had decided then and there. It was time her husband knew that she was "back." It was time to make her move.

As soon as Rudolph had left for the office late yesterday morning, she placed a call to her friend, who promised to have a crew available by three.

"No, not today," she had said, wanting time to prepare. "Tomorrow morning—say, ten?"

She set about organizing a set of tasks for Agnes, all of which would involve long errands into the city for most of the day. She knew she had to be careful. She had important information to relay and spent the rest of Thursday rehearsing her "performance" over and over in front of her bedroom mirror. She improved with every run-through. Topher would have been proud.

If she was right, and she had a feeling she was, she held the power to destroy the Martin woman and everything she represented. She just had to keep her nerve and let this thing play out one word at a time. Rudi would be so proud.

So here she sat, all coiffed and coutured herself in a pale blue Chanel with appropriate flesh-colored nail polish, situated directly in front of her prize pale cerise roses, sipping mineral water with a twist of lemon. She looked at the discovery sitting innocently, powerfully, on the table beside her and then took a few long, deep breaths to calm herself before the cameras started to roll.

24

"Come on, Joseph," he yelled. "You can do it, buddy. That's it. Eye on the ball."

He did not know it then, but she was watching him from the top of the hill.

Whack.

Joseph Mannix Jr. hit it to the left, over the head of the kid on third base, sending a scramble of little fielders chasing the ball before all three runners made it home.

"Good swing, Joseph. Come on, buddy, bring it home."

"He's good."

Joe Mannix turned to see Loretta Scaturro standing behind him. At first he didn't recognize her in blue track pants and a white windbreaker with a Boston Red Sox baseball cap securing her thick, dark hair in a short ponytail out the back.

"Better than his old man ever was. But don't tell him that." Joe smiled at the DA, not sure what to make of this meeting—chance, coincidence, whatever it was.

They both turned back to the game to see Joseph slide over home plate and then drown in a sea of yellow and red uniforms as his fellow teammates crowded around to congratulate their star player on a home run, which pretty much stitched up the game for the home team.

"You follow the Sox?" said Joe, trying to fill the awkward silence.

"A little. My dad used to take me to Fenway every week-

end when I was a kid. Just don't seem to have the time anymore."

"I know what you mean."

Another pause.

"Ms. Scaturro—"

"Loretta. It is Saturday, after all, Joe."

"Loretta, you know someone playing here today?"

"No, this is no coincidence. I called your home and your
wife told me you'd be here."

"Okay, well . . . here I am."

Joe was now more than just a little uncomfortable. It wasn't
that the DA's office and the police had ever been enemies; it
was just that a meeting like this was highly unusual. Their
relationship was a professional one and Mannix respected
Scaturro's ability as an attorney, but there was still some tension. Four years ago Scaturro had made a very vocal electoral
promise to "fight police brutality" which had pretty much
rubbed everyone in uniform, including Joe and his homicide
team, the wrong way.

Joe also knew that Scaturro's office had been guilty of using the police as scapegoats when a trial turned against them.
Nothing new in that, and more often than not it was ADA
Katz who was guilty of suggesting police incompetence every
time he managed to lose a case. But Scaturro was the boss
and she could at least have attempted to pull in the reins on
her ambitious deputy.

Scaturro nodded toward a bench next to the mound and
Joe followed her to sit.

"I respect you, Joe. I trust you—otherwise I wouldn't be
here."

"Okay."

Joe always limited his responses to one or two words when
he wanted the other party to provide as much information as
possible. It never failed.

"I'm worried about the Haynes case."

A pause—with no response from Mannix.

"I am concerned that it might spiral out of control."

"Isn't it the DA's job to control a case at trial?"

"Yes. Yes, it is; that's why I am so worried. I fear that
this one—the press, the public interest, the issues between

my deputy and opposing counsel." She paused again, but Joe was giving her nothing. "And the people involved—the family of the victim." She turned to look at him, taking off her sunglasses. "Look, Joe, you and I have always been straight with each other. This isn't easy for me; believe it or not, I don't often frequent Saturday Little League."

Joe smiled. "I guessed as much. What is it, Loretta?"

"You read Rigotti's piece?"

"Yeah, I saw it."

"Then you can imagine the past few days have been . . . difficult."

Another pause.

"I'm nervous, Joe. I fear this one is going to claim more victims than just Christina Haynes."

"Some would say Rayna Martin has already been played as a victim," he said.

"True, but a girl is dead and Rayna Martin was responsible for her . . . but that's not my point." She turned toward him. "I need your help, Joe. I might have to ask a favor or two as we get closer to trial. I might need you to make some discreet investigations for me, off the record, if you like."

"Loretta, I can't—"

"They won't influence the facts of the case—I give you my word on that. If anything, it could mean making sure no one else can unduly interfere with the judicial process. I just might need some . . . protec—collateral."

Joe noted her slip.

"I'm not a PI, Loretta, and my team isn't for hire."

"Of course not. But you are a decent man." She put her sunglasses on again as if preparing to leave. "Bottom line—I'm scared, Joe."

He looked at her and saw she was telling the truth. Maybe even understating it a little.

"So will you?" she began.

"Let's just say I'll listen to you if and when the time comes."

"All right, that's fair enough," she said, her shoulders relaxing with at least some sense of relief.

"He is good," she said, signaling toward Joseph junior, who was now on the bench waving at his dad.

"Yeah. Maybe one day he'll be a big baseball star so the whole family can retire and live like royalty."

"Now wouldn't that be nice." -

• • •

It was late afternoon on the first day of summer, and the weather was perfect.

As the sun started its inland decent, the vacationers at Cape Ann looked satisfied and refreshed as they lingered in holiday mode licking gelatos, strolling the waterside galleries and sipping iced coffee under colorful umbrellas outside colorful cafés.

In any other universe, thought David, who was himself downing a cold Coke as he waited for Sara at the Madfish Grille, a popular dockside café at Rocky Neck across from Gloucester Harbor. The Madfish was on Art Gallery Way, a picturesque strip littered with multihued weatherboard huts, each selling original arts and crafts, antiques, gifts and other pretty knickknacks.

Here I am, sitting in one of the most interesting seaports in the country, sipping a cold Coke on a hot day and waiting for a very beautiful girl . . .

It had been a good week. First, there was Teesha's recollection of possible witnesses, followed by Rigotti's editorial, and then Rayna's memory of Christina's missing anklet and his subsequent theory that the anklet might have caught on some of the old trawler nets.

He had been right. The autopsy report had noted "evidence of significant subcutaneous bleeding on the lower right leg with grazes on the ankle forming several circular impressions around the upper foot." It also suggested that an "exterior constrictor contributed to the numerous small abrasions." There was even a photo of the ankle injury to match.

David blamed himself. He and Sara had read the report that morning at Myrtle's, but they had only focused on the details relating to the drowning, and the fact that the coroner could not find any other probable cause of death. And maybe he had been too distracted by his partner to . . .

Despite the fact that he was angry at himself for missing such a detail, he could not help but think that this trip to Gloucester was key to their making a break in the case. With any luck, the next two days would not only see them find evidence of the Asian couple's identity and whereabouts, but also give them some indication of Christina's cause of death. Both were long shots, but at the very least they felt as if they were physically doing something. And "doing" felt good—especially after the setbacks and delays of the past weeks.

"Hi," Sara said, collapsing into the blue canvas chair opposite him. She reached across the table, grabbed his half-drunk, ice-filled, tall glass of Coke and downed it in a matter of seconds. Then she bent down and took off her shoes. David saw the name Manolo Blahnik on the inside label and recalled that Blahnik was one of those much celebrated European geniuses who made big money by torturing the feet of beautiful, shoe-obsessed women.

"Better," she said, wiping some brown bubbles from her top lip and smiling.

In any other universe, he thought again.

"You first," she said, plonking her bag on the table with various tour brochures spilling from its mouth.

"Okay, I visited forty-five businesses and was offered everything from top-class cruiser rental to a five-dollar foot massage from the wife of a very dodgy operator known as Discount Dick. Twenty-five of the forty-five open for business in mid-May. Of the remaining twenty, seven offer structured cruises where the tourists stay on board all day, which, obviously, rules them out.

"That leaves thirteen, five of which operate only in the immediate cape area and do not travel as far west as Turtle Beach, where Teesha saw her witnesses. The remaining eight do operate in early May, do offer tours to Essex Bay and did allow me to look at their booking sheets, none of which showed any reservations for anyone with an Asian name."

"And none of them remembered meeting the couple?"

"No. I'm afraid I've come up blank. What about you?" said

David, signaling the brightly attired waiter that the two fresh Cokes belonged to them.

"Forty-three negatives, I'm afraid. But," she said, thanking the waiter, taking the cold fizzy drink and discarding the straw before swallowing half the glass, "I did meet with one guy who had some pretty interesting offers."

"Tell him you're taken," said David, regretting it as soon as it came out. "Sorry, I didn't mean—"

"It's okay." She smiled. "Believe me, he was no competition." She shuffled the brochures in front of her.

"His name was Tom Cruise—seriously, Tom Cruise."

David laughed, grateful for the comic relief.

"Any resemblance?"

"Only to his mother." She smiled again.

"Anyway, he runs a small business out of Gloucester called The Top Gun, which offers helicopter drops—you know, take a couple up, set them on a deserted beach with a hamper, leave them alone for the day, pick them up and charge a couple of hundred for the pleasure. He says the tours are particularly popular with Japanese visitors."

"Was he operating the first week of May?"

"Legally, no; illegally, yes. He doesn't actually have a license."

"He told you this?"

"I told you he made me a few offers; I just delayed my polite refusals until we had finished our chat."

"Sara Davis!"

"Don't knock it, Mr. Forty-five Operators with Nothing to Show."

"Point taken. Okay, so—"

"So he admits he hires a bunch of renegade pilots, guys who might not have up-to-date licenses themselves. Pays them cash, by the day, no questions asked."

"And on May fourth?"

"On May fourth Mr. Cruise sold a two-hundred-fifty-dollar romantic getaway package to Mr. and Mrs. Sato Kyoji, the pickup at Beverly Airport and the drop-off at Turtle Beach, which is illegal in itself, given that the beach is private. That would have put them right in front of where our teenagers went overboard, and the timing could not be more perfect."

"Sara, I don't believe it."

"Wait, it gets better." She smiled.

"According to Mr. Cruise, and I quote, 'The missus had a bun in the oven.' "

. . .

"So what you're saying is," said Ewan Jordan as he stood to pour them another glass of Dutton Ranch Chardonnay, "you could have a cause of death."

It was just past eight and David and Sara were sitting at a foldaway dinner table on the front deck of Ewan's Beneteau 321, now moored at Gloucester Marina. Ewan, who had offered to be their guide on this fact-finding mission, had just cooked some fresh mackerel, marinated in lemon juice and white wine, on the top-deck grill, before serving it with a green salad with light vinaigrette and crisp, fresh rolls on the side.

"That's a good thing, right?" said their host, taking a seat across from them.

David and Sara looked at each other before turning back to Ewan.

"Yes and no," answered Sara. "We're surmising that the anklet got caught in the netting and pulled her under. She was a little drunk, so her senses were not one hundred percent. She probably tugged at the netting and that's why the anklet cut into her skin."

"Right," said Ewan, ready and willing to help play supersleuth.

"But that doesn't necessarily improve our case," Sara went on. "The prosecution will just say her foot got caught before Rayna saw her, which still leaves them to argue she was unconscious and could have been revived. We can claim her foot was caught *after* the conversation, but we can't prove it. None of this wins us any brownie points with the jury."

And David knew she was right.

"Hold on now," said Ewan, shifting his tall frame forward in the green canvas deck chair. "My experience is pretty much with creatures of the four-legged variety, but it seems to me your advantage could be in the timing."

"How so?" asked David.

"Take an animal, say a dog or a rabbit caught in a trap. It's a slow way to die; they tug at what holds them so long and so hard that often times they end up amputating themselves."

They all looked at him blankly.

"That takes some doing—hours, in fact," he said, only to see more blank stares.

"Okay, help me out here," he went on. "How much time elapsed between when Rayna lost sight of the girls and when she saw Christina near the cruiser?"

"Ah, ten, fifteen minutes max," said David.

"Right, so in that time the girls down a drink or two, capsize the boat and then Christina makes the swim."

"Right," said David.

"So those cuts on her ankle—they took time to procure. She must have tugged at those nets until she bled, till her skin was raw, poor kid. Just like the rabbit and the dog except that she also had to struggle to keep her head above water."

"So," said David, now following his lead. "That struggle had to happen *after* Rayna left her simply because there was no time for it to happen beforehand."

"If the autopsy report is accurate—and you have to assume it is—those cuts took at least five minutes to procure. Ask your coroner; I am sure they would agree. The human body doesn't lie," said Ewan.

"He's right," said David, looking at Sara.

"Ewan," said Sara. "You're a genius."

"Nah," said Ewan. "But I once cured a twenty-year-old turtle of depression, and that was pretty cool."

• • •

Three hours later Ewan had retired to a makeshift bed on the top deck. He had offered to bunk under the stars to give the two below-deck quarters to David and Sara.

The pair were now sitting at the back of the yacht, their feet dangling over the edge, the water lapping peacefully against the hull and the moon providing enough light for them to see each other's faces.

"They hurt, don't they?" said David.

"What?"

"Your feet. They hurt."

"They do not."

"Yes, they do. Those shoes cost you a fortune and you won't admit that they cut off your circulation."

"Well," she smiled, "maybe just a little."

They sat in silence for a minute longer, looking at the stars, enjoying the peace. David noted that despite the fact that they had spent many working hours alone together over the past weeks, tonight felt different. Maybe it was the moonlight setting or the fact that their investigations were finally getting somewhere, but whatever the case, he knew the growing attraction he felt toward Sara was becoming more and more difficult to suppress. Just sitting next to her made him want to lean across and kiss her, to run his hands through her hair, to feel her breath against his skin. It took all of his strength not to turn to her and tell her how much he wanted her. The only compensation was a sense of hope that she felt the same way.

"More wine?" he asked at last.

"No, thanks," she said, smiling.

"Big day."

"Yeah, we got lucky. Feels good."

"Finding the Satos won't be easy," he went on, trying to get his thoughts back on track. "They are probably back in Tokyo by now."

"We just have to pray the details on the card are enough."

The Satos had completed a registration card when they booked the helicopter tour. Their names were in English, but the information for their address was limited to one or two words written in Japanese. It appeared as though they were from Tokyo, but David planned to find a translator as soon as possible and hoped there was enough detail to give them solid contact information.

"It's incredible out here at night," Sara said, looking upward, her long neck stretching gracefully, her profile a perfect silhouette against the reflected moonlight that bounced off the water and softened as it dispersed upward toward her face.

"Incredible," he said, looking at her.

"It's strange, isn't it, that Christina's death has resulted in our being here in this beautiful place. I almost feel guilty." She turned to face him then, her eyes a brilliant blue.

"Don't," he said, his fingertips now resting against hers, their slightest touch providing a mixture of comfort and exhilaration. "There is nothing we could have done."

They sat in silence for a while, their fingers now entwined, listening to the soothing sound of the water, cooled by the slight breeze that had finally arrived to temper the memory of the day's summer sun. David had no idea how he managed to "leave it at that," but he realized that as much as he wanted to make love to Sara right then and there, he wanted *her* to want it more—and if that meant waiting until this trial was over, then so be it.

"Timing is everything," she said at last, as if reading his mind.

"What do you mean?" he asked.

"Well, you know, we all stumble through life trying to get it right—pacing things, making decisions, forming priorities, influencing our so-called fate. Sometimes I think we can be too cautious. Sometimes I just think we should say 'What the hell.'"

"I know what you mean," he said. And he did.

"I was thinking tonight how the small decisions we make can change everything," she said. "I mean, if Christina hadn't argued with her parents, not gone to the party, not worn that bracelet on her ankle . . . if she had obeyed them, she would still be alive."

"Yes, but she was reaching a stage in her life where she was questioning their beliefs. She was filled with idealism and stifled by their narrow-mindedness; she was on her way to breaking out."

"You think so?" she said.

"You don't?"

"Well, I don't want you to think I am some sort of pessimist and I don't want to dampen your positive perspective on life. I think that is what I like most about you." She smiled at him as she said this. "But you don't just break away from being a Haynes. She would have gone through her idealistic teenage years, given her parents a few headaches, caused them a few sleepless nights. But she would have come back into the fold, probably gone to Wellesley, attended country club parties, married a nice white Ivy League boy. And most likely, her three friends would be nothing more than names with addresses she sent Christmas cards to each December."

25

The weather had turned. The sky was gray and the wind fresh with a light rain kissing the water's surface, making millions of dissolving concentric circles. They had set sail after breakfast, heading north up the Annisquam to Ipswich Bay and then west toward Castle Neck Peninsula. They took it slowly, retracing Rayna's voyage, willing to wait until the tide was low enough for them to re-create the events of May 4.

"What time is it?" asked Ewan.

"Almost two," said David.

"I think this is as low as it's gonna get today."

The conditions were vastly different from those on the day of the accident, but they wanted to see if the old fishing nets were visible beneath the choppy surface.

"I can't see a thing," said Sara, pulling the hood of her white sailing jacket over her head.

"Me neither," said Ewan. "The swell is lifting the sand and silt off the seabed floor. Visibility is zero."

"Ewan," said David. "You mentioned there were some snorkels and masks on board."

"Sure are."

"It's probably freezing in there," said Sara.

"Actually," said Ewan, "it's not too bad, probably about seventy degrees."

"Well?" said David.

"What are we waiting for?" said Ewan, already pulling his windbreaker over his head.

For a big man, Ewan was very agile. He wore swim shorts and a wet suit vest and handed David a "short john," or sleeveless wet suit. David stripped down to his shorts, pulling the wet suit up and over his shoulders. Sara zipped him up at the back, and he pulled the snorkel and mask over his head.

"Here goes nothing," he said as they jumped over the side.

They swam out from the yacht, disturbing the pretty patterns made by the rain with strong determined strokes. Sara could not help but feel anxious as she watched them swim farther away. She knew this was where Christina had lost her life and felt an illogical desire to scream for David to get back on board. For the next thirty minutes she watched them snorkel, dive and swim—every now and again shouting and signaling to each other, the wind and rain making it impossible for her to hear what they were saying. As they turned back toward the yacht, Sara grabbed two large beach towels to have ready to hand to them as they climbed back on board.

"Thanks," said David. "Ewan lied about the temperature being comfortable."

"Ah, come on," said Ewan with a smile. "It wasn't so bad."

"Cut it out, you two. Just tell me what you saw."

"Okay, okay," said David. "It's the nets . . . they're everywhere."

"One big fat tangled mess down there," confirmed Ewan.

"And they are just below the surface," said David. "My feet got caught a few times—had to shake them loose. If her anklet was caught, even trying to undo the clasp would have been close to impossible. Especially for a panicked teenager who had had a few drinks."

"You were right then," said Sara.

"No question," said David. "It's like net soup out there. Once she was caught, Christina didn't stand a chance."

26

"So why now?"

David and his journalist friend Marc Rigotti had just been served two cold beers after sitting in the far corner of Bristow's Bar and Steakhouse, a small but popular downtown bar with a predictable but satisfying menu of grills, all served with a generous serving of chunky-style French fries and crisp green salad.

"What do you mean?" said Rigotti, obviously knowing exactly what David meant.

"Come on, Marc. That editorial was a probing mission. You were trying to get a reaction and my guess is you got it."

"You're here, aren't you?"

"Exactly. And I would imagine there was a similar perhaps more spirited response from the opposing team?"

If this was a question, Rigotti's only answer was a shrug.

"Okay," said David, knowing the gesture itself meant Rigotti had had to deflect a few swipes from the commonwealth. "But you still haven't answered my question."

"I thought I was the one who was supposed to be asking the questions."

David threw up his hands in frustration.

"All right, all right," said Rigotti, obviously knowing when he had reached his limit. "You wanna know why now?"

Marc was a born-and-bred New Yorker and his accent betrayed him. He had that sharp edge they bred in the Big Apple, that brazenness that comes from growing up in the world's biggest metropolis and knowing it. David had known the *Tribune*'s legal writer for years and they had always been straight with each other.

"I have a source," he began. "Not necessarily a willing one . . . more, shall we say, a person who gave me some information freely without realizing its significance."

"Okay." David was anxious to hear more.

"This source didn't as much tell me anything of note as suggest that a certain chain of events had taken place—that he was steered in a certain direction by someone with certain interests and now things were out of his control."

"And these events are detrimental to my client?"

"Ah . . ."

David knew Marc had to be careful; he would be mindful of his obligation as a journalist to protect his sources and would know he was walking a fine line here.

"Let's just say my editorial, the issues in it, were prompted by a conversation with the said source."

"The hate thing is a setup," said David.

"Well, one would think your team would have carried that opinion from the very beginning."

"Yes, but we need proof that the charge of murder two is bullshit. Hell, involuntary man is bullshit. From what you wrote, I'd say we were of the same mind regarding the motives of the prosecution, or rather, who is driving them."

"My opinion doesn't count."

"But your readers' opinions do. Whether we like it or not, the public is going to have a big effect on this trial."

"I thought you were trying to prevent that, keep it simple. Isn't that why you haven't returned my calls?"

"Yes, but that was before you set the cat among the pigeons," said David.

"I didn't do it for you."

"Hey, you really know how to hurt a guy. So why?"

"Because I'm a sap. I couldn't have lived with myself if I *hadn't* written it. Nothing pisses me off more than watching our so-called democratic system of justice screw itself and some poor innocent bastard in the process."

"My point exactly," said David. "You want your story,

you'll have it. The first posttrial interview with Rayna Martin guaranteed."

"And updates during the trial."

"Okay, but within legal reason."

"All right. So what's the catch?"

"No catch, just an opportunity," David replied. "You say you want to make sure an innocent person doesn't get screwed; well, I'm giving you the chance to help."

"I'm listening."

"I need to find a man and his wife."

"You have a name?" Marc fished for his notepad.

"Yes. It's Sato. S-a-t-o."

"Address?"

"Sure." David had to stifle a laugh. "They could still be vacationing somewhere along the eastern seaboard or be back home."

"And home is—"

"Tokyo."

Rigotti looked up, his face saying it all.

"You want me to find two people in a city of thirteen million?"

"Yeah. And Marc, I need you to find them now."

27

As Roger Katz shut his office door to show himself out (was it his imagination or had he actually backed out of the room with his head slightly bowed?), Rudolph Haynes could not help but smile. He looked at his watch. It was still early and he had at least another half hour before Louise and the rest of his staff rattled in to add their usual list of irrelevant items to his already cluttered agenda. His idea was actually quite remarkable—very confident, extremely bold. Katz wanted to go for all or nothing. He wanted to strike the count of involuntary manslaughter. He wanted to go for murder two and murder two alone.

Haynes stood up, out of his chair, pulled back the navy-blue drapes and looked out of his sun-drenched high-rise windows, surveying his city, his small antlike subjects scurrying obediently below. He had to admit the idea excited him. It had been a horrible week and this audacious, ambitious suggestion had sent a rush of adrenaline through his veins. *Careful,* he chided himself. He had to think this through. He took his seat again, closing his eyes, clearing his brain.

Part of the thought process, when considering any new variation to his plan, was to reflect upon the strategies of the greats: warriors like Alexander, Khan, Bonaparte, Nelson, Patton and MacArthur. Their philosophies often helped clarify his thoughts, guide his line of approach and, ultimately, strengthen his resolve, but, of course, none of them came close to Caesar. Gaius Julius Caesar was the greatest of them all, not because of the number of battles he had won but because of his all-around brilliance and his, dare he think it, similarities to Haynes himself.

Caesar lost his beloved father at sixteen. Haynes was only twenty-three when his father died. Caesar was tall and fair and well built, a remarkable resemblance to the senator himself. Caesar was a brilliant lawyer, with rich and powerful clients. He studied rhetoric at Rhodes and became a first-class public speaker. He mastered the art of politics, culminating in his receiving the highest political honor the Roman state could offer at the very young age of thirty-nine—the same age at which Haynes himself was first elected a U.S. senator. He possessed great magnetism, personal charm, masterful wit and, above all, led tens of thousands of loyal soldiers into battle, defeating millions and expanding the Roman Empire to include a landscape so vast that no one in history could compare.

And so to Caesar. What would the great Roman emperor think of Katz's suggestion?

Caesar once said: "I would rather be first in a little Iberian village than second in Rome." Meaning winning was everything; there was no room for second best. A conviction on the lesser sentence may be a conviction, but it would still be a defeat.

He also said: "Men freely believe that which they wish to be the truth." Men in general were a feeble species that would rather entertain an "acceptable" notion than one that was more abhorrent but closer to the truth. Katz, in fact, had made this point. He quite rightly pointed out that involuntary manslaughter gave the jury an out. If the jury so abhorred the Martin woman's actions that they preferred not to believe a woman could murder a teenager because of her skin color, they could subconsciously defer to the charge of involuntary manslaughter simply because it sat easier with their idealistic view of what the world should be. With only one charge to consider, the jury would have to convict on second degree murder, for they could not allow the murder of an innocent teenage girl to go unpunished.

Caesar also said: "He has not learned the lesson of life who does not every day surmount a fear." Right again. There was no challenge without fear. The risk made the victory all the sweeter. This was the part that Katz had liked the best. The abolition of the count of involuntary manslaughter meant there was only one alternative, and one sentence. When found guilty, Rayna Martin would be sentenced to life without parole and Katz would be the man who put her there, demolishing Cavanaugh's career in the process.

It was interesting how Scaturro barely entered the conversation. But then she was digging her own grave with her lack of dedication to the cause. She would be gone by the end of the year, replaced by her second in command, and Haynes would have the new DA tucked neatly in his pocket. *Perfect.*

He smiled slightly at this thought before refocusing on the issue at hand. They would have to time this correctly and file the motion at just the right moment. Katz was right—they needed a swing back in their favor. They needed the public back in their camp and this would be Katz's immediate priority. Once this was achieved, they could file the motion just

prior to jury selection, catching the defense on the hop. In the
meantime, Cavanaugh and his team could use a few more
obstacles in their course.

Haynes thought back to something Katz had told him
weeks earlier when he had asked why Cavanaugh hated him
so much—something about Katz defeating him in that murder trial, the case which ended in a girl's suicide. Cavanaugh
was attached to the defendant, and he blamed Katz for her
demise. There was something there, something Vincent could
use, manipulate, exploit. He would speak with him immediately. He would know what to do.

He could hear Louise enter the outer office and allowed
himself one final thought of Caesar before she knocked on his
door. Caesar had once said: *"Veni, vidi, vici"*—"I came, I
saw, I conquered."

Haynes smiled again. And so to war.

• • •

It was a macabre job. Trying to match the impressions on
Christina's skin with the piece of jewelry she had in common with her friends. But the markings were there, and quite
deep. The proofs not only corresponded with their theory,
they pretty much confirmed it.

"I think I can make out a heart shape; and look here—this
impression has to be the miniature peace sign. See?" said
David.

"Yes, I see."

Boston Chief Medical Examiner Gustav Svenson was a
man of few words. The Swedish-born Svenson was tall, over
six four, with a lithe frame and Nordic features. David handed
him Teesha's bracelet and he turned the shapes over in his
large hands, his long delicate fingers rotating the charms as
he looked at the photographs he had taken of Christina's right
foot a few weeks ago.

Svenson was practical and efficient. His reputation, like
that of most MEs, was one of proprosecution. But this was
somewhat unfair. Medical examiners, by the very nature of
their job, often provided the meat for the commonwealth's
case—the details of the nitty-gritty of murder—and thus
came across as antidefense.

David knew Svenson was unbiased and that despite his

low-key demeanor, he was relatively upbeat for a man who spent his life in the cold reality of mortuary rooms.

"So what do you think?" asked David. "Do we have a cause of death, or at least a probable one?"

"No, asphyxiation was the cause of death and drowning was the basis for such asphyxiation. But if you are asking me if this piece of jewelry acted as a trigger that led to such events, I would have to say, for want of any other logical explanation, that the scenario you describe is a plausible one."

They looked at the shots a minute longer before David broached the subject.

"So Gus, have you had any other ah . . . inquiries about—"

"David, you know it is not my job to give you information on what the prosecution may or may not have been asking of me."

"I know."

Another pause.

"I suppose you want to take these photographs with you," said Svenson.

"Yes."

"I'll need some time to make copies. I have only these originals."

Usually the prosecution made use of copied proofs in their investigations, keeping the originals under lock and key for trial. If Katz had requested copies, Gus would have made more than one, assuming the defense would want a set too. These were the originals, so Katz had not yet asked for another set. The commonwealth still didn't know, and Gus was giving him the tip.

"No doubt you will have some questions about this at trial," said Svenson.

"Yes."

This was an awkward point for Svenson. David knew he would not want to be put in a position whereby the prosecution could claim he withheld information. He now knew of the anklet and David was worried about what he would do with this information. Rumor had it there was no love lost between Svenson and Katz, but Gus played it straight and David respected him too much to cause him any trouble with the DA.

"You realize that if I am asked about these injuries, I must share my knowledge of the trinket," he said, as if reading his mind.

"Yes. But what if no one asks the question?"

"Hm," said Gus, removing a cream-colored rubber glove and tossing it into a nearby medical disposal unit. "The information on the ankle markings is in the report. Yes?"

"Yes."

"Of which Mr. Katz has a copy."

"Sure."

"This ornament does not belong to the victim. No?"

"No."

"It was given to you voluntarily."

"Yes."

"So it was not part of reclaimed evidence."

"No."

"You will make this piece of jewelry known to the prosecution."

"Ah, yeah," said David. "Eventually, sure."

"Well, then. This is your responsibility. Nothing to do with me."

"Thanks, Gus."

"Do not thank me. Like I say. They ask, I tell."

* * *

It was late when David left the ME's office, but he had one more stop to make before heading home. Joe Mannix had left a message saying he needed to talk, and David knew that when Joe left such a message, it was something important.

Joe had chosen a quiet Irish pub in South Boston, a place named the Idle Hour. It was a run-down, cozy joint filled with locals smoking and listening to Tommy Dorsey playing on an old jukebox.

"Nice place," said David, with just a hint of sarcasm, sliding onto a well-worn stool in the far back corner.

"I like it. Makes me feel anonymous."

They ordered a couple of beers and sat listening to Dorsey a minute longer before Mannix looked up at his friend.

"So how's it going?"

"Better, if that's what you mean."

"I heard about your mother."

So that was it.

"Harry McNally at Newark PD is an old friend. I went to the academy with his brother."

"It's all sorted out, Joe."

They drank some of their beer before Joe went on.

"You know, the better it gets for you guys, the worse it gets for you guys."

"I'm not scared of him, Joe. He messed with my family; you have no idea of the pleasure I will get in bringing this guy down."

"You going to ignore my warnings? The DA . . ." Mannix did not want to betray Scaturro's confidence, but he didn't know any other way to get through to his friend.

"What about the DA?" David looked at his friend. He was tired of being treated like a naive apprentice.

"Joe, I know what you are saying, but can't you see? There is no halfway with this. The only way to set Rayna Martin free is to expose this guy and everything he stands for."

They drank some more, leaving David's words hanging, a stark and dire reality.

"You need my help?" asked Mannix.

"I thought the cops worked for the DA's office."

"You know better than that."

"Do I? Maybe you should ask Paul Petri who he's working for."

It was a low blow and David regretted it as soon as it left his mouth. But all this to-ing and fro-ing was starting to wear him down.

"I told you," said Mannix. "Petri's going through a tough time. His wife is dying. She's up at Ashleighford—cancer."

"I'm sorry, Joe, but Ashleighford? On a cop's wage?"

Joe looked at his friend, obviously hoping beyond all hope that he was wrong.

"Petri's a cop's cop. He wouldn't cross the line; he doesn't know any other way."

"Yeah, well, I know of at least one uniform who would disagree with you."

Joe looked David in the eye as if willing him to elaborate. David knew he had to make a decision then and there. He had known Joe for almost ten years and had grown to trust and respect him. He was afraid of putting Tommy Wu in danger, but maybe not saying anything was taking an even bigger risk. More important, his primary obligation was to Rayna. She was his client and she was the one he was supposed to be defending to the best of his ability. He realized he had spent the past few weeks tiptoeing around everyone else's sensibilities, and time was running out. Maybe he had to stop playing it so safe and start trying to win this case—no concessions, no compromises.

"If I tell you this," he started, "you have to promise to tread softly. Don't go shooting your mouth off, don't go playing hero, not just for our sakes."

"What is it, David?"

"You were the one who warned me about Haynes in the first place. Did you think I would be his only target?"

"No. But I didn't—"

"The thing is, you were right. I thought you were exaggerating just to keep me on my toes, but it wasn't a cloak and dagger routine, was it, Joe? And you know it."

"Is Petri in trouble?"

"Probably, but more than likely for all the wrong reasons. The person I am worried about is Tommy Wu."

"What? Tommy's a good kid, how in the hell—"

"He has become involved with the case."

"He was the attending officer."

"One of them."

"And?"

"Let's just say he may have some information to our benefit that he is unwilling to part with. You see, Tommy has a sister who has a kid and—"

"Shit," said Joe. "Shit, David. Shit. Why the hell didn't you tell me sooner?"

"Because I knew you would act like this and because I didn't want to take advantage of our friendship and because, as you said, Tommy is a good kid."

"And still a little green around the ears, and dedicated and idealistic."

"Well, maybe his ideals have lost a little of their shine of late."

Joe shook his head.

"Joe, I know you, and your first instinct is to go and smash someone's head in, but you have to handle this carefully, for Tommy's sake. He doesn't want to talk about it. Believe me, I've tried, and I don't blame him."

"So where does Petri come into all of this?"

"I'm not sure, but as I said, Ashleighford Private Clinic ain't no public facility."

They finished their drinks, not knowing what to say from there.

"Leave it with me," said Joe, pulling a twenty from his pocket and wiping his mouth with the back of his hand.

"Joe, don't . . ."

"I know, I know. I just wish you had told me sooner."

28

"Sweet Jesus." Tyrone Banks let out a sigh. "That tastes good."

Tyrone had just downed one of Mick's large, fresh orange, grapefruit and honeydew melon juices, and he was already ordering another.

"I'm outta shape. Exactly how far did we run?"

"I'd say about seven miles, give or take," said David, finishing his own orange and pineapple concoction.

"These are the best, Mr. McGee," said Tyrone.

"Thank you, sir, and it's Mick," said the Irishman, pouring Tyrone a second juice. "So he dragged you on one of his crazy rampages around our fair city I gather?"

"Dragged, heaved, lugged—I'll be hurting tomorrow."

"Don't listen to him, Mick. He'd still be going if we hadn't got thirsty." They all laughed.

"You in town long, Tyrone?" asked Mick.

"Yeah, I've moved back to Boston for the next month or so, to be with the family during the trial."

"You sure your office is okay with this?" asked David, fearing he had put too much pressure on him to help.

"Absolutely and, to be honest with you, if they're not, they're just gonna have to deal with it. I've given them more than my pound of flesh over the years."

"We'll see you again then," said Mick shaking his hand.

"You can count on it."

David and Tyrone moved to a small side table, allowing Mick to serve his other customers. They took a seat by the window, taking in the green and blue expanse of the Boston Harbor foreshore and beyond.

"So you're staying at Delia's?" asked David.

"Yeah. Delia's set me up in the spare room and Teesha unpacked all my stuff and moved me in true and proper."

"You're a good uncle to her, probably the most important man in her life."

"Well, they're just as important to me," Tyrone went on. "I've screwed up in the past, David, acted like a perfect ass putting work before everything and everybody. I thought I was doing myself a favor, but as it turned out, the joke was on me. This whole thing with Rayna has made me realize how important family is. I want to help them, David, and I thought that"—Tyrone put down his juice and fished into the pocket of his shorts—"maybe this is a good way to start."

Tyrone pulled out three pieces of paper, folded in quarters and stapled together at the top left-hand corner. David took the sheets and opened them up, seeing what at first glance appeared to be a list of names, or couples.

"What is it?" he asked.

"It's the Republican Party's invitation list for Rudolph Haynes's banquet, which I believe is being held at the Haynes's Chestnut Hill estate in two weeks' time."

"How did you get this?"

"Not all my friends are Democrats, David. I do know a few who bat for the other team."

"So how can this help?"

"Well, from my experience you can learn a lot about people—who they are and what they believe—by looking at those they invite to dinner, so to speak. Even more telling could be what we learn from who *isn't* on this list."

"You know who all these people are?"

"Pretty much. If not, I can find out."

"You had this in your pocket all morning?"

"Yep. In fact, the extra weight was what probably slowed me down those last coupla miles."

This was just what David needed after his conversation with Joe last night. A new lead. A reason to keep fighting.

• • •

"It will be a nightmare. I can't believe he is actually going ahead with this dinner. You would have thought that after the funeral—"

"I know," said Loretta Scaturro, sitting across from Joe Mannix and Roger Katz in her basic but comfortable office on the fifth floor of a rather nondescript building near Government Center known as One Bulfinch Place.

"The senator shouldn't have to stop his life just because he has been victimized."

"You got some details you wanna give me?" Joe couldn't help it; he had to cut off the Kat. *There are five unsolved homicides on our books and here I am talking to the DA and her idiot offsider about the ribbons and bows on a dinner party, for Christ's sake. And all in honor of that bastard.* "I don't mean to rush you, but I hadn't planned on being called here this afternoon and we're kinda backed up downtown."

"Of course, Joe," said Loretta casting a quick frown in Roger's direction. "We appreciate that this isn't your area—not ours either, to be honest—but under the circumstances we thought it best that we all have our heads around what will take place in two weeks."

"Sure. So?"

"So the majority of guests are staying at the Regency Plaza. Their rooms have been booked and paid for by the Republican Party, and we will provide you with a list by early next week."

"How many of them are there?"

"About three hundred and fifty."

"Sounds like a check-in nightmare and an anti-Republican sniper's dream," said Mannix.

"Ah, no, the guests get their room numbers in advance. They don't even have to check in. Each will be sent a key card in the days prior to the function. There won't be any lobby backlog. The Party's in-house security thought this best, considering there will be a lot of big names milling around on that night."

"Good thinking. What about transport?"

"Well, as you know, the banquet itself is at Highgrove, the Haynes's home in Chestnut Hill. It was originally planned for the Regency Plaza ballroom, but it was felt security would be easier to control on a private estate where we can block off streets without having to reroute copious city traffic. As for the order of the evening, drinks will be held under a big canopy in the garden and dinner in their ballroom."

"They have their own ballroom?"

"Apparently so."

"Good for them."

"Lieutenant Mannix, I really don't think these little digs are—" Katz began.

"What about transport?" Joe interrupted again.

"The guests will be transported from the hotel to Highgrove in a series of circling limousines. The trip only takes about twenty minutes. Each guest will be given a time to be in the lobby, and departures to the banquet will be staggered. Chief Mahoney has assured me he will have two precincts at the hotel, on top of extra hotel security, and another two shifts at the house for arrivals and then departures later in the evening. The departures will be staggered too. On top of all this, Haynes will have his own private security team at the house for a full twenty-four hours leading up to and during the event."

"What's the rough start/finish?"

"Eight and midnight."

"And you want me?"

"At the house."

Joe couldn't think of anything worse. "What? Don't you think that's a bad idea? The press know who I am and are gonna be wondering why the head of Homicide is playing security guard at a party."

"You'll be inside."

"Did Haynes request this?"

"No, I did. I mean, I am, if that's okay?"

When she looked at him, Mannix saw the same apprehension he had seen in her eyes at the ballpark. She didn't want anything going wrong at that party for fear Haynes would find a way to blame her. She was nervous. She wanted backup.

"Sure," he said, watching her shoulders relax just a little. "You gonna be there?"

"No. We thought it best under the circumstances. We do not want the guests to be asking any uncomfortable questions. This night should have nothing to do with the impending trial. It is a political tribute, nothing more."

Katz made a huffing sound, just like a child who had been told he could not attend his best friend's birthday party. Scaturro ignored him. She was getting good at that, thought Joe. Good for her.

"You'll have a full list of attendees just in case, although I am sure the gate and door security will be tight and efficient."

"So what's the bottom line?"

"Excuse me?"

"What do you think is gonna go down? You must be afraid of something, otherwise I wouldn't be here."

Silence.

"Look," Joe went on. "I can't see the Martin woman breakin' out of jail with a posse, and Haynes is a little too subtle to invite the KKK for a bonfire on his front lawn, so—"

"Really," Katz jumped in. "This is going too far. This is slander."

"Which part, Katz?" asked Mannix, turning quickly toward the ADA. "The part about Martin and the posse or Haynes and the Klan?"

"Of course not," said Scaturro, trying to calm them down. "The press will have to be controlled, and the extra precautions are simply in place to thwart any unlikely disturbance by, ah . . . how should I put this—"

"African American extremists," said Katz.

"Well, I wouldn't have put it quite so strongly, Roger."

"Okay," said Joe, up and out of his chair. "That it?"

"Yes. Thanks, Joe."

"Sure." And he was out the door before Katz had a chance to say another word.

. . .

Senator Theodore Buford felt the fire rise inside his chest as beads of sweat broke out on his furrowed brow. *I should have been born in California,* he thought to himself. Lettuce leaves and cranberry juice would be a lot better for his aging constitution than his homegrown Louisiana fare. Still, he thought, his wife's Cajun cooking was delicious, and he would rather go to his grave with the taste of crawfish in his mouth than live an extra ten years on tofu and pumpkin seeds.

The Republican senator had represented his state for some thirty-five years and was proud of it. He was proud of his people and his party, and even prouder of his wife of forty years, who had been there with him for the entire term. Now, at this late hour, he sat at his study desk to open the remainder of the day's mail. The subtle green lamp was casting just enough light to read without attracting the summer bugs that still managed to break into the house despite the numerous screens and pest control lamps.

"*Well, I'll be . . .*" he said to himself as he opened the final letter, a thick cream-colored envelope of top stock with the red, white and blue Republican insignia centered on the back flap.

"*Well, I'll be . . .*" he said again, and this time loud enough for Meredith to poke her head around the study door.

"What is it, Ted?"

"An invitation."

"And a good one by the sounds of things?"

"No, well, yes. Good as in a good laugh, unbelievable really."

He had her now. "Go on then," she said. "What's all the fuss?"

"It's an invitation for us to attend Rudolph Haynes's banquet. Friday, the twenty-eighth."

"Well, I'll be . . ." she said, repeating his words.

"Exactly."

"Must be a mistake."

"Yes, and a doozie."

Despite the fact that Buford and Haynes were both Republicans, they had been adversaries, some would even say enemies, for years. Haynes thought Buford a liberal wimp, a naive idealist who deferred realistic action for noninterventionist pacifism. Buford thought Haynes a narrow-minded thug, a hard-nosed bigot who hid his intolerance in PR campaigns and calculated lobbying.

At one time he had even made up his own little joke about the senator:

Q: What did Rudolph Haynes say to the little people he
    stepped on as he made his way up the ladder?
A: A little less wax on the toe and a little more elbow
    grease on the heel.

"A little rude, isn't it?" said Meredith.

"What's that?"

"Sending such an invitation only two weeks before the event."

"Yes, I see what you mean. It must have been a clerical gaffe. Don't think old Haynes would appreciate my walking into his big social soiree."

Meredith moved into the room and stood next to her husband, looking down at the invitation.

"I feel for them, though, losing a daughter."

"Of course, but I also feel for that poor woman sitting in a jail cell awaiting trial for murder. It's preposterous."

Meredith moved behind her husband and started to massage his still strong shoulders.

"Anyway," she said. "I have more important business on . . ." She looked over his shoulder at the invitation again. "Friday, June twenty-eighth."

"What's that, my dear?"

"Hanging the picture rails in the family room and making my husband some good old-fashioned étouffée."

"Well said," he replied, reaching up to pat her hand. "But let's go a little lighter on the spices next time, eh?"

She smiled, bent to kiss him on his forehead and pointed at the invitation.

"Put that where it belongs then, and come on up."

And with that he tossed the invitation into the wastepaper basket, took his wife's hand and headed upstairs for bed.

29

Lisa Cavanaugh was worried. It was ten past nine in the morning and David's cell was ringing out. She had tried home and gotten the machine and had just hung up a call with Nora, who promised to grab him by the ear as soon as he got in. They hadn't spoken since that morning at Myrtle's, almost two weeks ago. She knew he was busy, but after their discussion in Newark, she thought he would at least have called.

She rubbed her temples. It wasn't just the lack of attention that worried Lisa today. It was the girl, her "patient." She was dirty and unkempt, a sad young woman who had entered the ER around eight this morning looking for treatment and asking for Lisa specifically.

"I'm not a doctor," Lisa explained. "If you're sick, you need to be examined by a resident."

"Well, I don't know if what I have can be treated," she had mumbled, head down, avoiding any eye contact. "I think I just need to talk to someone, and I thought you would understand."

"I'm sorry," said Lisa, taking the girl's large clammy hand. "Do I know you?"

"No," said the girl. "But I know your brother."

Lisa led the girl into a private room and sat her down. She got her some coffee, pulled another chair from the corner and sat across from her, not wanting to push but curious as to where this was going.

"How can I help you?" she said.

"I'm not sure that you can. I'm not sure anyone can. It's too late."

"It's never too late. What did you say your name was?"

"Yes, it is, it has always been too late for me," said the girl. "Your brother said he would help, but he let me down."

Then it hit her. "Oh, you know my brother through his work. Is he your attorney?"

"He was. Not anymore."

The girl lifted her head and Lisa saw something else besides sadness in her large green eyes. She saw anger, or something stronger, and it sent a chill through her body.

The girl took a deep breath. "I want you to give him a message from me. I came to you because you are his sister and I know how much a sister can mean to someone. Tell him he let me down. Tell him I hold him responsible for not working it out." The girl started to get up.

"Look," said Lisa. "I know my brother. He just isn't like that. I am sure there is some explanation. Please, sit down, I want to help."

Lisa put her hand on the girl's shoulder, and the girl turned sharply, grabbing her wrist and holding it tightly.

"Don't you see. It's beyond that."

Lisa held her breath.

"Make sure you tell him," she said in a cold, firm voice, her eyes never leaving Lisa's.

"Tell him what?" Lisa said, unable to move.

"Remind him how important sisters are. Mine is dead. So I know. Your brother has no idea what I went through—watching my little sister die in a pool of her own blood. Does your brother love you, Lisa? Because if he does, I am sure he'd hate to see the same thing happen to you. But then again, he was the one who screwed up, so maybe it's time he paid the price." She finally released Lisa's hand and turned to leave.

"Wait, I don't understand. Why are you saying this? I don't even know your name."

"My name?" she said. "He should know who I am. My name is Pepper. Stacey Pepper."

• • •

"I just think that if I see someone, they might be able to help me remember an important detail—something that's locked in my head."

"It's not a bad idea," said David.

"Can't hurt," said Tyrone.

Rayna was worried about herself. She was forgetting things. First the reindeer references, and then the anklet. These were important details, but they had been temporarily locked in her subconscious, eventually trickling to the front of her brain in spurts. She now feared that there were other details she was overlooking—pieces of information that could save her, or worse, others that could condemn her. And that's when she came up with the idea of hypnotherapy.

"I've used it before," she said. "I had a client, a young girl. She blocked out the memory of a domestic dispute in which her stepfather put her mom in the hospital. The hypnotherapist worked with her over several weeks until eventually the girl remembered every detail, without having a nervous breakdown."

"I'll arrange it."

"Thanks, David. At this stage anything's worth a shot."

They were interrupted by the beep of Tyrone's pager. "David, is your cell on?"

"No, they make you turn it off before you come in. In fact," he said, patting his jacket pockets. "I think I left it at the office."

"It's Arthur. It says, *'Return to office, urgent.'*"

David felt a surge of panic rise from the pit of his stomach. They both looked at Rayna.

"Go, go," she said. "But promise me you'll let me know—"

"We will, we promise," said David.

"Okay. Just go."

■ ■ ■

It was late afternoon and she was starting to get nervous. Rudolph had decided to work from home, but he was expected back at the office later that night for an important budget meeting and had decided to get as much done as possible in the privacy of his study without all the usual distractions. His door had been shut all day. Obviously, she was seen as one of those distractions, which was no wonder, considering her recent pitiable behavior. No matter, everything would be different after tonight; she just had to stay calm, focused. She wanted her husband to include her in his quest, or at the very least share what he felt he could, just as he always had, and undoubtedly would do again.

He was on the phone to Vincent. She knew this because Vincent was the only man Rudolph would talk to in such a tone—with authority but comradeship. A father to son.

"I want you around at the banquet," he said. "Yes, at the Regency Plaza and then here, in the background. Yes, that's right, Theodore Buford."

Ted Buford. *Good God,* she thought. Her husband had not mentioned that tree-hugging radical for years. What did he have to do with any of this?

And then they moved on to a man named Tyrone Banks. He was, from what she could gather, related to the Martin woman, an in-law. He was becoming a pest, a problem. He was asking a lot of questions, digging up a lot of dirt. He was a Democrat.

But then the sound became muffled as Rudi obviously stood from his desk and moved toward the window. She decided she would go to the kitchen to prepare her husband a late afternoon tea—and maybe even an early drink? A few stiff whiskeys might take the edge off what she knew would be a surprise turn of events later on that evening. The "surprise" had been largely her doing. She had made Caroline promise that there would be no prepromotion for tonight's show. She knew her husband would have prevented the interview from going to air if he had had any warning of its existence. *But he will be thanking me tonight,* she thought. *He will be proud of me tonight.*

. . .

"How dangerous is he?" said Haynes into the telephone. This Banks sounded like a problem—and one he needed to address with haste.

"He's been making inquiries regarding your colleagues and enemies," answered Verne immediately. "He sought out the banquet guest list. He wants to know who is in your camp and who is not."

"Good Lord, how dare he," said Haynes, his blood beginning to boil. "What the hell is he playing at? That is none of his business."

"I believe he is interested in locating those willing to speak against you, Senator. Those willing to slander your reputation in an effort to shift sympathy toward his sister-in-law," replied Verne.

"For God's sake, Vincent, what are you doing about it?"

"Banks is tricky, Senator. He is well respected—and, unfortunately, has a reputation for being determined, ruthless even, in his pursuit of information."

And in the moment Haynes was surprised at how quickly the thought came to him, how easily it had slid into his brain.

"Then perhaps he needs a reminder, Vincent, of how dangerous such meddling can be. He must remember that I have many supporters; most are intelligent, rational people. But there are others who have been deeply affected by my daughter's untimely death and what it means to people like us as a whole.

"People like that," Haynes continued as he looked out upon the extensive gardens beyond, "might have a tendency to act on emotion rather than reason—and sadly, their actions are beyond our control."

And then there was a pause, when Haynes knew his prodigy was taking it all in.

"How strong a reminder would you suggest a man like Banks would require, Senator?" asked Verne after a time.

"Strong enough to contain him but gentle enough to prevent any repurcussions at trial."

And Haynes knew that Verne would understand.

"Senator," said Verne after a pause.

"What is it Vincent?" said Haynes, now moving from the window to pace about the room.

"I was just thinking, sir, about the earliest principles of justice—about the law of retaliation, or as it was first expressed in Latin, *lex talionis.*"

"Retributive justice," said Haynes, and the thought filled his soul. "Or as the Hebrews put it, an eye for an eye."

"Yes, sir. It was all about proportionate punishment, equitable retaliation, relief for those who had suffered in the form of allowing punishment to fit the crime."

Haynes knew what Verne was suggesting and as much as it appealed to him at some deep primal level of the purest of satisfaction, he could not allow this train of thought to continue. Haynes knew that Verne loved Christina as a sister, and in turn, he knew how much Christina had cared for him. But he also knew that at the end of the day, they must act within the perimeters of their circumstance, and forgo such primordial desires for a more sophisticated approach to revenge.

"Vincent," he said quietly, "I understand what you are saying, but when it comes down to it, you must know that *lex talionis* is not an option here. It wins us nothing but the knowledge that Rayna Martin suffers in kind. You are talking about payback, payback in its most primitive and perhaps gratifying form; and if circumstances were different, if there came a time when I thought it was doable, then believe me I would ask you to act in kind.

"But we cannot afford payback, at least not at this point. For it would afford us nothing but complications. But I do promise you, Vincent, that when all is said and done, victory will be ours. I am sure of it."

· · ·

David pushed open their office door with Tyrone fast behind him. "What is it?" he said.

And then he saw her, his sister Lisa, her green eyes red with panic, her normally smooth brow distorted in folds of concern. She was seated on the sofa with Sara on one side and Nora perched on the armrest to her left. She looked up at him as he rushed in. "I'm okay, David. I'm all right."

"No, no, you're not," he said kneeling in front of her. "What the hell happened?"

"Take a seat, son," said Arthur, pulling a chair over to where David was perched. "Lisa has something to tell you, and I think you'd better hear it from the beginning."

And that's where she started, from when the "patient" had entered the ER and asked specifically for her. She spoke of her depleted appearance and dour demeanor, of her cryptic dialogue and seeming reluctance to explain exactly why she was there.

David listened to every word, his emerald eyes focusing on the replica of his own. Lisa watched him as she let the story unfold, finishing with the girl's veiled threats and finally with the name she had given her. As the words Stacey Pepper left her lips, David clenched his hands and felt a hot flow of blood rush into the veins in his temples.

"Lisa," he said slowly, "I need you to listen to me."

"Okay," she said, obviously terrified of what he may be about to say.

"That girl, she wasn't really Stacey Pepper. She was an actress playing Stacey Pepper. Stacey was my client. She was also a good person, but she is dead."

"Oh, David."

"The woman was an impostor sent to scare you. That is my fault and I am sorry." He took her hand and went on. "I want you to do something for me. I need you to go home and pack your bags. I want you to stay the night at a friend's place. And tomorrow I want you to go home to Jersey. Don't argue, just do it. Ring Sean and get him to pick you up at the station."

"David, I can't just leave, I have work and—"

"Do it," he said, before realizing he was scaring her. "Please, Lisa, I'll explain later; just promise me you will go."

"Okay, okay. I'm owed some free time. But what about you?"

"I have to go see someone and kick his ass to hell and back."

．．．

Five minutes and forty-two seconds. That is the time it took for David to walk/run from his offices on Congress Street to the DA's offices near Government Center. Two minutes and nine seconds is how long it took for the elevator to arrive at the bottom floor—with most elevators on their way down, delivering workers to ground level and freedom from their daily grind for another sweet weekend. One minute and twenty-six seconds is the time it took for him to reach the fifth floor, and twenty-two seconds is the time it took for David to leave the elevator, run down the corridor to Katz's office, bypass his sour-looking secretary, who was still at her desk even at this late hour, and barge through Katz's door. Two seconds is all it took for him to leap across Roger Katz's pristine desk, grab his shirt front and deliver his first blow squarely in the ADA's right eye.

"You *fucking asshole.*"

Katz was in shock, his arms and hands now trying to cover his face and ward off the blows.

"Shelley, Shelley, call security," Katz whimpered, slinking from his chair and trying to escape into the corner behind the bookshelf.

"Shut the fuck up. This is between you and me."

David looked across to see the secretary just sitting there (was that a slight smile on her face?), glued to her seat as the noise attracted other late workers in neighboring cubicles.

"Shelley, for *Christ's sake!*"

It was then that Katz noticed the "audience" gathering at his office door. Clerks, secretaries, even the office janitor. It was as if the director had called *"Action"* as the ADA sprang back off the wall to deliver a blow to David's ribs and a subsequent uppercut under his jaw. The punches weren't those of an experienced fighter, but the Kat worked out, so they were strong enough to send David flying back across the office and into the filing cabinet on the far wall.

"How dare you come in here and attack me like this," said Katz, panting and adjusting his tie and fixing his hair all at the same time. "What the hell is this about? Have you gone completely insane, Cavanaugh? I'll have you up for assault with grievous bodily harm before the night is over, and I've got at least five witnesses to back me up."

"I told you, Katz; this is personal," David said, before bounding off the cabinet and throwing a low punch into Katz's stomach. He felt the air leave the ADA's lungs as he stepped back, ready to go at him again.

"It's between you and me and a girl named Stacey Pepper, whom you as good as murdered."

"What? What in God's name has that retard got to do with anything?"

"Don't play dumb with me. He couldn't have done this without your help. You told him about Stacey and he went after my sister."

"Cavanaugh, for Christ's sake. I have no idea what you're talking about."

David steadied himself on Katz's desk and looked straight into his eyes. He hated to admit it, but his face was a blank. In that instant he realized the ADA had no idea what he was talking about. Then he saw something register in Katz's eyes. He was thinking the same thing—it had to be.

"What the hell is going on here?" Loretta Scaturro pushed past the crowd huddled in the doorway and bounded into the ADA's office. "Shut up both of you and turn on CBC *now*."

"What?"

"Just do it, Roger. Turn it on. Turn on *Newsline*."

Katz fumbled for his remote and flicked on the TV, and then the three of them stood there in silence, in disbelief, in shock.

There was Caroline Croft, superimposed in front of artwork depicting a vibrant Christina Haynes, introducing the

story as an exclusive, stressing that this was not only the first
interview with Mrs. Elizabeth Haynes, but also the first time
one of the principals affected by the case had spoken to the
media.

She went on to give the background to the story: the
details of the charge, the motive of hate, the effect the case
was having on the city of Boston and the country as a
whole.

Then after giving the obligatory narrative on the Hayneses
and their standing in society, she cut to the interview, which
she explained was recorded very recently at the Haynes's
stunning estate in Chestnut Hill.

It was sunny. Elizabeth Haynes sat in front of a rosebush,
the pale pink flowers in full bloom. She wore pastel, with the
lightest tinge of makeup on her face and the slightest glisten
of grief in her eyes. Her hair was up in a soft French roll just
like Grace Kelly's, with the sun's natural backlight forming a
halo effect around her head. In short, Elizabeth Haynes
looked saintly.

> *Caroline Croft: Elizabeth, I think we can all appreci-*
> *ate how hard this must be for you and I want to*
> *thank you for speaking with us today.*

Elizabeth did not reply, just gave a slight nod and even
slighter smile.

> *CC: Let's start at the beginning.*
> *Elizabeth Haynes: All right.*
> *CC: On the morning of Saturday May fourth, your*
> *daughter left the house to attend a birthday party*
> *for Layteesha Martin.*
> *EH: That's right.*
> *CC: It was a sailing party, and Rayna Martin, Teesha's*
> *mother, was the sole parent responsible for four*
> *teenagers on that day. Did you know Mrs. Martin?*
> *EH: Not really. I knew of her through Christina, but*
> *she did not seem to be . . . she did not seem to be*
> *socially active with a lot of the other mothers I knew*
> *from Christina's school.*

CC: *Did you have concerns about Christina attending the party?*

EH: *Yes. In fact, I had told Christina she could not attend. I felt the girls were too young to go sailing on their own outboard. On this particular morning we had a slight argument, as mothers and sixteen-year-old girls tend to do—nothing serious. And Christina left as an act of . . . I suppose you would call it teenage rebellion.*

CC: *I am sure many parents would identify with that. What was the argument about?*

EH: *Shopping. It sounds so ridiculous now. I wanted her to go shopping with me so we could choose a dress for her to wear to my husband's honorary banquet. She wanted to go to Teesha Martin's party.*

CC: *Given these circumstances, does this make it harder on you, knowing your last conversation was in the form of an altercation?*

EH: *(pause) First of all, let me explain, there is no "harder"; there can be no "harder." This is as hard as it gets, losing a child. Of course, I have pondered this question, and the fact that our last morning together was spent squabbling over something as trivial as a party dress. But if I had allowed her to go to Teesha's party, she would have gone with my permission and maybe, perhaps in that case, it would have felt slightly worse . . . if that is at all possible.*

CC: *Why is that?*

EH: *Because I would have been giving her my blessing to go to her death.*

Caroline went on to talk about Elizabeth's initial reaction to the news of her daughter's death (shock, disbelief, devastation), her husband's love for his daughter (she was the light of his life), her horror at discovering the subsequent charge was race related (inconceivable) and her attempts to get through each subsequent day, before moving on to the funeral.

CC: *Elizabeth, we have all seen the pictures, read the conjecture, heard the gossip about what occurred at Christina's funeral. Perhaps you can tell us what really happened between you and Teesha Martin.*

EH: *Yes. (Elizabeth shifts slightly in her seat.) First allow me to say that I bear no ill feeling toward Teesha Martin. She was my daughter's friend. What happened was not her fault. I feel for her under the circumstances.*

CC: *Then how do you explain the reports that there was an altercation between you and Teesha at Christina's funeral?*

EH: *There was no altercation. I know now that all Teesha was trying to do was explain how sorry she was for what had come to pass—how much she missed Christina. It was a distressing morning for me, as you can appreciate, so I am sorry if I was not perhaps as compassionate as I should have been.*

CC: *Do you think she was speaking on behalf of her mother?*

EH: *I do not know.*

CC: *So what caused all the commotion?*

EH: *Well, while Teesha Martin was speaking to me, I believe that a commotion started elsewhere. A reaction to the appearance of the defense team.*

CC: *You are talking about Rayna Martin's attorneys, David Cavanaugh and Sara Davis.*

EH: *Yes. They went to approach my husband and I believe the assistant district attorney, Mr. Roger Katz, attempted to deter them.*

CC: *Why were they at the funeral?*

EH: *I have no idea. I still cannot fathom the insensitivity of their actions.*

From here they moved on to the motive of hate and the public interest in a race-related trial that was becoming as big as OJ or Rodney King. Caroline asked how Elizabeth felt about such a motive.

EH: As a human being, I cannot understand it. I cannot conceive such levels of intolerance.

CC: You must be aware that there has been some speculation from prodefense sectors that perhaps you and your husband "exist" in a racially limited social infrastructure, and that perhaps the charge against Mrs. Martin is fueled by . . . shall we say, a racially limited perspective.

If Elizabeth was shocked by the question, she did not show it. All she did was lift her right hand to brush a wisp of hair from her forehead.

EH: I have heard such rumors and in all honesty, find them ludicrous and hurtful. First, my husband and I are not the prosecutors; we are the victims. We do not run the DA's office, and to suggest this is an insult to Loretta Scaturro, whom I believe to be a highly intelligent and capable attorney. Second, my husband has done so much for this city, this state . . . this country. He is a man of the highest integrity, a decent person, a wonderful husband, a doting father. Third, I have spent many, many years involved with charitable organizations that assist minority groups. To say we are intolerant is both insulting and disappointing. (A pause.) We have been lucky in life—true—and perhaps such comments come from jealousy. But I do not understand why anyone would be jealous of us now. For we are in hell.

CC: So if you cannot conceive of anyone committing murder based on racial intolerance, does this mean perhaps you hold doubts about Mrs. Martin's guilt?

EH: Initially, yes, because as you say, to me the concept was unthinkable. I refused to believe a woman, a mother, could abandon another girl . . . leave her to die just because her skin was a lighter color than that of her own daughter and her daughter's other

> *friends. But (another pause) subsequent informa-*
> *tion has led me to believe otherwise.*
> *CC: Which brings us to a conversation we had this*
> *morning. Elizabeth (Caroline tilted her head to the*
> *left, allowing her cropped blond hair to fall over*
> *her shoulder, and paused for impact), just before we*
> *sat down here together, you told me you had discov-*
> *ered evidence, new evidence, that this crime was*
> *indeed motivated by hate.*
> *EH: Yes.*
> *CC: And this evidence comes from—*
> *EH: My daughter—Christina.*
> *CC: Elizabeth, once again I want you to know we*
> *understand how difficult this must be, but can you*
> *tell us how Christina "told" you this, gave you this*
> *information, this message . . . I suppose it is from*
> *her grave? (Caroline had obviously decided it was*
> *time to build the drama to its emotional cre-*
> *scendo.)*

Elizabeth looked down into her lap, twisted her white
hanky and then turned to pick up a small sheet of pink paper
from the pretty, round garden table beside her.

> *EH: I found a letter in Christina's bedroom drawer. It*
> *is a note she wrote to Teesha Martin. A birthday*
> *message. She must have written it only days before*
> *her . . . her passing.*
> *CC: Do you think you could read this letter for us, and*
> *perhaps shed some light on exactly what happened*
> *the day your daughter died?*
> *EH: Yes . . . I, I'll try.*

Elizabeth straightened in her chair, took a breath and un-
folded the delicate sheet of stationery. She took a pair of
round reading glasses and placed them on the bridge of her
petite nose.

Dear Teesha
Happy, Happy Birthday!!!!

Can you believe we are turning 17—seriously.

*We'll be seniors in a few months. We'll be going to the
    prom next year and doing our SATs (oh my God!)
    and then college . . . (can't wait).*

*I just wanted to say—about all the other stuff. PLEASE
    don't worry about it. Parents can be weird some-
    times. She gives me such a hard time—and there's
    nothing you or I can do about it (I can't change who
    I am . . . obviously) and it is NOT YOUR FAULT.*

*That's why it's best I don't come to your party—I can't
    handle that "look" anymore, you know what I
    mean? She doesn't want me there in any case.*

*Anyway, we'll celebrate heaps more birthdays together
and pig out on our own cake next week.*

> *Love, your friend forever,*
> *C xxxxx*

*CC: Elizabeth, you must realize the significance of this
    letter. It basically tells you Christina knew Mrs.
    Martin did not like her and suggests the reasons for
    such dislike were based on race.*

EH: Yes.

*CC: But you have not handed this letter over to the
    DA?*

*EH: I only found the letter very recently and I think, at
    first, I wanted to hold onto it because it was proba-
    bly the last thing my daughter wrote. It was a letter
    she was sharing with her friend and I felt—I still
    feel to some degree—that it was her private busi-
    ness and unfair to her to make it public. I was also
    concerned about what it would do to Teesha. She is
    only seventeen and has had a lot to deal with in re-
    cent weeks. I did not want to destroy another young
    life.*

David listened to this line and flinched; this woman
was scaring the hell out of him. He did not know whether
she was lying with ease or actually believed what she was
saying. *Whatever the case*, he thought, *she is going to
bury us.*

CC: But . . .

EH: But I also appreciate its significance; that is why I speak of it today and why, after this interview goes to air, I will hand it over to the DA.

CC: Finally, Elizabeth, is there anything, anything at all, that you want to say to Rayna Martin?

EH: I . . . ah . . . It is strange. I have had dreams about coming face-to-face with her and in these dreams I am struck dumb, as there are no words—no words to express . . . But I suppose I want to ask her why. Why my daughter, my beautiful, young, vibrant, clever, happy daughter?

Elizabeth starts to cry freely.

EH: I want to say . . . that I try . . . I have always tried to be a kind, understanding, generous person. I taught my daughter these values, and she carried them with dignity. But I am finding it very hard . . . so hard . . . to forgive her. Perhaps in time.

CC: Elizabeth Haynes, thank you so much.

• • •

Roger Katz, his right eye starting to swell, the blood on his face now dry and cracking against the stretch of his smile, looked at David Cavanaugh and said just two words, "You're screwed."

• • •

Tyrone and Delia Banks watched the program in Delia's family room.

"My God," said Delia, her body shaking.

Tyrone put his arm around her and felt immense relief that Teesha was upstairs listening to her CDs, not that she wouldn't have to deal with this tomorrow, and the next day.

"The woman," she said. "She is . . ."

"Either a brilliant liar or so influenced by her husband's bigotry that she is no longer capable of seeing the truth," finished Tyrone.

"Yes," said Delia, now starting to cry. "They are going to

win this thing, Tyrone. They are going to win this thing and damn my poor sister to hell."

. . .

Moses and Sophia Novelli sat on their living room couch together, their wine untouched.

"That Caroline," said Sophia. "I have never trusted her. Poor Elizabeth. She must have talked her into this."

"No, Sophia." Moses shook his head. "Elizabeth knows what she is doing. She is Rudolph's wife, after all."

. . .

"I was right all along," said Ed Washington to his wife and daughter as they sat glued to the big-screen TV in Ed's billiards room. "That woman is a goddamned murderer."

Ed did not admit it to his family, but he was privately relieved at this latest revelation because it gave him an excuse to push all his recent fears and doubts to the back of his brain.

"The Hayneses are good, honest people—like us. They need our support. Decent people should stick together."

"Amen," said Harriet Washington, taking her daughter's right hand in her own.

"Amen," said her husband, taking his daughter's left and consolidating the family bond.

"Amen," said Francie Washington, simply because she could think of nothing else to say.

. . .

"Where is she?"

Rudolph Haynes had seen the story in all its "exclusive" glory on his office TV. He had called home immediately and Agnes had told him his wife was in his study, waiting for him and, dare she say it, drinking his black label Bourbon. He made it home in a record fourteen minutes, running two red lights on the way.

"Elizabeth."

"You're here," she said, now pushing herself to her feet. She was unsteady. She was drunk. She was looking at him with an expression of anticipation, of eagerness, of hope.

"You saw it then?" she said, steadying herself on the white oak side table.

"Yes."

"Rudi," she said, moving toward him now. "I know you are angry that I did not tell you sooner. But when I found the letter, the proof of the depth of that woman's evil prejudices, I wanted to show you that I was all right. That I could fight. With you. As a team. Just like always."

And he looked at her then, shaking his head. Realizing just how naive she was. She did not see it. She did not see that this letter, this weapon she had just pointed squarely at Rayna Martin, initially had been aimed somewhere else.

The note was a coup, a brilliant twist of fate that could definitely be used to sway things their way, but his wife's releasing it—on national television no less—would also open a can of worms he was not sure even he could contain.

"Elizabeth," he began. "The letter is a revelation. But you should have given it to me the minute you found it."

"Yes, yes," she said, taking a step back as she nodded her head in agreement. "But you would have forbade the interview and at least this way I did not disobey you. I was brilliant, Rudolph. I was my old self: poised, gracious, eloquent. At last we have proof of that woman's motives. She had been treating our daughter as an outcast from the onset, and now it is time for her to pay."

"Elizabeth," he said at last, walking toward her then, knowing that despite the devastation it would cause, he had no choice but to tell her the truth. "That letter," he began. "Christina's words. She was not talking about Rayna Martin, and I am afraid in releasing the note as you have, the defense and all her supporters will now be searching endlessly for another piece of evidence to tear our whole 'hate' case apart."

"What?" she began, losing her footing again as she reached out for his hand and looked confusedly into his eyes. "Rudi, I . . . I don't understand. What Christina said is clear—about the Martin woman's intolerance, the looks she gave her, the fact that Christina could not help who she was."

"*No*," he said loudly, now moving forward to grab both of her forearms with force. "Don't you see, Elizabeth. She was talking about you. She was calling you—calling *us*—the bigots. Christina wanted to go to that party because she felt more at home with them than she did with us. She was confused, she had forgotten her standing in life. And this letter—well, unless we are careful, there will be others that see the truth in it too."

But Elizabeth had heard nothing past the word *bigots*. And the depth of it all finally hit her. Her daughter—her miracle, her heart, her soul—the little girl who had looked up to her her entire life, the blessing she had loved more than she had ever loved anything in her entire life, had grown up to discover that her mother was not the person she wanted her to be.

Oh, God, she thought to herself as the tears began to track down her still flawless face. *She went to that party because of us.*

And then she looked up at her husband, wanting beyond all else for him to understand. And as he pulled her close, she knew that his embrace was just a poor attempt at placating her rather than one intended for comfort. And in that moment, with his limp arms resting dutifully around her shoulders, she felt more cold and vulnerable and alone than she had ever felt in her entire life.

What have we done? she whispered to herself, her own private agony now beyond anything she had experienced before. *Dear God, forgive us. What in the hell have we done?*

30

Loretta Scaturro had learned a lot about herself in the past eighteen hours. All this time she had convinced herself that the reason she was so nervous was because her conscience, her sense of morality, saw her sickened by recent events and the part she had to play in them. This was true, but she was surprised to realize that despite her desire to remain true to her convictions, she was not beyond compromising such scruples when it came to protecting her career.

Certainly her uneasiness had arisen from her ethical sense of responsibility, but it was amazing how the definition of said responsibility could change when influenced by the dire need for self-preservation. She had been so terrified of losing this case—and what such a loss would do to her professional standing—that she was preparing herself for defeat by justifying it on the grounds of principle. She hated to admit it, but last night, when she saw her first real chance to win this thing, she felt *good*.

I must not be so hard on myself, she thought. *Winning is my job; it is what I am paid to do. Defense attorneys are paid, in turn, to offer the alternative argument, and in the end the verdict lies with the jury.*

She had built her career on taking the higher moral ground, but the higher moral ground had always been a matter of conjecture. Much of the community would argue she was performing her duties with integrity and honor—fighting against the ugliness of bigotry, representing those too young or weak, or in this case, too white and unable to stand up for themselves. Bottom line, despite her own selfish internal skirmishes, she could come out of this looking better than ever. Especially now.

So as Judge Walter Fitzgerald, with new evidence in the form of the aforementioned letter in hand, passed their motion to strike the count of involuntary manslaughter and go for the single count of murder two, she decided to at least try to put her own views on the matter aside and uphold her legal responsibility as district attorney. They had filed late Friday night, requesting an urgent hearing the following morning (it did not hurt that Judge Stein was at a legal conference in Washington on this particular weekend) so as to secure the strike prior to jury selection, which began on Monday.

It was an unusual move to say the least. Normally it was the defense filing motions to strike in an effort to reduce their client's chances of a conviction on a list of counts. But this case was anything but usual. One glance across the Saturday morning closed court at David Cavanaugh's colorless expression told her they were going to win. And once again, she hated to admit, *it felt good*.

31

"Look at me," he said, reaching across the table to grab both of her hands. "Rayna, look at me."

She looked up then and he expected to see tears in her eyes, but what he saw was even worse; he saw nothing, a blank expression of total defeat.

"You cannot give up now," said David. "I know the letter is a setback, and the striking of the lesser charge appears to be a blow, but we can't look at it that way."

Rayna stared back at him and he could tell she was unconvinced.

"David's right," said Sara, pulling her chair around the table to sit next to their client. "When you think about it, they are actually doing us a favor. Now we only have one charge to defend rather than spreading our resources across the two."

"And they have removed any fallback for the jury," said David. "If you are found not guilty of murder two, there is no second charge to face. In other words, we win—you walk. And that is exactly what is going to happen."

Rayna said nothing, just looked down at her hands now enveloped in David's before removing them gently and bringing them close to her face. "Look at these," she said, holding them up, her fingers widespread. "Dry, chapped. Look at these fingernails: chipped, chewed, uneven." She turned them over, examining her palms as if she had never set eyes on them before.

"These don't belong to me," she said at last. "These are not the same hands that caressed my husband, bathed my baby girl, carried documents into court. I don't know who I am anymore, David. I have no idea."

"Stop," he said, grabbing her hands from her once again and forcing her to focus on him. "Listen to me, Rayna, I am going to do everything in my power to get you out of here, but I can't do it without you. *I need you* in and outside of that courtroom, listening, thinking, helping me win this thing. I have been tossing around how much to involve you in all of this—not wanting to apply too much pressure, careful to make sure your emotional needs are met, but the truth is we can't afford such sensitivity. I know you don't have a lot of experience with jury trials and that your background is more in civil proceedings, but you are a strong, smart attorney and an important part of our team. Jurors can smell defeat, and right now you reek of it."

He stopped before going on, knowing this had to be said. "We have so much to do and we're running out of time. Jury selection starts in less than two hours and I'll be depending on your opinion. In other words, if you can't do this for yourself, then do it for me and for Sara and, more important, for Teesha."

She looked at him then, small pools of water forming in her large brown eyes, and he was relieved to see at least some form of reaction to his impromptu tirade. She raised her hands once again to her face, wiped away the tears and took a deep breath. "All right," she said, sitting up in her seat. "I'm here. What do you need me to do?"

David began with the letter. While he knew this latest piece of "evidence" was devastating for the defense, he thought that if he could find some positives in its release, he might drag Rayna out of her depression and get her back on track.

"The letter is a one-off," he said, "a lucky break for the prosecution. There is no way the Hayneses could have more than one ambiguous note. Teesha said it herself—Christina never spoke of her parents' bigotry, so this was a first—and a last.

"Second, you'll be pleased to hear that Stein has upheld my motion to place a gag order on Mrs. Haynes and anyone else who attempts to pervert the course of justice and taint the potential jury pool by taking 'evidence' directly to the press. One step out of line and he'll slap an injunction on them and their media outlet of choice." David looked directly at Rayna. "And we'll sue for libel on your behalf. Finally, we know who the real subjects of that letter are, and we are going to prove it. In the end, that note is going to work in our favor. I'm sure of it."

It was working. Rayna was sitting straight up in her seat, her eyes alert, her concentration focused. He needed her to make the decision to stay involved. For her, and just as important, for him.

"Okay," she said. "So take me through the jury selection process. As you said, my criminal law is rusty. Where do we stand?"

"Well, we're starting at an advantage," he said, trying to remain positive. "Remember, in Massachusetts, unlike most other states, the potential pool is not just limited to registered voters but comes from a much bigger census list."

"Which means," said Sara, "that it gives us a broader base to work from and a system that is ultimately fairer for the defendant."

"In our case," David went on, "the court has dispatched four hundred summonses, and the recipients are currently on their way to the superior court, where they'll start by filling out questionnaires. They'll be asked about their views on race-related crimes, the potential penalty of life imprisonment, what they have heard or read about the case, and whether they know any of the possible potential witnesses."

"We figure that close to half of these potential jurors will be excused for hardship," Sara went on, "medical, financial or personal, and others will be eliminated by Judge Stein, who'll have the first look at their questionnaires. This first week will probably see us narrow the pool down to about sixty."

"And by the end of next week," finished David, "we should have our final twelve, plus four alternates."

"And peremptory challenges?" asked Rayna, now getting into the swing of things. "It's three apiece, right?"

"Right," said David. "You'll be there throughout the entire process. This week Arthur, Con and Samantha will be with you constantly while Sara and I continue work on the defense. Next week we'll all be on deck full-time, playing the vital game of jury chess with Scaturro and Katz."

"So who is our perfect juror?" asked Rayna. "Female, middle-aged, a mother, a minority?"

"At first glance you would think so," answered David. "But in reality you're way off."

"I don't understand." Rayna looked to Sara.

"You're right on one count," said Sara. "Our preferred juror will be from a minority, preferably African American, but the rest of your description pretty much describes the perfect juror for the state."

"I know it sounds crazy, but think about it," David told Rayna. "Scaturro will favor middle- to upper-class white jurors with a bias toward women—preferably mothers who would sympathize with Elizabeth Haynes as they picture their own children placed in a similar situation to Christina's.

"As for us, we want the men, and we prefer them young and black. You have to remember that young people have been raised in an era of political correctness and are more likely to find the entire hate issue ludicrous. Young male jurors tend to favor logic over emotion, and they would regard your actions as just that: logical under the circumstances."

"Of course, what we want and what we end up getting could be two totally different things," said Sara. "And that's why the peremptory challenge are so important—and where we should get an advantage over the commonwealth."

"An advantage?" said Rayna, now even more confused. "I would have thought we were at a *disadvantage* when it came to challenging jurors. We have to assume the minority jurors will be just that—in a minority. So we are sure to be faced with scores of white jurors—with only three vetoes to play with."

"No," said David. "It's the state that has the problem here. The minute they strike a black juror, they will have to *prove* their challenge is not based on color. Which won't be easy."

"Because if they don't," Rayna surmised, "and we lose, I could file an appeal saying the prosecution's challenges were racially motivated."

"You got it," said David. "Jury selection is a tournament with both sides fighting to the death to secure their magic circle of twelve."

"What about the Japanese couple?" asked Rayna, changing tack.

"Rigotti is on the case. He's enlisted the help of a friend by the name of Ricky Suma, who works for the *Tokyo Times*. Suma is going to run a series of classifieds to see what they turn up. Our only problem is that Sato is the Japanese equivalent of the American Smith or Jones, so sorting through any responses will be tedious. The city may be big, but our search is wide so let's not give up hope just yet."

At the word *hope* David saw Rayna flinch and he immediately stepped in to bring her back. "This isn't over by a long shot, Rayna. The prosecution may have played a couple of trump cards over the past few days, but they've played them early and now their hand is revealed. So let them have their day in the sun because I can promise you it's about to get cloudy. I will make this go away if it's the last thing that I do."

32

Rudolph had been sympathetic but firm. He had told her, in no uncertain terms, that this was "no time for instability." He had reasoned that Christina was a teenager "corrupted by a group of unsuitable peers" and that the letter was a result of

negative influences that they would have "terminated over
time."

"My priority now is making sure the letter is a one of a
kind," and she knew that despite the fact that he was convers-
ing with her, he was really only thinking aloud, as he did not
need her advice on how to proceed and even if she had any,
would not have taken it. "It is a catch-22," he had said. "The
letter gives the prosecution an unprecedented advantage, but
given that we are aware of its true meaning, it leaves us vulnerable to a similar discovery that could destroy our case and
us in the process."

He was right. And there was more—the other item she had
confiscated, not realizing its significance at the time. But she
would never speak of it. Never open it even. For doing so
would betray her daughter and her husband all at the same
time.

"Then how do we make sure the Martin girl does not
present such evidence in court?" she had asked, simply because it seemed like the correct question to ask at the time.

And then, of course, he had set her straight, putting her
promptly back in her place.

"That is not your concern, Elizabeth. You must promise
me you will not meddle in areas you are unequipped to handle. Knowing your boundaries has always been one of your
major strengths. Just leave this one to me."

And so now, as Elizabeth sat at her sunroom window, staring at the grainy front page photograph of Teesha Martin entering the superior court building, a photograph juxtaposed
with a smiling school photo of Christina, she ran her manicured fingers across the grain of the paper—from black to
white and back again.

And then it hit her, that now familiar wave of nostalgia,
this time tinged with a sense of déjà vu. The two girls—black
white, white black—they reminded her of the characters in
that old Hollywood movie—*Imitation of Life*—where Lana
Turner played a struggling single mother who went on to become a big movie star and Sandra Dee played her sweet but
sometimes lonely daughter swept aside in her mother's rise to
fame. The black girl in the movie was Dee's childhood
girlfriend—a pale brown girl who was determined to fit into

Turner's seemingly wonderful world of "white." She spent the entire back end of the movie denying her dark-skinned housekeeper mother and pretending she was something she was not.

And then Elizabeth tried to remember who ended up happy in the movie and decided the answer was pretty much no one. Because the demands of what life expected had consumed them and robbed them of their ability to *see*.

Of course, it wasn't just the photo that had made her think of that movie this morning. She often thought of it. It was, in fact, the last movie she and Topher had seen together, in 1959.

Things were different back then. She had realized from a very early age that her family was in the higher echelons of Westport society. It was not something her parents told her—just something she and her sisters knew and expected and took great pleasure in. They possessed all the social standing that prominent, wealthy Connecticut WASPs could afford, with her father smart enough to widen his circle to include appropriate Catholics, such as the Kennedys of Massachusetts.

The girls were seen as society princesses, all purity and class. They attended the right schools, went to country club dances, sailed on weekends and attracted the attention of an endless number of eligible bachelors who, with their hair slicked back, wearing white knit vests and comfortable pleat-cut pants, came in droves.

In the late 1950s, Elizabeth knew she was viewed as the catch of the bunch. It was not a conceited viewpoint, just a reality she accepted as just. Three of her older sisters were already married and Evelyn was close to being engaged to Edgar Pound III, a large boy who was not much to look at but came from a family so wealthy that her father used to joke that every cell in Edgar's body was worth at least his namesake times three.

As such, Elizabeth was the only Whitman left, the prettiest of the bunch with the biggest smile, the quickest wit and the best legs on the tennis court. Thus it was both easier and necessary to play down her "friendship" with Topher, for what was seen as acceptable (charitable) as children was now not so suitable after all.

Topher, she whispered quietly to herself as she closed her eyes and released her grip on the newspaper, allowing it to fall back onto the pretty white cane sunroom table. Topher Bloom, all dark and brooding and quiet and sensitive—a million miles from Edgar Pound and all his Ivy League friends.

She loved him, that was true, perhaps because he wasn't consumed by what should be but simply by what was. But in the end she also knew that there would come a time when they would all have to wake up and stop playing this little game of Hollywood romance and make-believe. And ironically it was Topher who set the whole thing in motion—by trusting her like no other—and surrendering to her his heart.

That night, after he had taken her to see the late screening of *Imitation of Life*, when she was enveloped in the warmth of his long gray coat and the mystery that was Topher and their forbidden romance, he told her that his mother had been black. And he knew, he said, that it would make no difference to her whatsoever. For he loved her and she loved him, and in the end they would be together no matter what.

Mere hours later, after she had gone to see her father in his study, and her mother had stood steadfast by her daddy's antique chair, she knew she had started something that could never be changed. And after her father made some calls and after Spence had been consulted, young Christopher Bloom was accepted as a late recruit to the United States Naval Academy at Annapolis, Maryland, and was to report for duty within the week. Its core values were Honor, Courage and Commitment. Spence's boy was making good. Everyone was so proud.

Spence thanked his old captain for the amazing opportunity; Percy patted his ex-lieutenant's bewildered son on the back, and Elizabeth's mother, Christine, started to knit him a navy-blue scarf with the appropriate gold trim.

As for Topher, he was lost in the whirlwind of it all, wondering what the hell was happening and why the youngest E—the same little girl whom he used to chase around the estate garages—was not crying, objecting, protesting with every inch of her being. But she didn't, and so he didn't, and in the end she never even came to say good-bye.

And so now as she opened her eyes and looked down at the newspaper photos of Teesha Martin and her daughter once again, Elizabeth realized one simple fact. As much as she loved him, she was glad she had never had to explain her actions, for he would not have liked what he heard. Because after everything that had happened, she knew that she had taken the road she was destined to take, simply because she knew no other path to follow.

33

"It's not enough, Ms. Scaturro, your reasoning is tenuous at best."

Loretta Scaturro was trying to persuade Judge Stein to dismiss juror number 21, a young man named Conrad Dale. Dale was a single, twenty-nine-year-old copywriter from Cambridge. He worked for a small but successful advertising agency whose clientele included major U.S. corporations. He had a degree in communications from Boston University and shared a rented apartment with his girlfriend, Leila Diablo. His father, Henry, owned a Cambridge news agency, his mother, Nina, was a part-time nurse at a local home for the aged and his younger sister, Anna, was a teacher at the local primary school. Dale was also an African American.

"Your Honor," said Scaturro, "Mr. Dale once worked on the BU newspaper *The Daily Free Press*. In his freshman year he wrote an article exploring the duties of local community service organizations. The article touched on the work done by AACSAM, of which Mrs. Martin is now deputy director."

The judge turned to Dale. "Mr. Dale, do you or did you know, ever meet or have contact with Mrs. Martin directly or indirectly?"

"No, sir. I didn't interview anyone at AACSAM. From memory, the story mentioned about twenty-five organizations. It was more a list than an article. I wasn't much of a writer back then, Judge." This brought laughs from the rest of the jury pool.

"Mr. Cavanaugh?"

"We have no problem with this juror, Your Honor." David glanced at Arthur. The guy was perfect.

"Ms. Scaturro," said Stein, "I tend to agree with the defense. So unless you are willing to use one of your peremptory challenges. . . ."

Scaturro bent down and whispered something to Katz. "Yes, Your Honor. The commonwealth would like to strike this juror from the panel due to possible predisposed opinions regarding the defendant's place of employment."

"Never mind he happens to be black," whispered Sara to David.

"All right then. Mr. Dale, I thank you for attending today. You are free to go."

And with that, David's "perfect" juror walked down the aisle of courtroom number 17, Suffolk County Superior Court, and out the back door.

Juror number 22 was Nancy Pirot, a forty-one-year-old widow from Boston's South End. Mrs. Pirot had two sons, one in junior high and the other about to travel to Germany on a senior high school student exchange program. She was an accountant, and since the death of her husband in a car accident five years before, she had set up her own small accounting firm at home, providing a bookkeeping service for small local businesses.

The prosecution liked her but was worried that her status as a widowed mother might evoke affinity for the defendant. Katz approached her.

"Mrs. Pirot, thanks for being here today; we can imagine how busy you are raising two boys, running your own business."

"Nonsense," said Pirot. "We do just fine, thank you."

"Can't be easy for a working mom, though."

"Nonsense," again. "With all due respect to my late husband, my business has flourished in the last five years and I get to work from home, see my sons every day."

"Best of both worlds."

"Exactly. The poor-widow argument just doesn't wash with me, Mr. Katz. You make your own happiness in this world."

"Thank you, Mrs. Pirot."

"That's *Ms.* Pirot."

"Forgive me, *Ms.* Pirot. We have no problem with this juror, Your Honor."

Stein nodded at David, but it was Arthur's turn to approach the potential juror. "Germany, eh? It's a great opportunity for your son," began Arthur.

"Yes, Mr. Wright." The woman had been listening. She remembered all of their names.

"Hard on you, though. You'll miss him." Arthur was concerned that Ms. Pirot, who was about to send her son into the arms of a student exchange family in Germany, would feel some animosity toward Rayna, whose responsibility it was, back on that fateful day in early May, to care for three teenagers who were not her own.

"Yes," she said, "but I have spoken at length with his sponsor family and have studied their student exchange information. I am confident he will be well looked after."

"Thank you, Ms. Pirot."

Arthur went back to speak with David and Sara. He was worried about this one. They had already used one peremptory challenge to strike a white, forty-six-year-old mother of twin twelve-year-old girls, from Back Bay, and there were forty-odd prospective jurors to go.

"I don't like her," said Arthur.

"Neither do I, but if we strike her, that only leaves us one more challenge and it's too early."

"I'm with David," said Sara. "She has sons not daughters, she seems more logical than emotional. It could be worse."

"Okay, two against three," said Arthur, who turned to Stein.

"We have no problem with this juror, Your Honor."

And with that, Nancy Pirot became juror number 5 in the matter of *Commonwealth of Massachusetts v. Martin.*

34

"I don't even know what it means. I hate to say it, but this could all be a waste of time."

Rayna looked exhausted. It was late and the four of them were sitting in interview room 3—the two women with their shoes off, the two men with their ties loosened.

"Rayna," said Sara. "It's a start. You've only had a few sessions. You told me yourself that hypnotherapy takes time."

"Which we don't have," said Rayna.

Rayna's latest session had revealed a memory of dull background noise just as Christina had reached the cruiser. She recalled straining to hear Christina over the din that she felt "came from above."

"It could only have been a light aircraft or helicopter," said Sara.

"Yes, but what difference does it make?" said Rayna. "Hearing the aircraft is one thing, seeing it is another. We have zero chance of working out what it was and even less of a chance of finding a miracle witness in the sky."

"Unless . . ." said David. "Unless it was the same pilot who dropped off the Satos."

"I doubt it," said Sara. "Their tour involved a morning drop-off and late afternoon pickup. The timing is off. Maybe, if we could find the Satos—"

"We might have some witnesses with their feet on the ground," he finished.

David was frustrated, as was everyone else in the room. The past three days had seen seven jurors selected, and so far the pool was looking very pro-commonwealth. Five of the seven were women and all were white except for an elderly Hispanic postal worker named José Renderra. David would be giving his opening statement in less than a week and at this point was cursing himself for his rash July first strategy.

"This is all my fault. If I hadn't asked for such an early date . . ."

"Don't," said Rayna. "It was my call."

"Come on now," said Arthur. "Regrets will get us nowhere. I'll bet the Kat would like a couple of extra weeks too."

But they all knew the scales of justice, like anything else, could be tipped one way or the other by that unpredictable element known as luck. Right now the prosecution was riding high and probably celebrating. Hell, they would be ecstatic about going into trial with such a judicial and popular lead.

"All right, let's all get some sleep," said Arthur. "Tomorrow will be a better day. I can feel it."

35

Foley Tibbs was a twenty-two-year-old mathematics major at Harvard. He was African American, born and bred in Memphis, the fifth child of George Tibbs, a part-time taxi driver/building super/handyman, and his wife, Beatrice, who was a homemaker and part-time seamstress.

"First up," said Foley as soon as he was sworn in. "I want to . . . *beeeep, beeeeeep.*"

"Mr. Tibbs," said Stein, covering his ears, "you do not

have to lean so close into the microphone. It will pick up your voice if you just sit back comfortably. That's it."

"Okay, cool, sorry. Anyway, Your Honor, sir, I just wanna say sorry for bein' late. You see, the bean heads had a keg party last night and I—"

"The bean heads?" said Stein, unable to resist.

"Ah, yeah, the accounting majors. Anyway, it was a big night and I slept past my alarm and I am sorry for holdin' people up."

Foley smiled and the whole courtroom smiled with him. David liked him immediately—not just because he started the day on such a bright note, but because he was their first "ideal" potential juror to appear before the court in days.

After a few preliminary questions from Stein, Katz approached the witness box.

"Mr. Tibbs."

"Yes, sir."

"Mr. Tibbs," he repeated. "How long have you lived in Boston?"

"Four years. I got myself a scholarship to Harvard fresh outta high school. Been livin' on campus ever since."

"Do you read the newspapers, Mr. Tibbs? Watch the TV news?" The question was actually very condescending and David noticed Scaturro squirm in her seat.

"Yes, sir, when I can, that is. Life's pretty full-on right now—classes, study, partaaays." He smiled.

"I'm sure. So you believe, given what you have read or heard about this case, that you could assess the evidence without bias or—"

Katz was prejudging this one already. David could see it and he stifled another smile.

"Oh, sure," Foley interrupted. "I would let the numbers fall, and then I'd make my call." He said this rhyme with a raplike rhythm.

"Excuse me?"

"The numbers, Mr. Prosecutor, sir. Life all comes down to numbers—the click of my dad's taxi meter, the mark on my latest exam, the probability of a crime bein' committed, the likelihood of the defendant being the bad guy."

"This is a murder trial, Mr. Tibbs, not a calculus class."

"No, sir, but I can see you're a numbers man, Mr. Prosecutor, just by lookin' at you."

"How so?" said Katz, now looking at Stein as if to say, "Oh, please."

"That suit you're wearin' cost you a pretty penny. It says 'I got more dollars than most of you in this courtroom.' You dress to impress, dude, and that's *all* about the numbers."

The entire room started laughing, even Scaturro could not hide her amusement.

"All right, all right," said Stein, calling for order. "Mr. Katz, is this almost over? We haven't got all day."

"Ah," said Katz, who had totally lost his train of thought but decided this young freak was no threat to the commonwealth. He looked at Scaturro and she nodded in agreement.

"We have no objection to Mr. Tibbs, Your Honor," said Katz.

"Mr. Cavanaugh?" said Stein.

"No objection, Your Honor."

"Thank you, Mr. Tibbs, you are welcomed as juror number eight. Please take a seat up in the stalls with the other members of the jury and we'll address you all very soon."

"Cool," said Foley Tibbs.

"Indeed," said Stein.

• • •

This was a rare meeting. Vince Verne had entered Highgrove through the rear gardens and gone completely unnoticed, blending into the background among a sea of caterers, gardeners and event planners who were busy setting up for the next night's festivities.

"Vincent," said Elizabeth, taking him in her arms. "It has been too long."

Elizabeth had obviously seen him approaching through the shadows of the back garden and gone to meet him at the large glass patio doors before her husband emerged from the library.

"Thank you, ma'am. I don't think I've actually had the opportunity to say how sorry I am for your loss."

"I know you are, Vincent, and I thank you for being there for Rudolph. He needs you. We both do."

"Anything I can do, ma'am, anything at all."

"I know, Vincent. I promise I will ask if something arises."

"There you are," said Haynes, emerging from the hallway.

He noticed Elizabeth still holding on to Verne's elbow, and it made him uncomfortable. It was not that he did not see Verne as a valuable asset to the family; it was just that he was more comfortable with Verne remaining in the background, away from close contact. One of the reasons their relationship had been so successful was because they kept their distance. This meeting was a risk, but given that the press had taken to following Haynes's movements, it seemed easier and safer to bring Vince into the circus that was the house and its grounds while there was so much going on.

"May I serve some refreshments?" asked Elizabeth.

"We'll be fine. Thank you, dear. I think Ms. Du Bois was asking for you."

"Oh yes, all right. It was lovely to see you, Vincent."

"Likewise, ma'am. Thank you."

And with that they went into the library and shut the door.

. . .

"You're all set then?" asked the senator, moving toward the back of the room to release the rear window curtains.

"Yes, I check in first thing tomorrow."

"You don't have to check in. I told you—"

"I know," Verne replied. "I have the key card. Straight to the room."

"I have arranged a special car for you. It will be parked on level B2, space 31. The keys will be left in your room, top left-hand desk drawer, behind the Bible. I want you here at seven. No later. And I don't want to see you all night."

"No problem."

"It is highly unlikely you will be needed at the banquet," said Haynes, now pacing. "This is just a precaution."

"Understood," said Verne, standing stock-still in the middle of the room as Haynes moved around him.

"I'll be very busy over the next thirty-six hours and I do not want to call you at the hotel, so if there are any further instructions, which would be highly unlikely and only in the case of an emergency change of plans, I will send them via message."

"Yes, sir."

"Don't use the hotel phone."

"No, sir."

"And take all the usual precautions."

Haynes knew there was no need to say these things, but for some reason, tonight he sought comfort in clarification. He also knew he was hovering around the other issue, the other task he had delegated—the one that would also be "executed" tomorrow night before the festivities began, an isolated incident far removed from all the tightly scheduled activities at the highly publicized banquet in his honor.

"And the Banks matter," Haynes began. "It is—"

"Under control," finished Verne.

"And it will be—"

"Quick, precise."

"And you will—"

"Make sure it appears to be an isolated incident. Untraceable. The act of a misguided supporter, angry at the injustice of it all."

"And it will—"

"Put an end to his meddling once and for all."

And Haynes nodded. There was nothing left to say. He trusted Verne completely.

They paused then, as Haynes walked back to the window and pulled the curtains aside slightly to see the large white canopy rise into the air like a circus tent, promising a night, as Ms. Du Bois had put it, "of magic and enchantment." He watched the caterers bringing in tables, the gardeners dressing the trees, the security personnel cordoning off walkways, the sound people laying their cables.

"Sir," said Verne at last, having walked toward his mentor to stand behind him, now taking in the same view that Haynes was watching with a strange sense of dull detachment. "I just wanted to say . . ." he began, as they watched the workmen lift four white poles that would fly the quartet of American flags to be posted at the corners of the rectangular canopy. "Congratulations."

"What? What for?" said Haynes, now dropping the drape he held in his right hand to look at his prodigy in confusion.

"The fifty years, sir."

And there it was. Haynes realized that tomorrow night he would be the guest of honor at a banquet celebrating a milestone so few had reached. It truly was an honor. He was an American institution. But Rayna Martin had stolen that from him too—the joy, the pride, the gratification he should be feeling at a time like this. He hated her. No question. He hated her and he hated her daughter and he hated her brother-in-law and her uncouth sister and everything they stood for.

"Thank you, Vincent," he said, before moving forward to shake Vincent's hand. And in that moment, as their palms met in a tight grip of understanding, they made a silent vow to make it right.

■ ■ ■

Seconds later, as Elizabeth Haynes finally recovered from the chill that had swept over her like an icy breeze on a hot summer night, she held her breath and rose up onto her toes before backing slowly away from her husband's library door.

And then, as if driven by a compulsion too powerful to ignore, she strode swiftly down the corridor and up the stairs to the room that had once belonged to her daughter—where she shut the door behind her and moved quickly to the hiding place Christina had never intended her to find.

36

The shrill of his bedside telephone rang long, sharp and loud.

Damn it! Who could be calling this late? David was so tired he woke thinking he had only been asleep for ten minutes, when in fact he had crashed at midnight and now saw his clock radio blink a bright red 6:05 AM.

Last night had been rough. Sam and Con had found no hard evidence that Petri was dirty, and Susan Leigh's biggest crime seemed to be her relentless ambition to reach commissioner by her twenty-sixth birthday. David had tried Ed Washington again with no luck, ditto for Tommy Wu and he hadn't spoken to Joe Mannix since their drink at the bar over a week ago.

"Who is it?" he croaked at the phone.

"And good morning to you too."

"Marc." David sat up, Marc Rigotti's voice breathing life and hope into his morning.

"We found them."

"I don't believe it."

"Sato Kyoji is a thirty-one-year-old quality controller who works for Coca-Cola. He is based in their Tokyo office. His wife Yoke is a research assistant at Coca-Cola— that's how they met. They've been married for three years and she is seven months pregnant with their first child. Both speak English, although his is a lot better than hers. Two months ago he was in New York for a conference at Coke's New York office. From there the couple rented a car, drove to Boston, stayed a few days and then went up to Cape Ann for the weekend before flying home."

"You've spoken to him?"

"Only briefly. I gotta be careful here, David. I'm meant to be neutral, remember."

"I know, Marc. I'm sorry."

"No, you're not."

"No. I'm not." They both laughed.

"So that's the good news. You wanna know the bad?"

"I knew this was going too well. Hit me."

"There is none. Just pulling your chain. This must be your lucky day. Mr. Sato makes regular trips to the United States. He says he is open to assisting you, but he needs to speak with you personally, find out more about the case and how, if at all, he can help. I've got his number. You can call him, set it up."

"Of course, but Marc, did he tell you—"

"Listen here, buddy. It took every inch of my professional restraint not to interview him then and there, but he's kind of a gentle-mannered dude, and I didn't want to scare him off."

"But—"

"But if it were my call, I'd say you had some bona fide witnesses on your hands."

"Marc, you are a legend."

"I know, mild-mannered reporter by day, legend by night. By the way, you owe Ricky Suma from the *Tokyo Times* a case of Veuve."

"No problem."

"And a case of black-label Walker for me."

"Goes without saying."

"And a case of that Guinness crap for Joe Mannix."

"What?"

"Mannix. If it weren't for him, I would never have found them."

"How—"

"I thought you knew. I mean, I assumed you asked him to call me. He was the one who tracked down the Satos on the police web. Turns out Kyoji has a few traffic violations, nothing serious, but Joe found him, called me back and I sent Ricky around for a chat."

"I didn't know."

"Well, in any case, you owe him."

"Thanks again, Marc."

"No problem. It's just what we legends do."

■ ■ ■

Sara had met Arthur in the elevator on the way up to their now routine 7:30 AM precourt briefing.

"Feeling positive today, are we?" smiled Sara at Nora as she walked past her desk and spotted the screensaver of the day. "Faith Will Move Mountains."

"Truer words have ne'er been spoken," said Nora with a prophetic smile on her face.

"Is he around?"

"Here already. I think he came in directly from his morning run. Something tells me he has some news."

Nora's words got them moving into Arthur's office, where David was sitting behind his boss's desk wearing a sweatshirt and running shorts.

"Well?" said Sara.

"I just left my third message for Mr. Sato Kyoji. He is in an all-day marketing conference at his office at Coca-Cola Tokyo. His secretary said he was expecting my call and would get back to me asap."

"At last," said Arthur, throwing his worn old briefcase on the office sofa, a huge grin on his face.

"Now don't get too excited; we don't know how much they saw." David's brow started to furrow.

"What is it?" asked Arthur.

"Well, I don't want to appear ungrateful for any form of good news, but to be honest, I'm pretty pissed that you went to Joe without telling me. We discussed all that and I thought we agreed not to."

David stole a glance at Sara, realizing he had just admitted to deciding upon their stance with Joe without consulting her.

"David, I have no idea what the hell you are talking about," said Arthur.

"Come on, Arthur, Marc told me. It was Joe who found the Satos. He used the police web and cross-referenced with Rigotti and his man in Tokyo. I thought we agreed not to involve Joe any more than we needed to. He's already stuck his neck out for us a number of times over the past few months."

"David, I can assure you I did not call Joe."

"For Christ's sake," said Sara. "It was me, okay. I called him."

"Sara," said David, "I can't believe you did this. We're a team and we make decisions as a group."

He realized what he had said—he had just chastised her for doing exactly what he had been doing with Arthur all along. But it was too late. He could see the color rising in her cheeks and braced himself for what was to come.

"What?" said Sara. "Do you know how hypocritical that sounds? I called him because I knew you wouldn't and because we needed the help."

"You shouldn't have made such a call without—"

"Without what? Without asking your permission. I don't work for you, David. I work for Rayna."

"Maybe so, but you should have spoken to us first."

"Is that so? Well, why is it I get the feeling you and Arthur have been speaking about Joe, but you have chosen not to include me? Anything else you been keeping from me, David?" Her look was cool, her voice on the rise.

David looked at Arthur. Taking his cue, Arthur turned and asked Nora if she would help him with the coffee machine. She nodded, almost pulling him from the room, and they left, shutting the door behind them.

The click of the lock acted as a starting gun, triggering a tide of emotion Sara and David had been suppressing for weeks. The accident, the charge, Katz, Tommy Wu, Paul Petri, Sara's brother, David's mother, Stacey Pepper, the letter, Haynes, what they almost did in David's apartment over a month ago.

"All right out with it," he said. "You have a problem with the way I am running things?"

"Frankly, yes. I have sat here for the past eight weeks watching you play your ridiculous game of moral hopscotch, protecting me, protecting Joe, protecting your family. That's all fine and good; you'll get a front-row seat in heaven, David, but it don't mean shit to Rayna Martin.

"Rayna is our client; she is our number-one priority, our *only* priority. You *know* that. I hate to say this, David, but Rayna's biggest problem right now is you, because you have the talent to win this thing, but you are unwilling to compromise your goddamned ideals to do it.

"The point is, David, no matter how honorable that may be, it makes for crap counsel. The only good thing about it is that if we do lose, Rayna could file for appeal on the grounds of inadequate counsel, because that's what you are right now, inadequate."

She took a breath, staring straight at him, as if willing him to respond, as if wanting him to shout back at her with all he had. They needed to yell, scream—they needed a physical release this last Friday before the trial began, before they walked that final mile that would carve out Rayna's destiny and, in a way, their own.

"Okay, Sara, you want the truth, you got it. I *am* trying to protect you," he began, his fists clenched, his chest tight. "There it is. I'm guilty as charged. But maybe I can't help it, and maybe you are the one who is losing out by not opening yourself up to something that could be."

"No, David. I don't want to hear it. You can't use that as an excuse. We both agreed we can't go there until this is over. At the very least you should have had the decency to treat me as an equal."

"Fine, but you can't have it both ways, Sara. You cannot stand there and accuse me of holding back on this case if you are unwilling to hear the reasons why. You can't tell me you value the fact that I'm an idealist and then abuse me for upholding those ideals.

"What do you want me to say?" he moved toward the window and then turned to face her before going on. "That you're right? Well, you *are* right, Sara. Seems I am stupid enough to believe that justice should be served with dignity. Seems I am even crazier for wanting to protect a girl I . . ." He stopped there, knowing she would want him to, and at that point, too afraid to hear what she might or might not say in return.

It took all of Sara's willpower not to move across the room. But even if she did, she was not sure if she wanted to hit him or hold him. After what seemed like an eternity, she took five slow steps toward him until they stood as close as they could without actually touching.

"Okay," she said quietly, lowering her voice. "Point taken. But don't you see? The reason I say all this is *because* of how I feel about you."

"You accuse me of being crap counsel because you have feelings for me?"

"No . . . I mean *yes*. I want you to win this case, David, more than *anything*, and not just for Rayna or for Teesha or for me, but for *you*. You *deserve* this, but you will give it all away if you don't stop worrying about me and Joe or anyone else, for that matter. You must do whatever it takes, because I promise you, if you don't, you will never forgive yourself."

And so they took a seat on Arthur's old leather couch, two feet and a million miles apart, and he told her everything. He told her about his guilt over the death of Stacey Pepper and how much he hated Katz; he told her about Joe's warnings that night at Myrtle's and of his fears for Tommy Wu and his family. He explained how he had asked for Joe's help with

Tommy and how he had accused one of his most experienced detectives of dealing with the devil. And he told her how he lived each day in fear of what was going to happen next.

. . .

Just after morning break, Scaturro made a strategic mistake. She used her last peremptory challenge to strike a thirty-eight-year-old black paramedic named Benjamin Boone.

At face value, Boone was a perfect juror for the defense: single, no kids, with a job that taught him how to shut the door on emotion. But a background check by Arthur's jury experts had revealed that Benjamin had lost a brother to a boating accident twenty years earlier, and this, teamed with the man's obvious discomfort in a courtroom, made Arthur nervous. Thus they weren't too distressed when Mr. Boone speed-walked to the back courtroom door and were even happier when the next prospective juror took the stand.

Amy Fae Basker was a bright and enthusiastic sixty-year-old widow. She had three children, six grandchildren and was a retired attorney who had served most of her career in the family court. By all accounts, Ms. Basker had the ability to separate emotion from logic with a swiftness that came from years of detachment necessary in her chosen profession. And the more Arthur questioned her, the more he liked her.

By this stage, Scaturro had realized she had made a serious mistake—and if she hadn't, Katz's glare would have told her. Her objections that Ms. Basker's previous profession would leave her with legal bias fell on deaf ears, and she was sworn in as juror number 11, only the second African American in the pool.

By midafternoon David had used his third and final challenge to veto a forty-one-year-old mother of two named Faith McGinty-Hill. McGinty-Hill, from Beacon Hill, was a wealthy homemaker who had listed her profession as charity adviser and was cut from exactly the same fine silk as Elizabeth Whitman Haynes. She swore she did not know Mrs. Haynes, but David was certain their paths must have crossed at some time. She was bursting to get on the jury, and took

David's challenge with all the distaste and disappointment her much practiced decorum could not hide.

By 4:30 PM all twelve jurors and four alternates had been selected, and Judge Stein took almost a half hour explaining the weight of their responsibilities before thanking them in advance for their time and dedication.

At exactly 4:52 PM the group of twelve (seven women and five men—nine white, two African American and one Latin American) and their four alternates (two women, two men—one white, two Latin Americans, one African American) stood, raised their right hands and were sworn in as jury members in the case of *Commonwealth of Massachusetts v. Martin* for the charge of second-degree murder.

• • •

Bristow's was unusually quiet for a Friday night, and the atmosphere uncharacteristically somber. It was as if the mood of the four forlorn souls in the far back corner had bleached into the surroundings, daring any happy-go-lucky Friday night reveler to interfere with anything resembling a smile.

"Four more," said Arthur, signaling the barman for beers.

They sat there in silence, all of them knowing the pool was a coup for the commonwealth. Only two African Americans among the twelve. Only two.

"It could be worse," said Sara.

"How exactly?" asked David.

"Well, at least the alternates are mostly minorities."

More silence. Truth was, the use of alternates was rare, especially in high profile cases where the twelve became heavily involved with their duties.

"We have the Satos," said Arthur.

"We *may* have them," corrected David. Mr. Sato had still not returned his call. "And we're still not sure what they saw, if anything."

"I'm so sorry," said Tyrone. "I thought the banquet invitation list might be more fruitful, but let's face it, I've been about as much use as a watering can in an inferno."

"That's not true," said David. "It's not your fault people are too frightened to be honest about him. Haynes might be the subject of gossip, but after the letter, no one is going to come forward with what they know."

"Wait a minute," said Sara. "What did you just say?"

"When? What? That it's one thing to gossip, and another to go on the record."

"Right," she said again, putting down her beer, her eyes lighting up. "So tell me, where do people gossip?"

"What?"

"When they are with friends, coworkers, socializing," interrupted Tyrone. "When they are with people who move in the same crowd, share similar opinions."

"Exactly," said Sara. "Like at a social gathering, for instance. A party, or a banquet."

"Sara," Arthur was reading Sara's mind. "No. *No way.*"

"We'd never get in," said David, a step ahead.

"Yes, we would." She was smiling now. "Arthur's invitation, remember? It's for two and it was transferable to other members of the firm if the principals could not attend."

"She's right," said David.

"No way," said Arthur again. "Are you insane? You'll be arrested."

"It's not trespassing if we were invited."

"You weren't invited," said Arthur, raising his voice.

"Yes, but you were." David smiled.

"The principals of my firm were invited as a matter of courtesy long before this thing erupted," countered Arthur. "Besides, I responded in the negative and I am sure they will have a guest list at the door."

"An invitation's an invitation," said David. "Worst case scenario, I'll claim they misread our response. They'll have security, but my guess is they'll have been told to be discreet. There is no way Haynes would insult his colleagues by having bouncers at the door."

"What could you hope to achieve?" asked Tyrone.

"We go in knowing we will probably come out with nothing. No one is going to talk on the record, but we can stay low, listen to the gossip. Maybe pry a few details out of the champagne-swilling masses, get some sort of lead."

"Come on, David," said Arthur. "Don't you remember

what happened at the funeral? It's too risky. Joe will kill you."

"Joe will never know," said David.

"Good Lord," said Tyrone, now grinning from ear to ear. "You people are truly crazy."

"What do you say, Ms. Davis?" David turned to Sara, pleased their morning confrontation had cleared the air and excited by her daring idea. "Wanna go to a party?"

"Why, Mr. Cavanaugh, I thought you'd never ask."

● ● ●

Two successive thoughts flowed through the mind of nineteen-year-old Amber Wells as she strolled down the classically decorated corridor on the tenth floor of the newly refurbished, highly respected Regency Plaza Hotel in Boston's upmarket Back Bay. The first was a sense of importance, a feeling of grandeur, that came with working for a "seriously la-di-da" establishment like the Regency. The second was a reflection on the clientele and came in the form of a sweeping deliberation regarding her current place of residence.

I am moving to Louisiana! she thought as the hot-looking politician opened his door. *If this is how they breed their senators down south, I am wasting my time with those conceited Harvard grads who are only after one thing. If this one was as good as he looked, well . . .*

But her mind was rambling again, and this was only her second week on the job. *Focus Amber. Focus.* "Good evening, Senator. On behalf of the Regency Plaza, I would like to welcome you to our fair city and offer you this complimentary bottle of champagne."

● ● ●

Verne was hamstrung. It was 6:45 PM and he had just opened his door to head down to the car in the basement when he was confronted by this waitress/hostess/room service maid, whatever she was, distributing bottles of Krug champagne. He was in the hotel as a measure of security. It was a big night for the senator, who did not want any unforeseen hiccup or resultant negative publicity in the beginning or the end, which meant Verne's participation across the entire event, blending with the other guests, slipping easily into the background.

"Thank you," he said. "But maybe later."

"Oh, you gotta take it," she said. "I mean, please accept this complimentary token, Senator. There is one for each guest and the manager will be very disappointed otherwise."

"All right. Thank you," he said, hearing other doors open down the hallway and not wanting to cause a scene. He took the bottle in his ungloved hands and made a mental note to wipe it—as he had done with everything else in the room—before he left.

"Sure. Say, you need anyone to show you around a little? I'm a Bostonian born and bred—know the Hub like the back of my hand."

"No. No, thanks," he said, starting to shut the door.

"Okay then, just offering. If you change your mind, my name is Amber and— Oh, *wait!*" she exclaimed, now placing her conservative uniform shoe in the doorjamb to prevent a now agitated Verne from closing it.

"I almost forgot. You have a message. I think they tried to ring it through to you, but you didn't pick up so—here," she said, taking a message pad from her jacket pocket and trying to lift the front sheet with her long-fingernailed thumb.

The girl put down the other two bottles of champagne she was carrying to attempt to tear the top slip from the vertical message booklet, doing an extremely poor job of ripping it along its perforated margin and lower edges.

"There you go." She smiled.

"Thank you," he offered, his radar for trouble now piqued. The senator had sworn he would only contact him by message if it was something untoward. He needed this girl to leave now so that he might adapt his course of actions to the senator's obviously urgent request.

And then Vincent Verne closed the door and read the ripped sheet of paper before him, the black ink clear on the pale blue rectangle now resting in his large, strong hand. And then he closed his eyes and nodded as if to clarify that he understood exactly what was being asked of him. And then he took a breath and put on his jacket and headed for the door once again.

• • •

It was like a chapter from a fairy tale. But instead of horse and carriage, the beautiful people arrived in sleek black limousines, the red-jacketed valets opening doors to couples dressed in all their finery.

The men were in dinner suits: the older generation opting for the traditional tuxedo and bow tie with the younger guests wearing more fashionable designer suits with straight ties in white or black or gray.

The women were their complement, making up for the color they lacked. Their dresses were long. Some were in full skirts which ballooned in the evening breeze as their wearers swept across the drive, and others hung comfortably on lithe frames shimmering in the light as they slid out of their cars and toward the music beckoning from the back of the house.

Each part of the journey was special. The walk down the side of the garden was under an arc of elms littered with fairy lights which weaved through their branches in perfect randomness. Once at the back of the main building, guests were led down through the gardens, which were backlighted with muted blue to soften the intensity of the strong pinks, blood reds and bright apricots of Elizabeth's prized roses.

From there it was over a temporary bridge constructed above the swimming pool, which was now littered with hundreds of white lily pads. The lilies, too, were backlighted by blue underwater lamps that created a muted Monet-like canvas on which they could settle. The bridge led to the main back gardens and up toward the canopy that looked like a huge, regal circus tent. Here the guests were met with tall flutes of Veuve, which they sipped politely before nodding to one of the many attentive waiters for a black-label whiskey or a perfectly mixed martini.

Inside, toward the front of the canopy that linked onto the opened folding doors at the side of the Hayneses' ballroom, was a small orchestra playing Brahms—the musicians dressed in short white coats with red, white and blue brocade around their collars.

The ballroom itself was an extension of the canopy and contained thirty-four round tables, each set for ten. Every table was covered in a crisp white tablecloth with the silver flatware arranged neatly for four courses. The name cards were centered perfectly between the crystal champagne flutes and the red and white wineglasses placed in front of each setting. The center pieces were simple, consisting of fresh white orchids in crystal vases, while the napkins gave the tables their color—one table all blue, the next all red.

But of course, the focus of the room was the main table—one long bench style arrangement with the guest of honor and his wife taking center stage. The napkins on this table were white with each of the ten places having a single crystal vase in front of it, carrying one orchid and one small American flag. Behind the table hung a royal blue curtain and behind the senator and his wife, a banner of the American flag and the Republican Party insignia.

In short, Ms. Du Bois had done an amazing job. It was a setting fit for a king and his queen and tonight, they certainly looked the part.

Haynes had never looked better. His gray hair was combed back but to the side—alleviating that sometimes cold look men took on when they combed their hair back "Gordon Gekko" style. He wore the traditional black dinner suit which shone with quality rather than age. His white shirt was starched to perfection, his black bow tie in the neatest of knots.

As for his wife, she was, as you would expect, absolutely stunning. Her hair was pulled back in a low bun which was set off with tiny white flowers woven in and out of her tresses with indiscriminate order. Her dress was also white—a scoop neck, fitted to the waist and then falling in a simple A-line skirt which, as it descended, contained a falling flow of white embroidered flowers matching those in her hair. Her shoes were of the same white silk—the toes of which peeked from beneath her skirt to reveal similar white embroidery but in a finer, more subtle pattern making the ensemble complete. She wore simple pearl earrings and a matching pearl pendant around her neck, and even at her age, shone far and beyond every other woman in the room.

Together they looked spectacular: the perfect combination of power and grace, strength and beauty, Grand Old Party royals, their poise and elegance offset by their love of the everyman. She was the Queen who would always be a Princess and he was the King who would always be King.

. . .

Vincent Verne stretched his left thigh a fraction of an inch and lifted his right shoulder a little higher before settling into position. He could not have been more fortunate. Delia Banks's multimillion-dollar home backed onto the Brookline Reservoir, a large parkland reserve filled with picnickers and joggers during the day but largely deserted at night. He was well hidden, with a perfect view of their five-bedroom colonial, which sat at the end of a quiet cul-de-sac.

He could see him now—Tyrone Banks's face lined up along the barrel of his SIG P210 semiautomatic, 9mm pistol. It was a beautiful weapon, a short recoil pistol with an innovative and rarely seen feature: a slide that ran along the inside of the frame, rather than the outside, which gave the bullet excellent support and contributed to its pin-point accuracy.

Verne had used a cheaper, lighter variation of the P210, the P225, when he was in the Secret Service and now remembered how much he had enjoyed the training. There was something satisfying about looking down the barrel as the delicate weapon aligned itself with a subject, as if capturing it in motion, like a moving portrait just waiting to be rendered immobile and transformed into a static work of art.

That thought aside, Vince had to admit that he was not entirely comfortable with the change in tonight's orders. Especially considering his recent discussions with the senator. They were extreme to say the least, and delivered in such an uncharacteristically hasty manner. They were, however, just that—orders—and as always he would carry them out with speed and efficiency.

He allowed his right elbow to relax and took a deep, slow breath before surveying the rest of the house's inhabitants. Three in total. Then he looked down the barrel again, found his target, held his breath, squeezed the trigger and fired. The bullet entered the victim's forehead, the silencer so efficient that the other two went about their business without even realizing one of their family was hit.

It would be some minutes before the discovery was made, and in that time the victim's breath would shrink below shallow and their heart would slow toward its final beat. And by that time Vince Verne would be long gone.

* * *

"Wow! You look amazing."

"Well," said Sara. "Just be grateful my roommate works at Calvin Klein and not Wal-Mart."

David admired the long, black fitted gown, cut low in the front and even lower in the back, with the bodice beaded with a shower of small blue-black glass drops. Her hair was down, dried perfectly straight, with small dark sapphire earrings and necklace offsetting the luminous makeup on her face. On her feet were simple black-strapped shoes made of the same material as the dress. Cindy had certainly come through with the goods.

"Too much?" asked Sara.

"Well, if our aim is *not* to draw attention, I think we are out of luck." He smiled when he said this, letting her know it was a compliment rather than a strategic concern.

"There is no way I am giving these back, by the way," she said, pointing at her shoes.

"I should think not," he said, taking her elbow to lead her to the car. "Just don't lose one at the ball, Cinderella. Something tells me our host is no Prince Charming."

"Agreed," she said, smiling at him before breaking into their fairy tale with mention of the harsh reality at hand. "What time is it?"

"Almost nine. We'll hang about a little because we can't walk in during dinner. We only have a small window of opportunity before someone recognizes us. When that happens, we have to leave fast before causing a scene. It's better that we arrive late, after everyone has had their chance to eat, drink—"

"And drink some more," she said.

"It will take us half an hour or so to get there."

"So let's go," she said. "I'm afraid if we wait any longer, we'll realize how insane we are and change our minds."

"Okay," he said as he started the engine. "Let's do it."

• • •

It was a major embarrassment, but it was averted quickly and with minimum fuss. Chairs were shuffled and seating cards rearranged with speed and discretion. Moses and Sophia Novelli had failed to show.

Haynes could not believe it. Sure Moses had had his little tantrum, but he always followed Clark—always—and this was seriously out of character. Still, no time to dwell on it now. Time for that later. Novelli would know there would be reprisals—hell, he would be expecting them. But tonight, Haynes realized, their absence could even play to his advantage.

Haynes had swapped Novelli's right-hand seat at the head table with that of Governor Elliot Frank from Oklahoma. Frank was as right-wing as they came and as black as the ace of spades. His wife was even blacker, so black, in fact, that her choice of fitted dark chocolate gown gave the illusion of her wearing nothing at all—which wasn't such a bad thing, considering that Talia Frank was Elliot's third wife and young enough to be his daughter. Sitting next to Elizabeth the two women looked like a politically correct Benetton commercial. Tomorrow's front page would show photos of the main table with the Hayneses framed by two of the darkest people in the room. Hell, it was brilliant; he should have thought of it sooner.

He turned to shake the hand of a salt-and-pepper-haired senator from Kentucky as he absorbed the awe and power of the room around him. It felt good. He was indeed Clark Kent. Superman in disguise. America's hero.

After dinner the beautiful people started to rise from their seats to mingle once again. The speeches had gone well, with various party notables paying tribute, sharing appropriate anecdotes and raising their glasses to the man of honor. There were video messages from past presidents, telegrams from others and, finally, the presentation of a gold plaque for fifty years of dedicated service to the Republican Party and the American people.

David and Sara entered from the back of the canopy at just after 9:30. Sara immediately noticed the stares, as did David. But he was relieved (if not a little put out) to realize the men in the room were staring at Sara because she was breathtaking and not because of who they were.

"Maybe you should . . . um."

"It's okay, David. I'll put my wrap on."

"I didn't mean to—"

"Yes you did." She smiled. "Never thought you'd turn out to be such a prude."

"I'm not, I was just trying to avoid unnecessary attention."

"Right."

They decided to split up, figuring they would be less noticeable as individuals. But after half an hour of listening to various conversations and asking a few discreet questions, they came up with the same conclusion: these people belonged to Haynes. Even if they suspected impropriety, they kept their opinions to themselves out of respect, loyalty or fear.

"We have to work quickly," said David, pulling Sara behind a hanging curtain beyond the bar. "I am sure some people recognize us but aren't too sure what to do about it. It won't take them long to raise the alarm."

"You're right. I'm sure I saw a few people point and whisper. If we get caught . . . if this goes public, we are in some serious trouble, and I'm not just talking about the hiding we'll get from Arthur and Joe. Maybe this was a mistake."

"I know. You're right, we'll get going asap. I'm coming up empty in any case. How about you?"

"Ditto. Except . . ." Sara paused, as if trying to make sense of the information she had gathered.

"What is it?"

"Well, there seems to be an undercurrent of gossip about the guest list."

"Who's here?" asked David, hoping she might have discovered a lead.

"Not who *is* here, who *isn't*." She lowered her voice. "As in Mayor Novelli. I get the feeling he was a late no-show, meant to be at the head table."

"That would make sense. Novelli and Haynes go way back, but I would imagine that these days their views on life are a little out of whack."

"From what I hear, Novelli is the genuine article," said Sara.

"Exactly. Worth checking out. What time is it?"

Sara looked at her watch. "Almost ten."

"Okay. You leave first. Just head back the way we came in. I'll see if there's a side way to the front of the house and meet you at the car. If anyone stops you, just say—"

David was interrupted by the ring of his cell. "Hold on," he said to Sara before picking up the call.

"Hello."

"David. It's Joe."

"Joe. What is it?"

"I thought you'd want to know right away."

"Know what?"

"I'm about to head out to Mass. General. You can meet me there."

"Joe, what is it?"

"It's Teesha Martin. She was shot through the head approximately one hour ago. And David, from what I'm hearing, it doesn't look good."

• • •

Haynes was shaking the hand of the slightly tipsy, and far too clingy governor's wife when he saw Verne standing at the edge of the canopy near the entrance to the ballroom. *What the hell?* He had been told to stay low, keep out of sight.

The senator excused himself and walked through the ballroom and around the waiters still clearing tables. Once at the canopy, he moved swiftly behind the orchestra, through a flap in the tent wall and out into the night air.

Careful to avoid the lights, he chose a slightly longer route down the right-hand side of his garden toward a set of sandstone stairs that descended to the back of the tennis courts. He could see him there, his shadow an odd twist of color under the green lights beyond the changing-room doors, and he felt himself getting angrier by the minute. It was not like Verne to defy an order; in fact, he had never done so before.

"What the hell are you doing?" asked Haynes.

"I'm sorry, sir. I just thought you would like confirmation that it was done."

This was a lie. Verne was not there to give confirmation of his deed; he was there because that uncomfortable sense of uncertainty he had felt when he first received the message had driven him. He wanted to check that he had followed the order correctly, that he had done the right thing. Because for the first time, this instruction felt—

"Confirmation? Why would I need confirmation? My instructions were clear. What the hell are you talking about, Vincent?"

• • •

No, he couldn't be, thought Mannix.

"David," he said, starting to panic. "David, where are you?"

Mannix could hear music in the background, beyond David's voice. It was orchestra music; they were playing Glenn Miller. He could hear the same tune himself, playing out back in the tent, "In the Mood," that was it.

David was here. He was at the banquet.

Shit!

David hung up before Mannix could say any more. He pocketed the phone and looked around the room. Haynes was gone.

"What is it?" said Sara, reading the shock, the anger in his face. "Tell me. *What is it?*"

"Sara, I need you to go out front and get the valet to call you a cab. Then I want you to go home, get changed and I'll pick you up in half an hour."

"*No way!* David, I thought we agreed, no more secrets."

"I know. I'll tell you everything, but for now I am asking you to trust me. There is no time. Please, *just go.*"

• • •

Haynes heard movement and looked up to see two men moving quickly toward the tennis courts—one coming down the sandstone stairs, the other down the pebbled pathway that led from the main house. Their shadows threw odd images in opposite directions, like two drifting ghosts set on a catastrophic course of confrontation.

"Impossible," said Haynes, squinting into the night. "I don't believe it. He's here. It's Cavanaugh. My God." He turned toward Cavanaugh, who was now entering the back gate of the court, and then back toward Verne.

"Leave. Go now," he whispered. "I don't want him to see you. You need to stay away, far away, until it is safe for me to contact you." Haynes could see Verne was torn. Should he go, or stay to defend his mentor?

"Mr. Cavanaugh," called Haynes. "This is a low move, even for you. Enjoy your last minutes of freedom because you are about to be arrested for trespassing. Better still," Haynes felt the blood rush to his head. "Allow me to remove you myself."

Cavanaugh moved quickly, so fast, in fact, that Haynes, he had to admit, felt a cold streak of fear steal into his brain and run down his spine like liquid silver. Cavanaugh was running now, and Haynes took an instinctive step backward before regaining his composure and standing his ground. Just then, Cavanaugh was hit hard from the side, tackled to the ground by the second man. Haynes heard a crack on impact and suspected the brazen attorney had just fractured a rib.

The next thing Haynes felt was a powerful pull from behind as Verne's training kicked in and he grabbed his superior, dragging him back and out of harm's way.

"For Christ's sake, Vincent," said Haynes, recognizing Mannix. "It's all right. It's the police. Just go," he said. "Go now."

Verne rose and ran, just as Mannix managed to contain David in a tight grip.

"Lieutenant Mannix, how nice of you to join us," said Haynes, straightening his jacket and managing a smile at the two so-called comrades writhing on the tennis court before him.

Joe pulled a struggling David to his feet, before David, still obviously boiling with fury, turned on Joe and pulled back his arm, ready to strike his friend in order to get free.

"David," said Joe, low enough for the senator not to

hear. "Not now. Don't screw this up. Think of Rayna, of Teesha."

David tensed and took a deep breath. He shook loose of Mannix's hold and wiped a streak of blood from his forehead, nodding at Mannix before turning to face Haynes. They stood there like that for a moment, saying nothing and everything, the steam from their breath forming muted green halos around their heads. Then David moved slowly forward and leaned toward the tall man who looked for all the world like a tower of strength but smelled of the sickly stench of fear.

"Remember this, Senator, I am not afraid of you." David leaned closer so that Haynes could feel the warmth of his words against his ear. "I promise you one thing. You will go down for this. You will fall so hard and fast that all this," David gestured back toward Haynes's grand house, "will be a distant memory." He pressed his clenched fist against the senator's chest before going on. "It is time for *you* to feel the fear, you heartless murdering bastard. I will make you pay if it is the last thing I do."

37

Teesha Martin was in a coma. The 9mm steel jacketed bullet had entered her brain just over her left eye. From there it had passed through the left cerebral hemisphere, the small section known as Broca's area, and on through the motor cortex and the primary somatic sensory cortex before exiting at the top of the parietal lobe and out the back of her skull.

"The left side of the brain typically controls the right side of the body and vice versa," Dr. Gad Kainer explained to a shaken Rayna, who had been granted special permission to visit her daughter at Massachusetts General's IC unit. "That's why the language control center for most right-handed people operates from the left side of the brain. Is Teesha right- or left-handed?"

"Right," said Rayna, knowing the answer was not what he wanted to hear.

"Okay," said Kainer, and Rayna could see that he was looking for a positive to counterbalance her fears. "The good news is that the path of the bullet appeared clean and there was no evidence of a stroke. I want to wait for the swelling to reduce and then I'll do some tests to gauge the extent of damage, if any—to her coordination, spatial orientation, eye movement, pain sensation.

"We must be aware of the worst and hope for the best," he said, then, obviously registering the terror in Rayna's eyes, added, "I have seen victims with more extensive brain trauma make a full recovery, but all we can do now is wait."

Wait.

Rayna—her two court-appointed security officers posted just outside the door—spent much of the weekend sitting by Teesha's bedside, talking, singing and stroking her daughter's smooth brown skin.

"I don't know if you can hear me, baby, but if you can, know that I love you," she said over and over again. "This is all my fault," she said for the hundredth time. "This is all my fault."

• • •

The shooter was a professional. Joe Mannix was sure of it.

The pistol and bullet were those of an accomplished marksman, and the precision had been faultless. The shooter had left no evidence. They had combed the reserve behind Delia's house and it was completely clean. The shooter's only error was a failure to finish the job, for Mannix was sure the bullet had been intended to kill and, fortunately, the unpredictable element of fate had been on their side.

The press was in a frenzy. Publications had printed close to entire issues on the Martin case and its latest macabre development. There was speculation as to the shooter's identity and motives, including extremist theories about vigilantism gone mad, neo-Nazis avenging the Aryan princess, the KKK returning and so on. A small group of extreme right-wing fascists known as the United American Protectors of White Supremacy even claimed responsibility, which was ridiculous given that the group was based in Utah, had a membership of twenty and none of them knew how to use a gun.

The defense team had set up shop in the hospital canteen. There they sat, reviewing evidence, rehearsing statements, preparing cross-examinations. David would have preferred being out with Joe, looking for Teesha's shooter—or better still, trying to link Haynes to the shooter. But he knew that now, more than ever, the trial must be his only priority.

Con Stipoulos was on his way to Tokyo. David had finally spoken to Sato Kyoji, but, unfortunately, his English was limited. Kyoji said he saw a "boat," but David was unsure if he was referring to the outboard or the cruiser. They had considered videoconferencing with an interpreter, but Mr. Sato seemed nervous, and given his importance as a potential witness, David believed that Con's calm demeanor would be more effective than the sterile use of computer technology.

He was concerned that if the Satos were in Teesha's line of vision, and Teesha could not see the cruiser, then the outcrop would also have prevented the Satos from seeing beyond the peninsula. That meant no clear picture of Christina—and no witness to any conversation.

Still, they realized that there was no point in speculating until Con and his interpreter met with the Japanese couple over the next few days. Until then, all they could do was pray.

38

Superior Court clerk Osmund Smead was a brave man, for it was he who had volunteered to make the suggestion. Judge Isaac Stein entered Suffolk County Superior Court, courtroom 17, and flipped his robe over the back of his chair before taking his seat. He could see him now, Clerk Smead, coming toward him, his feet leaving temporary impressions in the newly shampooed carpet, and Stein knew what he was going to say. Smead, a stickler for order, would be recommending that they move to the larger courtroom 9 immediately after lunch recess, and of course he would agree.

Seventeen was Stein's favorite, for it was small and, as such, it kept the press numbers down and the riffraff out. But now, looking out across the room at this crowd of sweaty, anxious spectators, he really had no choice. There were just too many of them, and the air-conditioning could not cope.

As he watched Smead negotiate the human obstacle course from the back of the room to the front, he took the opportunity to scan the crowd before him. There was the barrage of media squashed into the stalls on his far right and the jury, a half-stunned group of innocents, as their complement on the far left.

Before him, center left, sat Scaturro and Katz, all serious faced but brimming with confidence. They were surrounded by assistants—the young men, all slicked-back hair and dark suits, and the young women, all slicked-back hair and dark suits.

Behind them sat the Hayneses—the senator the picture of stoic determination, his wife the complement of pathos, poise and perfection.

Cavanaugh and Wright were huddled at the defense table to his right, and the girl, Davis, sat next to them whispering some last words of encouragement into the defendant's ear.

And there she was, Rayna Martin, her hair styled softly around her face, her emerald-green dress all crisp and cool, defying the heat and camouflaging her torment. But her eyes said it all, and in that instant he turned away for fear of meeting them and forming a bias he could not afford to entertain.

And so he agreed with Smead, and they would move to number 9 after lunch and make room for the rest of the voyeurs who had come to watch the show and retell the story to whoever cared to listen.

Stein took a deep breath and called the court to order. And so it began.

"'I consider trial by jury as the only anchor yet imagined by man by which a government can be held to the principles of its constitution.' Those words, ladies and gentlemen, were spoken by Thomas Jefferson and they still hold true today, perhaps now more than ever." Stein peered over the rim of his glasses and down toward the twelve men and women who sat straight, at attention, excited, anxious, terrified.

"I understand that this case has become a national issue. It has been the subject of many a newspaper and magazine article, hundreds of television and radio reports, endless speculation.

"But from this moment on, right now, from this second, you must eliminate all the conjecture, editorializing, loose comment and opinion from your minds." The judge, firm but considerate, serious but sincere, paused to let this sink in.

"Over the next two weeks you will hear conflicting presentations from the prosecution and the defense. It will be difficult—close to impossible even—to remove yourself from the emotion of their arguments. But, ladies and gentlemen, I ask you to keep your minds on the facts as they are presented. I ask you to listen carefully to each piece of evidence. I ask you to remember that a guilty verdict requires a belief in guilt beyond all reasonable doubt.

"Above all, I need you to remember that you are here as officers of the court, as guardians of our Constitution. Mr. Jefferson was talking about you, each and every one of you, when he spoke those words I quoted a few moments ago.

"Finally, I want to thank you in advance for your time, your learned considerations and your dedication to justice. Your duty is a serious one and your unselfish execution of it is most appreciated."

The main purpose of an opening statement was to give the jury a broad understanding of the case. It was more often taut than verbose, factual than emotional, and structured so that each of the twelve would begin the trial with a general understanding of what was about to occur. Both the prosecution and defense would stick to the facts as they saw them but also try to reach into the hearts of the twelve people before them, for, above all, trials were essentially vigorously contested competitions, where fact came with feeling and winner inevitably took all.

Knowing all of this, DA Scaturro also knew that she had a specific problem. For the past two months the prosecution had worked on a case based on fact but driven by emotion. They had gathered their evidence, but they knew they would have to manipulate the aesthetics of the situation in order to gain a guilty verdict. Which, at face value, should not be too hard.

Christina Haynes had looked like an angel. She'd been young, vibrant and beautiful, and the very fact that she no longer breathed seemed like a crime against humanity. Then there were the faces of her grieving mother, her brave but broken-hearted father, and the inevitable conclusion that someone had to pay.

For two months the DA had been mentally preparing an opening statement in which she had planned to draw on such emotions. She would be careful to stress that the facts would show Rayna Martin to be a murderer (for she must not contradict Stein's instructions to consider fact over sentiment), but she would also cautiously interweave words and phrases that were designed to set up her canvas for the colors of loss and grief, and finally conviction and punishment.

But now she faced a dilemma. The passion was still there to draw on, no doubt about that. But there was now a fresh dose of sentiment thrown into the ring: the feelings of loss and regret for Rayna Martin, the defendant, whose own long-haired, big-eyed, straight-A daughter, Layteesha, was lying in a coma at Massachusetts General Hospital.

Thank God she had been revived, at least Christina was one step higher—or lower—on the ladder of tragedy. Still, the shooting was a major setback for their case, and she would now have to paint the Hayneses as the greater victims and Rayna as a casualty of her original wrongdoing.

So after she had laid out the facts, and guaranteed that they would be supported by evidence, she endeavored to talk to the jury on a more personal level. For she knew dazzling them with promises was one thing, but winning their hearts was another.

"As hard as this may be for you all," she went on, "you must not—I repeat, *you must not*—allow events of recent days to affect your view on this case."

She had almost gotten through her entire opening statement without mentioning Teesha's name.

"These events have no bearing on *this* case. This case is about the death—the intentional killing—of Christina Haynes, nothing more, nothing less. You may be asking how you can rule out introducing emotion into your deliberations when the motive itself, the reason why Rayna Martin murdered Christina Haynes, was due to an emotion—the heinous, intolerable emotion of hate. This is a fair question, even reasonable. And I am not sure I can answer it with any great degree of reliability."

Scaturro paused, and shook her head before raising a finger to say: "But perhaps I can reassure you when I promise that we will provide evidence to show beyond any reasonable doubt that this woman did in fact kill out of hate, a hate so deep and so strong that a beautiful young woman was robbed of all of life's opportunities just because her skin was white."

Another pause as she shook her head yet again and made eye contact with individual jurors, stopping on Nancy Pirot.

"We are all human, and our justice system, as cold as it

may sometimes seem, is based on the principles of humanity. All I ask is that you seek the same foundations when casting your vote. Thank you."

• • •

"Accidental death," said David as he rose from his chair, trying to swallow his nerves and forget the fact that Loretta Scaturro had just given a flawless opening statement for the commonwealth. "Accident," he held up his left hand. "Death," he held up his right, and then he shook his head as if it did not make sense.

"Accidents are when your two-year-old toddler spills her milk, when your teenage son backs into the neighbor's car, when you trip on the ladder and spill house paint on the carpet."

The jurors gave a nod of agreement; Jose Renderra even let out a small laugh. At least one of these three events had happened to all of them at some given time in their lives.

"Accidents should have nothing to do with anything as serious as death. But sometimes, unfortunately, accidents *do* end in tragedy. It doesn't happen very often, and when it does, our heart goes out to those involved."

David paused, his expression one of acceptance of the harsh realities of life, before moving closer toward the jury with slow, calm steps.

"Ms. Scaturro is right, we *are* all human, and every now and again one of us is placed in a situation where a chain of events comes into play, events beyond our control, events that end in the ultimate catastrophe. That is what happened to Rayna Martin the day Christina Haynes died, and, unfortunately, there is nothing we can do to change that."

Another pause.

"But while we have no power to change what happened, and while none of us can ease the pain felt by everyone who knew Christina, we do have the power to break the chain here."

David looked at the jury. It was a look that said, "I understand the depth of your responsibility and I know you will stand up to the challenge."

"Rayna Martin did not kill Christina Haynes. It may be easier, even more popular, to say that she did. It would give us someone to blame, to punish, to *hate,* to put away in a box and forget about. But—and this is the most important thing of all—no matter how good it may feel to blame someone, *there is no one to blame.*"

David went on to summarize the basic elements of their case, realizing that before his opening statement was over he had to encourage these people to adhere to the facts without alienating them with a sense of coldness or insensitivity. He told them he would prove that the conversation Rayna had had with Christina just before she drowned had taken place, not yet knowing exactly how he would do this, and show them that Rayna Martin had made the logical decision under very difficult circumstances.

"Judge Stein was right when he told you to listen to the facts, and Ms. Scaturro told you the same thing—so here are a few to get us started.

"Rayna Martin is a good mother.

"Rayna Martin has spent her entire career making sure that people less fortunate than most have an equal chance at life.

"Rayna Martin is not a bigot.

"Rayna Martin *did not* kill Christina Haynes."

He paused as he rested his hands gently on the jury rail, talking to these men and women as friends, as if he were number thirteen to their twelve.

"As a lawyer, I have built a living investigating and presenting facts, and I am proud to work in a system where facts count, for what is the alternative?"

Another pause as he looked down and shook his head.

"But," he said, looking up at the twelve once more, "I disagree with Ms. Scaturro that justice is cold. Facts are not cold or hard. Facts represent the truth, and the truth is not sterile or insensitive or indifferent. Facts, about Rayna Martin, such as those I just mentioned, are warm, and good and true, and that is what our system of justice is all about."

David turned to gesture toward Judge Stein.

"Earlier today the judge spoke of Thomas Jefferson and his belief in the jury system of justice. So let me borrow from another of our forefathers when I say: 'There comes a time when one must take a position that is neither safe, nor politic, nor popular—but one must take it because it is right.'

"That, ladies and gentlemen, was from Martin Luther King Jr., and *that* is your moral responsibility."

• • •

Under Massachusetts law, the party bringing the case to court, in other words the prosecution, had both the opportunity and the responsibility to present its case first. Because it held the burden of proof, it would begin by calling its list of witnesses, with the defense maintaining the right to cross-examine.

Each witness was called with a specific game plan in mind—one jigsaw piece at a time—so that by the time they had all testified, the jury would have the full picture from a pro-commonwealth perspective.

Scaturro's first witness was, however, unconventional to say the least, for he was a friend of the defendant. Austin Malfrey, Rayna and Teesha's sailing instructor, was originally on David's list of witnesses, but when the count of involuntary manslaughter was dropped, the defense surmised that they no longer needed his testimony on Rayna's keen sense of water safety. So when Malfrey, a kind-faced man of about fifty, took the stand, he immediately looked at Rayna. He had no idea why he was being called and was obviously feeling as guilty as hell about it.

Scaturro began by asking Malfrey to summarize his extensive experience as a sailing instructor and outline exactly what his courses entailed. She then went on to question him regarding the generally accepted rules that come into play when there is a "man overboard"—the general term for someone who is in the water at sea. Next she moved on to the twelve-week course undertaken by Rayna and Teesha at Cape Ann the summer before last: specifically the ground they covered, including the practical aspects of sailing and the more theoretical lessons on water-safety regulations and rescue procedures.

"Mr. Malfrey, would you say Mrs. Martin was a good student?"

"Yes. Very good. She was smart and attentive, and her daughter . . ." Malfrey looked down as he mentioned Teesha, "she was pretty good too."

"And how many were in this group that included the two Martins?" Scaturro looked at her notes. "I believe the course ran for twelve consecutive Saturdays."

"That's right. There were about ten. In fact, Mrs. Martin was the one who set it up. She called and asked if I would consider taking on a class of young people who couldn't afford such a program under normal circumstances. I said sure and cut my price so that AACSAM could cover the total cost."

"I see. And these would be ten African Americans?"

"Well, I preferred to think of them as ten budding sailors."

This brought a snigger from the gallery and a small smile to David's face.

"Just answer the question, Mr. Malfrey."

"Yes, I believe they were all African American."

"Did Mrs. Martin pass the course, Mr. Malfrey?"

"Yes. Like I said, she did very well."

"So she understood the general procedures regarding 'man overboard,' or more specifically, the widely accepted protocol to help, retrieve and assist anyone in the water onto your craft."

Malfrey knew where this was going. "Yes, but—"

"Then how would you explain her leaving an unconscious teenager in the waters off Castle Neck Peninsula?"

David went to object, but Arthur held him back. "Malfrey is on our side; let him handle this one," he whispered.

"First of all, personally, I do not think the girl was unconscious because if she was, I know Mrs. Martin would have—"

"You do not *know* that Miss Haynes was not unconscious, do you, Mr. Malfrey?"

"Well, no, but—"

"Then please just answer the question. If in the event Miss Haynes was unconscious, can you think of any reason why Mrs. Martin would abandon her?"

"Well, no."

"You have never witnessed Mrs. Martin's preference for those of African American descent?"

"No, of course not."

"Mr. Malfrey, do you remember a student in that group of ten named May Robinson, and if so, could you tell us about her?"

Malfrey looked across at David, obviously unsure where this was going.

"Yes. May was one of the group. She was about fifteen, came from a troubled background. She had no interest in learning at first, but I went out of my way to try to get through to her, and by the end of the course, she'd gotten the knack of it—passed with flying colors," said Malfrey, a half smile on his face.

"Do you remember an incident in the earlier weeks when, and correct me if I am wrong, Mr. Malfrey, Miss Robinson called you a . . . I believe it was a . . . *'No good white-assed Nazi'*?"

There was a murmur in the courtroom, but a panoramic glare from Stein was enough to contain it.

"Well, yes. It was something like that. I was trying to show her how to draw in a sail and she was having trouble, got a little embarrassed. So she gave me some lip to . . . you know, cover it up. I didn't take it to heart. Mrs. Martin explained that the kid was abused. Her mother's boyfriend was white and he used to—"

"So that was a *yes*. Do you also remember what Mrs. Martin told Miss Robinson to calm her down that morning?"

Malfrey paused. He was trapped.

"Mr. Malfrey? Do you remember what Mrs. Martin told Miss Robinson to calm her down that morning?"

"I . . . ah . . ."

"Mr. Malfrey, may I remind you that you are under oath."

"Yes," said Malfrey, shifting uncomfortably in his seat. "I believe she said something to the effect of cutting me some slack."

"Did she not say, and I quote: 'May, give the white guy a break, will you? He is outnumbered after all and we don't want to scare him, now do we?' Is that what she said, Mr. Malfrey?"

"Your Honor." David was on his feet. "This incident, if it happened at all, occurred two years ago; Mr. Malfrey cannot be expected to—"

"No, Mr. Cavanaugh, the witness obviously has a good recollection of the sailing course and I want to hear the answer to this one. Objection overruled. You may answer the question, Mr. Malfrey."

Malfrey, now sweating profusely, looked at Rayna again as if begging for forgiveness.

"She said something like that, yes, but it was tongue-in-cheek."

"Thank you, Mr. Malfrey. Just one further question. Would you consider Mrs. Martin a friend?"

"Well, yes, I would. In fact, I would be proud to call her friend."

"Do you see her regularly?"

"Well, no. But we're both busy, and I'm based up at the cape."

"Has Mrs. Martin ever invited you to her house, out on a social gathering—barbecue, picnic, sailing party?"

"No, but—"

"Probably a good thing, Mr. Malfrey, for you would almost certainly be outnumbered."

"Objection," said David.

"Sustained. Watch it, Ms. Scaturro."

"I'm sorry, Mr. Malfrey, allow me to rephrase," said Scaturro, drumming home her point. "You consider Mrs. Martin a friend; could you perhaps define that friendship for us?"

"Well, I like her. I think she is a good person. But we don't see each other socially, if that's what you mean."

"It was, and I didn't think so. No further questions, Your Honor." And with that Scaturro returned to her seat with her head held high and a new bounce in her step.

"Your witness, Mr. Cavanaugh," said Stein, looking at David.

Rayna had reached across to whisper something to him just as he was about to rise.

"One moment, Your Honor," said David, before huddling

with his client once again and then standing to approach the witness.

"Mr. Malfrey, you described Mrs. Martin as a competent sailor?"

"Yes."

"One that stuck to the rules and knew her water safety procedures well?"

"Yes."

"So let me rephrase Ms. Scaturro's question. How would you explain Mrs. Martin's leaving Christina Haynes in the water on Saturday, May fourth?"

"Well, first up, as I was trying to say earlier," Malfrey stole a glance at Scaturro, "rules are important, no doubt about it, and ninety-nine percent of the time, sticking to them is the right thing to do. Then there are exceptions to the rules that become necessary in extreme circumstances. From what I can tell, Mrs. Martin had to make a choice without knowing all the facts. She chose to take the advice of the only person who did know what was going on—the young Haynes girl."

"Objection."

"Don't even think about it, Ms. Scaturro. You've had more than your share of wiggle room," said Stein. "Go on, Counselor."

"Mr. Malfrey, knowing what you know about water safety, and given your years of experience, what would you have done in Rayna Martin's shoes?"

Malfrey paused before answering.

"In all honesty, I'm not sure. And all this is easy to say in hindsight. But I cannot say I *wouldn't* have done what Mrs. Martin did. I guess what I *am* saying is I understand her decision." David let this last answer sink in, turning to make eye contact with juror Amy Fae Basker before changing tack.

"Mr. Malfrey, was Mrs. Martin's treatment of you any different from what it was toward the nine African Americans in your course?"

"No. Certainly not."

"She was not demanding, aggressive, derogatory?"

"No, not at all; on the contrary, she was pleasant, helpful, interested."

"Did you ever hear her make any racially motivated comments about you to the others on board, apart from that one comment to May, which you took as a comment in jest?"

"I did not."

"Did you ever witness Mrs. Martin in the company of any other white people?"

"Well, actually, yes, I did. One of the young people."

"I thought you said the entire group was African American?"

"Yes, it was. Except for one Saturday about six weeks in."

"Another AACSAM recruit?"

"No, one of Teesha Martin's friends. She was a lovely girl, just came for the day."

"And how did Mrs. Martin treat this member of the group?"

"Just the same as all the others, with caring and respect."

"This white girl was not ostracized by the group?"

"No. She got in there with the best of them."

"And you all had a good day together?"

"A good day. Yeah, we did."

"And do you remember this girl's name, Mr. Malfrey?"

"I sure do. She was a good kid. Her name was Christina Haynes."

* * *

After lunch, and now seated in the larger courtroom 9, Scaturro called her second witness. Jessica Jones was one of two paramedics who attended to Christina on the way back to Gloucester Marina. Jones was tall and strong with a determined face and self-assured manner. She had a matter-of-fact confidence accentuated by her cool demeanor and serious expression. She made the defense nervous from the minute she entered the courtroom, for Jessica Jones was also African American.

Scaturro began by setting the scene: the call from the Coast Guard, the trip out to meet the cruiser, the transfer onto *The Cruisader,* the evaluation of the patient.

"Her lungs had filled with water, her vitals were down. We instituted advanced cardio life support immediately, including the use of the Lifespan 12, a defibrillator monitor. This effectively gave us a computerized twelve-lead electrocardiograph, or ECG. We gave supplemental oxygen via endotracheal intubation, but there was no response."

"In other words?"

"In other words, she was dead when we got there. She ran out of time."

"Does that mean that Miss Haynes may have had a chance for survival if she had been treated earlier?"

"Definitely," said Jones. "The primary focus of the resuscitation of the near-drowning victim is prompt initiation of respiratory support. The standard of care involves rapid and safe extrication, cervical-spine immobilization, and early initiation of cardiopulmonary resuscitation, or CPR."

"I'm sorry, Ms. Jones, you may have to slow down a little for us amateurs," said Scaturro.

"I'm sorry. Basically, the sooner CPR is applied, the greater the chance of survival. Once you get a pulse, you are pretty much home. More than ninety percent of victims who arrive at the emergency room with a pulse survive neurologically intact."

"I see." Scaturro had made her first point and now moved on. "During your trip back to port, did you ask Mrs. Martin and the other three girls a series of questions regarding Christina's condition?"

"Yes."

"And they told you of the alcohol consumption, Christina's above-average swimming ability?"

"Yes."

"And did Mrs. Martin at any time refer to her alleged conversation with Christina Haynes."

"No."

"Did any of the other three girls refer to this supposed conversation?"

"No."

"Were you given any indication that this conversation even took place?"

"No."

"Objection, Your Honor." It was David. "The witness has just told the court of all the medical procedures she performed in a space of less than fifteen minutes. I would suggest that she was in no position to sit down for a chat with Mrs. Martin or anyone else."

"Fair comment, Mr. Cavanaugh, but the witness has testified that she asked the group a number of questions, and her testimony regarding the information contained or not contained in their answers is valid. Objection overruled. Go on, Ms. Scaturro."

"I'm almost done, Ms. Jones. Did any of the passengers make any other comments that, in hindsight, may have shed some light on the drowning death of Christina Haynes?"

"Yes."

David was perched on the edge of his seat, scared as hell and bursting to object again.

"Could you tell us about these comments and who made them?"

"Yes. It was Francine Washington. Just as we were disembarking with the stretcher carrying Miss Haynes, she came alongside me and said something to the effect of "She drank too much and then she had to go prove herself. She just wanted to impress. She was desperate to impress."

"Did you understand these comments at the time, Ms. Jones?"

"No, not really, but in hindsight—"

"What do you take their meaning to be in hindsight?"

"I believe Miss Washington was telling me Miss Haynes made that swim to impress Mrs. Martin. She obviously wanted to appear the heroine to win Mrs. Martin's approval."

"*Objection*. Your Honor, this is pure speculation," said David. "Those words, if they were spoken at all, could be interpreted in a million different ways."

"Mr. Cavanaugh is right, Ms. Scaturro. The jury is to disregard the witness's last comments."

"I'm sorry, Your Honor," said Scaturro, trying, but not succeeding, to hide the satisfaction on her face. Her point had been made. "No further questions."

David was on his feet before Scaturro hit her chair. He had

the feeling there was only one way to deal with Ms. Jones. Fast and furiously.

"Ms. Jones, when you reached Mrs. Martin's cruiser, what was she doing?"

"I'm sorry?"

"What was she doing? Was she standing still, steering the cruiser, soaking in the sun?"

"No." Jones got the sarcasm and did not appreciate it. "I believe she was administering CPR to the victim."

"Right. Was she doing this correctly?"

"Yes, I believe the technique was correct. Not, as it turned out, successful, but correct."

"Were your attempts to revive Ms. Haynes successful, Ms. Jones?"

"Well, no, but—"

"Did Mrs. Martin in any way hinder your work on board *The Cruisader*?"

"No."

"Did she attempt to give reasons for Miss Haynes's condition? In other words, did she seem anxious to explain or exonerate herself from any wrongdoing?"

"Well, no."

"Did you ask her if she had any final conversation with Ms. Haynes?"

"No."

"Did you ask any of the girls about any final conversation?"

"No, I was too busy trying to—"

He had her.

"Exactly. *You were too busy.* We understand completely, Ms. Jones."

David paused, allowing his point to sink in.

"Now as for Miss Washington. Did you know that it was she who brought the alcohol that Saturday?"

"No."

"Did you also know that Francine Washington was known to be jealous of Christina Haynes and her various talents?"

"Objection." This from Katz. "Speculation."

"He's right, Mr. Cavanaugh. Sustained."

It didn't matter. The jury had heard the question.

"Are you in the habit of passing judgment on others, Ms. Jones?"

"Objection," Katz again.

"Watch it, Mr. Cavanaugh. You do not have to answer that question, Ms. Jones," said Stein.

But Jones was angry and not one to give up a fight. "I just don't like seeing equality set back a hundred years by one bad seed."

"Ms. Jones," said Stein, this time using his gavel to quiet the courtroom. "Please refrain from making uncalled-for conjecture and stick to answering the questions."

"Finally, Ms. Jones," David didn't miss a beat. "Did Rayna Martin say anything to you as you disembarked from the cruiser that day?"

"Ah, I . . . I believe she may have."

"Yes or no, Ms. Jones?"

"Yes."

"And do you remember what she said?"

"Ah, I am not sure."

"Didn't she say . . ." David referred to his notes. " 'Thank you, thank you for helping her. Please do whatever you can.' "

"That might have been it."

"Yes or no, Ms. Jones?"

"Yes." Jones looked down, as if defeated. "That was what she said."

• • •

His media advisers were unanimous. During trial they should arrive and leave through the front door. They should not talk to the press—a series of polite "no comments" would do. They should not look down or around, but forward. They should not rush or saunter, but move assuredly to their town car, which would have special permission to park right at the bottom of the main front steps.

But this afternoon Rudolph Haynes wished it were otherwise. He was the first to acknowledge the benefits of media manipulation, and this first day at trial had gone reasonably well, but the tide had taken a serious turn last Friday night and he sensed the danger of an unpredictable influence he had not contemplated.

And so he held his wife tightly at the elbow as they left the courtroom and headed down the high-ceilinged corridors that led to the elevators, all the time their private security trying desperately to protect them from the barrage of media that hovered like moths to the flame. As soon as they hit the ground floor, it got worse, the *ding* of their elevator acting as an impetus for scores of additional insatiable scavengers to join the swell and press in on them from all sides, yelling questions, flashing bulbs, shoving, pushing.

"How do you think it is going, Senator?"

"What is your take on the first day at trial?"

The first thing he noticed was that Elizabeth was not leaning into him. She was, in fact, pulling away from him, ever so slightly. She even paused briefly to greet Caroline Croft, kissing her lightly on both cheeks before moving on.

By the time they reached the front doors, the swarm had grown tenfold. The security team tightened their circle and the questions flew thick and fast. A young reporter to their left was the first to ask it. He knew it was coming, of course, but they were almost to their car. "Mrs. Haynes, Mrs. Haynes, do you have any comment on the shooting of Teesha Martin?"

And she released—*pulled*—herself from his grip to stop and speak.

"I just want to say that my heart goes out to Teesha Martin and her family. It is . . . the attack on her was . . . an unforgivable act by someone who obviously . . ." She paused again as if not knowing how to put her feelings into words. "My husband and I pray for her full and fast recovery." And then an anxious Haynes took her arm again and steered her into the car.

The senator was completely lost for words and all he could do was turn to look at her, this woman, this stranger, his wife.

"What is it, Rudolph?" she asked. "It was the correct thing to say, was it not?" she said, her expression strangely unreadable.

"Yes," he replied.

"Good. Then perhaps when I am called upon to speak again, you will remember that I only have your best interests at heart and if we are to survive this, you are going to need me more than you think."

39

"Talk about a fish out of water," whispered Arthur, as the prosecution's third witness took the stand.

Frasier Kemp's sea legs looked particularly wobbly as he stood to be sworn in, grabbing the seat beneath him to steady his descent on the way down. Kemp was the command chief of the U.S. Coast Guard station at Gloucester, an old salt who was obviously less than happy with his current predicament.

The defense knew that the prosecution probably won the major points on day one, but felt that under the circumstances, they had kept things under control. They guessed that Kemp would be used to back up Jones's comments regarding the lack of referral to the conversation, but Kemp was the driver of the Coast Guard vessel so there was no way Scaturro could justify suggesting he should have been in the loop regarding the conversation. So they were not too sure where this was going but sat at the ready to object.

Scaturro began by asking Kemp to tell the court about his job, knowing it would be the quickest way to put him at ease.

"And you have been with the U.S. Coast Guard for—"

"Twenty years, ma'am, the first few in Hawaii, the next two down in Florida, and the last fifteen in Gloucester."

"Twenty years—amazing. You must have attended hundreds of untoward water and boating incidents in your time."

"Yes, ma'am, in fact we worked through the so-called perfect storm of 1991. They made a movie about it, starring that fella who started out on *ER*."

"Ah, yes, they did, Mr. Kemp."

Scaturro looked up to see jurors 1 and 2, Melissa Proctor and Roslyn Jones, look at each other and whisper "George Clooney" before suppressing their grins and refocusing on the witness.

"That's right, George Clooney," echoed Scaturro with a smile, looking at the pair and sharing in their girls' club before moving on. "And given your extensive experience, you must have also garnered an ability to, shall we say, assess a situation, read between the lines?"

"I suppose you could say that."

"Then tell us, Mr. Kemp, after receiving the first distress call from Teesha Martin, what was the first thing that went through your mind?"

"Alcohol."

"You needed a drink, Mr. Kemp?" Scaturro threw this in for a little light relief; she could see Kemp relaxing and wanted to help him on his way.

"No, ma'am," he said with a half smile. "But I could sure use one about now."

This brought a peal of laughter from the entire room, and a welcome reprieve from the tension.

"Fair enough, Mr. Kemp, but back to May fourth."

"Yes . . . ah . . . alcohol use is a key associated risk factor, noted in forty to fifty percent of drownings. And even more common when it comes to young people, particularly teenagers."

"And you were right, Mr. Kemp. Christina Haynes had been drinking."

"Yes."

Scaturro paused here, walking in slow circles around the front of the room and nodding her head just a little. She was taking her time with this one and David sensed it was because she wanted the jury to like this man. Likability often translated to believability and Kemp obviously had something important to say.

"I've got a bad feeling about this one," David whispered to Arthur.

"Me too," answered his boss.

"So you got the distress call," Scaturro finally went on,

"informed the paramedics and arranged for them to meet you on your vessel moored at Gloucester Marina, would that be right, Mr. Kemp?"

"That's right. There is an advance life support paramedics unit based on Eastern Avenue, so they were only a couple of minutes away."

"So from the time you took the distress call to the time you reached *The Cruisader*—what was it—almost to the point where the Annisquam meets Ipswich Bay would be—?"

"No more than fifteen minutes, maybe less."

"All right. What were you doing in that fifteen minutes, Mr. Kemp?"

"Maintaining radio contact with Miss Martin, rechecking their location, trying to get as much detail as possible so that the paramedics would be well informed prior to their arrival."

"I see. Now Mr. Kemp, you are no doubt aware of the two contrasting theories being presented by the prosecution and the defense in this matter, and the debate over the alleged conversation."

"Yes."

"The commonwealth maintains Miss Haynes was unconscious when Mrs. Martin saw her from the cruiser while the defense alleges Miss Haynes instructed Mrs. Martin to desert her."

"Objection." David was up. "Your Honor, Ms. Scaturro is not only trying to put words into the witness's mouth, she is trying to rewrite our stance on the case."

"He's right, Ms. Scaturro. Sustained."

"I'm sorry, Your Honor. The defense maintains Christina Haynes suggested Mrs. Martin leave her in the water." It wasn't much better, but a second objection would have appeared cantankerous.

"I realize that," said Kemp.

"Given that you were there on that day, Mr. Kemp, and involved with the incident firsthand, did you and do you still have an informed personal take on how the situation developed?"

"Yes."

"Which is?"

"I believe that Miss Haynes was most likely unconscious when discovered by Mrs. Martin."

This blatant statement sent a wave of contention through the courtroom and Stein was forced to call for order. Scaturro allowed the noise to settle before asking Kemp to explain.

"I believe that to be the case because that is the information I was given."

"Information? By whom, Mr. Kemp?"

"By Teesha Martin—the daughter."

Another wave of disbelief. Another call for order. David felt his heart skip a beat.

"Your Honor, at this point I would ask the court's permission to play a portion of the taped distress call between Miss Layteesha Martin and Mr. Kemp."

David immediately turned in his seat to look at Samantha Bale, who was seated behind him. She had listened to the tape as part of their initial discovery and had not found anything untoward.

Sam looked back and shrugged in disbelief, her red curls framing her now extremely worried expression.

"I am going to start the tape close to the beginning, Mr. Kemp. I will ask you to listen and then comment when I turn the tape off."

"All right."

The entire courtroom seemed to lean forward, as if posturing on the edges of their seats would improve their chances of hearing. But there was no need, the tape was loud and crisp and clear and everyone, including Rayna who fought back tears at the sound of her daughter's voice, could hear it.

"I ... we need help; this is an emergency," said Teesha.

"All right, Miss, calm down. First tell me your name and then tell me exactly what has happened?"

"My name is Teesha, Layteesha Martin, and ... my girlfriend—we found her in the water. She isn't breathing. She—"

"Where are you, Teesha?"

Teesha explained they were on *The Cruisader* heading back to port, and she gave their coordinates before going on.

"*Is there an adult with you, Teesha?*"
"*Yes, my mom is here. She's administering CPR, but I
     don't know if it's working.*"
"*Are you okay handling the cruiser, honey?*"
"*Yes . . . I have training.*"
"*Good. Now I've already placed an automatic call to
     the paramedics who will meet me here in minutes
     and then I'll head straight out to you, okay?*"
"*Okay, but please hurry.*"
"*We will, Teesha.*"

Kemp spent another minute or two rechecking Teesha's exact location. During this time the paramedics had arrived at the marina and jumped on board and Kemp raised his voice over the patrol boat's engines, which he revved up to full throttle before pulling out into the harbor.

"*What is your friend's name, Teesha?*" Kemp went on,
     keeping Teesha focused.
"*Christina Haynes.*"
"*And how old is Christina, Teesha?*"
"*Sixteen.*"
"*Has Christina been drinking, Teesha?*"
"*Yes, but . . . not that much. God, I don't believe this.*"
"*It's okay, Teesha, stay with me, honey. Stay close to
     the radio. We are on our way.*"
"*Okay.*"
"*What happened to Christina, Teesha?*"
"*I . . . I don't know. We were on an outboard and we
     putted into Essex Bay and our boat capsized and
     Chrissie swam out to get my mom and—*"
"*Your mom was on the cruiser?*"
"*Yes. But then the next thing we know, Christina is
     unconscious and Mom comes to get us and we can't
     find her and then we do and . . . and . . . we drag
     her on board and we try to . . .*"

Teesha's voice faltered. It was obvious she was fighting back tears and the entire courtroom sat silent, stunned with the reality of it all. Kemp checked her location again and told them they were minutes away.

> *"It's all right, honey, we're almost there . . . in fact, we can see you now. Can you see us, Teesha? Look south, honey, toward the mouth of the river."*
> *"Yes, yes. Thank God."*
> *"Okay, honey, we're gonna pull alongside as soon as we reach you, so start to slow down a little, okay?"*
> *"Okay."*

And then Scaturro turned off the tape.

It was a disaster. There it was plain and clear—a sequence of events in Teesha's own words.

> *". . . the next thing we know, Christina is unconscious and Mom comes to get us . . . and we can't find her and then we do and . . . and . . ."*

Of course the defense knew that Teesha had been confused, going into shock, rattling out details at random, and they would argue this on cross, but the evidence was still extremely damaging and they knew it. A shocked Rayna looked at David, who mouthed the words *"Don't panic"* before squeezing her hand under the table.

Scaturro rewound the tape and replayed the relevant section before reinforcing the sequence with Kemp. "It is clear, isn't it, Mr. Kemp? Teesha Martin says Christina was unconscious *before* her mother came to get them. The sequence is undeniable. 'Christina is unconscious and Mom comes to get us. . . .' "

So by the time she handed the witness over to the defense, everyone in the courtroom was contemplating the tragic irony that the defendant's own daughter had unwittingly sold her out.

· · ·

"I am sorry. I am *so* sorry."

It was late and they were now all back at the office, Nora

sitting quietly on the top corner of Arthur's couch, her hand resting softly on Samantha Bale's shoulder. Sam obviously felt terrible, worse than terrible. She felt solely responsible for the rapid demise of their case.

"I know you've had a lot on your plate, Sam," said David, who, he had to admit, was finding it difficult to curb his anger. "But this one was . . . well, it's a detail we couldn't afford to miss."

"I know, I screwed up," Sam said, her cheeks flush, her hair seeming to take on a life of its own. "I was trying to multitask. I was listening to the tape while looking up phone numbers for tour operators at the cape. But I should have—"

"You should have realized that the tape was on the prosecution's evidence list. And everything on that list is there for a reason. That's why we asked you to triple-check it in the first place."

"I know," said Sam.

David saw the distress in the young associate's eyes and realized there was no point in making the girl feel any worse. Besides, he was actually just as angry with himself. Sam had assured him that the tape was clean. She had even said it acted as a piece of evidence in the defense's favor because it showed how Rayna and her daughter had followed rescue procedures to a T. But given her history of hiccups, he should have found the time to check it personally.

Time, he thought, *and our lack of it is starting to prove a major liability.*

"I'm so sorry," she said again.

"It's okay, Sam," he said at last. "What's done is done. We're all under a lot of pressure."

Kemp's testimony had taken up the entire day, with Scaturro spending most of the morning playing and replaying the tape. Arthur made the cross after lunch and regained some ground by focusing on Teesha's state of mind. She was sixteen, going into shock, terrified, confused, and had also drunk a couple of glasses of champagne.

He reminded Kemp that the very nature of a distress call

meant that the caller was in a situation involving distress, and he asked him to call on his years of experience and admit that such calls were often littered with small discrepancies and misnomers.

In the end, they had gotten Kemp to concede that the chain of events could have differed from Teesha's specified order, but it was a small concession and the damage had been done. All they could do now was brace themselves for the next day's witnesses, who, they had to admit, held the potential to be even worse. Tomorrow they faced the double-barrel of Officer Susan Leigh and Detective Paul Petri.

"There's still time, David," said Sara, now reading his mind. "We can turn this thing around."

But he did not answer. In fact, no one said a thing. And then Samantha Bale leaned against Nora's comforting hand and started to cry.

40

Officer Susan Leigh had been called a lot of things during the course of her career as a Boston police officer: driven, focused, determined, thorough, persistent, tough and ambitious. But never stupid, no one had ever called her stupid.

She knew that success in any profession came down to fifty percent hard work and fifty percent politics. The hard work was easy—all you needed was the initiative and the energy. The politics were a little trickier because they were ever changing, creating heroes and victims along the way. And Leigh was no victim and had no intention of becoming one.

The lay of the land had certainly shifted over the past

weeks . . . hell, over the past few days. Two months earlier she felt sure she had put her eggs in the right basket. First of all, she had been lucky enough to be on duty on that Saturday, and not just on duty but up at Gloucester, of all places, on that goddamned water safety course that had turned out to be a windfall. Who would have thought?

Then she had spent that rather intense evening at the hospital, catching a lift back to Boston with some dumb-assed cop from the Gloucester PD who had no idea what he was missing. Next, she'd arrived at headquarters to find she was the star attraction with the commander of the Homicide Unit and the DA, both of whom were very interested in everything she had to say. Then there had been the meetings in subsequent days with Katz almost courting her, for Christ's sake. Not that she couldn't see through his posturing—he had his own political agenda, which was fair enough.

But then came the chance meeting with Lieutenant Mannix, and that had gotten her thinking: She had to be careful. She could not allow herself to be used as a pawn.

At first she had been delighted at the opportunity to ingratiate herself with a powerful U.S. senator. Who wouldn't be? But the Teesha Martin shooting had confused things a little and gotten her thinking that maybe the prosecution was not such a sure thing after all. And Lord knows she wanted to be on the winning team.

Not that the defense was looking very solid either, but there had been rumblings and she knew better than to ignore them. For starters, Lieutenant Mannix was said to be prodefense. Just a rumor, of course, but his earlier "advice" had suggested an aversion to the ADA and she knew he was tight with Cavanaugh. It would not do her career any good to piss off the chief.

Then there was the whole hate thing. The bigwigs at Boston PD were determined to stress their intolerance for racially motivated crimes. The department's mission statement was based on "neighborhood policing," and the guys who mattered were always going on about the department's desire to help "break down cultural barriers." It certainly wouldn't do her any good to be seen as having racial issues. The deputy commissioner was African American, after all, and this city was obsessed with political correctness, at least at face value.

So the question here was how to negotiate some very clever fence-sitting. Maybe feed the defense a little crumb or two. This would be difficult. There probably wasn't any way *not* to piss off the ADA, because he and his boss were certainly under the impression that her testimony would carry them a little further down their shiny white road to victory. But Leigh was a good tap dancer and when push came to shove, she knew she had to look after number one.

"Number one," she said to focus herself as the court clerk called her name and she stood to enter the heavy cedar double doors of courtroom number 9. *"Number one."*

• • •

Roger Katz looked particularly pleased with himself this morning, like a prima donna on opening night, a quarter-back before the Super Bowl. He glowed with promise and anticipation, shaking the senator's hand as he took his regular seat behind the prosecution's table, whispering words of advice in his associates' ears. Truth be told, it was making Scaturro sick to her stomach, but she allowed him this little presession performance if for no other reason than she knew he needed to do his best work today, and Katz was always at his best when he felt like the most important person in the room.

Officer Susan Leigh was sworn in and began by stating her rank and station in the Boston Police Department. She then confirmed that she had been on duty on Saturday, May 4, and in Cape Ann for the newly introduced water safety course, which was to be conducted at Gloucester Harbor.

There were ten officers undertaking the course that day, two from Ipswich, six from Gloucester and two from Boston PD: Leigh and her partner, Officer Thomas Wu. The morning session involved a series of lectures and video presentations given at the Gloucester police station, and the afternoon was to consist of the practical section, which would be carried out at Gloucester Marina.

The Coast Guard's call came in just as she and Officer Wu had got into their car to go to the marina. They picked up the emergency transmission on their scanner and headed straight for the wharf, awaiting the arrival of *The Cruisader.*

Yes, Gloucester had its own police force, but it soon became apparent that the people involved were from Boston, and the identity of the victim would require some special handling. No, this does not mean that this case received preferential treatment just because the victim was the offspring of a public figure, but it did necessitate immediate control in order to avoid a media frenzy and any violation of the victim's and/or the defendant's rights.

"So how soon did you realize the victim was Christina Haynes?" asked Katz.

"Almost immediately. The Coast Guard had her name, and Officer Wu and I put two and two together. We called it in to our plainclothes detectives, who suggested that we get Mrs. Martin back to headquarters asap."

"And the detective who gave this advice and subsequently handled the case was?"

"Detective Paul Petri. But once again, given the high profile nature of the deceased, the commander of the Homicide Unit, Lieutenant Joseph Mannix, also became involved with the case."

"So the head of *Homicide* was involved from the onset?"

"That's right."

"Is the commander of the Homicide Unit usually involved in fatalities that are anything but homicides?"

"Not usually. No."

Katz paused, allowing this to sink in. He then went on to ask Leigh to describe the arrival of *The Cruisader* in port and the victim's transfer to Addison Gilbert Hospital by a local ambulance. Leigh further explained how she had traveled in a second ambulance with the three girls, who were taken to the hospital to be examined and, if necessary, treated for shock.

"And did you speak with the three girls—Layteesha Martin, Mariah Jordan and Francine Washington—both at Gloucester Marina and at Addison Gilbert?"

"Yes."

Katz then launched into a rather tedious sequence of questions regarding Leigh's individual interrogation of the three girls. Even Stein was starting to get bored and at one point asked the ADA if his line of questioning was ever going to shed new light on the situation.

"I'm sorry, Your Honor, but Officer Leigh is a decorated officer with a fine record of successful interrogation. I believe this line of questioning goes to show the officer's thorough approach to the investigation."

"All right, but you've made your point, Mr. Katz, now move on," said Stein.

And he did: "Officer Leigh, did any of the three girls give details of the alleged conversation between Miss Haynes and Mrs. Martin?"

"No."

"Did any of the three girls at any time quote what was supposed to have been said by Miss Haynes in the alleged exchange?"

"No."

"Did any of the three girls quote Mrs. Martin's version of said discussion?"

"No."

Katz turned to walk slowly toward the jury.

"Did any of the three g . . ."

"But I got the impression they believed the conversation took place."

Katz stopped in his tracks. Scaturro looked up. This was not how they had discussed her testimony. Worse still, Leigh went on—largely because Katz seemed to have been struck dumb by her previous comments.

"The girls did not mention the contents of the alleged exchange, but I think they assumed it took place."

"Officer Leigh, you just testified that the girls made no reference to this supposed conversation."

"That's right."

"With all due respect, Officer, we do not require your opinion on the . . ."

"Objection." David was up, Scatturo knowing he would take advantage of the unforgivable blunder by her second in command. "ADA Katz has gone out of his way to stress Officer Leigh's excellent interrogation skills; I would think the court should be allowed to hear her expert take on the situation, given that she was the first to interview the three girls."

"He's right, Mr. Katz. Sustained. Go on, Officer."

Officer Leigh continued, much to Katz's obvious chagrin.

"The girls gave direct evidence regarding the portions of the day in which they were immediately involved, but there was a short period when this alleged discussion was supposedly taking place, for which they could not provide firsthand accounts, simply because they were not there. But each girl assumed Miss Haynes had told Mrs. Martin to go to them, for this was part of their original plan.

"They had *no reason* to doubt this did not occur, *no reason* to assume Christina did not deliver the message to rescue them, and *no reason* to believe Mrs. Martin would leave Christina in the water without Christina advising her to do so."

Scaturro knew Katz was in a hole, and could see from his expression that he knew it too but, ever clever on his feet, he quickly found a way out.

"Did they plan on Miss Haynes drowning, Officer?"

"No, of course not."

"Did they plan on spending that evening in the hospital?"

"I'm sure they didn't."

"Or being interrogated by a police officer? Or losing one of their best friends?"

"No."

"So things do not always go to plan, do they, Officer?"

"No, Mr. Katz, they do not." This was aimed at him, and Scaturro knew it.

"All right then, Officer Leigh, let me ask you one more time. Did any of the girls give any reference, no matter how small, to the alleged conversation between Mrs. Martin and Miss Haynes?"

"No."

"Thank you, Officer Leigh. No further questions."

"Then let's break for lunch," said Stein, indicating to Officer Leigh that she would be needed after lunch for cross.

And with that Leigh stood and started to make her way toward the back of the courtroom. Loretta Scaturro followed her with her eyes and realized her anger was not targeted at the ambitious young officer. Leigh had got the better of that exchange and in other circumstances she might have even championed the woman's ability to tie Katz into a knot.

But not now. Now she was furious at her ADA for allowing one of their key witnesses to parade as a poster girl for the defense. Cavanaugh was not stupid; he would read the girl's testimony for exactly what it was: an invitation to court her favor on the stand.

This is not good, Loretta said to herself just as a red-faced Katz returned to his seat. Officer Leigh had wielded the proverbial dagger and worse still, she suspected, the young woman was about to give it a twist.

• • •

David had a hunch.

He could have sworn that for a split second, just as Susan Leigh was passing the defense table on her way toward the back courtroom doors, she made eye contact with him and smiled.

The look said: *I have opened the door for you, now it's up to you to walk on in.* He sensed Susan Leigh had just given them something, but he couldn't put his finger on exactly what it was.

During the lunch break he asked for a court transcript of Leigh's testimony, and he wanted it on tape, not on paper, so he could hear the intonation in her voice. She kept emphasizing the word *reason,* and he got the feeling it wasn't by chance.

"What are you looking for, some sort of cryptic clue? Sounds a little cloak-and-dagger to me, David," said Sara, chewing on a chicken salad sandwich from the court cafeteria.

"No, nothing that obvious, more like a . . . a perspective."

"Well, whatever it is," said Arthur, throwing most of his egg and lettuce on rye in the rubbish, "we don't have much time."

"I know," said David, inserting the tape into a player.

Rayna had been given permission to place a call to the hospital during the lunch recess, so they sat listening to

Leigh's clear and decisive voice as they awaited her return. David played it and replayed it, focusing on the section where Leigh rattled the ADA by suggesting the girls assumed the conversation took place.

"That's it," he said, just as they were called into court.

"*No reason*—do you hear how she emphasized these words? They had *'no reason'* to think otherwise, and when you think about it, neither did anyone else."

- - -

"Officer Leigh, this morning you told the court you believed the three girls—and I'll quote you here—'assumed Miss Haynes had told Mrs. Martin to go to them, for this was part of their original plan, and they had no reason to doubt this did not occur.' Is that correct?"

"Yes."

"Officer Leigh, why wasn't Mrs. Martin charged with any crime the night of May fourth?"

"Because at that stage we did not have the evidence to confirm a crime had taken place."

"In other words, you had *no reason* to charge her."

"That is another way of putting it, I suppose."

"So at that point," said David, now moving slowly from the middle of the room toward the witness stand, "even several hours after the event, the incident was being viewed as a tragic accident, would that be correct?"

"Not necessarily, but I suppose our earliest assumptions leaned in that direction."

"Because you had *no reason* to think otherwise."

"That's right."

"Officer," David now changed course slightly, making his direction diagonal, toward the front of the jury panel. "Why do you think the head of Homicide was involved with the case from the onset?"

"As I said earlier, this was going to be a high profile case."

"So you believed Lieutenant Mannix was involved due to the victim's identity rather than the nature of the case."

"Initially, yes."

"In fact, that night at Boston Police headquarters, did you

not spend several hours with the district attorney, Ms. Scaturro, and Lieutenant Mannix?"

"Yes."

"And even then, after many hours of discussion with two of this city's top crime officials, you all still found *no reason* to charge her."

"Not at that point. No."

"In fact, Mrs. Martin was not charged until the following day, and at that point the charge was the lesser charge of involuntary manslaughter, isn't that correct, Officer Leigh?"

"Yes."

"And even then, when this lesser but still irrelevant charge was made, there was still *no reason* to suggest the incident was in any way a hate-related homicide."

David stopped short, now only two feet from his witness and the foreman of the jury, waiting for Scaturro's objection.

"Objection," said Scaturro. "Your Honor, the defense may believe the original charge was irrelevant, and that may be their prerogative, but it is inappropriate for them to put such words into the witness's mouth."

"Your Honor," David was quick to refute, "the prosecution effectively made the charge of involuntary manslaughter irrelevant when, at the end of last week, they filed their motion to strike it."

"Touché, Mr. Cavanaugh. You asked for that one, Ms. Scaturro. Go on, Mr. Cavanaugh."

"Officer Leigh, let me rephrase the question. When Mrs. Martin was arrested on the charge of involuntary manslaughter on Sunday, May fifth, was there any indication at that stage that the charge would be extended to murder two?"

"I do not believe so."

"Because there was *no reason* for anyone to view this as a hate-related murder."

"Not at that stage. No."

David was now at the front of the jury. He rested his hands on the railing before shaking his head. Then he turned toward his client, Rayna Martin, taking the jurors' eyes with him.

"So to your knowledge, what happened to change all of

that? What amazing piece of evidence suddenly gave everybody the reason to arrest this innocent woman," he said, gesturing at Rayna, "for the very serious crime of second-degree murder?"

"I believe it was new evidence provided by one of the girls—Francine Washington."

"Yes, yes, Miss Washington. One frightened sixteen-year-old girl suddenly came up with something that you, Officer Wu, Detective Petri, Lieutenant Mannix and DA Scaturro could not."

"Witnesses come in all shapes and forms, Mr. Cavanaugh."

"True, Officer. So tell us, given your stellar record of police interrogation, how would you describe Francine Washington?"

"Well, you must take into account that all the girls were distressed. But I found her to be scared, insecure, nervous, self-centered and . . ." Leigh paused.

"And what, Officer Leigh?" David quickly turned his attention back to Leigh, willing her answer to be as he hoped.

"Well, initially she lied about being the one who supplied the champagne, so I was going to say—"

"You were going to call her a liar."

"Well, yes. Yes, I was."

41

"This is unbelievable," he had said, looking at his daughter but speaking to his wife.

Elizabeth's eyes were closed, but even now, so many years later, she could see the pain, the anger, the disillusionment on her father's face—little Lizzy, his unspoken favorite, had disappointed her daddy.

She opened them now and looked at the clock by her bed. Twelve-twenty-two. Rudi was still up.

Elizabeth closed her eyes again and found it so easy to slip back, the years disappearing in seconds. Her breathing slowed. She was there now.

She heard the old eighteenth-century Britannia clock chime on the wall, its last note hanging in the air before dissipating into silence.

She looked at her mother and saw so much and not enough.

Her mother's face screamed of a need to reach out to her daughter, to ease her obvious pain, to mend her breaking heart, but her body stood firm, behind her husband's deep green leather chair, as if it knew no other place to be.

Elizabeth Whitman felt a wave of regret wash into her consciousness. She had made a mistake. She should not have told them. She loved Topher and now she was betraying him. But she had said what she had said and knew that there was no point in denying it now, for even if she tried to take it all back, they would know the truth of it soon.

And so she told them about her "attachment" to Christopher Bloom and how neither of them had intended to hurt anybody. And when her father concluded that the boy must be sent away, she did not object.

For as much as she hated to admit it, her father was giving her an out. Her heart, like her mother's, may have wanted to reach out—in Elizabeth's case to Topher—but her mind and body stood firm, in front of her father's antique mahogany desk, knowing this was, in the long run, for the best.

"This is a good opportunity for the boy," he said, as if reading her thoughts, and she nodded.

The phone rang and she heard Agnes pick it up in the hallway. It would be for her father and herald an end to this conversation and the matter as a whole.

"David Morgan-Bryant called this morning," said her mother, as if this were the best news they had heard

all day. "I think he wants to ask you to his parents' an-
niversary dinner."

She did not answer.

Agnes knocked at the door.

"Is that the last of it then?" her father asked, want-
ing one last confirmation that they could close this
rather unfortunate chapter for good.

"Not quite," said Elizabeth. "There is one other
thing."

42

While most of America was loading up the family car for a
long, sunny summer weekend, the players and spectators at
the trial of Rayna Martin had taken their seats as usual. It was
as if the holiday had leapfrogged courtroom 9, leaving everybody in it to their own important piece of business, too pressing to postpone, too mesmerizing to miss.

The defense had been buoyed by Officer Leigh's testimony
the day before and was not surprised when the state had asked
for an early adjournment, preferring to begin afresh with Detective Paul Petri this morning. But it was all over before it
began.

As soon as Stein entered the room, a nervous Scaturro
asked for a sidebar and David followed the DA and Katz toward the judge at the front of the room.

"What is it, Ms. Scaturro?"

"Your Honor, I am sorry to say the state would like to request a twenty-four-hour recess due to some unforeseen delays regarding our next witness."

"I gave you an early mark yesterday, Ms. Scaturro. What
is it this time?"

"I am afraid Detective Petri's wife passed away last night, Your Honor, and under the circumstances—"

"Who is your next witness?"

"Dr. Gustav Svenson, Your Honor."

"I suppose he has the day off too?"

"Actually, no. He is working, but they are very short staffed at the ME's office this week, as you can well imagine, and Dr. Svenson had to pull some strings to make himself available for tomorrow. I am afraid there is no way—"

"Mr. Cavanaugh, what do you have to say about this?"

David's head was still processing the news that Paul Petri's wife had died, and as much as he felt for the poor woman, he could not help but wonder what this might mean to the defense.

"Mr. Cavanaugh?"

"Obviously, we are disappointed with the delay, Your Honor. But under the circumstances, the defense would concede to a day's stay for compassionate reasons."

In reality, David was delighted with the request. He could think of a million things he could do today, the main ones being setting up a conference call with Con Stipoulos in Tokyo and catching up with Joe Mannix.

"All right then. Please pass my condolences to your witness, but I am afraid I want either him or Dr. Svenson on that stand by nine tomorrow morning."

"Yes, Your Honor," said Scaturro. "Thank you."

And with that, like a king over his country, Judge Stein wielded his gavel and told his audience—like it or not—they had the day off. "Go home to your families," he said. "And have a safe and happy Independence Day."

● ● ●

Bessie was late again. Yesterday she had come in with three horrible welts on her neck. Welts! Disgusting. They were love bites, or what Ed had called hickeys as a young man. He hated the look of them then, and hated them even more now.

It was Bessie's job to open up, tidy his desk and bring in the mail, including the morning paper that he had missed reading at home this morning because he'd slept past his alarm. He had worked late the night before, showing some useless wannabe a house there was no way he could afford. Why did people do that, he always wondered—ask to view homes they could only dream about buying? Goddamned voyeurs, good-for-nothing dreamers who had nothing better to do than waste his precious time. But his mind was rambling.

He took off his coat, cleared his desk and made himself a nice warm cup of coffee before sitting down to catch up on the latest from the trial. He heard his wife, who often brought her own car (so she could leave early), come in the back door, and cursed her for disturbing his peace and being late all at the same time.

"Coffee, dear?" she asked.

To which Ed gave no reply except to hold up his cup and give her a stern look which said, "Well, if you hadn't spent twenty minutes on the phone with your mother this morning you wouldn't have been late and you could have made me this cup and saved me another valuable five minutes."

"I'll take that as a no," she said, before turning to make one for herself.

"Holy God the Father!" said Ed, spraying his desk with a shower of milky coffee. "How dare she! Harriet, have you read this? She called our daughter a liar. For God's sake. That, that . . ."

Harriet Washington came running out of the coffee room, a chocolate Twinkie protruding from her mouth.

"Wha is i' 'oney?"

"That policewoman . . . Officer Leigh. Francine told us how nice she was. Well, more likely a wolf in sheep's clothing, or so it seems. She called our Francie a liar—in court."

Harriet Washington was obviously beside herself.

"Yes," said Ed. "The hide! Well, I'll show her who's the liar. That no good Judas, pretending to befriend a frightened young girl, taking advantage of her being in a state of distress. It just isn't Christian. I'm going to call the DA. Let's just see who—"

But Harriet Washington wasn't listening. She had obviously had enough.

"Eddie, please. I'm so tired of this. Francie is too. I'm not so sure we are doing the right thing—by Francie, I mean. It just isn't fair."

Ed Washington looked at his wife and in that moment knew she was right, even if he wasn't yet ready to admit it.

"We've set our course, Harriet. Washingtons are not quitters, Francie included. No matter what the cost, we stand up for what is right."

"Yes, I know," she said, looking him square in the eye. "So what the hell are we doing?"

* * *

"Unfortunately, David was right," said Con Stipoulos on the line from Tokyo. "The Satos's line of vision was blocked by the headland. They could see the girls on the outboard but not out to the cruiser."

"So when Christina swam beyond the peninsula, they lost sight of her?" Sara asked, leaning into the speaker phone in Arthur's office.

"I'm afraid so."

The four of them exchanged glances of disappointment. They knew that if the Satos were in Teesha's line of vision it was unlikely they could have seen beyond the outcrop, but it was hard news to hear nevertheless.

"But . . ." said Con.

"We're listening," said David.

"Well, it isn't all bad news. You see, when the Satos were dropped on the beach, the helicopter pilot gave them a cell number to call if they had any problems or wanted to be picked up early.

"When the Satos saw the girls capsize and Christina swim out to the cruiser, they called the number. Kyoji said he couldn't get through, but he left a message on his voice mail. A few moments later Rayna came to pick up the girls so they didn't bother calling again."

"Did Mr. Sato say he saw the chopper do a sweep?"

"No, but he did say he heard a chopper in the area minutes after he made the call. There is a chance this pilot got the message and went to check it out. If he was flying low, beyond the headland, the Satos might not have seen him."

"Hang on a minute," said Tyrone. "Rayna said she heard a 'white noise' above the cruiser. Maybe it was the Satos' chopper after all."

"Maybe," said David. "Con, did Mr. Sato know the name of the pilot?"

"Not exactly. But he said the tour operator—a Mr. Cruise—called him Kooriya."

"Kooriya? Was the pilot Japanese too?"

"No, Mr. Sato was giving me the Japanese translation of his English name. Our interpreter told us what it means but it doesn't really make sense."

"What is it?" said Sara.

"Kooriya means, *'Iceman.'*"

"What?" said David. "You're right, it doesn't make sense."

David looked at Arthur and Tyrone, who both shrugged, coming up blank. Then he looked at Sara.

"For God's sake." She smiled. "Did all of you guys sleep through the eighties? Mr. Cruise called his pilot Iceman, just like Val Kilmer's hot-shot pilot in *Top Gun*. My guess is, gentlemen, that Mr. Cruise and this pilot are tight—two unlicensed Mavericks flying low under the legal radar. I'll bet Mr. Cruise will know how to track down our Iceman, and maybe our Iceman got a real nice view of our conversation."

"Sara, you are amazing," said David.

"Nah, just an average American girl who saw *Top Gun* at least five times."

"Con," said David. "Did the Satos agree to fly here next week?"

"Well, Mrs. Sato is only weeks away from delivery, but Kyoji said he would come if we needed him. I told him about Christina and Rayna and Teesha. He wants to help."

"Okay, tell him to pack his bags. I think we are going to need him."

"What about our Iceman?" asked Tyrone.

"I'll call Mr. Cruise right away," said David.

"No," said Sara, catching their attention again. "Something tells me Tom might respond better to a face-to-face visit."

"She's right," said David, looking at Arthur, who jumped to his feet and rubbed his hands together.

"Ms. Davis, what do you say about a day trip to sunny Gloucester?" said Arthur.

"Why, Mr. Wright, I cannot think of a nicer way to spend Independence Day."

"That's settled then," he said. "Let's just hope for my sake that Kelly McGillis is still in the picture."

"You *have* seen *Top Gun*," said Sara, grabbing her bag and swinging it over her shoulder.

"Seen it?" Arthur grinned, before pointing at David. "Why, I taught that young Maverick everything he knows."

• • •

Each night for the past week David had called Joe Mannix for an update on the Teesha Martin investigation. Unfortunately, Joe had had little to report. He had no doubt the shooter was a gun for hire, and he knew that criminals such as these had a talent for disappearing after the act, leaving a cold trail and few clues as to who had hired them.

The pair may have had their suspicions, but there was no evidence linking Haynes to the shooting. David urged his friend to confront the senator, but Mannix had to remind him that it was he, not Haynes who had been outwardly breaking the law on Friday night.

"You were trespassing," said Joe. "Even worse, you crashed the party and then tried to attack the guest of honor. You were lucky I persuaded him not to press charges."

One thing they did agree on was a need to find out the identity of the dark man under the green tennis court lights. Initially Joe had surmised that he was part of the security team hired by the Republican Party for the night of the banquet, but a discreet call to Parkside Security turned up nothing. In fact, the firm's general manager confirmed that all of his men were in uniform and none of them had been detailed anywhere near the tennis courts.

David then countered that the dark man had to be linked to Haynes directly—a personal security guard or a friend. But once again there was no point in asking Haynes. In the first place, if this man had anything to do with the shooting, they did not want to tip off the senator to their suspicions.

And secondly, they doubted they would get an honest answer from him anyway.

David could not get rid of the nagging feeling that he had seen this man somewhere before, and he was telling Tyrone as much when Nora interrupted their conversation. It was Joe returning his call.

"I heard they gave you the day off. What did you do, win some brownie points with old Stein?"

"Very funny. How is Petri, by the way?"

"As you would expect. Busy with funeral arrangements."

"Joe," David had to ask. "Do you think this might make a difference?"

"Leave it with me, okay."

"Okay, but he's due on the stand tomorrow."

"Maybe, maybe not."

David knew when it was best to lay off, so he tried another tack. "What about Tommy?"

"Tommy will testify. He has to. It's part of his job."

"I know. But I am not as much concerned about what he will say, as what he won't."

"Like I said. Leave it with me."

"Okay. But time is tight, Joe."

"I know."

They paused before David went on. "Anything new on the shooting?"

"Nada. And it doesn't help that I have a double homicide on my hands this morning."

"What happened?"

"Some gun nut had a domestic with his lady at a two-bit motel in Mattapan. He missed his girlfriend but shot four bullets through the paper-thin wall into the next room. Killed a woman and her ten-year-old kid in the process."

"Shit."

"Yeah. We'll find the son of a bitch, though. The cleaning woman gave us a nice description, and his prints are all over the room."

"You up for a Fourth of July drink after work?" said David, realizing they were on a police department line and wary of pushing his friend any further.

"Not tonight. Marie is pissed that I got called in to work today."

"Fair enough, tomorrow then. Why don't you come up here?"

"Arthur still got a thing for those cold beers?"

"What do you think?"

"Okay, you're on. Tomorrow, about seven. I'll see you then."

• • •

"So nothing new on our mystery guy?" asked Tyrone.

"No," answered David. "I wish to hell I could remember where I'd seen him before."

"Okay," said Tyrone, standing to stretch his legs. "Let's think about this for a minute. If this guy is linked to Haynes, you had to have seen him in context with Haynes."

"But the senator and I have never really been formally introduced. Let's just say we don't move in the same social circles."

"David, from what I've seen, you don't have any social circles, but that's another story." Tyrone smiled before going on. "When have you and Haynes been at the same place at the same time?"

"Um, well . . . in court?"

"No way. Something tells me this dark dude is one for the shadows. Haynes isn't going to parade him in public."

Then it hit him. "That's it," said David. "It was in public, but Haynes signaled him to move back into the shadows, so to speak."

"What? Where?"

"At the funeral. He was at the funeral."

"Okay, good," Tyrone was pacing now. "That's a start. So . . . how does this help us?"

"I'm not so sure it does . . . unless, maybe . . . Nora," David called out, bringing Nora to the office door. "Can you find Marc Rigotti? Tell him I need to see him at his office—urgently."

"Done," she said.

Tyrone got it in one. "Of course, the media. They were all over the funeral. You think maybe some photographer caught our dark man on film?"

"I don't know, but it's worth a shot. At the very least it would give Joe something to work with. Maybe someone saw the guy near Delia's house last Friday night?"

"Should we call Joe? He might want to meet us."

"Nah. Joe's busy on a new case, a double shooting." David told Tyrone about the hotel homicides.

"Jeez, on the Fourth of July. What the hell is wrong with this country?"

"Good question, lad," said Nora from the office doorway. "But you've no time to ponder such grand dilemmas right now. Mr. Rigotti is in and expecting you."

"Thanks, Nora," said David, before turning to Tyrone. "So what are we waiting for? Let's go."

43

"Basically, the drowning process includes a series of seven destructive progressive stages: struggle, aspiration of water, laryngospasm, hypoxia, unconsciousness, respiratory arrest and finally cardiac arrest. One stage will progress to the other and ultimately end in death if rapid and effective intervention is not provided by appropriately trained personnel."

Boston medical examiner Gustav Svenson was on the stand, and the room was hanging on his every word. Scaturro had spent over an hour questioning him on the adverse effects of alcohol and the specific biological consequences of the level in Christina's blood. And now she was moving on to the physical description of the drowning itself.

The prosecution did not know what caused Christina to drown but figured that if the testimony on the alcohol was juxtaposed with that on the process of drowning, the jury would connect the two as cause and effect. One thing was for sure: although the commonwealth could not use Dr. Svenson to prove its motive of hate, it could certainly milk his medically sound, visually graphic and emotionally disturbing testimony to raise the level of sympathy for the victim and, in turn, the level of disdain for the defendant.

"Dr. Svenson," continued Scaturro, "do you think you could elaborate on these stages so that we might understand exactly what happened to Christina Haynes on that afternoon?"

"Well, first of all, it must be remembered that the drowning process is a very silent one. The conscious victim may only struggle at the surface for twenty to sixty seconds, and during that struggle, he or she rarely makes a sound; the victim is straining just to breathe. The arms are typically placed laterally to the side as he or she attempts to keep his or her head out of the water."

Typical Gus, thought David, *straight from the textbook.* This was going to hurt.

"To the untrained person, the victim appears to be playing in the water, when in reality he or she is engaged in a life and death struggle. This is referred to as the instinctive drowning response, or IDR."

"Right, so that is stage one, the struggle."

Scaturro turned to the jury as she said this, making eye contact with jurors 6 and 7, Lily Butterfield and Bonnie Sullivan. Lily was an interior designer and Bonnie an arts supplies shopkeeper. Neither were used to such descriptions and she wanted to work their distress for all it was worth.

"What about stage two, aspiration?"

"During the victim's struggle to remain at the surface and to keep his or her head and mouth above the surface of the water, the victim will gasp for air and ingest water. This aspiration of water into the lungs results in a decrease in buoyancy."

"And stage three, laryngospasm?"

"Yes, this term is self-explanatory. It refers to a spasm of the larynx. Basically, in a reflexive response to prevent additional water from entering the lungs, the larynx will spasm. This reflex spasm, however, also prevents air from entering the lungs. This, in turn, results in a lack of oxygen to the brain and other vital organs and tissues, so the victim becomes hypoxic, which leads to unconsciousness."

"Stages four and five."

"That's right."

Scaturro looked at the jury again, her pained expression highlighting the tragedy of it all. Then she turned slowly, encouraging them to follow her eyes across the room to Elizabeth Haynes.

It was a clever move. If this was hard for them to hear, imagine how difficult it was for the girl's mother.

"Go on, Doctor," she said, knowing she had them.

"By now the victim is usually situated either at the surface or submerged below the surface of the water with his or her face immersed in the water. The victim is not breathing and is considered to be in respiratory arrest, stage six. If rescue occurs at this point, assisted breathing will be required to adequately ventilate the patient's lungs."

"And the final stage, stage seven, cardiac arrest?"

"The heart may continue to beat for up to several minutes after the onset of respiratory arrest. However, as a result of a lack of oxygen to the brain and heart, the victim's condition deteriorates, resulting in cardiac arrest. If rescue occurs at this point, CPR must be immediately initiated and maintained until the patient can be defibrillated."

David looked at Sara, who returned his look of concern and grasped Rayna's hand underneath the defense table. It was a perfect description of drowning, a perfect visual portrait for the jury, a perfect play for the prosecution.

"So basically, what you are saying, Dr. Svenson, is that if Miss Haynes had received help minutes earlier, if Mrs. Martin had rescued her before attending the other three girls, if Christina Haynes had been pulled from the water as soon as Mrs. Martin saw her from the cruiser, she would still be alive today."

"Most likely, yes."

Scaturro paused, bowed her head and shook it ever so

slightly before looking back at the witness again. "Thank you, Dr. Svenson. No further questions, Your Honor."

Scaturro had timed her finish perfectly—just before lunch. She knew the jury would spend the next hour visualizing the drowning death of Christina Haynes in all its graphic, heart-wrenching detail, and there was nothing the defense could do about it. At the very least they had an hour to go over their plans for Svenson's cross-examination, which was for them, in many ways, the most important part of the trial to date.

For starters, it was their first opportunity to introduce their own new evidence in the form of the markings on Christina's ankle and the yet-to-be-mentioned silver anklet. They had considered hiring divers to search for the missing piece of jewelry, but time was short and they knew in the end it would have been like trying to find a needle in a haystack.

They were hoping Svenson's evaluation of the charm-shaped abrasions on Christina's skin would be enough to prove the anklet was tangled for several minutes, thus enabling them to build the groundwork for Ewan Jordan's "lack of time" theory and setting the stage for Sato Kyoji. They could then use Mr. Sato's eyewitness account to prove Christina must have fought her battle with the nets after Rayna left to rescue the three girls, considering there was no time before. This wasn't going to be easy. David would have to tread carefully, leaving the door open for Kyoji to close later next week.

Last night they had agreed that they might not find the Iceman in time for trial. While Sara and Arthur had found Mr. Cruise, who confirmed that his friend Iceman had dropped the Satos on the beach, Cruise claimed to be "unsure" of Iceman's real name and was even more vague about his current whereabouts.

Sara was sure he was lying, no doubt in an attempt to protect his renegade, unlicensed pilot friend. She could only hope that Mr. Cruise would follow through on his promise to try to locate the Iceman and ask him to come forward with what he knew.

"*Tom,*" she had said, looking at him with her large blue eyes, "I cannot tell you how much this would mean to us. I promise you we are not interested in the whole license issue. This is about saving an innocent woman. I can see you are a man of integrity, Mr. Cruise." She took his hand and shook it. "And for anything you can do, we would be eternally grateful."

Arthur was impressed. Cruise even more so. And now all they could do was wait.

In the meantime, Samantha Bale, determined to redeem herself after the setback of Frasier Kemp's Coast Guard tape, had gone to Cape Ann for the weekend. Characters like the Iceman tended to make an impression, and Sam was hoping someone else might know where the elusive pilot could be. It was worth a shot.

Marc Rigotti had come up blank. They looked at every frame taken by the *Tribune*'s photographer on the day of the funeral, but there were no shots of the dark man. None.

Marc promised to rally some media mates, both in the press and electronic media, to see if anyone had caught their mystery man on film. In the meantime, they realized that their priority was the Martin trial and at least for the time being, their efforts on the Teesha shooting would have to take a backseat.

. . .

"Dr. Svenson, did Christina Haynes drown because she was drunk?" David came straight out with it, knowing he had to shatter the prosecution's cause-and-effect scenario quickly.

"No."

The jury sat up straight. They were interested now—confused.

"But this morning you gave evidence of the dangers of drinking, and the statistical links between alcohol and drowning."

"Yes. But alcohol is a contributing factor, not a cause."

David put on his best puzzled face, urging the ME to go on.

"The early stages of drowning are much less likely to progress to the later stages if the victim remains calm, maintains clarity and introduces problem-solving techniques," explained Svenson. "Alcohol dampens such abilities—makes it difficult for the victim to act rationally, increases the likelihood of panic, distress and disorientation. But it does not cause someone to drown.

"Further," Svenson went on, "I would not necessarily classify Ms. Haynes as drunk. She was under the influence of alcohol, certainly, but the fact that she managed to swim some distance in a relatively straight line suggests the alcohol had not completely diminished her cognitive abilities." This last comment was a gift and David was grateful.

"So just to clarify, Dr. Svenson, you have not so far given testimony on the probable physical cause of the drowning?"

"No."

"All right."

The point was made and the jury was looking at him, interested in hearing more.

"Dr. Svenson, could you please turn to page nine of your report, and read for us the paragraph under section 5 (b)."

Svenson read from the document that Scaturro had tabled this morning. It was the same paragraph he had studied a few weeks earlier concerning Christina's right ankle and the series of circular abrasions around it.

"In other words?"

"In other words, the victim had a series of overlapping cuts on her right ankle and foot. They were circular in nature, some longer than others."

"Which suggests?"

"Some form of constraint and an attempt to free herself from the constraint."

"Objection." Katz leaped out of his chair before his boss had the chance. "Your Honor, this is new evidence. Dr. Svenson gave no reference to these so-called cuts this morning. I do not think—"

"Mr. Katz," said Stein, "did you and Ms. Scaturro have access to the full autopsy report before this morning's testimony?"

"Well, yes."

"And did Ms. Scaturro ask Dr. Svenson about these cuts?"

"No, but—"

"Well, now he *has* been asked the question. I want to see where this goes. Objection overruled. Sit down, Mr. Katz."

At this point David requested that a wooden stand be moved from the corner to the center of the courtroom. On it he placed a postmortem enlargement of Christina's right ankle.

"Dr. Svenson," said David, holding a pointer toward the large, imposing photograph, "what, in your opinion, caused these indentations?"

"It appears that whatever was constraining Miss Haynes's foot was not one hundred percent consistent. In other words, it contained irregular bumps or protrusions that left small engravings in the victim's skin."

David then moved back to the defense table to collect a small shiny object that he held up high in his right hand. The bracelet caught the sunlight streaming through the upper western windows, the reflections sending scores of brilliant colored rays bouncing around the room.

The jury, the entire courtroom, was mesmerized.

Those closest to Elizabeth Haynes heard a short, sharp gasp escape from her mouth. Katz turned to look and jumped to his feet.

"Your Honor, the state is appalled. This is a brazen disregard for the law. If the defense has an item of the victim's property in its possession, they should not only be disqualified from this court for failure to disclose this discovery, they should also be prosecuted for theft."

At that point David looked across the room and noticed that one of the colored lights was resting on Senator Haynes's face. In that moment, as the small blue crystal of light danced over his hard and determined features, David saw pure hatred and knew there was no choice but to win this thing, for if he did not, he would bear the consequences of it forever.

"Mr. Cavanaugh." It was Stein. "Mr. Katz is right. If this item belonged to the victim, I will have no choice but to instigate legal proceedings against defense counsel."

"It is not hers."

The people in courtroom 9 could not believe it. Rayna

Martin had risen quietly to her feet, standing tall, defiant, with the hint of a tear in her left eye. Stein should have stopped her right away, but he was caught by surprise, just like everyone else.

"This bracelet belongs to my daughter. She cannot wear it right now because both her arms are attached to IV units."

"Mrs. Martin." Stein was out of his trance and banging his gavel.

"They all have one . . . all of Teesha's friends."

"Counselor, control your client," said Stein to David just as Sara rose to gently pull Rayna back into her seat. But before she did, Rayna spoke once more.

"Teesha has one, Mariah has one, Francie has one . . . and her best friend, her *best* friend Christina . . . she had one too."

Stein had had enough. His gavel echoed above the murmur of disbelief building throughout the room. He called for a recess to meet with counsel in his chambers, rising from his chair and storming through the back left-hand door.

David looked at Sara and Arthur just as they stood to accompany him behind the courtroom. Their look said it all.

They were proud of their client, proud to be representing her, proud to even know her and more determined than ever to see her walk from this room a free woman.

■ ■ ■

"Je-sus!" said Rhett Lafayette, swatting another swamp fly off his right arm. "They're breedin' 'em as big as catfish this year."

"Know what you mean, Rhett," said Ted Buford, fanning himself with the handkerchief in his right hand, while sipping an iced tea with the slightest hint of whiskey that he held in his left.

"It's this dang heat. Brings 'em out in swarms," said Rhett.

"Right again, Rhett. Right again."

Senator Theodore Buford was enjoying his ritual Friday evening drink with his oldest friend, Baton Rouge barber Rhett Lafayette. The pair had been close since childhood, with Buford's political success never causing a problem between them. In fact, Lafayette was a Democrat, of all things.

That's why he still charged his Republican pal five dollars every time he wanted a three-dollar cut and shave.

"It's your contribution to the Democratic Party," he would joke, before laughing long and hard.

"Just don't expect a tip," Ted would counter.

"Ah, you conservatives," Rhett would continue the script. "Tight as a string o' dried molasses."

"Ted!"

It was Buford's wife, Meredith. They heard her call from inside the house, listened to her footsteps on the aged hardwood floor as she approached the front porch, and saw her poke her head around the old screen door as it squeaked in protest at being pushed from its rest.

"Phone for you," she said, surveying the two old comrades in their favorite chairs.

"Who is it, honey? If it's Merlin, tell him to come on over, have a drink or two."

"It isn't your brother, Ted, it's a man from Boston. A Mr. Tyrone Banks."

"Boston, eh?"

"Never been to Boston," said Rhett, taking another sip of iced tea.

"Well, you ain't missing much, old friend."

Ted Buford rose from his seat and walked into his nineteenth-century home to take the call in his study.

"Hello. This is Theodore Buford. What can I do for you, Mr. Banks is it?"

"Yes, sir. Tyrone Banks. I am research director for the Democratic Party."

"Good Lord, son, this some kinda joke? Rhett put you up to this?"

"Rhett? No, sir."

"I'm sorry, Mr. Banks." Buford let out a chuckle. "What can I do for you?"

"Senator, have you heard of Rayna Martin?"

"Who hasn't, son?"

"I am her brother-in-law."

"I see." Buford paused, taking this in. "Like I said. What can I do for you, Mr. Banks?"

It had been bothering Tyrone for weeks. Senator Theo-

dore Buford, Rudolph Haynes's oldest adversary, invited to
his honorary banquet. It just didn't make sense unless . . .
Had the pair mended their fences, made their peace, come
to some sort of truce? So Tyrone made the call from Massachusetts General while Delia was at their niece's bedside,
and he asked the questions: Was Senator Buford invited to
last Friday night's honorary banquet? And did he indeed
attend?

"Hm, well. Yes, Mr. Banks, I was invited. The strangest
thing I ever did see. Meredith and I . . . we assumed it was
some sort of joke. You see, Rudolph Haynes and I have never
seen eye to eye. I suppose that's no secret. He would not have
expected us to attend. Unless he was planning to kick us out
at the front door, which is really not his style. Rudolph is
nothing if not discreet, even when it comes to his
adversaries—especially when it comes to his adversaries. No,
sir, Mr. Banks. Last Friday night I was pretty much doin' the
same as I am doin' right now: drinking slightly spiked iced
teas with my old friend Rhett Lafayette."

"The Democrat."

"Yes, Mr. Banks." Buford laughed again. "The Democrat.
Is there anything else I can help you with, Mr. Banks?"

"Not unless you can tell me who checked into Boston's
Regency Plaza Hotel in your name last Friday night, sir."

"Hm," said Buford. "Now that is what is known as a mystery, Mr. Banks."

"Yes, sir."

"And I hate mysteries, Mr. Banks."

"Not as much as I do, sir."

"Then let's solve this mystery, shall we?"

■ ■ ■

He had done it. David had set them up. Stein had allowed the
bracelet into evidence; David had gotten Svenson to testify
that a similar bracelet was most likely the object that had
caused the abrasions on Christina's ankle, and more important, the ME told the court that such cuts most likely took at
least five minutes to develop.

But the commonwealth didn't take this new piece of evidence lying down. While they were not aware that the defense
would be producing evidence regarding the old fishing nets

and could not know the significance of the upcoming Sato testimony, they realized that David's aim was to establish a pattern in timing.

So as soon as David took his seat, Loretta Scaturro requested a countercross, during which she took Svenson to task on the issue. In the end she had gotten him to admit that while it was unlikely, there was a possibility that the ankle injury was sustained over a shorter period of time—perhaps four minutes or maybe even three. This counterattack certainly worked to water down the strength of David's theory, but at the very least the defense had started to build a scenario that would provide the jury with grounds for reasonable doubt on the whole "unconscious versus conversation" issue.

"I wonder if we aren't setting ourselves up for bigger problems here," said Sara, dropping onto Arthur's couch while David pulled out three cold beers.

"How so?" asked Arthur.

"Well, what if we *do* prove Christina's struggle started after she reached the cruiser? What if they decide to change tack and agree with us?"

They both looked at her.

"If we prove the struggle started later, they could turn around and claim Rayna *witnessed* the struggle and still chose to abandon her. They could also claim there was a conversation but of a very different nature: Christina begging Rayna for help, only to have her turn the boat around and head toward shore. Which makes our client look even worse."

"Yes, but you're forgetting their whole case for murder two is based on Francine Washington's account that Rayna said Christina was "floating" next to the cruiser. And then there was Kemp's tape, in which Teesha put Christina's unconscious state prior to their rescue," said David.

"David's right," said Arthur. "Katz would probably love to nail Rayna for turning her back on a drowning girl, but if they abandon the whole unconscious theory, they basically destroy the foundations for their original charge."

"I guess so," said Sara. "It's just that once we go the whole 'timing' route, I think they will find it hard to resist countering with the argument that there is a possibility

Rayna abandoned Christina midstruggle. Because, bottom line, we *still* don't have any proof that the conversation took place."

"David." It was Nora at Arthur's office door. "Some people to see you—I put them in your office."

"Thanks, Nora." David looked at his watch, seven-thirty. "That'll be Joe."

"Good," said Sara, on her feet.

"I'll get another beer," said Arthur.

"Think you might need more than one." Nora smiled.

David looked at his friends, and all three headed to the office next door to see Joe Mannix standing by the back window.

"Sorry I'm late. Got held up. Had to wait for my friends here."

All three moved into the room and turned to look at the two people sitting in the chairs across from David's messy desk. They could not believe it. Never in a million years would they have expected to see these two men sitting voluntarily side by side. Tommy Wu and Paul Petri.

"You'd better pick your jaws up off the floor, hand us a beer and sit down," said Joe. "We got a few things to discuss."

44

Tick, tock, tick, tock, tick, tock . . .

He was making them wait on purpose. This was all part of his plan. He had told them to meet him at his office at 8:00 AM sharp. On a Saturday. And they had been here at ten to. Leanne, Lorraine, Louise—whatever her name was—had let them in.

Loretta Scaturro looked at the digital desk clock

again—8:27. It made no sound. They never did. But she was imagining the ticking in her head.

Tick, tock, tick, tock, flap—8:28.

Katz had been pacing since 8:16. He was wearing his "weekend Lauren," as Loretta liked to call it. But the ice-blue Polo and cool cologne fell short of concealing his anxiety today. He was sweating on the inside. No doubt about it.

She wore a suit. She thought it might help with the air of authority she would need for this meeting. She knew Haynes would be wearing a suit. He wanted psychological advantage, and as she turned to watch him stride into the reception area outside his office, she saw that she was right—dark gray, subtle tie, crisp white shirt.

You have to control this meeting, she told herself. *Don't let him walk all over you.*

Tick, tock, tick, tock, flap—8:29.

■ ■ ■

"Hello," David croaked into the receiver, jolted from his sleep by the persistent ring of his bedside telephone. "What time is it?"

"Mr. Cavanaugh, I have wakened you."

David sat up in bed and picked up his watch from his side table drawer—8:30 AM.

"No, I just . . . I slept late. It was a long night and I thought you were my colleague. I'm sorry, who . . ."

"No, I'm sorry, Mr. Cavanaugh. Moses Novelli returning your call. I apologize for not getting back to you sooner and for calling you at home so early on the weekend. This is probably the only chance I will get to make a call today—Fourth of July weekend and all. The city is a hive of activity and for better or for worse, I'm in the thick of it."

"Mayor Novelli, don't apologize. Thanks for calling." David was wide awake now. He had been trying to reach Novelli all week. "I . . . ah, I'm not too sure where to start."

"Maybe this is a conversation better held in person."

"I'd appreciate it."

"How do you feel about lunch tomorrow? And don't say yes until I explain the circumstances. It's the annual Novelli family barbecue—just a whole lot of Italian Americans downing a few beers and trying not to burn the sausages. Nothing flash, I'm afraid, but you're more than welcome."

"I'd love to, Mr. Mayor. Thanks."

"All right then, I'll tell Sophia. I'll get my assistant to call you back with the address and directions. About twelve, okay?"

"Yes. Thanks again."

"Don't thank me yet, Counselor. I don't know if I can help you."

"But you're offering."

"I'm offering to cook you a few overdone *salsicce*." He laughed. "As for anything else, we'll just have to wait and see."

• • •

"You've had the ME's report for weeks. How in the hell could you have missed it?"

Haynes had taken off his jacket and now sat behind his oversize desk. His chair was at least a few inches higher than all the others in the room—establishing his dominance, diminishing the power of those before him and consolidating Scaturro and Katz as subservients who had failed to deliver.

"With all due respect, Senator," said Scaturro. "We didn't miss it; we just failed to recognize the significance of the ankle injuries."

"How else did you think she got them—at ballet class, for Christ's sake?"

Haynes was furious. The velvet gloves were off. They were here for some serious browbeating and Scaturro started to feel the perspiration underneath her arms tingle against her silk shirt.

"Senator," she countered, "even if we did miss the injuries, I can promise you that they will have no bearing on the final result. The point is not in the cause of death but in Rayna Martin's reluctance to prevent it. Alcohol, anklet . . . it really doesn't matter. The woman abandoned your daughter, Senator, and without trying to sound callous, I believe that whatever caused Christina to drown is irrelevant."

"Brave words, Ms. Scaturro, but the defense obviously sees it differently. They are trying to force us into a corner on timing. I need to know why this is so important to them. They must have a witness, someone who can spell out the chain of events in minutes."

"Yesterday they added a new name to their witness list," she said. "A Mr. Sato Kyoji. He may be their witness, but I do not believe he saw their 'conversation.' If he did, they would not have to set up an argument on timing. They would just produce him and let him tell what he saw."

Haynes looked at her. She could tell by his expression that he knew she was right. But she could also read the concern on his face—concern that if this Sato could set up a time frame, it could tear their "unconscious" theory to shreds.

"How solid is the Washington girl?" he asked.

"Solid," said Scaturro.

"In all honesty, Senator, I have some concerns," said Katz, speaking for the first time.

What! Scaturro was in shock. She could not believe what she was hearing. He had spent the past month convincing her that Francine Washington was ironclad. She looked at him, but he avoided her glare. *What the hell is he up to?*

"I'm listening, Katz," said Haynes.

Katz stood. A daring move in itself and one which, Scaturro now knew, was all part of a preconceived performance he had rehearsed for this morning's audience with the king. She had always humored Katz's arrogance, largely because he was good at his job, but right now, at this very moment, she had to admit that she hated him more than ever.

"Senator, I share your concerns regarding the defense's obvious maneuvering to establish some sort of timetable. I also agree that this Mr. Sato could well have witnessed events from the periphery. But like Loretta, I do not believe they have an eyewitness to establish the existence of their conversation. So where does this leave us?" he asked rhetorically, the orator giving his speech.

Jesus!

"Given our motive—that of hate—I am starting to wonder whether we could not use their timing theory to our advantage."

"Go on," said Haynes.

"What if Francine Washington got it a little wrong? What

if Christina was not actually unconscious when Martin saw her, but on her way to becoming so? Martin told the other three that Christina was 'floating' next to the cruiser. That could be because subconsciously she knew, by the time she had reached the other girls, that Christina would have been unconscious."

Haynes looked at him. Scaturro could see his mind considering the new theory. Katz went on. "All I am saying is that we have to be prepared for what the defense may have up their sleeves. We have to face the fact that Cavanaugh's timing theory could kill our 'unconscious' scenario and we have to have a plan in place to turn it to our advantage."

"And I suppose you have come up with a way to do that?" said Haynes.

"Well . . ."

Act 1, scene 2, thought Scaturro.

"Let's look at this hypothetically. What if the defense uses its timing theory to convince the jury that Christina was conscious when she reached the cruiser and, worse still, that a conversation took place. We just need to make sure we control the content of that conversation.

"The defense will claim her ankle was caught on something—plant life, nets, whatever—it really doesn't matter. But they will claim this happened *after* Martin left to fetch the three girls. We claim Christina is caught up *as* she reaches the cruiser and that she asks Martin for help. Martin demands to know what happened to the other three and then turns her back on the struggling white girl to go to their aid.

"All I am saying is," Katz went on, "if we need to, we give them their conversation but change its content. *Then* the defense will be screwed and the jury, who spent all of yesterday morning listening to the horrors of Christina's final moments, will want to put Martin away for good."

"What about the Washington girl?" asked Haynes.

"We can still use her. We just paint a picture that says Martin used the word *'floating'* because she jumped ahead in her own mind, which is even worse because it spells premeditation. Don't forget that the Washington kid will testify that Martin favored the black girls over Christina."

No one said anything. Scaturro was still in shock. Haynes was mentally dissecting Katz's argument.

"That's all fine and good, Katz, but as far as I am aware, the defense has no witness to their conversation. What makes you think they are going to find one?"

"I am afraid they may be closer than we think, Senator."

Haynes was on the edge of his seat. Scaturro was ready to strangle Katz.

"Yesterday I dispatched one of our associates to Gloucester, basically to find out more about this Mr. Sato and look into where the defense might be going with their anklet theory. The associate called me last night. He says the defense had also dispatched an investigator to the area. A young lawyer named Samantha Bale—totally second-rate, but that's beside the point. My associate questioned the same people Bale spoke with shortly after she moved on. It seems Bale has been seeking a helicopter pilot with the moniker of 'Iceman' who, from what we can gather, may have been in the air at the time of the incident."

"A witness."

"Potentially, yes."

"We have to find him first."

"I agree. In fact, my associate says he might have a lead. He was drinking late into the night with a fisherman from Rockport whose brother runs a charter company in Beverly. He says he has heard of this Iceman—a dodgy type—an unlicensed pilot who shops his services to less than reputable operators."

"Do we know how to find him?"

"Better than that. We know his name and his place of residence."

Katz pulled out a piece of white notepaper he had tucked neatly in the back pocket of his perfectly pressed chinos.

"Gabriel Jackson. He rents a duplex in Essex."

"Does Cavanaugh's girl have this information?"

"We don't think so. At least not yet."

"What makes you think this Jackson will see things our way?" asked Haynes, his full focus now on the ADA with Scaturro all but forgotten.

"Two previous counts for unlicensed piloting," Katz began, "and at least four outstanding warrants in three different states for misdemeanors, such as assault with grievous bodily harm, drunk and disorderly and aggravated assault."

"He's ours," said Haynes, a broad smile of triumph now spreading across his face.

"Yes, sir," smiled Katz in return. "I believe he is."

• • •

Paul Petri had been working for Rudolph Haynes for a little over two years. He had been recruited, over the telephone, shortly before his transfer from general duties to Homicide and shortly after his wife had been diagnosed with breast cancer. He had been an honest cop for more than twenty years and accepted Haynes' offer, via proxy, for one reason and one reason alone: he needed the money.

Rebecca Petri's cancer was advanced and Petri was determined to seek out the best care available. That meant several specialists, experimental drugs, chemotherapy and monthly admission to Ashleighford Clinic for biopsies, blood counts and intermittent transfusions. At the very least, the four thousand dollars in cash that Petri picked up each month from a previously arranged deposit box at the Bank of America in Somerville had probably prolonged his wife's life for at least twelve months.

So would he do it again? Shit, yeah. No question.

But now that she was gone, and in the wake of the Martin girl's shooting, Petri was feeling the weight of his part in the whole charade and wanted to make a deal. He was willing to tell the defense everything he knew, but in return he wanted them to keep what he told them within the four walls of David's office. In other words, they had his information but not his testimony.

"I am six months from retirement," he told them. "I got no kids, I just lost the one thing that I gave a damn about and I have sixty bucks in the bank. I need my pension." Petri took a long wheezy breath before going on. "This gets out, I get prosecuted and the deal is off. I'll deny everything, and when it comes down to it, you have no proof. So," he said, looking tired and drained and festering with guilt, "that is my offer. Simple as that. Take it or leave it."

Time was short. He was their only link to Haynes's illegal activities. There was no discussion needed. They took it.

Joe Mannix didn't appreciate one of his men turning dirty, and had certainly never brokered such a deal before. He may have understood Petri's motives, but his actions still made him sick to his stomach. However, the trail to Teesha's shooter was growing cold and he knew this might be his only opportunity to link Haynes to the elusive gunman. Sometimes you had to take the sour with the sweet. Life was like that.

As for Tommy Wu, he was terrified. He told them about the photograph of Vanessa and Mikey, and the accompanying threat. Petri admitted putting the envelope containing the items in Wu's locker but assured them he was unaware of what it had contained and was sorry for the distress it had caused.

"I am afraid I need to make a deal too, David," said Tommy. "Believe me, I want to help, but there is no way on God's earth I will put my family at risk. I'll give you my testimony, but there will be no mention of Haynes or the note or Petri's reindeer references. I promise to tell the truth—that I found Mrs. Martin cooperative and compassionate and that I did not and still do not believe her to be a murderer. But I'm afraid that's as far as I go."

And so they had worked on into Friday night, Wu recounting the events of May 4 and Petri explaining how the whole thing worked. They sat and listened until midnight, until Petri had finished and their brains could not absorb any more.

And now, on Saturday morning, after a long, hard first week at trial, the three of them were going through it all step by step. Working out what it meant to this case and to Teesha's shooting, the two events sickeningly interwoven in a web of escalating horror. It was nothing short of amazing— complex, calculated, clever, contrived—a chain of events that had started over two years before and worked itself into the frenzy of recent weeks.

As for their deal with Petri, which at first had sounded stacked in his favor, it was fortunately more even than they had first suspected, for Petri gave them a major piece of their puzzle. He gave them a link to Haynes's right-hand man. He gave them his recruiter, his conduit—*a name*. He gave them Vincent Bartholomew Verne.

Two and a half years before, Detective Petri had received a call from an unidentified man asking him if he was interested in working for a prominent U.S. senator.

The "job," it was made clear from the start, would be viewed by some as illegal; however, it was to be passive rather than active, meaning that the detective would simply pass on information and encourage certain courses of action rather than directly influence any specific legal chain of events.

It was enough to get Petri listening. They had sought him out, after all.

He asked for details and the conduit was quick and specific in reply. Petri would be required to collect data, undertake a monthly drop of the information, advise on the status of any investigations of specific interest to the senator, and occasionally pursue selected individuals or issues at the senator's request.

The fee was four thousand dollars a month cash, and with Petri's wife now in the throes of her first round of chemotherapy, he did not hesitate.

Petri had never met his conduit. But he was a cop, curious by trade. Call it collateral, call it watching your own back, but he needed to know who his go-between was. He started by staking out the Somerville safety deposit box, hoping to see his contact in the flesh. But after months of surveillance, he realized that the conduit had several dummies: average Joes and Joans who would empty his box, go to the closest post office and redirect his drop via mail. The same people delivered his cash—a different person each month.

Petri would follow them home to their average homes on average streets, but he knew there was no point in approaching them. They would not know the name of his contact and he certainly did not want to tip them off to his curiosity.

Then, one week Petri came up with the idea of making his drop larger than usual—too big for the messenger who picked up the package to drop it in the mailbox, making it necessary for him to leave it at the post office counter for postage. So when the overweight, bald-headed courier left the Somerville post office, Petri went inside, showed his badge and asked to see the package that had been readdressed to a security box in Chelsea.

He then took two days' sick leave to stake out the new box, and a little over twenty-four hours later, he saw his contact for the first time—tall, dark, clean cut. He looked like CIA, FBI or maybe even Secret Service.

Next, he followed the man to a café where he saw him order coffee and a bagel. He waited on the street until the man left, then swept inside and stole the cup for prints. It was that easy.

From there it was a matter of running the prints through the local police computer—no match. State police—no match. Interpol—no match. Finally, he followed through on his hunch by asking a federal cop, a friend, to run the prints through the government system. It took his friend twenty minutes to come up with a match. The guy was ex-Secret Service. He was thirty-four, six three, 180 pounds, current address not listed—and his name was Vincent Bartholomew Verne.

Then came Saturday, May 4. This was a memorable day for many reasons, but for Petri its significance was magnified because it was the day he would speak to his employer for the first time.

When Susan Leigh radioed to report the suspected and then confirmed death of Christina Haynes, Detective Paul Petri faced the biggest dilemma of his illegal career. The information was critical, personal, but its delivery was problematic considering his usual directive and as such both awkward and unnerving. Normally, if he had an urgent message, he would call Verne on a prearranged number and leave a message—and then wait for the return call. But when Christina Haynes was DOA at Gloucester Harbor, Petri knew he had to act immediately. This was not the sort of news that could wait, and he knew it would be "safer" if it came from him rather than Joe Mannix.

So he decided to bypass Verne and call the senator direct. The housekeeper answered, and after a short pause Senator Haynes was on the end of the line saying four words: "This better be good."

It was—and it wasn't.

So Haynes knew his daughter was dead half an hour before Joe Mannix knocked on his door. Enough time for him to pack his pain, instruct Petri to do whatever he could to nail the "black bitch" to the wall, and feign surprise when the head of Homicide came to his door.

Petri then called Wu and forced the race issue at his boss's request to try to secure an arrest before midnight. Unfortunately, the perp clammed up and by that stage Mannix and the DA were involved, leaving the detective a way down in the pecking order of power, which in this case suited him just fine.

From there it became a matter of following orders from Verne, including dropping the newly arrested Rayna at the front of headquarters and planting drugs in Jake Davis's car. He had also been at Katz's beck and call. He had even been told to keep an eye on his boss, Joe Mannix, whom Katz suspected was sympathetic to the defense.

And so he had reported every time David had visited or called and monitored the defendant's activities, including her hypnotherapy sessions. Up until last week he had also attended regular weekly meetings with the ADA to rehearse his testimony, in which he would state that he had found Rayna Martin to be a difficult, disobliging and uncooperative suspect.

His appearance in court had been avoided with the death of his wife and his subsequent claim to having had chest pains requiring urgent medical attention. This last detail was a lie, although Petri felt as if his heart had broken, so perhaps it was not so far from the truth after all.

The bottom line was that they weren't too sure how any of this could help Rayna in the short term. It did not prove the conversation took place, and it did not provide tangible evidence against Haynes. It suggested Haynes could be guilty of anything and everything from corruption of justice to conspiracy to commit murder, but as yet there was nothing concrete.

At the very least, they were a few steps ahead of where they were this time yesterday. They had avoided Petri's testimony and he had given them Verne. But finding him and building solid evidence against him and his powerful boss was not going to be easy, for men like Verne knew how to disappear.

• • •

"How's Teesha?" said Sara, turning toward Tyrone as he walked through Arthur's office door.

Tyrone had been meant to join them three hours earlier, but when he didn't show, they assumed he was at the hospital.

"I saw her last night—good news, in fact. Her neurosurgeon says the latest tests show definite signs of brain activity."

"That's great," said David.

"I dropped Delia at the hospital this morning and then I had a last-minute breakfast engagement."

They all looked at him, urging him to continue.

"Actually, I spent the morning in a very nice hotel room, the Regency Plaza executive suite 1025, to be exact."

"Come again?" said David.

"Now don't jump to any conclusions." Tyrone couldn't resist. "There was no hanky-panky involved; in fact, my companion was none other than Joe Mannix, and he's really not my type. He's on his way up here right now."

"What is going on?" asked Arthur.

"Well, I guess it all started a couple of weeks ago, when I first saw the banquet guest list. Something on it—or rather someone—didn't make sense, and that's when I started to put two and two together."

Tyrone explained how he had noticed Ted Buford's name on the list and thought it strange, given that he and Haynes had been enemies for over twenty years. He then told them of last night's conversation with Buford and the revelation that someone had indeed checked into the hotel under his name.

"Then there was something David said last Thursday. It stuck in my mind. It was Joe's latest homicide. Remember David, the double shooting at the hotel?"

"Sure."

"Well, you said Joe was confident he would catch the guy because the maid had given him an ID. I figured if our guy was at the Regency Plaza—and we are guessing he was the mystery man who checked into suite 1025—then maybe someone could give us a positive ID too."

They all looked at one another. It was a good idea.

"So this morning I called Joe and arranged to meet him at the Regency Plaza for breakfast with the hotel's manager, a very helpful guy named Gaylord Brewster. I would have called, but I knew you guys would be hard at it and I wanted to see if there was anything there before I got you all excited."

"And?" asked Sara.

"And according to Brewster, Buford's suite was definitely occupied last Friday night, and he knows this for sure because the occupant accepted a bottle of complimentary champagne from one of his room service hostesses."

"Someone *did* see him," said Sara.

"Yes, a young girl named Amber Wells. She apparently told everyone in the kitchen that the senator from Louisiana was the 'hottest piece of ass' in the building. A compliment I am sure sixty-eight-year-old Ted Buford would appreciate." Tyrone smiled again; he was on a roll. "Anyway, Wells, unfortunately, is away for the holiday, but she has a shift on Tuesday evening, during which Brewster assures us we can speak to her. He is even keeping 1025 free just in case we need it. Joe is having it dusted as we speak."

"Verne," said David, looking at Arthur and Sara.

"Could be," said Tyrone, Joe having filled him in on Petri's revelations on the drive back from the hotel.

"So," said Arthur, "now we have four people who have seen this guy: Petri, David, Joe and this Amber Wells."

"Yes," said Tyrone. "Petri knows him as Verne, so he gives us the name; hopefully, Wells can put him at the hotel before the banquet, and Joe and David can link him to Haynes following the funeral and the altercation on the tennis courts."

"But," said Sara, "we still don't have anyone to put him at Delia's house at the time of the shooting."

"No," said Joe, walking through the office door to join the conversation. "But there is at least a tenuous link. The shooter used a weapon known as the SIG P210, a forerunner to a similar weapon used by the Secret Service."

"So Verne was used to using such a pistol," said Sara.

"More than that," said Joe. "He was trained to kill with it if necessary. Of course, it would be easier if we could get a witness to place him at the scene."

"How is Rigotti going with getting us a funeral shot of this guy?" asked Arthur. "If we had a shot by Tuesday, we could show Petri and Miss Wells and at the very least confirm we are all talking about the same man."

"I'll call him again," said David. "So all this may go toward nailing him as the shooter. But how do we prove it was Haynes who gave the order?"

"First things first," said Joe. "Let's start with Rigotti. We get a shot of this guy, we have something to work with."

45

Elizabeth Haynes waited until the large, gaudily dressed aunt had left the room and then she walked slowly toward the door and opened it. It was exactly as she had imagined. Quiet except for the beep of the various machinery. Pale green walls, sterile smell, fluorescent lighting, white bedding.

Teesha Martin lay there—still, the only dark-colored thing in the room. She had IVs in both her hands, tubes coming out of her nose, another larger one from her mouth and a large bandage covering her head, which had been shaved.

She did not know why she was here. She simply got up this morning, ate a light breakfast, showered and dressed in a pale apricot summer suit with suitable flesh-colored shoes and a Gucci bag. Then she left via the garden, not bothering to say good-bye to her husband, who was in the study, or Agnes, who was in the kitchen, got into her silver Volvo sedan, drove to Massachusetts General and followed the ward signs to ICU.

She did not ask for Layteesha Martin's room, simply

walked through the corridors of the intensive care unit look-ing as if she knew where she were going. Within minutes she had spotted Delia Banks through the glass portion of the door to room 10B, after which she took a seat at the far end of the corridor and waited for her to leave.

And so here she was, standing in front of the girl, looking at her for the first time with different eyes—with those of her daughter's—as Christina had seen her, and cared for her, and looked up to the girl's family as the antithesis of her own.

Strangely enough, she noticed that being here now she did not feel the anger that had seethed inside her for weeks. She had entered stage three—bargaining—her grief now playing politician with her brain. She found herself brokering a deal with God. *Dear Lord, please do not take this girl. One loss is enough. If you spare her I shall—I shall try to learn from what they have both taught me.*

But Teesha Martin's fate was out of her hands. She had done her best to prevent the tragedy, but her husband was the man he was, just like her father before him, and she had never had the power nor the courage to defy either of them.

And so as she looked down upon the small, narrow-faced girl before her, her tiny frame engulfed by machines and tubes and lifelines, her brain made that leap again, back to the other time. And she wondered if Topher Bloom—all tall and thin and exhausted—had also been hooked up to technology that pulsated and beeped. But she doubted that they had had such medical facilities at Khe Sanh in 1968, when six thousand U.S. marines were bombarded by a force of more than twenty thousand Vietcong. And she guessed that the fire-power that sliced into twenty-eight-year-old Topher had left little to work with, in any case.

Had she killed him? Probably. Indirectly, but probably. He would not have gone but for her. So yes, she had done it. Cast her shadow on another life.

So why was she here? She was not sure. Perhaps to see the extent of the damage for herself. And in that moment she re-alized that just as she had forced Topher from her life, she had used the same principles of "appropriateness" to alienate her own flesh and blood. And despite her sadness, despite her re-gret, she took solace in the knowledge that her daughter—if she had grown to be the woman she was destined to be—would have been nothing like her mother . . . whatsoever.

• • •

"This is Anthony," said Moses Novelli. "He's my eldest, a lawyer like his old man."

Anthony Novelli, a foot taller than his father, stood to give David a strong handshake. "Nice to meet you," he said. "I guess everyone says this, but I've been following the case and I admire your work."

"No, they don't, so thanks," said David.

"And over there by the barbecue is my daughter Donna with her fiancé, Michael. Donna is the creative one in the family; she is a curator at the Isabella Stewart Gardner Museum. And there is my baby." Novelli pointed to a pretty young woman talking to Sophia Novelli in the far corner of the large rooftop terrace. "Natalie is second-year med at BU. She is the one we'll all depend on when this rich Italian food catches up with us."

"My pop is meant to be on a low cholesterol diet," said Anthony Novelli, stealing a cheese stick from his father's hand.

"Ah, kids . . . since when did they become the parents?"

Moses Novelli was the consummate politician, thought David. From the minute the mayor greeted him at the front door and led him through his palatial home in an upper-class section of the South End, he was made to feel at home. This was his job, David knew, making people feel comfortable in his presence, but Novelli's hospitality certainly seemed sincere, meaning he was either very good at his chosen career or the guy was the genuine article.

The house was large and comfortable, clean without being sterile, tidy without looking austere. It was decorated in milky creams with splashes of warm naturals picked up in the original art, plush rugs and upholstered chairs covered by cozy throws.

It said money, but it smelled of everyday life—Sophia's perfume, fresh-cut flowers, in herbs from the kitchen and the inviting aroma of barbecued meat mixed with Parmesan cheese and garlic bread wafting from the rooftop terrace.

As ridiculous as it seemed, considering the comparison by scale and grandeur, it reminded David of his home in Newark, a home with a history of family. And it crossed David's mind what an odd couple they must have made in college—Haynes and Novelli—for they appeared to be of different stock, living by opposing principles.

David entered the roof from the third-floor sitting room and was immediately overwhelmed by the feeling of warmth, not just from the midday sunshine but from the smiles and ambience that permeated this annual gathering of the extensive *famiglia Novelli*. There must have been over a hundred people on Novelli's roof—young, old, short, tall, family and friends—all eating, drinking, celebrating the holiday.

"I hope you're hungry."

"Yes, sir. I'm afraid I skipped breakfast."

"Good. Then you have some catching up to do. Sophia!"

Novelli signaled to his wife, who stocked up two large plates of sausages and salad and approached them, handing David the bigger of the two.

"It's nice to meet you, Mr. Cavanaugh." Sophia Novelli wiped her hand on the towel over her shoulder before extending her right arm and taking David's hand.

"It's David, please."

"David it is. Please enjoy. Moses can lead you to the far corner of the terrace. It's a little quieter over there, and don't feel obliged to remember everyone's names along the way."

"Thanks, Mrs. Novelli."

"Uh-uh, you call me Mrs. Novelli around here and at least ten women will answer," she said. "It's Sophia."

"Thanks, Sophia . . . for the invitation, the hospitality, the food."

"Don't be silly; you look as if you could use a good meal. Just make sure my husband goes heavy on the salad and not so heavy on the pork."

"For God's sake, it's a conspiracy," said Novelli, putting his arm around his wife just as she flicked her towel at him in lighthearted rebuke.

"Get out of here," she said, smiling. "Grab a drink from the ice buckets under the umbrella on your way." And Sophia went back to her guests.

Fifteen minutes later, after at least fifty introductions—Uncle Vinnie; Cousin Luca; his wife, Anna; Aunt Marisa; Grandpa de Pietra and so on—David and Novelli took a seat on outdoor furniture next to some potted gardenias in full bloom at the corner of the terrace.

"You have a wonderful home, Mr. Mayor," said David, relaxing in the man's company.

"Today it's just Moses and thanks, we like it. Been here for almost fifteen years now. The kids are all gone, of course, which makes us wonder if we should downsize, but it's home, you know?"

"Yes, I do. I've lived in Boston for over ten years but still consider home to be a small, but much loved duplex in Newark."

"My point exactly," said Novelli, putting aside his plate for a moment. "But I don't suppose you've been calling me all week to talk family."

"Wish I had, sir."

"Hm, so do I."

"Mr. Mayor . . . Moses, I . . . we don't have much time."

"I know."

"Let me ask, sir, given your legal experience, your knowledge of this city. How do you call it? Do you think we have a chance?"

"Everyone has a chance, son. But if you are asking me if I think you will win, I have to say the odds are against you."

Novelli was known for his straightforwardness, a trait David always admired in lawyers and even more in politicians who, more often than not, built a career on whitewash and euphemisms. But the mayor's words were hard to hear nevertheless.

"You've had a tough week. The state has done a damned fine job of hammering home the facts—the Coast Guard, the police, the medical experts. Scaturro is good, very good in fact, and I am afraid next week will be even worse because they will introduce witnesses to support their motive—people who will call your client a bigot. That kind of hatred is hard to listen to, sometimes even harder than the details of death.

"It goes against everything we like to call American,"

Novelli went on. "There are corners of this country that seethe with hatred, David, but none of us likes to admit it."

He was right. Scaturro's witness list contained at least ten names of people Rayna once knew—or knew of—who could be called to twist the nature of Rayna's work and lifestyle and push the commonwealth's racist agenda. They were old college acquaintances, ex-clients, mothers of white girls at Tee-sha's predominantly white school. None of them appeared particularly dangerous, but put together they could do some serious damage.

"And then there is the Washington girl and, of course, that letter," said Novelli.

"Francine Washington is an insecure, confused young girl," said David. "The fact that the commonwealth is using her to support their ridiculous charge is bordering on child abuse."

"Strong words, David."

"Dire consequences, Moses."

"Too true. Too true. But bottom line, she will most likely give their case a nice boost and set the scene for their most potent piece of evidence."

"The letter."

"Yes, the letter."

David paused before going on.

While he was comfortable with Novelli, he knew he had to be careful. This man was in the business of winning votes and David had yet to meet a politician who didn't have an agenda. He was also supposed to be one of Haynes's oldest friends. Rumors of their recent falling-out were rife, fueled by his no-show at the banquet, but David didn't want to give too much away just in case Novelli's loyalties still lay in the past. It was as if the mayor had read his mind.

"Rudolph Haynes and I have been friends for many years, and what I say here, David, cannot be repeated . . ."

"No, sir."

"There comes a time in every man's life when the fog lifts from his eyes and he sees the world, and those in it, with clarity. Needless to say, he does not always like what he sees, especially when he looks at those closest to him."

Novelli paused before going on.

"You look at me and see a man of commitment, family, achievement, confidence; but it wasn't always like this. There was a time when I was content to bask in the glow of others, even when their light was ill conceived. I've made mistakes, David, most of them due to my lack of self-esteem. But my days of sycophancy are over and I suppose, somewhat sadly, along with them a good deal of my tolerance. I no longer pander to the conceited, David. I don't have to and, in all honesty, it feels good."

David said nothing, just looked directly into Novelli's eyes and saw the anger, the determination and perhaps even some form of satisfaction in finally being able to speak, if indirectly, of his soured relationship with Haynes. Whatever had occurred between them, it had been serious.

More important, David knew Novelli was letting him know he could be trusted, and considering that time was so short, he also knew he had no choice but to believe him.

"Forgive me, Moses, but time is a luxury we can't afford, so I'll be frank. Rayna Martin is innocent. Christina Haynes's death was a tragic accident. The charge of involuntary manslaughter was preposterous and the charge of murder two is criminal.

"We believe Senator Haynes is not only responsible for driving the prosecution to press these charges but is also—and I, too, must stress here that my words must never be repeated—in some way linked to the shooting of Teesha Martin.

"As for the letter, it is a scam—one big lie—or I should say a truth turned into a lie. You and I both know the parents Christina was referring to in the letter were her own. Your old friend is a bigot of the worst kind, Mr. Mayor, and I think you know it, and have known it for some time."

Moses Novelli looked at David, his eyes filled with recognition and perhaps some trace of regret. The mayor nodded his head slowly and opened his mouth to say one more thing before standing and indicating the meeting was over.

"You're digging in the wrong garden."

"What?" said David, tired of people suggesting he was

missing something when he knew Haynes was impenetrable. "Rudolph Haynes is protected. It doesn't matter how deep we dig, we still won't get anyone to . . ."

"No, you're not listening to me, Cavanaugh," said the mayor. "You're digging in the wrong garden."

"I don't understand."

"Stop trying to dig up the old oak tree. It is deep rooted and stubborn and cosseted by age—an impossible task. Focus on the roses, for they are beautiful to look at and when the sun stops shining in one end of the garden, they can be moved, and replanted, and live to bloom again."

"I am not sure I understand, sir," said a now confused David.

And Novelli looked upward, toward the clear blue sky, as if deciding how far he might go. "Loss is a terrible thing, David, but in many ways it can also bring new life, or at the very least, force those affected by it to reassess their loyalties and question where they stand.

"This takes tremendous courage, for change is a terrifying thing, but perhaps if one were to show such a person that there is light beyond the darkness, then maybe, just maybe, that person might be persuaded to take a leap of faith."

And then David looked directly at this perceptive man before him, realizing exactly what he had said.

"Where do I start?"

"In the past. You were right about history, Counselor. That is where the answers lie."

"With all due respect, Moses, that's not enough. I'm running out of time."

And Moses Novelli nodded.

"My old college friend once told me it was important to know your enemies, and he was right. Public record is an amazing resource, Counselor, if you know where to look."

"Please, Mr. Mayor. I—"

"In 1968, a young U.S. Marine was killed in Vietnam. His name was Christopher Bloom."

"And—"

"And as mayor, I have a legal and moral obligation not to

pervert the course of justice, and that includes assisting your case."

"Please, Moses, if the man is dead, how can he help me?"

"History, Mr. Cavanaugh. As I said, the answers are in the past."

• • •

The shrill of the telephone jolted her from sleep. Sara had no idea what time it was, only that she had fallen asleep, her head resting upon the reams of paperwork on the breakfast table before her.

"Sara," said David as soon as she picked up.

"Yeah, um. Hey."

"I'm sorry. You were sleeping."

"No, no . . . at least not intentionally. I was just writing down some last-minute thoughts for the next two days. Scaturro's next witnesses and . . . Anyway, I've been trying to reach you all evening. What time is it?"

"Eleven. Sorry to call so late."

"That's okay, just tell me, how did it go with Novelli?"

"Sara, I need you to do something for me."

"Sure."

"It will mean missing the next few days of the trial, and it may be a total waste of time. But I need someone I can trust."

"Of course."

"But you must promise me you will be careful," he said. "Digging this deep may be dangerous."

"David, what is it?"

"I need you to find out about a man named Christopher Bloom."

"Okay, okay," she said, reaching across her kitchen table for a pen. "Who is he, what does he know and where can I find him?"

"That's just it. I don't know, I have no idea and he died in Vietnam in 1968."

"David, for God's sake."

"I know. It sounds—"

"Ridiculous. Crazy."

"Exactly."

"This come from Novelli?" she asked.

"Yes."

"All right then." She paused before going on. "You know, you might as well ask me to find the man in the moon."

"At least we know where he lives."

46

Moses Novelli was right, Monday and Tuesday were damaging. The state marched out witness after witness in a series of short, sharp testimonies all with one agenda—to brand Rayna Martin as a racist. Individually, their evidence was weak, but cumulatively they painted an ugly picture.

There was the old Boston University professor who testified that a young, idealistic Rayna had belonged to an African American activist group that organized equal rights rallies on college grounds. There was a former next-door neighbor who said Rayna did not allow Teesha to play with her white children. Then came a former AACSAM employee who claimed he was fired because he was half white; he was followed by a former client, a young, black drug dealer, who said Rayna Martin promised to get the "white-trash bastards" who had set him up just because he was a "brother." An interesting claim given that the state had offered the young man a walk on a possession charge for his testimony.

Tuesday brought more of the same: the PTA mom who said Rayna refused to be involved in school activities because the ladies on the committee were white, and the former housekeeper, a bitter, elderly white woman who accused Rayna of underpaying and overworking her because she enjoyed "lording it over the white folks in revenge for those years of black slavery."

David and Arthur worked each witness on cross, eating away at their petty little stories, trying to expose hidden agendas, tarnish their credibility, question their own racial sensibilities. But Scaturro was operating on the theory that there was strength in numbers, and in the end she was right.

Put together, this contemptible collection persuaded the jury to at least consider that Rayna Martin was capable of a murder motivated by hate. And the defense knew their acceptance of this possibility opened their minds to the prospect of delivering a guilty verdict. They could see it on their faces.

• • •

"Yeah. Yeah, that's him," said Amber Wells, not knowing what she had done to receive this much attention from so many men. The guy asking the questions was particularly cute. She normally went for the dark and mysterious type, but for this one she'd make an exception.

"I'm sure of it," she said, looking at the paused shot on the TV. "That's the guy, Mr. . . . ."

"Cavanaugh, but you can call me David."

"Thanks, David," said Amber, with the coyest of smiles. "What did he do? Kill somebody?" It was meant as a joke, but nobody laughed and Amber responded by saying "Oh, shit."

Marc Rigotti had managed a miracle. He had called a cameraman friend from Channel 4 who had spent most of the funeral taping outside Trinity Church. Most of the film showed mourners entering and leaving the church, but there was a lot of tape in the middle focusing on the people out front: the blocked traffic, the passersby, the curious onlookers.

Just before the film turned back on the congregation pouring from the front doors, the camera swung right and caught about three seconds of a tall, well-groomed, dark-haired man sitting inside a dark blue sedan across the road and up Boylston Street to the right of the church's main entrance, exactly where David had seen him start to get out of his car before being waved off by Haynes. The make and registration number of the car were not visible.

"Senator Buford! My mom always says it's always the ones you least expect," said Amber.

"It wasn't the real Senator Buford, Amber," said David.

"Right, I get you, sure. I should have guessed something

was up when his wife was a no-show and he started giving off signals . . . you know. But I am a professional and would never date a guest. You're not staying at the hotel, are you, David?"

"Ah, no."

"Good. Then maybe—"

"What else can you tell us about him?" asked Joe Mannix.

Amber didn't think the detective was anywhere near as cute as the lawyer, and it was obvious to her by the way he had interrupted that he was jealous of their "chemistry."

"Well, he looked kinda tight."

"Tight?"

"Yeah, you know . . . serious. He didn't even want the champagne."

"But Mr. Brewster told us he took it." Joe looked at Brewster. "He said you returned to the kitchen with every bottle delivered."

"Yeah, but I had to practically shove it down his throat."

"I don't suppose you know where that bottle is now?" asked Mannix.

"If the bottle was unopened," Brewster explained, "we would have returned it to our kitchen, making sure, of course, that it was not damaged or tampered with in any way. The bed was not slept in—housekeeping confirmed that—so we can assume the supposed Senator Buford did not return to his room that evening and probably did not drink his champagne. Given that we are now talking ten days ago, the bottle would most likely have been resold or presented again in a complimentary basket."

"So we have him here," said Arthur. "The same man David and Joe saw at the funeral, the same man Petri identifies as Verne. But we still have no evidence he was acting under orders. Mr. Brewster, are you sure there were no calls made to this room last Friday night?"

"Yes. The switchboard has a record of all incoming calls and the room extension to which they are connected. There were no calls put through to room 1025 on Friday, the twenty-eighth, or Saturday, the twenty-ninth."

"Sure," said Amber. "But those records would not have

shown the internal call made from the front desk to the senator's room. Am I right, Mr. Brewster?"

And they all looked at her—dumbstruck—and Amber's heart leaped once again as she realized they were hanging on her every word.

"Internal call?" said the hot one named David, now leaning even closer toward her. "Are you saying the front desk called the senator's room, Amber—and if so, do you know why?"

"Sure," she said again, this time with a smile. "Friday night was superbusy. The guys on the switchboard were shorthanded, so the crew at the front desk, who were actually kind of free because everyone had been checked in electronically before arrival, helped take some calls.

"Anyway," she went on, "when I went to the front desk to get the list of room numbers so I could deliver the champagne, Brad asked me if I would deliver a message to Senator Buford's room because he wasn't picking up."

"And this message, Amber," said Joe. "Do you know who it was from; did you read it?"

"No, sir," said the girl, knowing such an intrusion of privacy would not be appreciated by her esteemed boss, who was now sitting mere feet away from her. "Brad gave me the entire pad because they have stacks at the desk, and I took it upstairs and ripped off the blue slip for the senator to read.

"In lots of ways I was grateful, considering that, well, the senator was starting to make advances—you know—but then I tore off the message and he looked kind of distracted and shut the door quickly. I guess so he could read it in private." She looked at Brewster, hoping her stellar work ethic would win her some brownie points.

"Can we find out where the original call came from?" Tyrone looked toward Brewster.

"We can certainly try," said Brewster. "Better still, if you have a number for us to check against, we can tell you if that specific number called into the hotel."

And Joe nodded, stealing a glance at David. "We can do that."

"And we will need to speak to Brad," added David. "If he

took the message, he may remember something about the caller."

"Of course," said Brewster. "I will get on it as soon as we leave here."

And David nodded.

"Mr. Brewster," Joe went on. "One more thing, your valets are sure this Senator Buford did not get into his allocated car to the banquet."

"That's right. He was unaccounted for."

"So you assumed . . .?"

"We assumed he made his own way there."

"He could have taken a taxi," said Arthur.

"I doubt it," said Joe. "He wouldn't have risked the ID."

"He must have had a car," said David.

"He . . ." Amber began, but then hesitated, wondering how much she should tell David with her boss in the room.

"What is it, Amber?" asked Joe.

"Amber," said Brewster, picking up on her concerns, "you're doing a great job here. I want you to help these people."

"Well about fifteen minutes after I dropped off the champagne, I kinda left the kitchen for a few moments and went up to his room to tell him his car was ready. But he wasn't there. So . . ."

"So . . ." said David.

"So on my way back to the kitchen, I saw the senator taking the service elevator down to the basement. I figured he must have gotten confused or something. I ran down the fire escape, wanting to help the guest as much as possible, just in case he was lost." She cast another glance at Brewster. "Anyway, just as I got there I saw him getting into a car, a classy black sedan—you know—like a banker would drive."

"Do you remember anything else about the car, Amber?" Joe spoke slowly. "This is very important. Someone else might have seen that car later that evening and it might help us solve a crime."

"No, not really. It was black, shiny, clean, four doors, kinda plain." The cute one—David—looked so disappointed. Those big green eyes turned all downcast and . . . *What the hell,* Amber thought, and dropped the bombshell. "But I got the plates if that helps. I figured he must have been driving to the banquet, and considering that we were told all guests had to arrive in the hired cars, I figured that if security didn't have his plates, they wouldn't let him in.

"I ran upstairs and told one of the security guys—his name was Kevin, I think. Yeah, Big Kev, if you know what I mean." She smiled to break the tension, not knowing whether she was doing something wonderful or seriously damaging her career.

"Anyway, Kevin said he would call ahead to the Haynes's house security so Senator Buford wouldn't have any hassles getting in. I told Kev to make sure the senator knew it was Amber from the hotel who had made his entrance as smooth as possible. Just wanted him to know that the Regency Plaza provides all kinds of services for our guests."

"Do you remember the plate number, Amber?" said green eyes, and Amber was excited to see him so hopeful.

"Sure, I wrote it on the message pad. It was the only paper I had on me at the time. I still have it in my jacket pocket, in fact . . ." She stopped before going on, pulling out the same message pad she had been handed on the night of the banquet. "Here it is: Massachusetts plates V106–9554. Does that help?" she asked, hoping David would be eternally grateful.

"Amber, you're worth your weight in gold," said David.

"My dad always said there was a reason I was named after a valuable substance. I guess they just picked the wrong one." She batted her eyelids again.

"Amber," said Brewster, and Amber realized, by the expression on her boss's face, that she had finally overstepped the mark. "The message pad," he said. "It is one of our old ones, before we changed to the smaller single-sheet books."

"Ah . . . yeah," said a confused Amber, wondering if this was a trick question. "That's what Brad gave me," she said, instinctively transferring any blame.

"Well, I'll be," said Brewster, now starting to smile as he reached across to take the message pad from her. "These books date back to when we used to keep manual records of our messages, before we started conserving paper and everything went electronic. So if we are lucky, we could well have . . ."

And Amber saw the other three exchange glances before standing to move quickly toward Brewster.

"I don't believe this," said Brewster. "It's here, in black and white—or black and yellow, to be more specific. The original sheet was backed in carbon, so it left a perfect replica of the senator's message."

And Amber, who hated to be left out, immediately joined the others behind her boss's shoulder and read:

> Room 1025. 6:30 PM.
> Cancel move on Banks.
> No time for payback.

"Except that when you tore off the slip, Amber," said an obviously excited David, now inches away from her, "you ripped off the first word from both the middle and the bottom lines."

David looked at Joe.

"She tore off the 'Cancel' and the 'No,' " said Joe.

"She changed the message entirely," said David.

"Somebody was calling Verne off," said Tyrone.

"But Amber here unwittingly ordered the hit," said Joe.

"*I what?*" said Amber, her skin now turning a sickly shade of gray despite the fake tan she had applied only hours before.

47

"I'm not one to complain about long working hours, Loretta, but seriously, this is ridiculous. Six AM, for God's sake. What's the matter, the stress affecting your sleep?"

Loretta Scaturro looked around the chic, early-opening downtown café known as Rise to check that their conversation was not being overheard. The sun was just up, the early morning air had yet to respond to the effects of its warmth, and the café, a tribute to the cold starkness of minimalism, was deserted apart from a few banker types who sat scattered at white marble tables, drinking black espressos and reading the business section of the *Tribune*.

Truth be told, Scaturro could hardly bear being in the same room with Roger Katz, let alone across the confines of a small table.

"Just shut up and listen, Roger. I am about to offer you the career opportunity of a lifetime, but first we need to get a few things straight."

The pair had hardly spoken since Saturday morning's "performance" in Haynes's office, the sting of the betrayal still fresh in Loretta's mind. After they had left Haynes's rooms, Scaturro had managed to contain her rage long enough for them to ride the elevator down to the basement, where they had both parked their cars. But by the time they were way beyond Haynes's earshot, she let loose at her lying, underhanded deputy.

She had never been so humiliated in her entire life. This two-timing, conceited, arrogant asshole had blatantly conspired to undermine her authority and displace her position in the eyes of one of the most powerful and terrifying men in the country. Katz knew what Haynes was capable of, and he was happy to lead her into his office like a lamb to the slaughter.

Bastard. Rat. *Son of a bitch.*

But the most frustrating thing of all was Katz's reaction—complete silence. He just didn't care. He didn't give a flying fuck what she thought of him and she knew he was mentally counting the days until the rug was pulled out from under her feet so that he might be crowned as her successor.

For Katz, it was a fait accompli—Scaturro was up for re-election in September, so all he had to do was humor her until the end of the trial and then maneuver for the top job with Haynes's gratitude and public support at the polls.

She knew how these things went. She could hear Haynes now: *You look tired, Loretta. The attorney general is an old friend of mine and we agree you have done a great job and*

*deserve a well-earned break. In fact, we think it best you do
not run in September. Probably best you step aside, "go out
on top," so to speak. I know Roger will welcome your support
and be forever grateful for all the experience he has gained
during your term. And by the way, how is Jim Elliot and his
fine fucking family?*

Well, now it was time for her to get some insurance of her
own. She had thought she would need Joe Mannix, but it was
way beyond that now. Things had gone too far, and only she
could save her own skin.

She had one bargaining chip left on the table—the exami-
nation of the last three witnesses—and if Katz was as narcis-
sistic as she knew him to be, she was fairly sure he would do
anything to be the one to ask the questions over the next two
days.

"All right," said Katz, who, waiting on his skinny milk
latte, turned to snap his fingers at the only waiter in the room.
"You have my attention. What do you want?"

"It's not about what I want, Roger; it's about what *you*
want—to question the next three witnesses: Francine Washington, Elizabeth Haynes and Gabe Jackson."

His face remained expressionless, but she did catch a tic
at the corner of his left eye. He wanted this, and he wanted it
badly.

"You and I both know that the case will be won over the
next two days . . . Washington, Mrs. Haynes and her letter . . .
and Jackson, the one that will seal the deal and give us head-
lines for months to come. But everything comes at a price,
Roger, and if you want this, you have to give me something in
return." She watched his eyes narrow, like a cat facing a prize
canary but still concerned the neighbor's dog might be just
around the corner. "So let's cut the crap, shall we, because
you know I still have the power to keep you on the bench. I
give you this trial on a silver platter, and you tell me everything you know."

Katz considered her for a moment just as the two lattes arrived at their table, Scaturro's placed carefully in front of her,
Katz's slapped roughly in the middle of the table. Touché.

"Shit," said Katz, mopping up the damage with his napkin.

Scaturro said nothing, just stared at him awaiting a response.

"Okay, you want honesty, let's talk straight shall we?" he said. "First of all, it's time you got off your goddamned high horse. You and I both know that sometimes you have to allow people like Haynes to push their agenda because in the end it works to your advantage. It's not the first time something like this has happened and it certainly won't be the last. He was only driving the bus in the same direction we intended to go. He just chose the route, and put our feet on the accelerator."

"And you approve of his methods?"

"I approve of any method that gets us a guilty verdict, Loretta. Because that's our job."

"I thought our job was about justice."

"Hm," he laughed. "Now that, my dear Loretta, is why Haynes confided in me and why you fell out of the loop."

"Well, I'm back in the loop now. In fact, I'm holding the goddamned rope. So if you want to be the one to finish this thing, if you want me to take a backseat at the climax of the trial of the decade, you need to tell me everything."

"What for, so you can go to the police?"

"Don't be ridiculous. I'm not stupid, Roger. I realize I am in this thing almost as deep as you are, although unwittingly."

"Bullshit, you knew what was going on. You let Haynes run this thing the minute he mentioned Jim Elliot's name."

So he knew about that.

"Turning a blind eye is just the piss-weak way of committing a crime," Katz went on. "You're still a criminal in the eyes of the law, just a pathetic one. At least I had the balls to follow this through."

In a way he was right and she hated herself for it.

"I just need to know. Call it conscience, call it closure, call it guilt . . . I don't care. I need to know for me."

Scaturro wondered if he suspected he was being taped. Probably. But she was banking on his realizing that she had nothing to gain and everything to lose by exposing him. If she gave any such recording to the police, she would not just be ratting out her ADA but also divulging her willingness to be steered by outside influences—by blackmail and her relationship with a man named Jim Elliot.

"So as I said, let's cut the crap," she said, knowing she had to force the issue now, before his sense of reason had time to overpower his first point of reference: vanity. "I want the whole story, from the beginning, every detail from the minute this woman was arrested. Otherwise, I keep holding the reins and you keep your ass firmly planted on the second chair."

She took a breath and held it. She was taking a huge risk. It all came down to Katz's insatiable quest for advancement. Hopefully, his ambition would cloud his judgment just enough for him to overlook the fact that he was handing her enough evidence to even up the odds.

Katz returned her glare and then she saw it—that look, that *need*. He wanted this more than anything he had ever wanted before. His ego would make this decision for him and for once she was grateful her second in charge was an arrogant, conceited pig.

"All right. You want to know the petty trivialities? Fine. But don't go playing all sanctimonious if some of them don't sit too well with your misguided sense of morality." He looked at his Rolex: 6:33 AM. "We don't have much time, so you get the edited version. Like it or lump it.

"And then, *boss*," his voice dripped with sarcasm. "Then I'm gonna give this city one of the best judicial finales in its extensive legal history. I'll win this thing, and in the process"— he smiled— "crush Cavanaugh's career beyond repair and put that black bitch away for good."

• • •

She was hot. *So* hot. Her stomach was cramping and her heart pumped so fast she could no longer distinguish the lulls between the beats. She felt her glasses slip on the sides of her sweating nose. She hated wearing her glasses, but she needed to keep her eyes on her parents, otherwise she doubted she could get through this.

"Just keep looking at us, Francie honey," her mom had said, using her lavender lace handkerchief to wipe the perspiration from her daughter's brow. She had gotten the feeling that her mom was unsure about what she had been asked to do, but her dad said they were "committed" so her mom had turned to her again and kept repeating it: "Focus on Mom and Dad and everything will be okay."

But now, up here on this isolated stand where important people sat to say important things, she found it hard to focus on them, for they were two faces in a sea of hundreds with every eye in the house fixed on her.

And so, just as creepy Mr. Katz—she thought it was going to be the woman, Miss Loretta, but they changed their minds at the last minute, making it even worse—got up to go through her questions, she allowed her eyes to drift across to the defense table . . . to the woman she had known since she was seven.

Their eyes met, just for a second, and what Francine Washington saw made her heart sink even lower. For Rayna Martin offered nothing but a smile. It was a smile that said "It's okay, honey," and Francine Washington swallowed the bile that rose like a traitor in her throat.

"Francine, let me start by saying thank you so much for being here today. We know this isn't easy and I want you to know you can ask me to stop or slow down at any time."

"Okay," she managed, clearing her throat.

She took a deep breath and pinched her own legs behind the partition, willing herself to stay calm for fear she would pass out. Mr. Katz was reading from the script and all she had to do was remember her lines—just like in the school play, one sentence at a time.

"All right then, we're going to begin by talking about your friends—specifically Layteesha Martin, Mariah Jordan and Christina Haynes. Is that all right?"

"Yes, sir."

"Good. Then let's get started."

Katz began by asking Francie how the four girls had met, and Francie, knowing her part by heart, recounted how she had known Teesha and Mariah from elementary school and befriended Christina much later, a few years ago, when they all attended Curtis. He then went on to ask her about Christina's part in the group—her relationship with the other three, and the possibility of any friction given her different racial denomination.

"It wasn't a problem for us," she said. "Chrissie was our friend, not our white friend."

Mr. Katz had told her to say that.

"But it was for some others. Some people thought it was inappropriate, her hanging out with us."

"When you say others, are you thinking of anyone in particular?"

She knew this question was coming and it made her catch her breath, her eyes downcast.

"Yes . . . um . . . Teesha's mom. Mrs. Martin."

Francine was getting nervous and was glad when Mr. Katz moved to his left, forming a human shield between her and Teesha's mom.

"Can you tell us what you mean when you say Mrs. Martin did not approve of your friendship with Christina?"

"Objection," said David. "The witness said no such thing."

"Perhaps not exactly, Mr. Cavanaugh," said Stein. "But the witness did say she believed Mrs. Martin found their friendship to be 'inappropriate.' So I'll allow it. Objection overruled. You may answer the question, Miss Washington."

"Well, Mrs. Martin always seemed to be a little cold around Chrissie. Often we'd be at Teesha's house—the three of us—and Teesha would make excuses as to why Chrissie wasn't there. She'd say she was at ballet or swimming or something. But I got the feeling she wasn't invited."

"Teesha didn't invite her?"

"Well, I'm sure *Teesha* wanted her to be there, but I don't think her mom approved."

"Objection," said David. "Speculation, Your Honor."

"Which is her right when asked her opinion, Counselor," said Stein. "Objection overruled."

"Go on, Francie," said Katz.

"Well, on the day of Teesha's birthday, for example. Teesha told us Christina couldn't come because she had to go shopping with her mom. But then Chrissie showed up."

"And you think Christina was not invited to the party but showed up at the last minute as a sign of friendship toward Teesha."

"Yeah. I could tell Mrs. Martin was put off. She was fairly

terse with Chrissie when she opened the door. But Teesha was happy. I was too."

Francine's eyes hit the floor again. This was a lie. Francie remembered feeling pissed that Christina had shown up, knowing her perfect persona would dominate the day. Sometimes she just wanted Teesha and Mariah to herself. But that was back in the old days, when Teesha could speak and Mariah gave her the time of day.

And so it went on, Katz probing carefully, Francine sticking to the script. A perfectly written piece of drama, fleshed out with little details, padded with points of purpose.

The ADA spent over an hour weaving his way in and out of the friends' history, stopping each time Francine made an observation that contributed to his picture of Rayna Martin "the bigot."

Both he and Scaturro had been careful not to set the girl up in a lie—Scaturro for moral reasons and Katz to save his own butt. If Francine Washington was caught in a direct lie that could be refuted by a believable Mariah Jordan, it could discredit her entire testimony.

Moreover, Katz had coached her to view each situation with an eye toward prejudice and the result was quite brilliant—a mélange of incidences painting the defendant as a narrow-minded racist who tried to manipulate her daughter's choice of friends. Katz was on a high, marveling at his own brilliance, and it felt good.

Finally, he got to the moments prior to Christina's death and the courtroom sat still, silent, hungry for every single word that spilled awkwardly from the mouth of the plain-looking, young girl.

It was at this moment that Francie realized she had gotten her wish. She was famous. She was the center of attention, the most important person in the room. Tomorrow morning she would be on the front page of every newspaper in the country . . . and she felt like she wanted to die.

"Yes, I brought the champagne and I still bear the guilt of doing so," she said as per instructions. "But I know I could not have stopped what happened. It was as if the four of us lost control of our friendship as soon as Christina swam off to alert Teesha's mom."

"And when did you first realize that Christina was in trouble?" asked Katz.

"After Mrs. Martin picked us up—when we could not see her in the water."

"But you later realized there were clues that pointed to her predicament a little earlier?"

"Yes, when Mrs. Martin first arrived at the outboard."

"How so?"

"Well, she specifically told us she saw Christina floating in the water. She did not mention any conversation with Christina and she suggested the three of us were rescued because we were black."

The courtroom broke its silence in a gush of disbelief just as David leaped to his feet.

"Objection. Your Honor, please, the witness is obviously regurgitating a list of prefabricated—"

"Your Honor," said Katz, "if the defense is suggesting that this witness has been coached, I take offense at the accusation."

The judge banged his gavel before the room had a chance to build on its growing buzz of conjecture.

"Mr. Katz, I will allow the witness to continue, but I warn you, if at any time I believe this young girl may have been schooled in her responses, I will throw her testimony out of court—and you and Ms. Scaturro with it." Stein turned to Francine.

"Miss Washington, I am sure you know that everything you say here has to be the truth. You are under no obligation to say anything you are uncomfortable with, and any attempt to do so could land both you and Mr. Katz here in some serious trouble. Do you understand?"

"Yes, sir," said Francine, the sweat now dribbling into her eyes and starting to fog her glasses. She clutched her stomach behind the bench, willing herself not to barf in front of all these people.

"We're nearly finished, Francine," said Katz.

"What gave you the impression Mrs. Martin made you a priority because of your color, Francie? Was it due to your past knowledge of her views on white people?"

"Yeah, but . . ." Francine Washington stopped and

coughed, wiping her mouth with a tissue she clutched tightly in her left hand. "But it was more in what she said when she came to pick us up and again later after we had pulled Teesha . . . I mean, Christina . . . up onto the outboard . . . I mean the cruiser."

Francine was fading.

"What did she say, Francine?"

"Well, first up . . . um . . . first up, she said we were lucky, you know, to be rescued, I guess because we were black."

"Objection!" David was up again. "Hearsay, speculation."

"He's right, Mr. Katz," said the judge. "I want the jury to discount the witness's last response."

But they had heard it, and that was enough.

"It's all right Francie," said Katz, pushing his witness over the line, hoping she could hold out for this one last, all-important response. "What did Mrs. Martin say when you helped pull the unconscious Christina onto the cruiser?"

"Well, I had a cramp and told her it hurt and . . . it did hurt, it really hurt. And . . ." Katz could see Francine trying to focus, the tears starting to mix with the perspiration, making it impossible for her to see.

"It's okay, Francine. Go on." The girl was about to lose it; he had to nail this fast.

"Well, she said . . . she said something like . . . 'For God's sake, Francie, look at yourself. You're not the one with the problem. You were never the one with the problem. So just snap out of it.' "

"And you took this to mean?"

"I was safe . . . I was never in any danger because I was African American."

"Thank you, Miss Washington," said Katz, trying his best to suppress a smile. "No further questions."

Across the room Rayna Martin said two words: "Oh, Francie . . ."—not even realizing they had left her lips. Not because she was shocked and not because Francie was lying, but because Francie had just recounted exactly what she had said: ". . . You were never the one with the problem. So just snap out of it." Her comments had nothing to do with racial preference, but she could see now how they could be twisted to hang her.

Dear God, she whispered to herself. *That poor child.* Francine was dying up there and she had to do something about it.

. . .

David could not believe what he was hearing.

He was furious, exasperated, mad enough to want to reach out across the interview room table and physically shake some sense into her. "I cannot believe this! Rayna, this is insane. We have come so far; you cannot give up now—you have to let me do this."

"No, David. *No.*"

"Do you have any idea how much damage her staged testimony did to us . . . *to you*? Do you know how weak our position will be if we don't . . ." David was so frustrated he had no choice but to tell her where they stood.

"Look, Rayna, we are in a serious situation here. The prosecution has done a damned fine job of painting you as the racist bitch from hell and they have Elizabeth Haynes and her precious letter to come. We have no witness to your conversation; we cannot find Gabriel Jackson and time is running out."

Samantha Bale had managed to discover the name of their Iceman but was unable to track his whereabouts. And given his long list of outstanding warrants and apparent abilities to evade the authorities, they did not like their chances of either (a) finding him any time soon or (b) presenting him as a credible witness, in any case.

"I don't want to scare you . . . No, on second thought, yes, I *do.* I want to scare the hell out of you because you and I both know we are losing this thing fast."

Rayna looked at him.

"I can take this girl," he said. "She is already shaken, and I can blow her story out of the water. You have to let me . . ."

"No, *stop,*" Rayna said. "You talk of damage, well . . . can't you see? I have done enough damage already. I let a sixteen-year-old girl persuade me to leave her in open water, and in effect I signed her death warrant. My own daughter is lying in a coma and may never fully recover, which is my doing as well—indirectly maybe, but I was the one who set this whole mess in motion. So no. I will not stand by and allow you to ruin another young life. I know Francine Washington, and she is dying up there. This girl lives every day on shaky ground, and this thing could damage her for the rest of her life, if it hasn't already. No, enough is enough."

"Rayna, please . . ." said Arthur.

"No, Arthur, that's it. End of discussion. No cross-examination. Let it go, David. Just let it go."

• • •

Roger Katz was in heaven. Bliss, ecstasy, rapture. He, along with everyone else in the courtroom, could not believe the nine words that had come out of his competitor's mouth a few minutes previously. "We have no questions for this witness, Your Honor." Unbelievable.

There was no doubt that Cavanaugh was unhappy. Even Stein, in his own way, tried to get him to at least consider a cross, as it was "within his client's rights to refute the commonwealth's line of questioning of this witness." But nothing. Nada. Zip.

Katz wondered what had happened at the defense team's lunchtime lovefest, but he knew it certainly hadn't anything to do with making fucking sense. His only guess was that the Martin woman wanted to save the Washington kid from any further distress. *Please!* These people should live in a monastery, because they certainly didn't operate in the real world.

But truth be told, he couldn't give a shit about their reasons. If they wanted to hand him this case on a silver platter—not that he needed their help—then that was their prerogative. More fool them. To the rich go the spoils.

And so here he stood, in his element, lording over the proceedings as he called his next witness to the stand.

"The state calls Elizabeth Whitman Haynes, Your Honor."

And as this elegant, graceful woman walked toward the witness stand, her large, innocent eyes offset by the pale blue flowers of her dress, her hair down, resting neatly but softly on her shoulders, he knew he had it won.

48

Elizabeth Haynes moved slowly toward the stand.

She had made a decision.

She had concluded, after much deliberation and soul-searching, that she was simply incapable of change.

She had spent the night alone in their bedroom, having retrieved her find from Christina's hiding place so that she might keep it close, to her chest, in the hope that it would inspire her. But in the end, despite her efforts, the fear had been all encompassing. She had tried to defy him, tried to take matters into her own hands, tried to prevent yet another senseless tragedy from exploding this already sinister chain of events into catastrophe, and that had backfired disastrously.

She would never be a leader—she was a follower born and bred—and the prospect of changing now, after all these years, seemed nothing short of impossible. No, she knew that to take another path would go against every grain of her being. And worse still, selfishly, she realized that exposing the truth would leave her completely and utterly alone. When Christina died, much of Elizabeth went with her, and what was left was dependent on her husband for companionship, for direction, for purpose.

And so she would do what was expected of her and stick to the preordained script. After all, she had been incapable of saving her daughter, so why on earth would she even consider that she would be able to save herself.

• • •

"Can you tell us about your relationship with your daughter, Mrs. Haynes?"

Elizabeth Haynes sat straight in her chair, her demeanor calm, her voice even.

"Certainly. It was a normal loving relationship. Of course we had our moments, as I suppose most mothers and teenage daughters do. But overall I believe we were very close. I loved her more than anything on this earth, Mr. Katz, as did my husband."

A dream witness, thought Katz.

"Did you and your daughter ever experience any friction over her choice of friends?" Katz was pacing slowly now, commanding the room with his relaxed but confident strides.

"No. I liked all of Christina's friends."

"What about Layteesha Martin?"

"My only regret is that I did not get to know Teesha better. She did not visit the house very often."

"Why was that?" he asked, a look of genuine interest on his face.

"Well, previously I suspected it was because her mother may have been protective of her. Some parents choose a more cloistered approach to teenage parenting and I respect their decision. But obviously, given the revelations of recent months, I now believe Mrs. Martin had a problem with Christina's racial denomination and as a flow onto that, a problem with me."

"When did you reach such a conclusion, Mrs. Haynes—was it immediately after Christina's death?"

The string of pearls shifted on Elizabeth's slender neck as she swallowed at the word death.

"I'm sorry, Mrs. Haynes." Katz stopped in front of the witness. "Please, take your time."

And Elizabeth Haynes nodded. "The answer to your question is no. Perhaps I am naive, but even when Mrs. Martin was charged with Christina's murder, I found the motive difficult to fathom. One always likes to think the best of people until proven otherwise. To be honest, I could not believe any woman—any mother—could leave a young girl to her death simply because her skin was of a different color than that of her own child."

"But a discovery in your daughter's own hand made you think otherwise?"

"Yes," she said, shifting slightly in her seat.

"A letter," said Katz.

"That is correct," said Elizabeth.

"Written by your daughter to Teesha Martin."

"Yes, a birthday note."

At that point Katz walked back to the prosecution's table to retrieve the letter that Elizabeth had provided to the DA some weeks previously.

"Is this the letter, Mrs. Haynes?"

"Yes, that's it," said Elizabeth, lifting her right hand to her forehead as if attempting to move an imaginary stray hair from her bright blue eyes. "I found it in Christina's dresser drawer in the weeks following her—"

"Would you mind reading it for us?"

"No . . . I . . ." Elizabeth took a deep breath.

"Mrs. Haynes, once again, if this is too—"

"No, I'm fine."

And so Elizabeth Haynes took out her glasses to read the letter once again. She read the note slowly and then removed her glasses at the same gentle speed before placing the note back in her lap and looking up again. And then she lifted her right hand to remove that imaginary strand once again.

And so it went on, the perfect questions were given their perfect answers with the witness pausing intermittently, just enough to win the sympathy of the jury but not enough for them to doubt her sincerity, or her sanity. Her testimony was merely a regurgitation of her *Newsline* performance, but it was all the more poignant given that this show was live and the stakes were much higher.

Finally, Katz tried to extinguish any hope the defense might have of claiming the letter referred to the Hayneses rather than Rayna Martin. He had told Elizabeth that this line of questioning was necessary because he needed to "put out their fire before they had a chance to light it."

"Mrs. Haynes, looking at the letter now, can you see how some people might come to the conclusion that the parent referred to by your daughter is not Rayna Martin, but is, in fact, yourself?"

Katz knew Elizabeth had been preparing for this question for weeks, and so he was a little unnerved when she paused—five seconds, ten, fifteen—before opening her mouth to speak.

"Mr. Katz, I know that from the outside looking in, it appears that we lead a privileged existence—and that is largely because we do.

"My husband's political and community achievements have been nothing short of amazing, but he has worked hard to get where he is and I am incredibly proud of his efforts." She glanced at her husband, a look of appropriate admiration in her eyes.

"It is true that we enjoy the spoils of a fortunate financial situation, we have traveled extensively, we live in a beautiful home, we enjoy all the trappings of a high profile life—and all the stresses that go with it." She attempted a smile then, and Katz sensed that perhaps the strain was getting to her after all. But then he looked across at the jury to see that at least half of them were smiling back, and so he relaxed into the rhythm this brave but sympathetic witness had set to perfection.

"So yes, we are lucky, very lucky but . . ." Now her face hardened a little as if she had to prepare herself for what was to come. "My husband believes that in life, happiness has a lot to do with achievement. Rudolph has his work and to a lesser degree I have my work in support of him, be it involvement with the community, raising money for charity or assisting in his campaign efforts.

"But if you ask me what was my greatest achievement, I would have no hesitation in saying . . . Christina." And she hesitated, looking at Katz as if willing him to prompt her to go on. And so Katz nodded, giving her a slight push of encouragement without breaking the momentum of her testimony, for he had learned a long time ago when not to interrupt, and given that the jury was mesmerized by this breathtaking witness before them, this was definitely one of those times.

"In my heart I know Christina was born special. It is no secret we tried for many, many years to conceive a child, and she came along when all hope was lost. I firmly believe she was born to greatness. She was bright and energetic and funny and sweet. She had such an incredible sense of compassion, and above all, she was my very best friend."

The jury sat in awe as this stunning creature wiped a single tear from her flawless left cheek.

"Do I wish we had more children? Yes, of course, but by the same token, I would have felt almost greedy wishing for another after God graced us with such a miracle." Elizabeth looked at the jury again, this time making eye contact with the women in the group. Katz could not be sure, but he believed Nancy Pirot was crying.

"All parents have regrets, Mr. Katz, and we are no exception. I am sure that my husband regrets having been unable to spend more time with his daughter. And I . . . my regrets, they . . ." Elizabeth paused then as if needing to steel herself before moving on. "My regrets lie in the little things . . . the time wasted arguing about a party dress, the ballet recital I missed because we were campaigning in Springfield, my inability to see my daughter as the incredible human being that she was . . ."

This last comment was not exactly to script, but Katz was not going to quibble over one off-the-cuff comment that was lost in the woman's obvious grief and sorrow.

"But I am afraid that is just the beginning because, you see, Mr. Katz, I am facing a lifetime of misgivings. I regret I will not see a nice young man pin a corsage on my daughter's prom dress. I regret I will not cry the day she leaves for college. I regret I will not cry again at her graduation. I regret I will not watch my husband give her away in marriage. I will never feel the warmth of my grandchild's cheek against my own, and I regret the fact that when I die, my daughter will not be shedding a tear for me." She took a deep breath.

"So . . . if you ask me how some could interpret the parent in the letter to be me, my only answer can be . . ." and then she stopped, completely, as if unable to find the words to continue. The tears flowed freely now, and Elizabeth made no effort to stop them, the trail of brown mascara now tracking slowly down her smooth white cheeks.

"Mrs. Haynes," said Katz, his voice appropriately soft and comforting.

"I am all right, Mr. Katz, and please," she turned to the jury, ". . . if you will allow me, I have one last thing to say. In the end I was powerless. In the end I could not protect her from principals so twisted by the bitterness of intolerance that their actions defy any form of logic. That is my one true failure, Mr. Katz. I am her mother and I could not save her from the world, and I have to live with that for the rest of my life."

And Katz, completely misreading his witness's intent, felt an unsurpassed surge of bliss flow through his entire body.

Nobody said a word. It was as if they were all suspended in time. It felt almost sacrilegious to break the silence. Even Stein felt disrespectful when he turned to the defense to say "Your witness, Mr. Cavanaugh."

• • •

They were words David was dreading, for Elizabeth Haynes's performance had been nothing short of spectacular. He had not objected throughout her entire testimony for fear the jury would hate him for doing so, and he would have been right.

They had run out of time.

If Moses Novelli had been right, if the answer did lie in the past and with the "roses," then they had no evidence to support it.

They still had no idea who had called off the hit on Tyrone Banks. While the phone logs were still being checked against the Hayneses' home number at Highgrove, the Regency Plaza front desk clerk known as Brad said he took hundreds of calls that evening and could not recall anything specific about the person who left the message for Senator Buford in room 1025. Brad did not even recall if the caller was male or female—the one distinction David hoped might offer them a glimmer of hope.

Sara had not phoned in all morning, which basically meant she had nothing to report. And so when it all came down to it, they had no evidence to prove either Rayna Martin's innocence or Rudolph Haynes's guilt—until David finally rose from his seat, only to be interrupted by a loud and unexpected noise from behind.

The bailiff entered the back of the courtroom with a bang, prompting every head in the house to turn and look and listen to his heavy footfalls as they made their way quickly up the center aisle toward the defense table.

He handed two small notes to David. One sealed in a blank envelope but written on a Boston PD notepad and the second on a piece of yellow message paper.

"One moment, Your Honor," said David, sitting back down to read them in a huddle with Arthur.

The first was from Joe Mannix. It read: "VV plates sighted Fri 28th—Brookline." Then on the next two lines there were two statements with an arrow between them: "Call 2 Hotel 6:30 PM > from Highgrove."

In other words, Joe had put Verne's car, with the plate number Amber Wells had provided, near Delia's house the night of the shooting. And even better, the telephone company had confirmed that someone from Highgrove had called the hotel at the exact time the message had been taken on Friday, June 28. They could not believe it. David needed to speak to Joe right away.

The second note was a message from Sara, taken by the court clerk. It read: "Stop. Wait. Don't cross EH. CB the key. Flying to Louisiana—need more time. S"

Here he sat, the entire courtroom, the entire city waiting to see how this day would pan out. He was thrilled with Joe's news and—given the power of Elizabeth Haynes's testimony—grateful for the interruption. But he also knew he and his team would be ridiculed for ducking one of the most difficult cross-examinations in the city's legal history. They would say he had given up the game, thrown in the towel, bowed out, lost his nerve.

But he had no choice. He had to trust Sara and hope beyond all hope that she had managed to save them from complete disaster.

"Your Honor, out of respect to Mrs. Haynes and given the late hour of the day, the defense would like to suspend its cross-examination of this witness until a later date."

Stein looked shocked. David could feel the air of derision spread throughout the room.

"The defense is due to start its case tomorrow, Mr. Cavanaugh; are you sure you don't want to question this witness while her testimony is still fresh in the jury's minds?"

"Yes, Your Honor, the defense has no questions for Mrs. Haynes at this time."

Stein paused, the courtroom buzzed, and members of the jury shook their heads in disbelief.

Katz could obviously not contain himself. David glanced across at the prosecution's table to see him grinning from ear to ear. Elizabeth Haynes remained composed.

"All right, Mr. Cavanaugh, as you wish. This court is adjourned until tomorrow morning, when the defense will call its first witness."

Stein held his gavel high, like an auctioneer hesitant to sell the merchandise, hankering for a buyer he knew had the goods to seal the deal. But David remained silent and Stein had no choice but to call it a day.

"Court is adjourned," he repeated, allowing his gavel to hit the bench with all the finality of an execution.

And with that he shook his head, flipped his robe up over the back of his chair and stormed out of the courtroom.

• • •

"There is a police camera on top of the traffic lights at the corner of Warren and Bolyston; that's one block from Delia's house," said Joe Mannix on the line to David, who was still in the office at 9:00 PM. "Luckily the car behind Verne's ran a red. The camera went off and caught Verne's plates leaving the frame."

"What time was it?"

"About seven-thirty. It fits. Gives him enough time to stake the place out, find his hiding place, settle in."

"So now we have him at the Regency Plaza, in the vicinity of the crime and back at Haynes's house later that night. And we have the direct call from Highgrove to the hotel," said David, thinking out loud.

"Yeah," said Joe. "But we still don't know who made that call—if it was Haynes backing away from his original order or someone else trying to prevent a disaster before it came to pass."

And David said nothing.

"I heard about her testimony, David," said Joe, reading his mind. "She'll never do it—she'll never turn. I know her type," he said. "Loyal to the end, no matter what the consequences."

"Maybe she's scared," said David then.

"Her husband is a scary guy."

"No, not just that—I mean maybe she's scared of being alone."

"Aren't we all," said Joe.

"It's not enough, is it, Joe?" asked David after a pause. "Verne, the message, the car near Delia's home, it's not enough, is it?"

And Joe hesitated before answering. "No," he said at last. "And even if it came close, Haynes knows—and can afford—the best lawyers in the country. We have to be careful we don't go on the attack without the full cavalry behind us."

"And what will that take?"

"We need to prove that Haynes gave the order on Banks. We need to know who left that message at the hotel."

And David said nothing.

"Failing that, a senatorial confession would do nicely," Joe said, managing a weary laugh.

They paused then, knowing each other well enough to lapse into silence and read each other's minds in the process.

"David?"

"Yeah."

"Maybe to most people it looked like you blew it in there today. And the press will most likely agree. But I just want you to know that, well, I believe you will find some way to see this thing through, some ace up your sleeve that hasn't revealed itself yet. And if you need my help, you know that you only need to—"

"Maybe I did blow it, Joe," said David, interrupting him.

"It's not over yet, David. What about that ace up your sleeve?"

"It's Sara. She could be my last hope."

"Well, don't worry, Bud. Something tells me she could be your lucky charm, in more ways than one."

DEFENSE SURRENDERS IN MARTIN TRIAL
CAVANAUGH CRUCIFIED BY PASSING ON CROSS
MARTIN GUILTY? ROGER THAT!

And Katz's personal favorite:

KATZ GLOATS AS CAVANAUGH CHOKES

Well, not the gloating part, but the choking, well, that was something.

It was late, very late, late enough for Roger Katz to be in his office when the early editions of the next day's papers were picked up by his PA, Shelley.

"Roger," said Loretta Scaturro, who had been arguing the point with him all evening. "Listen to me, we have to stop here. We don't need Gabe Jackson. Look at the papers; they all agree we have this thing won."

"Ah, Loretta. Ye of little faith."

"This has nothing to do with faith, Roger. Does Haynes know you intend to call him?"

"He trusts me."

"Yeah, right." She shook her head again. "Look, if we introduce Jackson, we have to renege on our 'unconscious' theory, the same theory that got us the charge of murder two in the first place, the same theory that is winning this trial for us. We start saying the Haynes girl was conscious when she reached the cruiser, we open the door to the defense's goddamned conversation.

"Secondly, Jackson is a liar—a slimy, two-faced criminal who will say anything to get the majority of his outstanding warrants washed away in return for his testimony. The defense may seem to have been struck mute, but that doesn't mean they are stupid. They could destroy Jackson on cross and our new argument with it.

"Finally, Roger, you have to ask yourself what your motives are for wanting to call Jackson. Is it because you believe he will drive the final nail into the coffin, or is it because of your personal vendetta against Cavanaugh—and your egotistical need to play the leading man in one final climax? Because if it is even one of the last two, then we are in big trouble. We've won it, Roger; just leave well enough alone."

He'd had enough. The ungrateful bitch should be kissing his feet not beating his brow for taking control and winning this trial in the space of a single day. Truth be told, he was in control. Haynes knew it, the press knew it and Scaturro knew it too. What she said didn't matter and she was seriously pissing him off.

"Loretta, do me a favor and shut the fuck up. It's over for you, and you seem to be the last one to get it. Go home, take a pill. Take two or three, for all I care. I'll do this tomorrow with or without you. Just don't expect to bask in my glory after the fact, because in all honesty your days are numbered. I just hope you have the sense to bow out gracefully."

49

"All right, Mr. Cavanaugh, let me make one thing clear." It was early. They were in the judge's chambers, just the two of them. "I called you in here this morning for one reason and one reason only."

David stood before a seated Stein, feeling like a naughty schoolboy before the principal. It was the last thing David needed, to be chastised by the master for a situation beyond his control barely an hour before he was due to begin their case in court.

"This is not going to be a conversation. In fact, I do not want you to say a word for fear of jeopardizing the legal process. Is that clear?"

"Yes . . . I . . ."

"Uh-uh, Mr. Cavanaugh. No words. Just nod if you understand."

David nodded.

"All right. Now I have no idea why you have suddenly decided to blow your case to hell by refusing to represent your client in cross-examinations. However, I will say this: if I discover that you have decided to drop out of this case on purpose for being incapable of proving your case, with a subsequent aim toward an appeal based on incompetent counsel, I will kick your ass so fast into a four by four cell, there will be no time to say 'appellate court.' "

David said nothing, but the expression on his face said it all: Stein thought he was taking a dive so Rayna would have a chance at appeal.

"CNN has been speculating on such a theory all morning, and the *New York Times* has alluded to it in an editorial."

David was mortified. He always thought he had Stein's respect. How could he think—

"Look, David," said the judge, reading his mind. "I did not . . . I do not think you are capable of such a low move, but it had to be said, nevertheless. Believe it or not, I thought you were the one person who could pull this off. I am just disappointed that such conjecture could damage one of the most promising legal careers this city has." Stein stood up and moved around his desk so that he could be at eye level with the young attorney in front of him.

"I see so much of myself in you, son. I just need to know that you are doing everything you can."

David looked at him again.

"Of course you are." Stein patted him on the shoulder like a mentor to a prodigy.

David wished he could explain, but he knew that was impossible—and Stein knew it too.

■ ■ ■

"Mr. Cavanaugh," said Stein, calling the room to order. "You may call your first . . ."

"Your Honor," Katz interrupted just as David was about to call Officer Tommy Wu to the stand.

"What is it, Mr. Katz? Correct me if I am wrong but defense counsel has not said anything as yet, so I can only assume you are rehearsing your intention to object before he even has the chance to get started."

"No, Your Honor, I am sorry, but the prosecution has one final witness."

"What?" said David.

"Conference," yelled the judge, looking directly at David. There was no doubt he had registered the shock and fury on

David's face and wanted to control this potentially turbulent sparring match from closer quarters.

David and Katz approached the bench.

"Mr. Katz," began Stein, now covering with his right hand the small microphone that sat before him. "Need I remind you that the commonwealth has a legal obligation to disclose every witness prior to . . ."

"Yes, Your Honor, but over the past twelve hours we have come into some fresh information that we believe will shed new light on the exact chain of events of Saturday, May fourth. We have found a witness, Your Honor, and if you will indulge us, I believe he can clear up a number of discrepancies within a matter of minutes."

"Your Honor," David said quickly. "This is beyond ridiculous. We have no idea who this mystery witness is, and we have had no time to prepare for cross-examination."

"As if that matters," said Katz under his breath.

"Mr. Katz," snapped Stein before David could react. "If this is some sort of joke—"

"No, sir. Believe me, we are completely serious."

"All right, Mr. Katz, but I warn you: this better be worthy of the disruption or I'll have you removed for contempt. Now step back."

"Yes, Your Honor." Katz tried as hard as he could to suppress a smile. "The commonwealth calls Gabriel Jackson," he said, loud and clear enough for everyone in the overcrowded room to hear.

"The Iceman," said Rayna.

"Shit," said Arthur.

"Jesus," said David, turning to his old friend. "They've bought the Iceman. They have us, Arthur. That's it. We're well and truly screwed."

* * *

Gabriel Jackson was a large, imposing man with tanned skin, close-cropped graying hair and small green eyes. He looked like a beat-up tank that had just been squeezed through a car wash—shiny faced, deodorized and wearing a dark blue suit that was two sizes too small. The witness box barely contained his generously muscled girth.

Katz hated to admit it, but he was nervous. Jackson was

not the sharpest tool in the shed and Katz was fervently hoping that he was capable of sticking to their story. Truth be told, Gabe did not remember all that much of the "truth" anyway, considering that on the day in question he was driving his chopper with one hand and nursing a bottle of Jack Daniel's with the other.

In the end, Katz was pretty sure he had convinced the big buffoon that the story he fed him was actually what he saw, or close enough to it. He hoped this was the case because most people, even two-bit criminals like Gabe Jackson, were very poor liars, and he desperately needed this one to at least look like he was telling the truth.

Katz began by asking Jackson his name, address and occupation. Jackson listed the latter as helicopter pilot, but was quick to point out that his license was currently in a state of temporary "lapse."

"I wasn't too well earlier in the year—medicinal problems—and I failed to renew, but I intend to reapply within the week," he said. "Got a few jobs lined up already."

Katz knew he had to air at least some of Jackson's dirty laundry so that the defense's attack on cross would not come as a complete shock to the jury. And so the ADA questioned his witness about some "outstanding legal matters," which Jackson assured him were being attended to.

"Mr. Jackson, regardless of your current legal situations, I know you are aware that everything you say here must be the truth and nothing but the truth."

"Yes, sir."

"All right then, Mr. Jackson, would you please tell us exactly what you were doing on Saturday, May fourth."

Jackson tugged at the too-tight tie and began to tell his story. He spoke of his under-the-table agreement with Top Gun Charters in Gloucester and the scenic tours he worked on, including the one-day picnic drop-offs on some of the quieter beaches in the greater Cape Ann area.

"May is still pretty quiet, so I remember the fourth pretty clearly. I only had the one job that day."

"Which was?"

"Meeting a Japanese couple at Beverly Airport, flying

them north, dropping them on Turtle Beach and coming back
for them later that afternoon."

"And this Japanese couple . . . they would be . . ." Katz
looked at his notes, "Mr. and Mrs. Sato Kyoji from Tokyo."

"Yeah, that's them. Nice people. The missus was knocked
up."

Lovely, thought Katz, who fired the next question as
quickly as possible.

"And you dropped them off at what time?"

"Eleven or a bit after. It was a nice day—warm, clear."

"And after that?"

"I headed back to Beverly."

"And did you see a cruiser beneath you on the way
back—specifically, *The Cruisader* being skippered by the defendant, Rayna Martin?"

"Yes, sir. The first time I saw them was just on the Ipswich
Bay side of Castle Neck; the girls were jumping into the outboard, looked like they were havin' a whole lot of fun. They
got in and started to putter into Essex Bay, toward Turtle
Beach. I remembered thinking the Satos's romantic hideaway
was about to be bombarded by a bunch of teenage girls and it
made me laugh." He smiled at his own thought. "Not so romantic after all," he chuckled, and Katz was pleased to see he
was following his orders.

One look at this witness had told the Kat that he would need
softening for the eyes of the jury. And as his appearance was
hardly going to achieve this, he had suggested that Jackson use
his hearty sense of humor to smooth out his rough edges. It was
working. Jurors Thomas Lawson and José Renderra shared a
half smile with the burly witness.

"Mr. Jackson, you said 'the first time' you saw them,
meaning you saw the party again?"

"Yeah, I got a call on my cell about an hour or so later. It
was Mr. Sato. He told me about a group of girls on a dinghy,
just off their beach. He said they had fallen out of their boat
but were okay. He was more concerned about the one girl who
had started swimming out into the bay. He couldn't see the
cruiser from the beach, so he didn't know where she was
headed."

"And what did you do, Mr. Jackson?"

"Well, I figured he was talkin' about the girls from before, and I guessed that one of them had made the swim out to the cruiser. So I took the chopper up to investigate."

"And what did you see, Mr. Jackson?"

"Well, first up I saw the girl swimming toward the outcrop; she was pretty good. Nice smooth stroke."

"And the cruiser?"

"Ah, yeah, I saw the defendant, ah . . . Mrs. Martin, sitting on a deck chair."

"Go on, Mr. Jackson."

"Right, well anyway, then Mrs. Martin over there," he said, pointing at Rayna, "then she looks up, as if she is trying to see the girls and, of course, they're around the outcrop."

"And what was the swimmer, Christina Haynes, doing at this point?"

"Ah, she was almost around the peninsula, so I hung around a bit to make sure she made it to the cruiser okay."

"And did she?"

"Um, well, yes and no." Jackson paused and closed his eyes trying to remember his lines.

Come on, thought Katz, *it isn't that difficult.*

"Well," said Jackson, opening his eyes again as if his head had been cleared. "Here's where it got a little tricky. After a bit, she just kinda stopped swimming."

"How far was she from the cruiser at this point?"

"About fifteen yards."

"And what was she doing?"

"Ah, well, she started flailing about, bobbing up and down in the water, like she was caught on something."

"She appeared to be in distress?"

"Yeah, she started flailing about, bobbing up and down, like she was caught on something."

Shit, the man has no ability to improvise. "And Mrs. Martin?"

"Oh, she saw her all right; she went over to the railing and said something. I assumed she was asking the white kid about her black friends."

"Objection," said David. "Speculation. And I would request this witness refrain from labeling the girls as black or white. Your Honor," David stood to point at Katz, "this whole line of questioning is nothing short of outrageous. The commonwealth's entire case has been based on a lack of communication between Mrs. Martin and Christina Haynes and now, all of a sudden, they concede a conversation took place? Well, ten points for finally seeing the light, but if they plan to use the testimony of this criminal to attempt to prove our client—"

"Mr. Cavanaugh." Stein was banging his gavel, preventing David from facing a charge of slander. "Counselors, please approach the bench."

David and Katz walked to the front of the room.

"What's going on, Mr. Katz? Mr. Cavanaugh is right; you have taken a serious about-face here. This type of diversion makes me very nervous."

"We are only interested in one thing, Your Honor, the truth. I can assure you that Mr. Jackson's revelations came as a great shock to us too, but there is no way we could continue claiming there was no conversation if new evidence shows this to be incorrect. It is, however, the content of this conversation that is of primary importance, and Mr. Jackson is the only one who can provide us with eyewitness testimony."

"Your Honor," said David, "you can't allow this to continue. The only reason they managed to secure the trumped up charge of murder two in the first place was because they claimed my client left an unconscious girl in the water. What about Francine Washington's testimony?" David turned to look at Katz. "We all know the girl is a liar, but you are the one who put her up to it. But I guess you're gonna screw her over too?"

Katz looked at Cavanaugh with complete contempt. He was not prone to the primitive urges of violence, but he felt like striking out at his moralistic opponent right then and there. He knew he was on the verge of a major victory and took comfort in knowing the judge would be forced to allow his witness's testimony; for Jackson was the first and only witness to the events of May 4, and to shut him down would be tantamount to judicial tampering.

"Gentlemen, enough," Stein whispered, covering his microphone once again, obviously trying not to raise his voice as the entire room strained to hear their private conversation.

"Truth be told, Mr. Katz, it all sounds a little too clever for me. You better know what you are doing, for I share Mr. Cavanaugh's suspicions." Stein looked at the two men again. "I'll allow you to continue, Mr. Katz, but be warned, you are walking on very thin ice. Now move back." Stein turned to the witness before going on.

"Mr. Jackson. First of all, I must ask you to desist from making assumptions about conversations you did not hear, and referring to the subjects in question by their racial origins. Secondly, I will remind you of the oath you took earlier regarding speaking nothing but the truth. I will assume you understand the consequences of perjury, sir."

"Yes, Judge," said Jackson, his thick neck taut as if he were trying to swallow the ball of nervousness stuck in his constricted throat.

"All right then. Go on, Mr. Katz."

"Mr. Jackson, allow me to recap," said Katz, trying to get his witness back on the page. "You saw Ms. Haynes struggling to keep her head above water, and you saw the defendant lean over the edge of *The Cruisader* to speak with the teenager."

"That's right."

"What happened next?"

"Well, ah . . . let's see . . . I, um . . . I left."

"You left?"

"Yeah, I mean, I assumed the white chick, I mean . . . the swimmer girl, was gonna be okay because Mrs. Martin would pick her up."

"Is that the only reason you left, Mr. Jackson?"

"Ah, no. You see, I was unlicensed at the time and there was the situation with those legal matters and, well, I really didn't want to have to converse with the local authorities."

"And how do you feel about that decision now, Mr. Jackson?"

"Aw, just horrible. Awful, sick to my stomach, Mr. Katz, swear to God. I coulda saved that pretty girl. But how was I to know the bla . . . I mean, the woman was gonna leave her there to die."

"Objection! Your Honor, *please*."

"All right, Mr. Cavanaugh, calm down," said Stein. "Mr. Jackson, whether or not Mrs. Martin is guilty of murder is a matter for the jury to decide. It is not your job to cast judgment; simply tell us what you saw."

"Yes, Your Highness."

"Just one more thing, Mr. Jackson," said Katz, now reveling in the greatest high of his career. "How far away were you when you saw all of this activity on and around the cruiser?"

"Above it to the left, about a hundred feet."

"So your view was—"

"Clear as a whistle. I got twenty-twenty vision, Mr. Katz. My gall bladder ain't so hot, but my eyes work as well as the day I was born."

"All right then. So, finally, let's make this clear. From your perspective, barely a hundred feet above the victim, with perfect vision on a clear and sunny day, Christina Haynes was alive but physically struggling in the water the last time you saw her."

"Yes, sir."

"And the defendant . . ." Katz pointed at Rayna. "She could see this young girl was in distress."

"Yes, sir. It was bloody obvious."

"And the next thing you knew, the Haynes girl was dead and Rayna Martin was charged with her murder."

"Yes, sir, and if you ask me—"

"Uh-uh, Mr. Jackson," said Stein. "Please just stick to answering the questions you are asked."

"Yes, Your Highness."

"So why, Mr. Jackson, did you not come forward with this information sooner?" The ADA was almost there, and despite some predictable hitches, it was all going to plan.

"Same reason as before, Mr. Katz. Like I said, I been in some trouble. But I'm here now, ain't I, trying to set things right."

"Yes, you are, Mr. Jackson, and for that the court thanks you wholeheartedly."

. . .

"Okay, Mr. Jackson. Let's cut the crap shall we?"

"Objection!" Katz had barely reached his seat before David was up and moving toward the witness.

"Mr. Cavanaugh," said Stein. "If you fail to treat this witness with respect, I will have no hesitation in asking security to remove you from my courtroom. Is that clear?"

"Yes, Your Honor." But David was furious and determined to show the jury what a slimeball this "witness" actually was.

"Mr. Jackson, let's start with those legal matters, shall we?" David retrieved some handwritten notes from his jacket pocket. "Would they include two counts for unlicensed piloting in the Commonwealth of Massachusetts, one outstanding warrant for assault with intent to do grievous bodily harm in the state of Connecticut, one outstanding warrant for aggravated assault in the state of Maine, two outstanding warrants for drunk and disorderly conduct in the state of Florida and two parole violations, once again in the Commonwealth of Massachusetts?"

"Ah, well, that sounds like an awful lot of—"

"Would you like me to read them again, Mr. Jackson?"

"Ah, no. That sounds about right."

"Right. Now, Mr. Jackson, did the district attorney's office offer to have some of these charges reduced to misdemeanors and others removed from your record in return for your testimony here this morning?"

"We had a discussion and—"

"Yes or no, sir?"

"Well, yes, but—"

"Do you like a drink, Mr. Jackson?"

"I enjoy the odd glass or two."

"Were you drinking the morning of May fourth?" This was a punt but a risk David had to take.

"I, ah . . . may have had a sip or two."

"Once again, yes or no, Mr. Jackson?"

"Yes. But as I explained, I have medicinal problems and—"

"What were you drinking that morning, Mr. Jackson—sherry, wine, beer?"

"Ah, I'm not sure, most likely bourbon."

"And were you drinking this bourbon while piloting your helicopter?"

Jackson looked at Katz in a plea for help. David saw it and the jury saw it too.

"Mr. Katz can't help you now, Mr. Jackson; do you want me to repeat the question?"

"Ah, no . . . I mean, yes. I keep a bottle of JD in the chopper."

"And JD would be Jack Daniel's?"

"Yes, that's right. But my gall bladder was playing up and the JD is the only thing that kills the stinging sensation and—"

"Mr. Jackson, regarding your helicopter license, you mentioned before that it had lapsed, but is it not the case that it was suspended when you failed a random blood alcohol test while working for American Charters three years ago?" Sam had found this gem during her research, and David was grateful.

"I was set up. I had taken some cough medicine that morning. How was I to know the stuff contained alcohol?"

"Finally, Mr. Jackson, did you have a drink before appearing in court this morning?" Another punt.

"Come on now." Jackson squirmed in his seat and twisted to look up at the judge. "This is below the belt; what I do outside of this room is no one else's business."

"When was the last time you had a drink, Mr. Jackson?"

Jackson hesitated, looking once more at Katz.

"Answer the question, Mr. Jackson," said Stein.

"The last time I took a drink . . . not sure I remember."

"Is that because it was a long time ago or because you are under the influence as we speak?"

"Objection," said Katz. "Counselor is badgering the witness."

"He's right, Mr. Cavanaugh. Watch it. Objection sustained."

"Let me put it another way for you, Mr. Jackson. If we had a Breathalyzer test brought into this courtroom right now, would it find any trace of alcohol in your system?"

A pause.

"Yes or no, Mr. Jackson?"

"Well, yes, I suppose it would."

"What was it this morning, sir? More JD?"

"No, no. I know better than to drink the hard stuff when it matters."

David glanced quickly at Katz, hoping to take the jurors' eyes with him. It worked—all twelve heads turned simultaneously just in time to see the ADA cringe.

"It was just a small flask of vodka," Jackson went on. "Just to calm my nerves."

"Well, I hope it worked, Mr. Jackson," said David.

Jackson snorted. "Yeah, right. Not bloody likely."

• • •

"Do you feel that?" said Scaturro, learning into her colleague's ear.

"What?" snapped Katz in a whisper.

"That burning sensation in the back of your head."

Katz did not reply, his blood boiling with rage and humiliation. Scaturro leaned a little closer.

"It's Haynes. His eyes are sending daggers into your skull. Problem with you, Roger, is you never know when to leave well enough alone." She leaned even closer now, looking for all the world as if she were consulting with her peer.

"I have wanted to tell you to go screw yourself for years, Roger, but today you didn't need any encouragement. You fucked up big time, and you have only yourself to blame."

• • •

"Amazing, my boy," said Arthur as David returned to his seat. "Well done."

It was just what David had needed, a glimpse of what was possible, a chance to get back in the fight.

"Thanks," he said, leaning across his employer to look at his client, hoping the last half hour had given her some new sense of hope. Her face said it all—for the first time in weeks he saw a trace of optimism, a hint of determination, a will to go on.

"It's not over, is it?" she said.

"No," said David, reaching for her hand under the table. "In fact . . ." he said, pausing to consider his latest thought.

"What is it?" asked Rayna.

"It's risky, but . . . I recommend we call for an adjournment, say we need more time to consider the state's change of tack."

"Hold on, my boy," said Arthur, unsure. "We are ready. We don't want to lose our momentum. We stall now and we look indecisive. All of our witnesses are ready to go."

"That's just it," he said. "We might not need them. Well, all but one. It's a gamble, but if Sara comes through—"

"What is it, David?" asked Arthur.

"I think it's time we go after him, Arthur."

"David, we've been over this. The man is a fortress."

"Maybe . . . and then again, maybe not."

• • •

"This is unbelievable," he had said, looking at his daughter but speaking to his wife.

Elizabeth's eyes were closed but even now, so many weeks later, she could see the anger, the disappointment, on his face. Christina, his only child, was lying to her father.

She opened her eyes now and looked at the alarm clock by her bed. Eleven-fifty-nine. Rudi had still not come to bed. She heard the old eighteenth-century Britannia chime on the wall downstairs in his study, its last note hanging in the air before dissipating into silence. She had taken it after her mother's passing. It was a powerful reminder of her father's influence and the presence he would always have in her life.

She closed her eyes again and found it so easy to slip back. Her breathing slowed. She was there now.

Christina looked at her and she could see in her eyes that she saw so much and not enough.

Her daughter screamed of a need for support, but Elizabeth stood firm, behind her husband's deep green leather chair, as if she knew no other place to be.

Christina must have known then that there was no point in denying it. For even if she continued the charade, she knew she could not hide the truth forever. And so her daughter had told them about her friends, how she sneaked out to see them, lied about where she was.

Of course, the next thing Elizabeth had expected was for Christina to apologize to her father and agree to go shopping with her. But this is where the story took a different turn.

"No, Dad. I'm sorry, but I'm going to Teesha's party."

"No you are not."

"Yes, Dad. Yes, I am."

"How dare you defy me? How dare you lie and sneak around while living under my roof? It is about time you learned what is appropriate and what is not, young lady, who is acceptable and who is not. No one treats me like an ignorant fool, Christina, least of all my own daughter."

"Ignorant fool?" said Christina, stealing a glimpse at her mother, perhaps hoping, wishing, longing for some sign of assistance. *"Father, do you know what ignorance means? Ignorance is about not accepting people for who and what they are. That may be fine for people who don't know any better, but you . . ."*

Elizabeth sensed that Christina could not stop herself now. It was as if someone had finally taken the gag from her daughter's mouth, allowing the months, the years of frustration to come rushing out.

"You with your Harvard degrees and your stuck-up friends. You with your empty campaign promises and socially acceptable agendas. You call me a liar, but don't you see? You live a lie, Father, each and every day."

And then Christina looked at her again. And despite what she knew to be the unfathomable depths of her daughter's disappointment, all she could do was return her gaze with an expression that begged Christina to stop.

And in that moment she saw how much Christina loved her, because at the age of sixteen, she finally understood—right then and there—how impossible it would be for Elizabeth to challenge her husband and side with the child she loved more than life itself.

"It's okay, Mom," she said, no doubt reading the terror in her mother's eyes. *"I know there is no other way for you. Somewhere inside I think you used to be different. I think once, long ago, you were actually happy, and I wish I had known you then."* She took a deep breath. *"But this is not your fault and I feel sorry for you. I forgive you, Mom, and I love you."*

And with that, her daughter turned and ran from her father's study.

She went to her bedroom and hurriedly packed her bag.
She ran down the corridor, keeping her head down.
And she rushed down the stairs and out the front door,
giving one quick look back before disappearing from view.

And so that was how it was. Elizabeth Haynes knew she
had become a shadow of her own mother and she felt the
deep, dark pain of regret. Her performance in court was
both brilliant and pathetic all at the same time, her resil-
ience hiding her weakness, her fortitude disguising her cow-
ardice.

And in that moment she realized she had sealed her
fate—to a life where every morning would begin as the last
had—predictably, reliably, safe. And as comfortable as it
sounded, she knew that that was the sentence she had given
herself for failing to be the person her daughter deserved.
Life in her own form of solitary confinement, a suitable punishment indeed.

. . .

They climbed out of his car and stood on the footpath under
the fluorescent umbrella of the street lamp that stood like a
sentry outside her house. The light caught the flyaway wisps
of her hair, creating the illusion of a halo around her head,
encircling her beautiful face, filled with anticipation but bur-
dened by the weight of exhaustion.

"Are you sure you want me to do this?" she said, for the
hundredth time.

"Yes," David answered.

"Are you sure it wouldn't be better if you—"

"No. You understand this better than anyone, Sara. Novelli
was right. This is the only way to get to him."

"Perhaps we should wait, call our witnesses."

"Sara, no matter how good our witnesses are, you and I
both know the jury is expecting proof of the conversation and
we still don't have it. No, the only way to destroy their case is
to expose that monster for what he really is."

She looked at him then, full of fear and self-doubt.

"I don't know if I can."

"You can do this, Sara. You can bring him down."

She paused then, looking up into his eyes. "I guess I should try to get some sleep. Tomorrow is going to be a big day," she said, attempting a smile.

"You mean today." He looked at his watch. It was ten after midnight.

She turned to him and brought up her hand to his shoulder and stood on her toes to kiss him on the cheek.

"Thank you."

"For what?"

"For believing I can do this. For having faith in me."

And then she turned to walk up her front stairs, one, two, three. He felt the loneliness inside him grow as she moved, step by step, farther away from him. It seemed so long ago since that first night when he had dropped her at her door, and even then, after having known her for less than a day, he had felt the urge to draw her back to him.

And so after she went inside, shutting the door behind her, he stood there under the light, until the smell of her perfume had dissipated and the magnitude of the day ahead consumed the warmth of her presence in one almighty swallow.

50

The sky was a bright magenta. The early morning humidity, heavy after a dawn shower, seemed to leach its way through the walls, bringing with it a damp feeling of disquiet. It was as if the gods had conspired to set the scene for a day of reckoning, for as the sun began its journey up the eastern windows, it formed radiant red caps on the hundreds of heads that bobbed and turned in anticipation as Judge Isaac Stein entered the room.

The fidgeting press settled on the edge of their seats; the jury took deep breaths, feeling the weight of responsibility on their shoulders; and the gallery cut short their whispers like an audience waiting for the concluding half of the show of a lifetime to begin.

"Mr. Cavanaugh," Stein began, "is the defense ready to call its first witness?"

"Yes, Your Honor," said Sara, standing to respond and providing the first surprise of the day. "But first we have to explain a slight change to today's agenda." Sara rose from her chair and moved to the middle of the room.

"The defense will not be calling Officer Tommy Wu today," she said, turning to face the jury. "Or Dr. Svenson or Mariah Jordan."

"Objection," said Katz. "Surely Counselor realizes that changing the order of witnesses at this late stage can be classified as unfair surprise."

"He's right, Ms. Davis," said Stein. "But I am willing to listen to your reasoning, especially considering the state's change of play a mere twenty-four hours ago. Sit down, Mr. Katz. Objection overruled."

"Thank you, Your Honor," said Sara. *One step at a time,* she reminded herself. *One step at a time.*

"We believe there is one witness who can help us clarify both the events of May fourth and those of subsequent weeks."

Sara then turned toward the prosecution's table to look squarely at Roger Katz. She saw his fear rise at the shocking prospect of being called to the stand himself. He was as guilty as those who controlled him, she thought, maybe even more so, considering his abuse of his office. His time would come, she knew, maybe not today or tomorrow, but his time would come.

"If you recall," she continued, "the defense reserved the right to cross-examine one of the commonwealth's final witnesses. And we would like to take the opportunity to cross-examine that witness now."

She allowed her gaze to move beyond Katz and settle on those immediately behind the prosecution's table—first on Rudolph Haynes and then on his wife, the elegant woman dressed in white.

"The defense calls Elizabeth Whitman Haynes," she said, and the courtroom inhaled as one, their gasp broken by a booming voice from the commonwealth's table.

"Objection," said Katz, regaining his composure. "Mrs. Haynes was not on the defense's witness list and—"

"True," said Stein. "But neither was Gabriel Jackson on yours, Mr. Katz, and Ms. Davis is right. They reserved the right to cross-examine this witness.

"Mrs. Haynes." The judge turned to Elizabeth. "Would you be kind enough to return to the stand, for I believe the defense is now ready to begin their cross-examination and complete your testimony."

Elizabeth turned to her husband, a look of pure confusion in her eyes, before turning back to Stein. "Of course, Your Honor," she said, before standing to move to the front of the room.

"Mrs. Haynes," Stein continued, "I know I do not need to remind you that you are still under oath."

"Yes, Your Honor." She managed a slight smile before turning to face Sara. "I am ready, Ms. Davis," she said.

"And I thank you in advance for your honesty, Mrs. Haynes," she said, letting this comment hang in the air. Sara knew she had to take this slowly, carefully, and do everything she could to bond with the witness, despite the fact that they were, at least theoretically, on diametrically opposed teams. "Let's get to it then, shall we?"

"All right."

"I would like to go back to May fourth, to the conversation you had with Christina before she left for Teesha Martin's party. Do you remember that conversation, Mrs. Haynes?"

Sara saw a small tic at the corner of Elizabeth's left eye.

"Ms. Davis," Elizabeth began. "It was the last conversation I ever had with my daughter and so it is branded on my memory forever."

"Of course," said Sara with a nod of understanding. "And would you mind telling the court exactly what you were discussing?"

And Elizabeth took a breath. "It is no secret that Christina and I exchanged different views on her plans for the day. She wanted to go to the party and I wanted her to go shopping with me for a new dress to wear to her father's upcoming honorary banquet."

"Christina did not want to go shopping?"

"No."

"Was there a reason that you preferred the shopping trip over the party? Couldn't you have taken her shopping on another day?"

"Perhaps, but I had other concerns about this party, such as the safety of the sailing vessel and the girls' intentions to get into their own outboard." Elizabeth's voice had now slipped into a monotone, and Sara sensed that the woman was tired, not just of repeating her story, but perhaps of regurgitating the facts as she had been told to represent them.

"So you disapproved of the nature of the party rather than the people involved in it?"

"Yes," she answered without hesitation. "Although, to be honest, I had not met Mrs. Martin, and so I was not one hundred percent sure of her dependability."

"I see. So you argued . . . you and Christina."

"And my husband. We both agreed she should not attend the party."

"Your husband . . . Tell me, Mrs. Haynes, how did your husband request that Christina not attend the party?"

"Ah . . ." Elizabeth hesitated, as if not sure what Sara was asking. "He was her father; he told her not to go."

"I'm sorry, Mrs. Haynes," said Sara, shaking her head in feigned self-admonishment. "I apologize for not being clear. Did your husband order her, forbid her? Did he give her reasons for his trepidation?"

"He suggested strongly that she not attend. He shared my concerns. He is her father and as such, had every right to make decisions that could affect his daughter's safety." Her voice was almost robotic now, Sara noticed, and she guessed by the sound of the shuffling behind her that the prosecution was picking up on it too.

Last night they agreed that Sara had to reach Elizabeth

Haynes on a level of understanding. For if their assumptions about the beautiful woman before them were correct, they reasoned that she was most likely crying out for someone to recognize why she had made the decisions she did.

And truth be told, despite Sara's distaste for the woman and all she represented, despite her inbuilt fury at the Hayneses and all others like them, she could see why Elizabeth had become the woman she had. She saw the regret in her eyes. And in spite of it all, she felt sorry for her.

"But she defied you both, by going to the party," Sara went on.

"Yes, Ms. Davis, as teenagers have a tendency to do," said Elizabeth, turning slightly toward her husband. "My husband explained that it was all part of growing up. He said rebellion, stretching boundaries, was normal at this age. He said every parent experiences similar problems. And that Christina would have grown to . . ."

And as Elizabeth's eyes locked firmly on her husband's, as if willing him to spur her on, Sara stole a glance at David, who gave her the slightest nod. They had discussed how, above all else, Sara must run interference between any connection Haynes might be trying to establish with his eternally dedicated wife. They needed Elizabeth to hold her own—to think, speak, decide without any prompting from her overbearing spouse. They needed to hit her square between the eyes with questions she would not be expecting—with queries she would be forced to answer independently. For as impossible as this sounded, they knew it was their only hope.

"Mrs. Haynes," said Sara then, physically placing herself between the witness and her now straight-backed husband. "Isn't it true that you and your husband did not want Christina to go to the party because Teesha and her friends were black?" And there it was.

"I . . . No!" Elizabeth held her hand to her throat and craned her neck ever so slightly in an attempt to make eye contact with her husband.

"Isn't it the case that Christina had been sneaking around behind both your backs because she knew you would not approve of her African American friends?"

"No!" Elizabeth said again, this time with force. But Sara saw it, the slightest hint of panic in her eyes.

"And isn't it the case that the letter you read for us in court, the same letter you claim brands Rayna Martin as a racist, is actually a note referring to Christina's frustration at the intolerance of her own parents? And isn't it also true that the reality of this—the heartfelt expression of your daughter's sadness at you and your husband's intolerance—pains you deeply, each and *every* day?"

"I . . ." began a now openly anxious Elizabeth, her hand now scratching at the pearls around her neck, her eyes blinking against the muted violet light.

"Objection." Katz was up, cutting his own star witness short. "Your Honor, this is preposterous. I understand that we have to allow Ms. Davis some leeway, given her inexperience, but not only is she badgering the witness, she is also on the edge of committing slander against one of this country's finest public figures."

"He's right, Ms. Davis. This better be moving somewhere fast."

"Yes, Your Honor."

Sara expected this. The main reason for asking the questions was both to set up an alternative scenario in the jurors' minds and to let Elizabeth know that she knew the truth—and that she *understood*.

"Mrs. Haynes, earlier this week you spoke of your impenetrable bond with your daughter."

"Yes."

"She was your miracle."

"Yes."

"Your only child."

"Yes."

"Your greatest achievement."

"Yes." Elizabeth shifted in her seat.

"But now you are alone."

"Yes . . . I mean, *no.* I have my husband," she said, still unable to lock eyes with the man who had controlled her every move, directly or otherwise, for the past forty years.

"Would you say you have a good memory, Mrs. Haynes?"

"I . . . well, yes, I suppose so."

"Short term? Long term?"

"Yes, yes. I don't understand, Ms. Davis. Is this some sort of cruel joke?"

Elizabeth's neck jolted left, as she finally managed to link eyes with her now red-faced husband. It was a quick glance, not seen by the majority of the gallery, but Sara caught it and she suspected that the jury caught it too.

"I am so sorry, Mrs. Haynes," said Sara, shifting her stance again to prevent a similar move from the witness. "I do not mean to appear harsh. I am just trying to establish the importance of a mother/daughter relationship, an unforgettable connection."

"Yes, yes," repeated Elizabeth, the first tear releasing itself from her right eye and now glistening softly on her smooth, pale cheek.

And then Elizabeth stopped short and watched Sara turn to nod at Tyrone Banks, who had moved to the back of the courtroom. She pulled out a white lace handkerchief from her white Escada suit jacket and began to twist it with her perfectly French-manicured hands.

Tyrone responded to Sara's signal by opening the large, cedar double doors, prompting every head in the room to swivel around, determined not to miss the next installment in this unbelievable chain of events. Four people entered the room and proceeded to move up the center aisle and toward the bench immediately behind the defense table.

The first to enter was a tall man with thick gray hair and a distinctively proud stride—Senator Theodore Buford. He led the group up the aisle like a guardian, assisting an older man who walked with one arm on Buford's elbow and the other on an old brown walking stick. This elderly man was of average height, with white hair and leathery skin. He walked slowly, but with his head held high.

The third to enter, behind Buford and the old man, was a woman of about forty. She was tall, attractive and well groomed, with coffee-colored skin, shoulder-length brown hair and blue eyes. Her right hand held the small dark hand of a little boy, aged about six, who seemed more than happy to be the center of attention.

Sara saw Haynes react immediately. He bent forward to whisper something in Scaturro's ear. Sara saw the senator's right index finger point toward Ted Buford, but she guessed he was having trouble identifying the three other members of the group.

Scaturro turned closer toward Haynes, Katz now out of their little huddle. Sara watched as the pair then turned to look at Elizabeth as if trying to ascertain if she could shed some light on the identity of the three strangers.

Elizabeth's normally creamy complexion had turned a sickly shade of gray. She recognized at least one of them, Sara was sure of it.

"Mrs. Haynes, do you recognize this man?" said Sara, pointing at Senator Buford. Elizabeth was starting to perspire.

"Yes," Elizabeth managed. "It is Ted Buford, from Louisiana. Mr. Buford is a Republican senator. He and my husband . . . they . . ."

"They what, Mrs. Haynes?"

Elizabeth's eyes flicked instinctively toward her husband, with no hope of connection, before returning to Sara.

"They do not see eye to eye," she said, her breaths now short.

"And what about the elderly gentleman seated next to Senator Buford? Do you recognize this man, Mrs. Haynes?"

"I . . ." Elizabeth stuttered. "No, I . . ."

"Yes or no, Mrs. Haynes."

"I am not sure. He is so . . . old I . . ."

"Mrs. Haynes, do you wear glasses?"

"Ah, yes."

"Would you mind putting them on now?"

"I . . ." Elizabeth looked up at Stein, who nodded for her to proceed. She fished into her large Chanel bag and retrieved a pair of petite mother-of-pearl YSL eyeglasses, unfolding their arms and bringing them up to her face. "Oh, God," she said.

"Hello, Beth," said the old man, rising from his seat.

"Spence. Spence, is that you?" she said, the slightest smile of recognition on her now tear-stained face.

"Yes, dear," he said.

"Mrs. Haynes," said Sara softly, trying not to break Elizabeth's focus. "This man is Spencer Bloom, who once worked for your father as a motor mechanic on your family's property at Greens Farms, Connecticut. Is that correct?"

"Yes . . . yes. But it was so long ago, I assumed he was . . ."

"Dead? No." Spencer smiled, now aged ninety-two. "I'm still here. It's family. They keep you going, give you a reason to go on living."

"Yes . . . I . . . know," Elizabeth began. "But I don't understand. Why—"

"Mrs. Haynes," Sara continued. "I know you have never seen the woman next to Mr. Bloom, but she has been waiting her entire life to meet you, so I will allow her to introduce herself."

Scaturro went to object, but Stein used his hand to signal a return to her seat. There was no way to stop this thing now, the entire room waited as the woman stood to say: "My name is Mary Beth Bloom McCarthy. Spencer Bloom is my grandfather; my father was killed in Vietnam, and my mother . . . well, my mother gave me up at birth and her name was . . . her name *is* . . . Elizabeth Whitman Haynes."

There were no words to describe what happened next as the noise in the room exploded. A court artist drew madly, trying to capture Elizabeth's shocked expression, making the most of the unusual light that had now turned her shiny skin a surreal shade of lilac.

Stein called for order and the racket subsided as quickly as it had risen, for they all wanted to hear how the witness would respond. But all she could manage was "I . . . I thought . . . I . . ."

"Mrs. Haynes," Mary Beth continued. "This is my son, Christopher. He was named after his father. Christopher," she said turning to the boy, "this is your grandmother."

The child looked up into this pale woman's eyes, confused by all the fuss and not knowing how to react.

"Hello, Grandmother," he said, and the crowd erupted again.

"*No!*" Rudolph Haynes was on his feet. The entire room turned to watch him. His hands were gripping the partition before him with a force so great that they had turned the purest shade of white. "This is a lie," he said. "She would never . . ."

"Rudi," Elizabeth called then and Sara moved, enabling them to make eye contact for the first time in moments. "I am sorry. I wanted to tell you. But I knew . . ." She took a breath. "It was a long time ago. Topher was my . . . he . . ." She faltered. "I told my father. He sent me away. To a clinic. To New Hampshire. I only saw her for a minute. I thought she was adopted. I held her. I *held* her," she repeated. "But she looked just like her father and I knew I could never have kept her. I did not know that Spencer took her. My father told me it had been taken care of. I . . ."

"*Shut up, Elizabeth,*" screamed Haynes, a spray of saliva now shooting from his mouth as he leaned forward toward the witness stand. "You have made your bed, now at least have the decency to respect all that I have made you. I am your husband. Christina was your daughter. Think of Christina and how she would appear standing next to . . ."

And as Haynes's eyes drifted across to Mary Beth Bloom McCarthy, and as her now terrified son clung tightly to his mother's thigh, Elizabeth fished into her bag once again, this time retrieving a small white notebook, its patent leather cover glistening in the pretty lilac light.

She got to her feet, and straightened her jacket, and pushed her mother-of-pearl glasses slightly up her nose. And then, for the first time that morning, she looked up and out, upon the now mesmerized masses before her, as if needing to take in each and every face, as if asking them to bear witness to what she had to say.

"January third," she began, the pretty white book now held high and open before her. "A new year and I am determined to make the best of it. Mariah and her mom drove up from Providence yesterday and stayed the night at Teesha's. Today we are going ice skating. I lied to Mom again. I said I was invited to Cassie's house. The Cummings went skiing for Christmas, so I figure it's safe as long as she doesn't call. Cassie continues to ask me over, which is really quite embarrassing. But Mom likes her because she is white."

And there it was, plain and clear, for all to hear.

"February twelfth." Elizabeth flipped forward, the entire

diary now committed to memory. "I am totally bummed. Agnes told my dad I had a friend over when they were out. Mariah came over for a second and they still found out. Father said our 'association' was 'inappropriate.' He said I had to 'learn my place.' He called me 'ungrateful.' I know Mom heard him, but she stayed in the kitchen. I love my mom," Elizabeth hesitated there, taking a long slow breath, "but she is a coward."

Elizabeth looked up then, as if making sure everyone had heard what she said. She glanced at her husband, the only member of the gallery now standing, before bending her head again to turn forward to the month of March.

"March fifth. Francie hates me. I try to befriend her, but she seems to find a million ways to put me down. I skipped out on ballet and went to Teesha's after school. Teesha told her mom how Francie had been giving me a hard time, and Mrs. Martin explained how Francie was just finding it a little hard to come to terms with who she was and where she fit in. So I guess that Francie and I aren't that different after all. Teesha says Francie is jealous of me, which is kind of ironic considering that deep down I think I am jealous of Teesha— and what she has with her mom.

"April nineteenth," Elizabeth moved on, her voice rising just a little. "Father has been in his study all night. I heard him on the phone to his campaign manager saying that he would make sure Uncle Moses was on board. He said the mayor would win him the Catholic vote and maybe even some minorities. It is such a joke. Father wants their votes but can't stand even to have them in the house. I am angry at him and feel sorry for him all at the very same time. I know they won't let me go to Teesha's party, so I haven't even asked. I am so tired of sneaking around. I can't help who I am."

Elizabeth shuddered then, her entire body shaking as if overcome by the harsh, cold truth of it all. She obviously knew Christina's words mirrored those in the letter, and she guessed everyone about her remembered them too.

"May second," she said at last, her voice now quivering. Her breaths coming in fits and starts, her hands now trembling as she lifted the shiny white book an inch closer toward her now tear-filled eyes. "I was at Father's office after school today and I heard him fire some campaign aide named Enrico. He was from Mexico. He told Enrico he wasn't pleased with his performance, but then later he told Mom that he was hiring some nephew of a rich white ex-governor in his place. He called Enrico a derogatory name. I don't want to repeat it here.

"My father scares a lot of people. He pretends to be all noble and inclusive but in truth he is just another prejudiced white guy with no clue as to how it all works. The weird thing is, I still love him and sometimes I think maybe, if I told him what I thought, he might understand how his bigotry is eating him up inside. But every time I go to say something, I see the fear in Mom's eyes. Like if I rock the boat she will be lost at sea forever."

Elizabeth broke down then, the irony of her daughter's words triggering a fresh flow of tears that began streaming down her cheeks and falling freely onto her crisp white suit lapels. Her shoulders convulsed as she swallowed the sobs, determined to finish her "reading" once and for all.

"It's Teesha's party on Saturday and I wrote a note explaining why I couldn't go. But I know the time is coming when I won't be able to hold it in any longer. A person can only lie and cheat for so long—until the truth comes out and fate comes into play. For sometimes, despite what I know it will do to my mom, I find myself on the verge of telling him what I think—and I feel a sense of freedom rise inside me, a force so strong that it takes all my strength to swallow it back inside. And that is when I know that it is just a matter of time before I break out of this prison I call home, and live the life I am meant to live."

And in that moment, as Rudolph Haynes fell back into his seat, his own eyes now bloodshot with what Sara suspected were the first tears the man had shed for his only child's passing, Sara approached the witness one last time.

She moved slowly, right up to the graceful woman before her, the diary now clutched close to Elizabeth's chest as she refocused on Sara and finally retook her seat.

"Mrs. Haynes," said Sara. "Did you make a call to the Boston Regency Plaza Hotel on the night of June twenty-eighth of this year to leave a message for an associate of your husband's by the name of Vincent Verne?"

"I . . . Yes," she said, the rumble in the courtroom now building once again.

"And did you intend Mr. Verne to believe this message came from your husband?"

"Objection," yelled Katz over the hubbub.

"The witness will answer the question," overruled Stein, now banging his gavel, demanding some quiet.

"Yes," she said, her voice now rising a notch.

"And this message, Mrs. Haynes, did it not involve you asking Mr. Verne to disregard a previous order to fire a bullet at Rayna Martin's brother-in-law, Mr. Tyrone Banks? A bullet intended to either assassinate or warn Mr. Banks, who was assisting the defense in its investigations, to stay away, to back off, to discontinue meddling in your husband's affairs? And did not this message backfire, resulting in Mr. Verne's driving to Delia Martin's Brookline home and shooting Teesha Martin in an act of open retaliation, intended as payback—an eye for an eye, a tooth for a tooth."

The gallery erupted. The members of the press were on their feet, the men and women of the jury now leaning over the partition before them, desperate to hear the witness's reply, determined to get to the truth.

A stunned Scaturro remained seated while her now desperate cohort was up and screaming objection after objection, all of which were overruled by Judge Stein, who seemed just as determined as everyone else to hear what the witness had to say.

And then it was as if the entire room held its breath as one, as the noise diminished and the strangest thing happened. Elizabeth Haynes looked at Stein. Then she faced forward and looked at Sara before turning to her left to look at the jury and smile. She got out her purse and began to check her face in a small tortoiseshell mirror. She used her right index finger to remove a breakaway wisp of hair from her left eyebrow and pursed her lips to smooth out her neutral-colored lipstick before shutting the mirror—*click*—returning it to her bag and shifting her gaze to look straight at her husband.

"Here," she said, holding the now infamous diary out before her.

"Here," she said again, as she looked directly at her husband. "Take it, Rudolph, and read it, and you will see that killing Mr. Banks or Teesha Martin would have solved nothing.

"It was an accident, Rudolph," she went on, her voice now strangely composed. "A terrible, tragic accident, and trying to prove otherwise *will not bring her back*."

Elizabeth paused for a moment, her chest rising slowly as she took a long, slow breath. "You see, Rudi, no matter how much we try to deny it, the truth is, it was just too late. We were losing her. She told us as much just before she ran out of the house. And it was not because she was growing up, although that was part of it. No, we were losing her because she was old enough to see us as human beings rather than just her parents. And sadly, my dear, she did not like what she saw.

"I understand now," she went on, taking a long, slow breath, "what Christina meant about freedom. About breaking out and acknowledging the truth and staring it boldly and bravely in the eye. And perhaps—if there is one saving grace in all of this—Christina died knowing the truth and defending it as only she knew how.

"She has taught me so much, Rudi," she said, straightening her back as she managed a smile. "She lived a better life than both of us, and for that . . . for *that*," she repeated with determination, "I shall be eternally proud."

51

It was early—4:00 AM. Rayna Martin could not sleep.

She twisted in her tiny bunk, trying to avoid the springs that dug into her ribs and attain some semblance of rest. She had become accustomed to sleeping in a building full of people, hearing their nighttime noises: their coughs, their sighs, their tears.

But tonight she reveled in the interruptions, for they came

in the form of checks every two hours of Teesha's blood pressure and heart rate and oxygen intake.

Her bunk sat a foot below Teesha's hospital bed, and every now and again she would sit up to look at the most beautiful face in the world.

"Teesha," she whispered, sure her daughter could hear her. "I am here, my darling. Mom is here and I will never, ever leave you again."

52

Two Months After Trial

She was back there again.

Outside the same room. Well, it wasn't exactly the same room, considering that the Martin girl had been moved out of intensive care, but it felt the same—pale green walls, sterile smell, fluorescent lighting, white bedding.

She had come at a bad time. The room was crowded. She looked through the glass partition to see the girl, now sitting up in bed and smiling, surrounded by her mother, her aunt and the man named Banks.

The two girls sat in the corner, the girl named Mariah and the other one, Francine, the one her husband had persuaded Mr. Katz to "use" at trial, the sad, nervous one who now appeared transformed as she joined the jovial team around her.

It was no use. She could not do it.

She straightened her pale pink blouse and turned to leave, but then, just as she started to move back down the corridor, the door opened and Rayna Martin called her name from behind. "Mrs. Haynes," she said.

Elizabeth was unsure what to do, and so she simply turned

to face the woman who a few weeks ago was standing trial for her daughter's murder.

"I am sorry. I . . . I did not wish to interrupt."

"No," said Rayna, now moving out into the hallway and allowing the air-controlled door to squeeze shut behind her. "You are not . . ." she began. "Teesha is going home today and I am afraid we are all a little overexcited."

"I see." Elizabeth managed a smile as Rayna Martin started toward her.

"You came to see her," said Rayna.

"I . . . Yes. I suppose I wanted to . . . I am sorry," she added after a beat, taking a step back. "This is highly inappropriate."

"It's not, and we're grateful," replied Rayna. "She knows, you know," Rayna continued after a pause.

"I beg your pardon," said a now confused Elizabeth.

"She knows—Christina. She knows what you did. How brave you were."

But Elizabeth shook her head. "I am many things, Mrs. Martin, but no one has ever called me brave. I am afraid that whatever courage I showed . . . it was a case of too little too late, at least for my daughter."

"She knows," Rayna said again. "As do I, and Teesha and everyone who witnessed your testimony. You saved my life, Mrs. Haynes, and in many ways my daughter's and Francine Washington's as well."

And Elizabeth responded with the slightest of nods.

"Do you want to come in?" asked Rayna after a moment.

"I . . . No, I don't think so. At least, not now, not today."

And Rayna nodded before stretching out her right arm in front of her.

"Thank you," she said, as Elizabeth looked down at the woman's long, slender hand, hesitating only a second before taking it in her own.

"Do you really think she knows?" asked Elizabeth, the two women now locked in a bond of loss and understanding.

"I am sure of it."

• • •

"Look," said Sara, hesitating as she rounded the ground floor corridor.

"What is it?" asked David, carrying a tray of coffee he had collected from the hospital canteen. And then he saw them, Elizabeth Haynes and Rayna Martin, their hands clenched in a bond of understanding.

"Let's let them be," said Sara then, pulling him aside toward a pair of double glass doors that led outside to the hospital gardens.

"Now that's a sight I never thought I'd see," he said.

"Sometimes things have a way of working out." She smiled, taking one of the cups of coffee as they sat on a green-painted garden bench. "I mean, I know it's not perfect: Verne is still at large, and it looks like Roger Katz is guaranteed his job for another term."

"I still can't believe she intends to keep him on," said David, speaking of DA Loretta Scaturro's decision to publically endorse Katz as her running mate for the upcoming November elections. By all accounts they were the front-runners, with Scaturro's reelection looking more like a sure thing by the minute. "I really thought that after all that's happened, she would have the guts to cut him loose."

"Katz is smart," said Sara, stirring her strong black coffee with a plastic spoon. "He wins trials. And I guess maybe, from where Scaturro stands, it was a case of better the devil you know."

And David nodded.

"Do you think, if Scaturro is reinstated, that Katz will prosecute the Haynes case?" asked Sara then, speaking of the impending conspiracy-to-commit-murder trial against the now-former Senator Rudolph Haynes.

"I think he'll do whatever he can to recover from his recent loss, even if it means turning on Haynes, who, obviously, is nowhere near the powerful force he used to be."

"But you're forgetting," said Sara with a half smile. "According to Roger, Rayna's dismissal wasn't a loss. The Kat has spent the past two months telling everyone who will listen that a not-guilty verdict would have been a loss—"

"But that his and Scaturro's decision to drop the charges was the responsible thing to do," finished David. "You have to hand it to him, the guy has some gall."

And Sara nodded, just as they watched Elizabeth Haynes move through the garden doors and head toward the exit.

"I'm going to miss you," he said then, taking her hand and squeezing it.

"I'll miss you too. But we'll talk every day. I promise." Sara was booked on a plane to Atlanta the very next morning, having decided to seek out her own birth mother.

"Mary Beth was inspiring," she said, referring to a conversation she'd had with Elizabeth's first daughter. "She and her mother have started to form some sort of friendship. Elizabeth isn't exactly embracing her with open arms, but they have met a number of times, and she has shown interest in getting to know her grandson."

"Sara," he said then, feeling that now-familiar need to protect her. "You must remember that your mother may not want to do any rebuilding."

"I know, but I have to try. I'll be back before you know it." She reached up to kiss him on the cheek. "Just don't meet any smart, attractive young cocounsels while I'm away."

"Don't worry, Arthur is definitely not my type."

"You know what I mean," she said, elbowing him in mock admonishment.

"Yes, I do, and no, I won't."

They sat quietly in silence for a while, watching two young boys play catch on the flower-bordered hospital lawn.

"Sara?" he asked.

"Yes."

"You do know how much I—"

"Yes." She turned to look up at him. "How could I not? You have shown me that sometimes the world really is as beautiful as it seems."

"Ah, what's this? My favorite cynic has become an idealist after all."

"Is that such a bad thing?" and she smiled.

"No," he replied, taking her in his arms. "Because right now I can't imagine the world being any other way."